# A Convenient Secret

## Merged Series

Maxine Henri

Copyright © 2025 by Maxine Henri

All rights reserved.

www.maxinehenri.com

Cover designed by Sweet 'N Spicy Designs

Edited by Indie Editing Chick

This book is a work of fiction. The characters, incidents and dialogue are drawn from the author's imagination and are not to be construed as real. Any resemblance to actual events or persons, living or dead is fictionalized or coincidental.

No part of this book may be reproduced in any form or by any electronic or mechanical means, including information storage and retrieval systems, without written permission from the author, except for the use of brief quotations in a book review.

ISBN: 978-80-69048-06-5

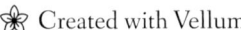 Created with Vellum

*For all you, ladies, who fear your truth might burn. Don't hide. Shine.
You're a Gift.*

# Chapter 1

## *Lily*

Voice.

His voice.

It always wraps around me like velvet, its timbre reverberating through every inch of my body. It speaks to all my desires. Desires I've not experienced before.

It's really quite ridiculous.

Confident, and often with a tinge of annoyance, his baritone has become my safety blanket. Like listening to him is the safest thing in the world.

My rational mind recognizes the madness of it. If I could afford a therapist, they would probably charge me double.

I'm twenty-five, and I'm infatuated with my client's voice.

It's pathetic.

There should be a support group for addicts like me. I can't shake it. Whenever his number flashes across the screen, all my previous self-pep talk goes down the drain.

He hasn't even said anything nice to me. I'm addicted to the melody, I guess. Because, for all its deep rumbling quality, his tone is aloof, most of the time, and quite often obnoxious.

Grumpy. Demanding. Brooding.

My colleagues hate him, and keep forwarding his calls to my line.

Outwardly, I roll my eyes, but secretly, I appreciate the opportunity to listen to him.

Not even a therapist could save me.

He's a single dad with a high-demanding job; he must be overwhelmed. That's my explanation for his abrupt behavior. Yes, I'm making excuses for him. I'm aware.

But if I was kind to myself about this thing, it's not like anything could ever happen between us, so my little crush is harmless. It makes the dull day at work more exciting.

Let's face it, being a concierge to the rich and powerful may sound thrilling, but it is not. Not at all. Most days, I keep answering the phone and cater to the whims of people who can throw money at any problem.

Not all of them are completely disconnected, but many are, which makes this gig a challenge.

Unlike my colleagues, I understand their needs, and I'm fairly good at providing solutions, so I guess my position here is safe.

Which is good, because as someone who needs to remain under the radar, I need a job that helps me blend into the crowd, remain fairly invisible. Beggars, choosers, and all that.

"Yoga and drinks tonight, bitch?" My colleague Aaron leans on the beige partition between our cubicles.

It took me a moment to get used to this open concept. But I appreciate the human interactions. It's something that has increased in value in my lonely life.

The beige monolithic decor, however, is worse than the open concept. While our furnishings are comfortable, and there are chill areas and a well-stocked cafeteria with mismatched, comfortable, wing chairs, reminding me of a hipster bistro, the concept itself just sucks your energy if you have to stay here longer than five minutes.

Or maybe it's the job that drains me.

At least Aaron is one of those people who brightens one's day.

"My friend has a barbecue, sorry." I shrug.

"Lily Thorne, I'm starting to think you don't want to hang out with me." He mock-scoffs.

I swallow, heat rising to my cheeks. "That's not true."

It's mostly correct. I don't mind Aaron at all. He's a great colleague. The problem is me. Or rather, my hermit ways.

Ever since I arrived in New York almost eighteen months ago, I've been looking over my shoulder. Like the past will catch up with me. It probably will, and I'm not ready to risk it.

Will I ever be?

"Even those friends of yours are probably made up," Aaron deadpans and taps his headset. "Summit Solutions, Aaron speaking." He dives back into his chair.

And now, I feel like shit. This is not the first time Aaron has voiced his opinion about my need to keep things private. As always, his words drop into my stomach like a lead ball.

I don't want to be that girl. But I don't have a choice.

Besides my three girlfriends, a group of women who accepted me, despite the odds, into their circle, Aaron is the only person who brings a bit of normal and a lot of fun into my life.

And yet I'm not ready for normal, or for ordinary. I

need to stay on the down low. Until I learn to trust again. Until I find my footing, and my purpose.

In the meantime, I have to do what I have to do. Be small and invisible. Be someone else. It's been eighteen months, and I've built a home here. A very fragile and not necessarily desired home.

But I have my friends and this work. Things that anchor me. For now.

My line blinks, and when I see the name, my heart rate spikes immediately, heat spreading across my face.

"Summit Solutions, Lily speaking. How may I help you today?" I smile. Not that he can see me, but I know a smile comes across in my voice.

"I need a sitter. Urgently. Full time," he spits out without a greeting.

"Of course. Have your needs changed since last time?"

Poor man hired a nanny not even six weeks ago. I know this, and not only because it's recorded in his file. I don't need to open his file to remember everything about him. I helped him with the task last time, and four times before.

I wonder if his kids are next-level brats or if he's an abusive employer. The turnover seems unreal. But perhaps the agency hasn't matched him with the right fit. He should be demanding when it comes to his own kids.

He sighs, and the load of it carries through the line, spearing me. I inhale and straighten my spine, like I can possibly carry his burden. I can't. And, more importantly, I shouldn't want to.

"Same prerequisites," he says.

Children's laughter echoes in the background. He must be home. Of course he is. It's a Saturday. Is he wearing a suit? Or what is his casual wear?

*Stop it, Lily!*

"I'll have an agency send you suitable resumes—"

"I don't have time for that," he interrupts. "I need someone to start on Monday at seven sharp."

"Understood." I run my fingers over the keyboard to open his file. "I see you had a runner-up selected last time. I will try to get them to start on Monday."

"Try isn't good enough," he snaps. "I need a nanny on Monday."

I close my eyes briefly and try to embrace his frustration with a smile. "Of course. We'll make sure a qualified nanny is at your house on Monday morning."

"Good. Do a thorough reference check."

"Daddy, Daddy—" a girl's voice interrupts.

"It wasn't my fault…" a boy cries.

"I need to go. Can I rely on you?" His voice is laced with something I haven't heard before.

It's not his usual *don't-bother-me* attitude; it's that

tired and resigned voice parents have when they're at the end of their rope.

A cry for help. Or I'm just projecting, probably.

"Of course. Is there anything—"

The line dies. I sigh and open the contacts to dial the childcare agency.

"You wouldn't believe what that old hag wanted." Aaron's head pops up again.

"Aaron!" I widen my eyes, grinning. "We don't gossip about clients."

He waves his hand. "It's not gossip if it's true. Listen to this: she requested I get her a new pool boy with a large dick."

I burst out laughing, and a few heads emerge from the cubicles around us. "She didn't," I laugh-whisper.

"Keep it quiet." Aaron glares at me and looks around, waiting for our colleagues to return to their jobs. "She sure did," he says through his teeth, his lips quirking up. "Like, what the fuck, that's not exactly on their resume." He shimmies his shoulders.

I turn my chair to him, chuckling. "What did you tell her?"

"That perhaps she should consider an escort service, and she got upset because she wouldn't want that on her husband's credit card."

I giggle again.

"Don't laugh, bitch; she's going to get me fired.

What was I supposed to do? Hire a pool boy and risk he has a small package?"

I can't hold it anymore and double over, laughing. We get eccentric requests often, but Aaron seems to get the best of them. "You could have screened the candidates for her."

"I'm in a committed, monogamous relationship with Jack. I'm not going to check other dicks."

I wipe a tear. "I don't know how you attract these demands."

"I can't wait to quit this place. I don't know how you maintain such a level of understanding with their fancies."

"They don't know any other way of life. Or they are unhinged, but that is not exclusive to the rich. There are worse jobs." Not that I would know. "Did you resolve her request at the end?" I try to divert his attention away from me.

"At the end, she agreed to interview ten candidates."

"Ten? They should be warned."

"Yeah, I hope she at least has a pool."

Another laugh escapes me, but it dies on my lips as a loud shrill fills the room. My body freezes completely, my eyes darting around.

On the edges of my paralyzed mind, I see everyone standing up and heading toward the exit.

"What are you doing, Lily? Move."

The words reach me, but I'm unable to execute the command.

There is a fire.

Fire.

Fire.

Someone yanks me to stand up and ushers me forward. I'm pulled into the staircase. I want to inhale and take charge of my body, but it's like I'm submerged underwater.

Unable to breathe. Unable to act. Unable to think.

The air outside is hot. Fire. Fire. Fire.

"What's wrong with you?" Someone shakes me, and I finally focus my sight.

"There is a fire." I'm pretty sure I said the words, but I don't recognize my voice.

"There is no fire." Aaron grips my shoulders, forcing me to look at him. "You're safe."

"There is no fire?" Oxygen floods my lungs, and I gasp.

"What the fuck, Lily? It was probably only a drill, and you completely panicked."

"I'm sorry. I-I—"

"I grabbed your purse. Your shift is over anyway. Are you okay?" He hands me my bag.

"I'm sorry."

"Stop saying that. It's okay. Do you want to talk about it?"

"No, thank you." I take the bag from him.

As my nerves and heart resume their normal function, I know I need to say something, but I don't want to lie to Aaron.

There have been enough lies in my life.

I ring the bell for the third time. My friend Saar and her husband, Corm, are hosting a barbecue I'm late for. Perhaps they all are in the back and don't hear the bell.

But I hear a commotion, and finally the door opens. Saar smiles at me.

I give her a hug. "I'm sorry I'm so late."

"How was it?" she asks, but turns away, distracted.

Oh, shit, I forgot I told my friends I'm breaking up with a boyfriend. An imaginary boyfriend. God, I hate to lie to them.

But when you're twenty-five, single, and new in town, people feel the need to partner you up. So I made up a dude. Not the finest moment of my life, but who's counting?

Who knew people would want to meet my fake boyfriend? So I had to dump him today.

I wish I could keep *him* around. He was a perfect

decoy when I didn't want to go somewhere. He was my perfect avoidance tactic. But unfortunately, there are too many secrets in my life already, and sprinkling them with this lie became too much.

Saar's cat Coco dashes from under the console table and practically flies up the stairs.

"Thewe she is." A little girl runs to the staircase, her ponytail bouncing.

"Zach, Zoya." Saar pulls me with her, away from the entrance. "Why don't we go make your burgers? Uncle Corm has a special sauce for you."

"But we want to play with the kitten." The girl frowns, already halfway up the stairs.

"*She* wants to play with her." A boy—with very similar features to the girl—puts his hands in his pockets with a bored expression.

And I realize who they are. I have never met these twins, but I've heard about them.

"Zoya, it's Coco's bedtime." Saar looks at me, desperate.

Zoya looks up, and then shrugs and bounces down. "What secwet sauce?"

"It wouldn't be a secret if she told you." Her brother shakes his head. "Let's go outside."

They start toward the patio, but then Zoya stops. "Auntie Saaw, I wish we had a kitten."

"Dad is allergic," her brother growls.

"Can I come and play with Coco tomowow?" Zoya's brown eyes widen, looking at Saar with expectation.

Saar goes white and glances at her beloved cat.

"Maybe Auntie can take you to the shelter where she volunteers, and you can help her with the kittens and puppies there," I offer, hoping I didn't overstep.

"That is a wonderful idea. I'll talk to your dad about it." Saar winks at me and mouths a thank you.

"Dope," Zoya cheers, and runs off.

I watch the little girl disappear outside. Funny how I just met her but I feel a kinship toward her. "Those are Declan's kids?"

"How do you know Declan?" Saar frowns, and for some outlandish reason, embarrassment warms my cheeks.

"From Celeste's Christmas party." I balance on one foot then another.

Celeste is our mutual friend, and half a year ago, her husband, Saar's brother, organized their vow-renewal Christmas party.

I now realize I'm going to see all the people I met there. My pulse quickens, and my mouth goes dry.

"Oh, I forgot about that. Come get a drink. How was it?" Saar asks, leading me toward their patio.

How was what? Oh shit, she's talking about my fake breakup.

"It was okay." Will the lies never cease? "I'm more shaken about a fire alarm at work."

"Oh no. Are you okay?"

I sigh. "I need a drink."

Saar wraps her arm around me, and we step outside.

"Lils," Cora calls as soon as she sees us.

I walk over to the makeshift bar in the corner and hug her. Cora is the first person in New York who showed me the kindness I didn't deserve.

She owns a bistro and hired me with no experience. I lasted a few weeks, and that was probably several days longer than I should have done. I couldn't figure out the coffee machine, or learn how to carry a tray without spilling everything.

Not something that was taught in my childhood home. I probably still owe Cora for the broken dishes. She let me take care of her social media to even out the score.

While she's a decade older, we became friends. And she introduced me to Celeste and Saar. And they became my people. I didn't believe I could trust anyone when I arrived here, but they proved me wrong.

"What are you drinking?" Cora asks.

"I'll have a glass of white."

"Coming right up," Xander says and winks at me.

Alexander Stone is a partner in Merged. Saar's

husband, Cormac, leads the company. Her brother, Caleb, has an equal share.

Xander gets my drink from the hired bartender. "Cheers. You ladies got even prettier since Christmas."

I giggle into my glass.

"Stone, Jesus, do those lines really work?" Cora laughs.

"I have money and looks, sweetheart; I don't need lines," he jokes.

"And he can get even more cringey," Cora teases him.

They fall into some sort of ridiculous sparring match, and I look around the large stone patio.

Celeste, heavily pregnant, stretches on a lounger while Caleb dotes on her like he always does.

Cormac's arms are wrapped around Saar, and he's whispering something to her while her face lights up.

The twins are by their father, Declan, the fourth partner at Merged. He's talking to Zoya, and there is a tiny smile on his face.

He's wearing a light blue polo shirt and navy slacks. His dark hair is slightly longer on the top, styled back. He's lean but muscular, with a trim waist, broad shoulders and strong legs.

And I should not be noticing these details about him.

His collar is open, and when he turns, I get a glimpse of his collarbone. Just a suggestion of a protruding bone and the dip around it. Who knew collarbones were sexy?

If it wasn't for the usual scowl on his face, he would be handsome. Who am I kidding? He's ridiculously attractive, even with that glower. Gorgeous.

The man has an aura of mystery around him. Like he doesn't want the world to really see him. And when they try, he scares them away quickly with his arrogant scrutiny.

We have that in common. The need to repel attention, not the scowl. I have yet to learn how to be or look mean. I lean into smiles and giggles when faced with something I want to avoid.

I understand this intense need for privacy. I wonder what he's hiding from. A person? A feeling? A danger?

"You're not drinking, Lils." Cora bumps her hip against mine, and the wine spills over my hand. "Oops, sorry."

"Here you go." Xander snatches some napkins and dabs my hand.

"Looks like I need to drink faster." I laugh, and before I turn, so Declan is out of my sphere of vision, I glance at him one last time.

Our gazes collide before I whip around, my heart

racing. Of course he was looking; I just spilled wine. People look when you do something klutzy.

And yet his attention, however brief or coincidental, makes me feel all hot.

I wish he wasn't here. I never know how to behave around him. Not that I met him more than that one time.

I wish he didn't belong to this circle. Not that he knows I even exist.

Which is a good thing, because if he tried to speak to me, I'd probably make a fool of myself.

And he might recognize my voice. Just like I'd recognize his anywhere.

His voice.

# Chapter 2

## *Lily*

CELESTE

I'm still pregnant. (crying emoji)

SAAR

Which means you can sleep.

CELESTE

Try to sleep when you can't even move.

> I'm sure the baby will come soon.

SAAR

Always looking at the bright side, @Lily.

CELESTE

Fuck wishful thinking. I want guarantees. NOW! (crying emoji)

CORA

Can you still waddle to come for a coffee?

## CELESTE

I'm not moving until this baby is out.

I sit up suddenly, my breath shallow and fast like I've been running for miles. The darkness presses in around me, heavy and suffocating. I clutch at the sheets and scan the room, searching for... what?

With a lavender sachet under my pillow, the distant hum of cars passing on the street outside, the warm yellow night-light plugged near the door, my brain slowly anchors me in my tiny spare room.

Shit. Another nightmare. As hard as I try to forget, to move on, to clear those memories, they persistently infiltrate my mind.

Days are good. I've always been a cheerful person. A bit too bubbly according to my parents. During the day, I stay grounded in the present.

Some pay hundreds or thousands to learn mindfulness. To stay present in the moment. I had to embrace the *here and now*, because I've had no alternative.

I don't want to remember my past, think about it, or revisit it—even when some memories try to bring me to my knees.

And my future is uncertain, so really, the present moment is what keeps me going.

*A Convenient Secret*

While my life over the past year has been nothing like the life I used to know, I've made it work.

Because, however unfortunate my life may look, it's mine. It's not decided for me. It's chosen by me. And that is priceless.

Yes, there is the unfortunate housing situation. But right now, I can't afford more than this room in Mrs. Whitaker's condo. Not ideal.

The cost of living in New York wasn't something I was prepared for. God, I used to be a naïve girl. My life till that moment forced me to mature in certain ways, but completely sheltered me from reality.

New York is where I want to be. It's vibrant and pulsing with life.

New York is where I need to be. It's large, anonymous, and far enough from home.

New York is where I belong now. Even in my isolation, missing my family. Some of them, anyway.

During the day, I learned to enjoy my life.

At night, the past persists in my dreams.

I sit up and press my palms against my thighs, grounding myself. "You're okay. You're okay," I whisper into the stillness, as if saying it out loud will make it true. My voice is hoarse, barely above a breath.

I switch the lamp on and pull out my journal from the nightstand. Scooting up, with my back against the headboard, I review the last few pages. All the things I'm grateful for.

My friends: Celeste, Saar, and Cora.

That I have work and a roof above my head.

That I joined a local gym.

That I saw butterflies on my way to a store.

That I bought myself a large iced coffee with extra whipped cream.

And several other entries of little things that made me smile, improved my day, and made me feel normal. Like I'm slaying this living-by-myself thing.

The tightness in my chest loosens, and the nightmare's aftertaste subsides. My heart is still racing, but it's no longer galloping. Just trotting.

I glance at the glowing red numbers of the clock on my nightstand. Almost three in the morning. Too early to be awake, too late to hope for a good night's sleep.

The weight of the dream is still there, lurking at the edges of my thoughts. I don't remember the details—I never do—but the feeling is always the same: the crushing certainty that I'm not safe, that the past is just waiting to catch up with me.

I put away the journal and lie back, staring at the cracked paint of the ceiling. I force my mind to remember more things that I enjoyed today, yesterday. Reliving the more recent past.

New York never sleeps, so here I am, wide awake. And alone in the quietest hours of the city.

Loneliness is new, but it also isn't. It's been over a year. I wasn't prepared for this feeling of isolation. But then, I wasn't prepared for any of it.

"It's just a bad dream. Tomorrow will be better." The words feel hollow, bouncing around in the empty space.

Outside, loud voices crescendo and quieten down again—perhaps a group of friends leaving a party. Life is still moving, even if I feel stuck.

I close my eyes carefully, because what I see in the darkness is often the worst. I feed my brain all the happy moments, hoping to fall into a dreamless abyss.

"What the hell, Lils?" Aaron says as soon as I answer the phone.

I blink a few times, turning in my twin bed. "Ouch," I murmur when my elbow connects with the wall.

"Ouch doesn't even cover it. The devil is beside himself."

I sit up, and the room spins from the sudden movement. "You make no sense."

Why is Aaron calling me so early in the morning? I

suppose it must be early in the morning since he woke me from a deep sleep.

Dust particles dance in the cone of light, seeping through an opening in the heavy curtains. The digital clock on my nightstand suggests it's five past seven.

"There is no memo on his file. You talked to him on Saturday. He's waiting for a nanny. I hope you only forgot to record it and the nanny is on their way. She is late already, anyway." Aaron talks in a hurried whisper, tripping over his words.

Words that cause a sober awakening and terrifying realization all at once. "Fuck."

I jump out of my bed and switch on my side lamp.

"Fuck is right. He's calling again, Lils. What should I tell him?" Aaron sounds panicked. And he never sounds panicked.

"Tell him his nanny got delayed in traffic but will be there in thirty minutes."

"How do you know that?"

"Answer the client's call, Aaron. The nanny will be there in thirty." I wish I had an ounce of the confidence I channel into my tone.

"Okay." Aaron hangs up.

I allow myself a moment of panic, standing by my bed, unsure where to go or what to do.

My hands shake.

My heart is trying to escape my chest.

My mind is racing.

I take a deep breath in and rush to my wardrobe. Grabbing jean shorts and a long-sleeved black T-shirt, I get dressed in record time.

I open my door carefully and tiptoe to the bathroom.

"Good morning, Lily."

Goddammit. "Good morning, Mrs. Whitaker."

My landlady stands in her kitchen doorway, sipping coffee. Rollers in her silver hair, she is wearing a pink housecoat and channeling all her nosy energy.

"You're up early. I thought you had a day off." She takes a sip.

The woman knows my schedule better than me. "I'm sorry, Mrs. Whitaker, but I'm in a hurry."

"I can make you breakfast."

She is nosy *and* lacks boundaries, but I guess it all stems from her loneliness. And while I indulge her more often than I want to, this morning is not one of those days.

"I'm sorry." I push the door to the bathroom open and grab my toothbrush.

How did I forget to book the nanny?

The fire alarm.

I practically scrape a layer of skin from my gums as I vigorously run the brush across my mouth. What am I going to do?

Brushing my hair, I regret for the gazillionth time that I chose a pixie cut when I decided my New York look. It would have been easier and faster to pull my hair back.

I've been trying to grow it, so I lose another precious second gathering it in my hands and pulling it back as if I could stretch it longer.

"It's still too short."

I jump and hit my elbow on the shower door. It's the same nerve I already abused this morning in my small bed. "You're here, Mrs. Whitaker," I state the obvious, rubbing my hurting arm.

"You know, Lily, I was so happy to share my home with you, but you're never here." She stands in the doorway, blocking my only way to escape. Her guilt-tripping is next-level passive-aggressive.

"I'll be here tonight. We can have dinner," I blurt out, more to get rid of her than because I really want to spend any time with her.

The problem is, Mrs. Whitaker is lonely because she's just not nice. And as much as I try to bring some positivity into her life, I've learned it's a lost cause.

"Will you bring takeout?" She finally moves, and I step around her. "Let me get you a flyer from this new place four blocks from here. It's Indonesian."

I get to my room and grab my glasses and my purse. Turning, I collide with Mrs. Whitaker. She pushes a leaflet into my hands. Using the time I don't have, I lock my room. I don't have proof she'll snoop around, but I'm not taking a chance.

Not that she will find anything.

"See you tonight." I practically sprint from the apartment.

Tonight is far away. I'll worry about it later. Right now, I need to figure out how the hell I'm going to solve my problem.

I open the app on my phone to order a taxi. Where am I even going? I put the phone away and run to the subway. By the time I reach the platform, I'm soaked in my own sweat.

The waiting makes me sweat even more. Summertime underground isn't fun. I roll up my sleeves a bit, but it's no help.

Twenty-five minutes since I spoke with Aaron. Not good. I dial the childcare agency but get their voicemail.

By the time I reach the Upper East Side, it's almost eight o'clock. My hair plastered on my forehead, I feel like I'm swimming in my own juices. Attractive as hell.

My phone rings. I don't want to answer, but Aaron doesn't deserve to carry the consequences of my actions.

"What's going on, Lils? He called again."

"It's not like I can get there any faster," I huff. *Shit*.

"You?"

"I mean I can't get her there any faster." *Wow, Lily, you've become quite a proficient liar.*

"What's going on, Lily?" Aaron's voice carries a hint of worry, and an equal amount of warning.

Too late for that.

"I got to go. I have it under control. Trust me." I hang up.

Panting, I get into the cool—freezing—lobby of a swanky condominium.

"I'm here for Mr. Quinn." I shiver as my body protests at the sudden dip in temperature.

"Who am I to announce?" The uniformed concierge smiles at me.

"Nanny."

The concierge puts the receiver down. "He's been expecting you. Come."

"Thank you..." I glimpse his name tag. "Karl."

"You're welcome. Good luck today. You might need it." He hands me a handkerchief.

I take the white linen from him, puzzled.

"It must be hot outside." He gives me a warm smile.

"Oh, yes, and I've been running to get here... very late." I wipe my face and my neck. "I'll wash it and get it back. Thank you."

"Keep it, no worries."

The door opens, and he steps in and taps his card on the panel before pressing "P".

I enter the car, and as the door closes, I try to take some courage from Karl's kind face.

What am I even going to say? I know nothing about childcare. Not in a responsible adult way, anyway.

But I may be able to find someone, and he may not even notice. And if he does, I'd just confess. Or come up with another lie.

My head is spinning by the time the elevator opens. I step out into a small foyer; it's all beige, and still completely different than our offices. Luxurious, soft, and welcoming.

Across from me is an arch that opens up into a living room, with a spectacular view of Central Park that stretches past the window wall on the other side.

I take a few steps. The living room is huge and pristine. Several large sofas create a focal point in the middle. There are pillars that break the open space, with twelve large chairs in a dining area on one side and a grand piano on the other side.

The entire room is lined with windows on all sides. It's like a large, elegant greenhouse. It's beautiful.

"Hello," I call, and jump back when a person moves to my left. Jesus. I didn't even notice someone was in the room.

My skittishness causes me to hit my elbow into the

arch's door frame. Third time is a charm. The pain reverberates up my arm.

The person crosses the room. It's Declan's mother. I saw her twice—the second time was just this Saturday at Saar's.

She is tall and slender, dressed in a camel pantsuit with her hair styled in a perfect blowout.

I'm suddenly double-aware of my sweaty, disheveled appearance.

"Oh, it's Lily, isn't it? Did Declan call you as well?" She narrows her eyebrows. "Come on in." She smiles at me.

I follow her around the sofas and the dining table into a large kitchen. While it's kind of separated with two smartly positioned walls, it's really a hidden part of the same open room. The spectacular view through the wall of windows is the dominant feature here as well.

"The mix-up with the nanny got him in a mood." She sighs. "Coffee?"

I can't imagine when her son isn't in a mood. I stop by the square kitchen island. "No, thank you, Mrs. Quinn." God, I need caffeine, but let's get the ugly over with first. "The mix-up is unfortunate. I'm the replacement nanny." My words come out in one rushed breath as I shrug.

She jerks her head and then smiles. "Oh, that's great. I'm sorry I never asked you what you do. This is fantastic. So much better than a stranger. And call me Dorothy."

I smile and hold my tongue, trying to limit how far my lie will stretch. Am I really becoming Declan's nanny?

No.

I will find someone by the end of the day, and then explain everything.

"Lily, awe we going to the sheltew with Auntie?" Zoya runs into the kitchen from behind the corner, her huge eyes full of excitement.

"Not right now, Zoya." I try to pretend I'm capable of this responsibility. "We need to get you to school." The confidence in my voice is at odds with my fingers rapidly tapping on the sides of my thighs.

"I don't want to go to school." Zoya pouts.

"Sweetheart, go get your backpack and your brother. We're running late as it is." Dorothy leans down and kisses the girl's head. Zoya opens her mouth, but her granny swats her bum gently. "Off you go. No arguments."

The little girl huffs but skips away.

"Declan is on a call. It's been a crazy morning, as you can imagine, but I cleared my calendar and got here shortly before you. We'll take the kids to school together, and then you can pick them up this afternoon."

"I hope your lateness is an exception." The velvety baritone wraps around me with its usual charm.

Its solace disappears as soon as I glimpse the owner. Declan walks into the kitchen, wearing a navy suit that hugs him like a second skin. He kisses his mother's cheek. "Thank you for coming to help. Again."

He's fidgeting with his cufflinks. His mom turns his hand and helps him to clasp them on. He hasn't looked at me yet. He still doesn't know I'm here. Or that I'm not a qualified nanny. Or that I exist.

His brief gaze at Saturday's party flashes through my memory. That wasn't attention; that was just a reaction to my clumsiness. I'm sure he doesn't even know my name.

If I'm lucky, my presence here today will go unnoticed, or at least unconnected to our friend's circle.

Though Dorothy may burst that sliver of hope.

He walks to the counter and puts a capsule into his Nespresso machine. "You've met my mother. She will show you the ropes with the school run. The housekeeper comes at eleven and will fill you in on the rest." He picks up his small cup and downs the coffee. "I'll be home by seven today, and we can talk then. Make sure—"

Our eyes meet. I swallow.

"I better go check on the kids." Dorothy leaves the kitchen.

Declan stands, the skyline of Manhattan behind him. It looks all bright and beautiful in contrast to his frown.

Frown?

It's not his typical scowl aimed at repelling people. It's something between shock and curiosity. Like he's trying to remember something.

Yep, we met before.

He holds the small, black cup in one hand and draws circles around the rim with his finger. The motion is painfully slow. It's not a mindless fidgeting; it's a deliberate move. Like I do when I think.

The few feet of the tiled floor stretch between us. The kitchen is spacious, but under his gaze I feel trapped. Like his eyes could make me smaller and more insignificant, so I straighten my spine and lift my chin.

I swear his lips quirk up for a millisecond before he schools his expression again. Is he amused? By my presence? By my chin-lifting act of defiance?

He moves his gaze slowly, languidly, down my body. It's not scrutiny; it's almost an indulgence. He enjoys what he sees.

And God help me, I enjoy his perusal. When I entered this penthouse, I was grateful for the pleasantly-set temperature. Right now, my T-shirt is absorbing my body's weight in sweat. I'll be seriously dehydrated after this morning.

The few moments of his attention feel like an eternity. His eyes linger on my naked legs for a moment, before he remembers all that's wrong with this situation.

"Are you even qualified to watch my children?" That puzzlement is back now, along with parental concern.

He should be concerned. I should be concerned.

But those thoughts are canceled because I nod. I freaking nod.

Well, let's be honest here, this man robbed me of my sanity the first time I heard his voice over the line at Summit Solutions.

"Okay." He nods curtly and leaves.

It's not lost on me that he doesn't walk past me but takes the trouble to back up and walk around the island from the other side. He may as well, as I'm in desperate need of a shower.

But more importantly, has he even recognized me?

# Chapter 3

## *Declan*

Fucking hell.

Lily is my new nanny. How did that happen?

How did I allow that to happen?

Ever since I saw her that first time at Caleb's Christmas vow renewal, she's invaded my every waking hour.

So I did the only reasonable thing. I've been pretending she doesn't exist. At least we didn't need to see each other again. Not that it helped my infatuation.

And now she is in my fucking kitchen. With her weirdly unkempt haircut, large unflattering glasses, and those legs.

Fucking hell.

She's in my kitchen in those indecently short

shorts, her tanned legs imprinted on my mind for an eternity.

But it's her eyes that grabbed my attention that first time. She hides them behind those glasses like she's trying to avoid attention.

But I saw those brown eyes. She is all smiles and kindness, but those eyes hide loss and pain.

I noticed way too much about her that first night. She talked to her friend about Greek gods. What an odd thing. What an intriguing thing.

"Daddy, do we weally need to go to school?" Zoya pulls at my jacket.

"Of course, sweetheart. You're already very late. You better hurry."

"But, Daddy—"

"Zoya—" I use my strict voice, and her little shoulders sag.

"Have a nice day, Dad." Zach extends his hand, and we shake.

"Are you okay?" Mom studies me.

I sigh. "It's been a hell of a morning."

"Daddy, money in a sweaw jar." Zoya practically dances with excitement that she caught me cussing.

"Let's go now," my mom says, and my twins bounce toward the elevator.

"See you later." Lily's voice comes from my side, and I whip my head toward her.

That voice. Jesus.

She smiles. It seems like it's a deliberate effort to form a smile, but it still comes out honest. Sunshine.

My jaw tightens, and I nod and then gesture toward the elevator, rushing her away. Pink ghosts her cheeks, and she hurries after my family.

I stare at the closed door of the elevator for way longer than I can afford.

Fucking hell. Lily is my new nanny.

I've successfully ignored her for half a year. Quite unsuccessfully, if I'm honest, since I still saw her everywhere, my mind completely ignoring any sensible notion of how wrong it was.

I have no right to think about her. She doesn't need an older man with family to derail her life. She's in her early twenties, for fuck's sake.

And even if she didn't mind that I'm at least a decade older, there is no room for any relationship in my life.

Between work and the kids, I have no time for anything else. We have a good routine. One that I fought hard to build. I can't have it disrupted. Zoya and Zach deserve stability.

It's one thing to fantasize about your friend's friend. But about my nanny?

Fuck. I need to fire her tonight.

\* \* \*

"I didn't think it's possible, but Declan actually can glower more." Xander takes a loud sip from his ridiculously large cold drink. What is he, twelve?

The youngest partner at Merged is a gifted child, but sometimes I wonder if he rigged the IQ tests.

"What's wrong?" my brother asks, and stands from behind his desk. Why we always have meetings in his office instead of a boardroom is beyond me.

"Nothing." I take a seat in a one-seater in the farthest corner, as far as possible from slurping Xander.

"I can't believe I'm saying this, but I side with Xander on this one; you look like a cat peed into your favorite Ferragamos. What pissed you off?" Cormac sits in the armchair beside me.

"Talking from experience?"

Corm recently adopted a cat. Well, more like his wife did. My brother is a different man in many ways since he settled down. Case in point: the large black-and-white photograph of Saar above the sofa beside me.

I have pictures of my kids on my desk, but his approach seems a bit over the top. Despite the fact that it's an art piece taken by a famous photographer that cost a high five-figures.

"I think he looks more like he had his wisdom tooth

extracted." Our office manager, Roxy, waltzes in and picks up the conversation—one I care little about—flawlessly. Does she have this office bugged?

She never removes her earpiece, and sometimes, I half wonder if she's listening to music while pretending to talk to us. But her productivity and ability to keep the office, and especially the four of us partners, organized is priceless, so she can listen to audiobooks for all I care.

What she shouldn't do is comment on my mood. Fuck them all. If they'd had the morning I had, they wouldn't even show up.

The most difficult part of being a father is having to constantly adjust the schedule. It doesn't matter how prepared I am to tackle everything, to be there for the kids' bedtime, to catch all the concerts and games, something always explodes.

"I think his new nanny quit." Caleb, our chief operating officer, walks in. Does this office have speakers all around the floor for everyone to listen in?

"She didn't quit," I snap.

Not that it hasn't been an issue before. At one point this past year, Zoya and Zach decided to drive all the nannies away. I hope it's just a phase. As soon as they start the first grade in September, they won't have time for their antics.

I need a stable nanny by then. Not that I have one

now. The woman in my home, probably talking to my housekeeper right now, can't stay there. I still don't understand how Lily ended up in my house in the first place.

"Not yet." Caleb chuckles and sits beside Xander.

"Let's start this meeting, shall we?" I flip my tablet's cover and click on my notes app.

"Let's start then." Corm sits, and even without looking, I can feel his eyes on me.

Okay, maybe I'm in a worse mood than usual. Again, with the morning I had...

"All right, let's get to the big item on the agenda. The London expansion," Xander announces with a self-satisfied grin. "I've looked at opportunities, and Declan ran the numbers. This is a no-brainer. London's financial district is primed for growth, and positioning ourselves there could increase our market share in Europe by at least twenty percent over the next two years."

"Primed for growth?" Corm raises an eyebrow. "How much of that twenty percent are you expecting to come out of our pockets first?"

"Initial investment isn't negligible," I say. "Office space in Canary Wharf isn't cheap, and we'd need to recruit locally—top talent only. But the long-term returns make it worth it. I sent you all the numbers, and I think we can all agree the time is right."

"If we want an aggressive expansion. We started this company a little over a year ago," Cal points out.

"Well, I'm all for aggressive growth. The question is, who will babysit this adventure?" Corm looks around the table.

"One of us should oversee it personally for at least the first year." Xander puts his drink down. "It's a critical move, and I don't trust an outsider to understand the intricacies of what we do."

"You mean the intricacies of how you want it done," Roxy snickers.

"It's not a bad strategy," I say. "Having one of us there ensures continuity and control."

Cal lets out a long puff of breath. "I'm all for sipping tea and watching cricket, but with the baby on the way and Mia living here with her mother, I can't relocate. Celeste and I need to stay here."

He recently found out he has a preteen daughter, so of course, he can't leave. Mentioning Celeste, who is a friend of Lily's, triggers images in my mind.

Lily in the summer dress at Corm's party on Saturday. The pang of jealousy I felt when she laughed at something Xander said. The moment of insanity when I wanted to walk over and talk to her myself.

Lily at my house. In the shortest fucking shorts ever. Fuck.

"Declan, are you listening?" Corm kicks the side of my seat.

"Of course I am," I lie.

I need to fire her today, and avoid all group activities with her friends. Not an easy feat, given that two of them are my partners' wives. But I can make up excuses those few times a year. Forever. Or until she gets married.

The thought squeezes at my stomach. I ignore it. Corm studies me with suspicion.

"It can't be me," he says, and as he's the CEO, he's right. "And Xander is nurturing several long-term projects that can't be handled from over there."

"What are you suggesting?" I smirk. "Because if it's what I think it is, you must be delusional."

"You're best suited for the job," Caleb says. "You would be signing off on all the expenses anyway, so why not do it from the ground?"

"So I'm expandable here?" Fuck, I hate being defensive.

"Hey, boys," Roxy interrupts. "Let's set the egos aside for a moment. Have your pissing contests in your free time. I have more important things to do."

"No, you don't," all four of us say in unison, and Roxy rolls her eyes.

"Declan, you have the operational background and

the strategic mindset for this. If anyone can set up London, it's you." Corm shrugs.

"And you're the least likely to punch a banker in the face at a networking event." Caleb chuckles.

"That's true." Roxy crosses one leg over the other. She's wearing workers' overalls with a formal jacket on top. The woman's wardrobe is atrocious. "You've got the whole 'serious CFO' thing going for you. You'd charm the pants off the London crowd." Her commentary is equally tragic.

"I'm flattered." I glower at her, and she shrugs, grinning.

"I get it, Declan," Xander says, a hint of frustration in his tone. "Family comes first. But this isn't just about any of us. It's about the future of Merged. The way I see it, you're the most qualified to handle this."

"That's true," Corm says.

"You really think I should move?" I look at my brother, a sense of betrayal coiling up my spine.

He sighs, pinching the bridge of his nose. "That's my opinion as the CEO. As your brother, I understand the twins come first. At the same time, they're starting a new school in September. Perhaps the best time to relocate."

"Are you fucking kidding me? You know how much it cost me to ensure stability for them." I seriously didn't think my day could get any worse. "So Caleb's family takes precedence, but mine is—"

"Yours is equally important," Corm jumps in.

"It sure feels that way," I growl, tapping my fingers on the armrest.

"Okay, gentlemen, I don't want to break up your bonding session, but it would be a big personal decision for any of you." Roxy sits up straight and stacks her pen into the dreadlock bun on top of her head. "Why don't we table this conversation for later?"

"What would be our plan B?" Corm looks at Xander, who pouts.

The fucker pouts.

"Don't tell me you didn't prepare a plan B?" Caleb gives him a side look.

"We bring in a managing director to oversee the office. Someone vetted, with a strong European network. But let's be honest—no outsider is going to care about this as much as we do."

"Okay, Roxy, put out feelers about potential candidates." Corm stands up. "Discreetly. Let's continue this riveting discussion in two to three days."

As everyone files out of the office, Corm stops me. "Think about it, Declan."

"I have nothing to think about." I march out of his office and across the floor to mine. "No interruptions," I bark at my assistant, and slam the door behind me.

Two hours later I've done nothing, because my mind is wandering in all directions, usually circling back to my new nanny with determination.

And without scruples, or consideration for the moral implications or the sanity of my actions, I log into my security system.

The living room cam streams into my work computer screen, and it's like I'm rewarded for my creepiness, and I spot her immediately.

Lily walks alongside the windows in the living room. Back and forth. She's on her phone. I can't zoom in closer, but she seems to talk with urgency.

Who is she talking to? I check my watch. She will leave to pick up the kids soon. Even her nervous pacing is elegant. She runs her hand through her messy hair and leans against the window.

I push my chair forward, my heart rate spiking. I know those windows are triple-glassed, reinforced to withstand pressure, but for some reason, anyone leaning against them makes me anxious.

It's completely irrational. Even if by some strange act the window broke, she would only fall onto the terrace. And yet I want to call to her to step away. To stay safe.

I wouldn't call her, of course, but the outlandish thought gives me pause. I don't have her number.

Usually, the agency copies me in on the email

when they send the paperwork to my accountant for the payroll. I didn't receive anything today. Strange.

I was so stressed about the no-show this morning, and then so shocked about Lily's presence, I didn't even realize the usual procedures were not followed. I left my kids with a person I have no means to contact. Fuck.

I look back at my screen. Lily shoves her phone into the back pocket of those indecently attractive shorts and covers her face in her palms. What's wrong?

Why do I need to know?

She drops her arms and looks up. She is not looking at the camera, but her gaze isn't that far off, angling toward me. One ankle casually crossed over the other, her slender frame calls to me seductively. I almost reach out and trace my finger on the image.

How is it I find a casually leaning woman so attractive that my cock twitches in my pants? That is a reaction I haven't had in such a long time. I need to get laid.

Her black shirt isn't tight, and yet it hugs her perfect tits. Fuck. I should have never noticed those, but I did. The first time I saw her.

Her eyes.

And those perfect tits.

I open the same app on my phone and screenshot the current view. I'm half-hard, and officially a stalker.

Another reason to fire her tonight.

*A Convenient Secret*

I drop my phone as someone knocks on the door and scramble to click out of the app on my large screen.

"I said no interruptions," I bark.

The door opens slightly regardless, and Corm pokes his head in. "Indulge me for a moment."

Not waiting for my response, he saunters in and sits on the dark leather chair across from me.

I pull my chair close and steeple my fingers, resting my forearms on my heavy mahogany desk.

"If you think you can sweet-talk me into moving to London—"

"Have you ever heard me sweet-talking?" He arches his eyebrow.

"Touché." I shrug.

Corm is more into manipulation with a side of blackmail. I know, I grew up with him. We couldn't be more different, but at almost thirty-seven, I still consider him my closest friend.

"I think I'm getting Saar a dog," Corm says.

I study him for a moment. "This really is a social visit? During work hours?"

"We own the shop." He deadpans.

"Fair enough. Congratulations. Now you will have a cat peeing in your shoes and a dog chewing on your ties."

"And yet she wants one, and I can't help myself." He groans.

"Pussy-whipped much?"

"You'll understand once you fall."

"I love my children, and a dog is a hard no."

"You'll understand one day... mark my words."

I glare at him, painfully aware that I'm having a conversation with my brother while hiding a semi behind the desk.

If I didn't have kids, I wouldn't have to go home and try to avoid her today. But then if I didn't have my kids, I wouldn't have my temptress nanny.

He leans back in his chair. "How are things with Kendra?"

My ex-wife's name induces instant heartburn, as usual, and with it goes my unsatisfied erection. "Her lawyer reached out again. My lawyer is reviewing options."

"She abandoned Zach and Zoya twice already. She can't win a custody battle." Corm picks up a stapler from my desk and clicks it a few times.

"Her new husband has all the means to sponsor her attempt." I watch the staples disappearing behind my desk, dropping to my office floor.

"But why now? It makes no sense. She is a heartless bitch." Click. Click. Click. "She doesn't want Zoya and Zach."

I reach out and snatch the stapler from him. "Do you think she's after money again?"

It wouldn't be the first time my ex-wife tried to extort money from me, but her recent nuptials removed her financial desperation. Though I guess there may be no limits to her greed and selfishness.

"I think you can find out easily."

"Yeah, I'm meeting my lawyer on Friday to discuss our options."

"Is that what put you in the mood today? If you need time off to sort things out—"

"I don't need time off," I snap.

This work is the only part of my life I'm not failing at. I failed as a husband. Or rather at choosing a partner. God knows I'm failing daily as a father, no matter how hard I try.

"So what's up your ass?"

"Just a shitty morning. The new nanny was late, and I had to scramble to get shit done."

Corm stands up and walks to the door. "Jesus, I hope she sticks around."

*That's not happening.* "Funny enough, the agency sent one of Saar's friends. The short one with glasses." *As if I didn't know her name.*

He frowns. "Lily? I thought she worked at Summit Solutions." He leaves, closing the door behind him.

*Me too. Me too.*

I leave my office with a sense of dread mixed with something akin to excitement. They turn into shock when I step into my home.

It's the screams and laughter that make me pause first as I exit the elevator. My kids can be loud, but never this loud. The sounds are coming from my living room.

What the hell?

They are usually in their rooms upstairs when I arrive. But it's the melody of laughter that isn't familiar in my home that makes me breathe faster.

I drop my keys on the console table and step forward. What the actual fuck?

The entire four thousand square feet of my living room is littered with confetti. It's like a rainbow died and dissolved all over my floors and furniture.

Zach and Zoya run around, spreading more little sparkly messes while Lily is chasing them.

I stay rooted to my spot, unsure how I feel. My kids are wild—it will be a nightmare to put them to sleep—and so happy that my chest squeezes, the reprimand for the mess and the raucous noise dying on my lips.

Zoya cackles like crazy, throwing around party ribbons. Zach, who is always serious, has jumped on the sofa and is now bouncing and tossing colorful shredded paper and yelling, "Let's get in trouble!"

Lily grabs him, tackling him to the sofa and tickling him. They both giggle like they're possessed.

"Me too, me too." Zoya launches at them, and they roll off the sofa in a heap of laughter.

I jerk forward. In my mind's eye, I'm already seeing one of them hitting the corner of the coffee table. But I realized it's just the carpet. Or rather, my rug is somewhere under the colorful mess.

"Have you moved my furniture around?" I bark. Really? That's what I focus on?

The three of them freeze. Zach's eyes widen, and he scrambles to his feet, wiping the confetti from his clothes.

Zoya smiles at me with that beautiful, innocent smile that has no boundaries. "Daddy!"

She sprints to me, running over the sofa and almost tripping. I squat to catch her as she wraps her little arms around my neck and gives me a kiss. "You awe home."

The uncensored honesty of her joy is like a kick at my solar plexus. Every. Single. Time. I'm pretty sure most of the time I'm disappointing my kids, and Zoya still accepts me with such enthusiasm.

It breaks my heart and mends it without failing.

On the periphery, I more sense than see Lily standing up. When I straighten, she is beside Zach, her arm protectively around his shoulders.

"Are we in trouble?" Zach asks, leaning toward Lily. She makes him feel safe. She's been with them for a few hours, and they've bonded already.

It hits me with a potent cocktail of emotions I don't want to dissect. All of them are overwhelmingly touching. I don't have time for touching.

"Why don't you both go get changed so we can have dinner?" I kiss Zoya's crown, and both kids shuffle toward the staircase while I avoid the nanny at all costs.

"I'll go help them," Lily says.

"We need to talk." I glance at her, and it's like being bathed by the first rays of sunshine after the darkest and gloomiest storm.

She looks so young and innocent in the middle of my party-littered home, I avert my eyes immediately.

I walk toward the windows. That way I can ensure my back is to her.

"What are you doing here, Lily?"

# Chapter 4

## *Lily*

He knows my name? He knows it's me.

"I mean, besides destroying my house and riling up my kids when they should be winding down," Declan continues.

His hands are in his pockets as he stands by the glass wall and stares outside while having a conversation with me. Fuck his voice. He really is a dick.

I look around at the mess, and I can see some of his annoyance may be justified.

"I didn't destroy your house. The kids had a bad day. They didn't know that in September, Ms. Corrine won't be their teacher anymore." It's like talking to a wall. His broad back visibly tenses. "So I wanted to cheer them up."

Okay, maybe I didn't think it through. When we entered the party store, I was planning to get balloons, but when Zoya suggested a confetti fight, I couldn't resist her pleading eyes. That girl is a serious charmer.

"I'm sure my housekeeper will appreciate your efforts."

"I'll clean it up." I pull at the sleeves of my T-shirt, shifting from one foot to the other, feeling like I'm being judged and scolded by my father. Only my father would never scold me, or talk to me with his back to me.

"Before you do that..." He turns around. "Answer my question."

Our eyes collide. His are so dark, they seem black. His gaze is so intense, I can practically feel myself shrinking under its ferocity. I regret all the times I wished he'd notice me.

My fingers drum on my thighs of their own accord. It's an alarm drumming. A call for capitulation.

But I'll be damned if this man makes me cower. I might have a crush on him—his voice—but I won't allow him to intimidate me.

I didn't escape my old life only to end up as someone's doormat.

And yet my pulse quickens, my breath comes out fast and shallow. And if I allowed myself to think about it, my pussy is clenching. My nervousness is laced with yearning.

There is something wrong with me.

*A Convenient Secret*

The air between us is charged with so many weird, unresolved feelings. Well, my conflicting feelings. Declan is just Declan—grumpy.

He takes a few steps, and now I can smell his intoxicating musk—sandalwood, and him. I almost step backward, but I stop myself. I'm not giving him the satisfaction.

"Answer the question." His voice is chocolate—decadently washing over me despite his tone.

I swallow.

One of us must have taken another step or two, because suddenly he's looming over me. I have to crane my neck to maintain the eye contact, and damn it, I'm not breaking it.

His jaw is tense. His gaze is burning. His presence is overwhelming.

"What was the question?" I croak.

He closes his eyes with his next deep breath and then bores his gaze back into me. "Why are you here?"

"I'm your nanny."

He furrows his eyebrows and looks almost menacing. I guess the answer isn't satisfactory. Oh hell, I know it isn't. If he knows who I am, then he must be wondering why I am here. I should just confess.

I spent the day calling the agency, but nobody can get a full-time nanny here before next week. They can send a temp, but I may as well stay myself. Before I went to pick up the kids, I panicked and called in sick at Summit Solutions.

I only have three sick days without a doctor's note, but with my days off this week, it may give me enough time until a real nanny is available.

I allowed myself a minor breakdown, because the idea of childcare scares me. I love kids and can play with them for a moment or two, but being responsible for two human beings seems daunting. Hopefully, as long as I keep them safe and entertained, I should be okay.

"Why?" he growls, losing patience.

"I work at Summit Solutions. You spoke with me on Friday, and I... well, I fucked up. The soonest I can get you a full-time nanny is next week, so here I am." I spread my arms and smile like I'm a true gift to him.

His jaw ticks, but that's the only movement. He doesn't even blink, I think. A solid statue, he's glaring at me like he's trying to catch up for all the times he didn't even glance my way.

Not that he had a reason to; that's always been just my fantasy. One I need to bury rather fast if I don't want to lose my job. Summit Solutions doesn't tolerate client dissatisfaction.

After what feels like several lifetimes, he nods. Before I even exhale my relief, he turns and walks toward the kitchen.

Before he disappears, he looks at me and grunts. "Follow me."

What? I rush behind him. He opens a door in the kitchen's corner and beckons me in with his head.

I stop abruptly, shelves with cleaning supplies in front of me. "You can't lock me in the closet," I blurt.

I swear his lips twitch a bit before he tames them back into his usual scowl. "I wasn't planning on it, but interesting where your mind went. You said you'll tidy up the mess."

Oh. I step in and reach for a broom.

"I'd use a vacuum." He sighs. "And please don't rile up the kids before my arrival again. I work long hours, and I need the kids well-behaved for the only two hours I can spend with them."

What a prick. I pick up the vacuum.

"Am I understood?" he demands, and goose bumps sprout on my skin. My body is making fun of me with these reactions.

"Yes, sir," I mock, but the joke is on me.

As soon as the words slip out of my mouth, while I'm passing him and my arm brushes his jacket, we both still. I chance a look-up and almost drop the vacuum.

Until today, Declan Quinn has never looked my way.

Today, he already looked at me with an intensity that probably scares the people he deals with.

Right now, he's looking at me with burning curiosity. Yearning, even.

It reverberates through me, catching my breath. My cheeks are aflame, and I look away, regretting it immediately. Because now, my gaze lands on the tent in his pants.

I should walk away, but I can't move my legs. I stare at the outline of his very hard cock, and it takes me several moments before I will my feet to move. I practically run to the living room, the large vacuum banging my leg, probably leaving a bruise.

What just happened? Yesterday I had a silly crush on the timbre of his voice, and today I call him sir, and... have I affected him like that?

I drop the appliance on the ground and rush to the powder room hidden under the stairs. Washing my face with cold water helps with the persistent blush, but does nothing to my racing heart.

I wish the odd situation would erase my stupid infatuation with him. It does the exact opposite. I'm way over my head with a man like Declan. And he probably got aroused by bossing me around... Did he?

I can't go back out there. Are we going to pretend I didn't see? That would probably be the best course of action.

*A Convenient Secret*

When I finally emerge from the bathroom, I find Declan vacuuming the large rug by his sofa. Pausing, I observe him for a moment. He shed his jacket and rolled up his sleeves, the sinews of his forearms bulging with every move.

I'm not sure what captivates me more… Seeing this man cleaning his house? Or just seeing him doing something, anything really?

And why on earth do I find him vacuuming so damn attractive? It's like I saw an outline of his cock, and I'm drawn to him by some potent mixture of pheromones.

This is a disaster. I will have to run into him for an entire week. Jesus.

I step from the shadows of the staircase, and he stops, tapping casually at the top of the appliance with his foot. The humming stops.

Declan doesn't look at me. That's more of a familiar dynamic between us.

"See you tomorrow at seven," he says, speaking to the space in front of him.

The scared, inexperienced girl in me is grateful he pretends nothing happened. Grateful he retreated back to being his usually aloof version of him.

Great. That's probably for the best.

"I'm going to say goodbye to the kids." I don't wait for his approval and run upstairs.

He doesn't start the vacuum until I turn the corner.

* * *

My heart is still pulsing chaotically from my encounter with Declan as I ride the subway back to Brooklyn.

What a day.

I can't wait for a nice long shower. The good thing is that I told him about the mix-up, and he seems to have accepted the situation. Also, he knows who I am, and even knows my name. That's a bit of a surprise.

Maybe his mom told him.

What's not so good? I'm still in charge of keeping his kids safe and alive for a week.

While they were in kindergarten, Declan's housekeeper showed me their rooms on the second floor, their playroom, and their schedule.

Color-coded on a board in the kitchen, it outlines all the activities. The kids have their own driver, and sometimes, when they each have a different activity, Declan's driver is in charge of getting Zach to and from his soccer practice. Is he there by himself? Is the driver helping him to get changed?

Jesus. Single parenting isn't easy. And I only got an overview on a piece of paper. It's overwhelming. I can't imagine how a busy man manages it all. No wonder he's in dire need of a nanny.

Maybe easing up on their schedule might help him. Not that I would suggest that ever.

Why do all their nannies quit? I wanted to ask the housekeeper, but it felt too nosy after only fifteen minutes with her.

I can't believe I ended up working for Declan. Only I can get into this kind of situation. Jesus.

What a day.

Though I did enjoy the confetti fight with the kids. I don't even remember when I was last silly like that. Probably never. It felt so liberating.

It was so nice to see them unleash their uncensored side. Declan may be upset about his precious carpet—arguably, there are less messy ways to have fun—but those kids needed to let go.

I don't know where their mother is, and obviously their father's time is limited. Still, they are adorable. Such beautiful little souls.

I try to think about them, because thinking about their father is super confusing. It makes me hot. It tingles between my legs. But mostly, it invades my mind with thoughts and images I have no right to think or picture.

It was easy to fantasize about him when he was just the voice. Even after I met him and realized he was the voice, he still felt like a fantasy.

But now? Now he's real. Within twelve hours

today, he looked at me, spoke to me, I spent a day in his house, I played with his children, and we had a moment.

I don't even know if it was a moment, but I had an impact on him. This is going to be an endless week.

I unlock the apartment, exhausted and heavy with all that happened today.

"Here you are," Mrs. Whitaker, in her typical pink robe, accosts me the minute I enter. "I thought you would make me starve."

Shit. I forgot about the dinner. She scans me with narrowed eyes, searching for the takeout bag.

"I'm sorry. It was one of those days—"

"You're just so selfish." She sniffles and almost produces actual tears of hurt.

"Look, Mrs. Whitaker, I'm sorry—"

"You know, Lily, I think I need to find another roommate. Someone more considerate." She crosses her arms over her chest. "I will have to ask you to move out by Friday."

I blink. "Our contract obliges you to give me a month's notice."

"Not if you break the tenant code of conduct." She purses her lips, the small line around her mouth wrinkling more.

"What code of conduct?"

"You broke clause seven..." She names several made-up accusations while I tune her out.

She's making everything up, but knowing her "sincere" personality, I don't think I will get too far pointing out her lies.

"You're really throwing me out because I forgot to get us takeout?" I try to appeal to her twisted common sense.

"Don't be ridiculous. It's the code of conduct." She maintains her ridiculous ploy. She really wants to taste that new restaurant.

"What if I went to get us that takeout?" I say, not because I want to eat or spend my evening in her company, but because I can't be homeless. How would I even find a new place within days? On my budget, no less?

"I might consider it." She lifts her chin.

I turn and march out.

What a day.

It takes me almost forty-five minutes before I trudge my feet back to my current home.

By the time I arrive, I'm so tired I don't want to eat or talk. Not even shower anymore, even though I'm grossly sweaty.

"Ooh, what did you get us?" Mrs. Whitaker coos and pulls out two plates.

"Enjoy your dinner. I'm going to sleep."

"Lily?" my landlady calls after me, but I'm already closing the door to my room. And I lock it.

* * *

My alarm goes off at five-thirty, and I spring out of bed. Mrs. Whitaker likes to sleep in, so if I'm lucky I'll be able to shower and leave without running into her.

I take a quick shower and brush my teeth. Not bothering with my hair, I just towel-dry it. It's hot outside, and it will be dry by the time I arrive in Manhattan. It's not like I can shape it into any style at this point.

I put on a short, flowery summer dress with long, voluminous sleeves that gather at my wrists. The dress is way above my knees, but it's been so hot. At least, that's what I tell myself. I'm definitely not wearing it for Declan.

I almost make it out of the door undetected. Almost.

"Lily, I think I'm going to insist you clear the room by Friday."

Her words startle me, and a gasp escapes me when I turn. Mrs. Whitaker stands at the end of the short corridor in shadow. A cone of light from the kitchen is splitting her face.

Something snaps inside me. My life here is meant

to be a fresh start, a step toward independence. This woman's demands push me to betray that. To betray myself. I'm done with her.

I leave without a word, my heart hammering.

My housing situation is concerning, but I can't be late. I might be an under-qualified nanny, but those kids don't need another stressful morning. And neither does Declan.

My consideration for him seems misplaced as soon as I arrive at his house.

"Lily!" Zoya shouts when I round the partition wall to enter the kitchen.

The family is sitting around the kitchen counter. Sweet vanilla and a hint of cinnamon permeate the air.

"Good morning." I smile at the kids. "Wow, pancakes on a school day."

They look delicious, but that's not what makes me pause. Declan is at my side, at the stove, flipping the golden batter. It's such a normal, human thing that I consider he may have a twin.

Equally gorgeous, but without a stick up his ass. When a handsome man makes pancakes for his kids, it's just plain attractive.

When Declan Quinn flips pancakes, it's slightly weird, like he's been replaced. But it's downright sexy.

And then I notice he is wearing his dress shirt. Open. Did he lose all the buttons? It's just a sliver of skin where the two sides almost meet. I can't even really see it, but I know it's there. Oh, my poor ovaries.

Our eyes meet for a beat, but we both look away like the sight could burn. Well, it does. My cheeks are aflame.

He serves more pancakes on the twins' plates and pivots to drop the pan in the sink. His shirt opens up wider, and I get a glimpse of his defined abs and chest. It's so quick, I hardly get a chance to ogle, which is probably even worse.

My fantasies used to be limited to his voice. Now that voice has a body, and even a glimpse leaves me aching in every neglected inch of me.

A few minutes into the day here and I'm sweating again.

"I'll shawe mine with you," Zoya offers.

"That's so kind, Zoya, but I already ate."

At that, because why not, my stomach rumbles. I haven't eaten since yesterday lunchtime when the housekeeper fixed me a sandwich.

"You lied?" Zach frowns.

Who knew I could blush more? Thank God for my darker skin, because I would look like a ripe tomato by now. "Maybe I'm extra hungry today after our fight yesterday."

Zach snorts.

"Okay, monsters, you need to get ready. Finish

your breakfast and go get your backpacks." Declan moves around the kitchen.

I try not to look at him. He didn't even greet me, so I guess the world is back to normal. I should be relieved. His ignoring me is something I'm used to.

But I'm not relieved. I'm annoyed with him, but there is nothing I can do about it in front of the kids. There is nothing I have the right to do anyway.

Since I have no plate in front of me, and I'm not quite sure what to do with myself, I decide to get a glass of juice.

Only Declan appears from somewhere and opens the fridge the moment I turn to it. While I was lying to Zach and Zoya about having breakfast, Declan buttoned up his shirt. Thankfully.

But even dressed, his closeness sends my fantasies on a wild ride. "Sorry." I step back.

"No, please, go ahead." He doesn't look at me.

I reach for the juice carton and pour myself a glass. He gets milk for his coffee and closes the fridge. The color-coded schedule glares at me from the board. Right. Let's focus on the job at hand.

Soccer practice for Zach after school, and swimming for both of them afterward. Good, at least there won't be room for silly ideas like a confetti fight.

"I finished. Thank you, Dad." Zach slides down from his stool and walks out.

"You're welcome," his father says from somewhere behind me. "Zoya, hurry up."

"I'm done. Can you dwive us, Daddy?" She tilts her head, her eyes pleading. But there is a hint of calculation she can't hide. She must know what effect she has on people.

"You know I can't," Declan says. I guess she doesn't affect all people.

"But why?" She pouts.

"Zoya, we can't talk about this every single morning. Lily will drop you off. Go get your things."

She pouts more, her lip practically covering her whole chin, but she doesn't argue and leaves.

The minute we're left alone, the air changes, charged with something. Something I'm surely imagining.

"I better go and get them to school." I don't look at him and start leaving.

"Lily," he says.

I pause. "Yes?" I breathe. I freaking breathe.

Is he going to talk about the confetti mess? About my nanny fuck-up? About his erection? *Don't be silly, Lils.* He may want to discuss the kids' schedule. Something normal. Like my employer. Jesus.

I turn.

"Your juice."

What? Declan is pointing at my still-full glass. In

my nervous awareness of his presence, I filled it to the rim and forgot to drink it.

I don't want the juice, but I don't want him to think I'm crazy. I take the glass gingerly, putting it to my lips, and really hoping I won't embarrass myself by spilling it all over me.

I gulp it down, painfully aware of Declan's gaze. So *now* he is staring at me? I turn slightly, and he disappears from my peripheral vision. There is a kitchen island between us, but he feels indecently close.

Can this morning be any more awkward?

Putting the glass down, I try to walk normally to finally get out of the kitchen.

But I learn that the morning can indeed get more awkward when Declan asks, "Is this what you are wearing?"

## Chapter 5

### *Declan*

Have I really just asked that?

What the fuck?

As if it wasn't enough I sported a semi in front of her yesterday, now I'm commenting on her clothes.

She looks hot in that dress. But for fuck's sake, everyone could almost see her... That dress is too short.

Longer than her shorts yesterday, but it's all flowy, and as she moves, it shimmies around her, drawing attention to her beautiful legs. But to her other parts, as well. They remain hidden, but so within reach in her indecent dress.

Or rather, my thoughts about her are indecent. It might be a normal summer dress, but it isn't innocent in my dirty thoughts.

I should have fired her yesterday. I didn't, because she's getting me a new nanny next week. One that isn't her. And I don't have time to find someone sooner, so having her here temporarily makes sense.

It made sense yesterday. In the light of this morning, I'm not so sure. It's going to be a long week.

"Obviously." She puts her hands on her hips.

The action lifts the dress slightly more. My gaze drops to the lightly tanned skin, but I catch myself and start moving around, tidying up after the kids.

When I say nothing—because, let's face it, haven't I said enough already—Lily steps in front of me, blocking my useless activity.

"This is what I am wearing. Sorry it's not up to your standards, but I wasn't aware there is a dress code. Anything else?"

Her nose is small and slightly curved to one side. I never noticed that before. The imperfection makes her even more interesting. I wish she would ditch those glasses. They hide half of her beautiful face.

I finally meet her eyes—something I try not to do for her own sake—and I find a challenge in them. Right, she asked something.

"Please don't move the furniture around, and don't lean against the windows." I guess we both can lead a successful passive-aggressive conversation.

"What?"

I close my eyes briefly and take a deep breath. Only now I'm engulfed in the subtle scent of coconut.

When I look down at her, she is glaring back.

"You heard me. Just do your job, and get me a permanent nanny." I look at my watch. "And you better leave so the kids are not late. *Again*."

It's much safer to repel her with my attitude.

A pink hue warms her cheeks. "As you wish." She smiles and leaves.

I know her obedience was as passive-aggressive as our conversation. I'm equally aware her agreement was to mock me.

And yet it does something to the deepest, darkest, depraved corners of my soul.

What if she was this pliable in... Fuck, don't go there.

I stare at the spreadsheet, the numbers blurring in front of my eyes. There is something wrong with these projections, but I can't point it out. I had the best people from my team on it, but I guess I can't trust anyone.

Fuck. I'm exhausted. I press the intercom,

connecting with my assistant. "Can you, please, get me another coffee?"

I haven't slept much this week. It's been a blur of meetings, calls, number crunching, and stolen glimpses of Lily. In reality, I have done nothing productive this week.

If I don't count a few satisfying jerk-off sessions. Courtesy of my nanny. Not that she knows—or could ever know.

Since I didn't fire Lily, I made myself scarce. I dove into work to avoid her. In the last few days, it also meant I didn't see my kids much. I miss them, and I really hate losing even the little time we have together.

But it's only for a week. Well, only for today, as it finally is Friday.

Not sure when I became the man who hides instead of attacking his problems head-on, but here we are.

I have no control around Lily. Or rather, the last threads of control I had burst the minute she walked into my penthouse.

She is too young. I come with all the complications of a busy man with a busy family. This makes no sense for either of us. I need to squash my infatuation and move on with life.

It's not like we could hook up. I'm not particularly attached to the group that formed because Cal and

Corm fell for their women, but having a one-night stand with Lily would only add unnecessary tension.

On Monday, I will get a new nanny, and then I can go back to the life I know. One where I have control. One that I've carefully crafted to make sure the kids don't suffer much from the absence of their mother.

One that, if I'm honest with myself, I arranged so I can deal with the demands I never saw myself addressing.

Back to safety and order.

One more day.

I will delete her footage from my security system tonight.

Yes, in the last few days I went into hiding, and into full-blown stalker mode. I've never logged into my home security as many times as this week. Who am I kidding? I haven't logged out this week.

Lily didn't destroy the house, and doesn't engage in any other outlandish entertainment ploys anymore.

She talks to the kids—more Zoya than Zach, which is not surprising—paying eager attention. I respect her for that.

She herds them around to do their homework with proficiency. I admire her for that.

She laughs with them a lot. Way more than they've ever laughed with me. I hate her for that a little.

But mostly, I just stare at her. She is clumsy, dropping things. She is giggly, chatting with my housekeeper. She is all bright and positive, but there is something behind those eyes. Something I want to unravel, and I have no idea why.

It's like I armor myself with a glower while she protects herself with a smile. And while I believe her smiles are genuine, I feel like they are her weapon as well.

Fuck. I'm really deep into this nonsense. A few more hours and she's gone.

My assistant knocks and enters with my coffee. "Mr. Quinn would like to see you in his office."

"We don't have a meeting." Why would my brother summon me?

"It's all partners for a few moments."

"Okay." I take my mug and walk over to Corm's office. "What's going on?"

Xander lounges on the sofa, and Corm is finishing a call. I guess we're waiting for Cal. I take a sip of my coffee.

"Good, you're here." Corm turns in his chair.

"Where is Cal? What's going on?" Xander plays with his phone, tapping it on his leg and flipping it over before he repeats the move. The kid is never still.

"Celeste's waters broke. Cal can't make it for the Aertech board meeting, which means I have to go instead. Someone needs to represent us at the mayor's dinner party."

"I'll go," I blurt, and both men turn their heads to me.

"You?" Corm frowns.

Okay, I guess his surprise is guaranteed since I never volunteer for any evening engagement, and even the obligatory ones I try to wriggle out from.

"Is this some sort of attempt to prove you're needed in the States?" Xander snorts.

Fucker. "This has nothing to do with your genius idea to ship me to London."

It has everything to do with avoiding my nanny. Even though it makes no sense, because she'll leave when I arrive home from work.

This way I'll have to ask her to stay longer. Like having her longer in my space—while I'm not there—would solve anything.

It would give the kids more time with her before she says goodbye. That's the only reason. One I can use when I look in a mirror. Fuck.

"Calm down, Dec, I'm not trying to ship you anywhere. I'd go in a heartbeat—a taste of English pussy is on my bucket list." He grins like he said something amusing. "But you know I can't leave at the moment."

"This is not about London. And for the record, I have nothing to prove." I start to leave. "Send me the details," I say to Corm.

"I guess I don't need to cancel my date," Xander's voice reaches me.

"What's going on?" Corm catches up with me as I enter my office.

"You need to be more specific."

"You hated these things even before you had kids." Corm sums up the truth. "Where are they tonight?"

"With the nanny."

"I didn't know she works evenings." Corm leans in my doorway.

"I thought you had a plane to catch to get to the board meeting." I sit behind my desk.

Corm steps in and closes the door behind him. "Why do you want to miss an evening with your kids? Like you've been doing all this week."

Fuck. "How do you know that?"

"Roxy." He shrugs.

Of course, nothing escapes her. "I'm not avoiding my kids," I growl.

"Interesting choice of words. *Who* are you avoiding?" He puts his hands in his pockets, a gleeful smirk on his face.

"Lily." I sigh.

Corm laughs. "Do you have a crush on your nanny?"

"Fuck off. What am I, fifteen?" Yes, if we consider my latest behavior. "She's just everywhere, invading my space."

"She is there for your kids."

"I know," I snap.

"You *are* attracted to her."

He sits down like he is expecting popcorn and a show. I hate how perceptive my brother is. When I don't answer, he laughs.

"Get out of my office." I open a folder and pretend to review whatever is in it.

"Look, if it was anyone else, I would tell you to fuck the nanny, have fun. God knows you've been living like a monk. A good shag is what you need."

"When you have kids, you'll definitely see sex with your nanny in a new light." I glower. "I have work to do."

If I hoped that would make him leave, I was wrong.

"Okay, sleeping with your nanny is complicated, but it's not like they stay around long enough," he dares to tease me. "What I wanted to say... This is not just your nanny. Lily is my wife's friend. Don't go there."

"I wasn't planning to."

It's true, but it tastes like a lie. I don't lie to my brother. But apparently, nothing is right today.

He stands up. "You know, Declan, you can have a woman in your life. You're single. Kendra has been gone for a long time. Maybe it's time to get back out there."

"You've been married for a minute, most of it faking, so I'll make sure to consider your advice."

"Dickhead." He shakes his head.

"Asshole," I counter, because apparently, we're both fifteen.

He smirks. "I'll send you the event details."

\* \* \*

It's almost eleven when I come home. The dinner, the small talk, and a few divorcees' advances made it a torturous night.

And for what? Okay, a few important connections, and valuable intel for Merged.

But mostly to keep Lily here longer. I think. It makes no sense. I hate when things make no sense.

I'm making nonsensical decisions. Nonsense leads to a lack of control. That's dangerous.

By the time I step into my house, I'm practically vibrating with annoyance.

The night started all wrong. Not only because I went to the event for all futile reasons, but because I met with my lawyer just before.

A custody battle is the last thing I need at the moment.

And his suggestions to bullet-proof my case were completely unacceptable. I wish I'd never met Kendra. The thought only deepens the darkness in my mind. Without Kendra, I wouldn't have Zoya and Zach. I can't imagine that.

I drop my keys by the elevator door and start undoing the stupid bow tie. I can feel her presence before I even cross the living room.

Pausing at the window, I contemplate if a third whiskey tonight is a good idea. Will I pay the price tomorrow when Zoya attacks me in my bed before dawn?

After the week I had—after the day I had—I need one more. Fuck it.

Walking over to a buffet table in the dining area, I open the bottom cabinet and take out a bottle of Macallan.

I pour myself an inch and take a sip. It spreads through my limbs in the expected languid way, but it doesn't give me the relief I seek.

I don't know where Lily is, but I know she is here.

That's enough to make my skin tingle, and not in the worst way. It gives my cock ideas, too. But it also makes me feel more at home than ever before. Perhaps because I know I can reclaim my home once she leaves. Yeah, let's go with that logical conclusion.

"Wow, the James Bond look suits you well."

I whip around and almost drop the glass. Lily stands across the room on the last step. Her eyes have a sleepy, glassy look, and her head is flat on one side. She is beautiful.

If this is her just-woken look, how would her just-fucked look compare? Something tells me it would be like a new potent hit. As if I wasn't addicted enough.

"You slept." It's an observation—because now I need to know where she slept, pervert that I am—but it comes out as an accusation.

Narrowing her eyes, she opens her mouth, but then she sighs like a comeback is not worth the trouble. Like I'm not worth the trouble.

"I fell asleep reading with Zoya."

We stand there in the large room, the lamp, the lights on the terrace, and the New York skyline casting shadows around us. Lily's eyes shine so brightly, I can't move my gaze away.

We don't move for I don't know how long, while I wish I was younger or she was older. While I wish I had no kids, or she would feel the same attraction. I wish for things that I can't control, and that scares me.

"Daddy." Zoya's sleepy voice snaps me back to reality.

"Zoya, sweetheart, did you have a bad dream?" I cross the floor.

I put my foot on the first step, and my arm brushes Lily's. An electric current zaps through me. It probably scorches vital gray cells in my brain because I hand her my whiskey. "I'll be right back."

I rush upstairs and scoop Zoya into my arms.

Why did I say that? I practically asked her to wait for me. Fuck.

I put my sleepy daughter in her bed and pick up her white, plush unicorn from the ground. "Did you lose Mr. Corny?"

She hugs the toy tight to her as I kiss her forehead.

"I want Lily to stay," Zoya whispers before I reach the door.

*So do I. So do I.*

"Sweetheart." I return and sit on her bed. "Lily has a different job. She was only helping us. She helped to find a new nanny."

"I don't want a new nanny. I like Lily. Even Zach likes hew, but he doesn't want to say it."

I sigh. "I like Lily, too, but she is not a nanny."

"I'll miss her." Zoya's eyes mist with unshed tears, and her typical pout makes its appearance. Only this time, I'm pretty sure it's not a manipulation tactic. And as if her sadness is contagious, suddenly I'm filled with regrets.

So many fucking regrets. About Lily. About my kids. Even about Kendra.

I wrap Zoya in my arms and kiss her crown. "It's late. Get some sleep, so we can chase pigeons tomorrow."

"It's Satuwday tomowow? No wowk?"

"No work tomorrow. Good night, Zoya."

"Good night, Daddy."

I look through the adjacent door at my sleeping son. *Even Zach likes her, but he doesn't want to say it.*

Just my luck that my kids would take to the one nanny I can't have. Goddamn Lily, with her sunshine personality, pulling people into her orbit.

By the time I get downstairs, my irritation seeps through me, and I'm ready to shove Lily out of the door and never see her again.

That determination dies a quick death when my gaze lands on her.

She sits on the armrest of the double-seater, her profile to me. She's staring at the flickering lights of the city, my glass in her hands.

I don't dare to move, rooted at the base of the staircase. She is completely still, as if mesmerized by the view, unaware of my presence.

I've been watching her through my cameras the whole week, but this genuine moment in time doesn't compare.

*A Convenient Secret*

She must have run her hand through her hair because it's slicked back, showing her exquisite cheekbones. She's not wearing glasses, which is probably why I noticed her sleepy eyes before.

With her imperfectly perfect crooked nose, her profile is arresting.

She lifts her hand and puts the glass to her lips, taking a sip from my drink. Her lips touch where mine were moments ago, and I hit a new low. I'm jealous of my own glass.

"I hope you don't mind. It's better than vodka."

I startle. "Of course."

She giggles and slides back, down across the armrest, plopping into the soft cushions of the sofa. "I don't drink hard alcohol, and Saar and Cora got me drunk on vodka once." She shivers. "But this is good." She takes another sip and sighs.

The sound is soft, and has nothing to do with me. And yet my body reacts, and my cock stirs. Fuck. My. Life.

Abandoning any remains of common sense, I walk over and sit beside her. It's a fucking two-seater, but somehow I feel indecently close. There are feet of sitting surfaces around us, and I choose to squeeze in with her here.

I take the glass from her. "You better pace yourself if you're not used to this."

"Fair enough, but I can see the appeal. It makes me feel lighter."

I take a sip and savor it, hoping to feel lighter. All I feel is coconut, her warmth, and persistent heaviness.

It's been a shitty week altogether.

I'm failing my firm, because I know I'm the best to run the London setup.

I'm failing my kids, because my work cuts into my time with them.

I'm failing to protect them from their viper of a mother.

And amid all these problems, instead of looking for solutions, I'm sitting here with a woman who makes me feel level, even though she's the reason I'm so unsettled.

I sigh.

"That kind of a day?" Lily takes my tumbler and puts it to her lips. I don't see it because I'm staring into the space in front of me, but I still see it in my mind. Her lips.

"That kind of a week," I murmur. *Just stand up and let her go.*

She chuckles. "I guess I started your hell of a week. I'm sorry."

*I'm not.*

"You're good with them. I'm glad they had you

while they couldn't have me." I don't tell her they didn't have much of me because of her. That's a confession I'm not yet admitting to myself. And obviously failing at that, too.

She reclines her head, resting it on the backrest. "I kept them safe and occupied."

I slide forward and mirror her position, closing my eyes, grateful for the strange sense of peace. "Stop being modest. It doesn't suit you."

She giggles. "Okay, I won't."

I turn my head to the side and look at her. The pretense at obedience again. She is mocking me, and I love it.

But even while teasing, her compliance makes all my hair stand on end, my body tingling with the need to dominate her in other ways.

She also turns her head, and now her face is just inches from mine. We inhale each other's breath, the taste of whiskey lingering between us.

My eyes drop to her lips.

She darts out her tongue.

I angle myself toward her and drape my arm over the backrest behind her. She is even closer now, as we stare at each other like this was the only thing on our agenda.

I don't think I ever allowed myself to look at her for

this long. It stirs something in me. It's like discovering a new painting, or finding a hidden gem of antiquity.

Like seeing the kids wild with joy I don't understand.

Like everything I ever enjoyed has collided in this moment, in the woman beside me, and I can finally breathe and allow myself to simply absorb this rare pause in my life.

To absorb the attractive and very young woman who shares whiskey with me.

Her crooked nose adds to her allure. That minor flaw makes her more approachable, real. I want to trace my finger down its curved outline.

The delicate column of her neck bobs. If I lean a few inches, our lips would meet. As if my thought had telepathic abilities, Lily's lips part. She swallows again.

Would it be possible that she wants the same as me?

That's preposterous.

And even if she does, I should know better. She's so young. I don't have room for a fling.

I jerk back against the backrest again, desperately searching for the train of our conversation.

"They will miss you," I say, hopefully picking up a reasonable thread.

Any thread that takes me away from her full lips.

That aristocratic jewel of a nose. Or those bewitchingly enigmatic eyes.

"I'll miss them too."

The honest regret in her voice shocks me. She spent a week with them, and she genuinely cares about them. Not because it's a job. Because she likes them as much as they like her.

"Lily," I groan, wishing I could stop her from bringing value to my life. Hoping against the odds that, somehow, she may just disappoint and make things easier for me.

"Declan," she sighs, mock-mirroring my desperation, and fuck, I want to hear my name on her lips more often. In different situations. "I'll be happy to hang out with them again. They are wonderful kids."

"You would do that?"

Is she just generous with her time, or does she want to spend time with us? Not that she should.

"Why not?" She hands me the glass.

"You spent a week with them; it's not like you have any obligations to my family."

Why am I talking her out of it? Zoya would be happy. And probably Zach. I would hate to... to love it. It's the worst idea.

I need her out of my life. Having her around and not having her is pure torture. It impacts me negatively... My time with the kids, my performance at work. It's a recipe for disaster.

"I wouldn't do it out of obligation. I had fun with them. I didn't think I could do it, but in the end, it was actually quite rewarding."

"Then stay." My brain-to-mouth filter is broken. Have I just said that?

# Chapter 6

## *Lily*

I shift and look at him wide-eyed. Has he just asked that? He wants me to stay?

Obviously he doesn't want his kids with yet another new nanny.

I actually enjoyed my week with them. More than I could ever imagine. Could I stay? Having Declan as my boss would be a challenge. But he wasn't here much. And perhaps, interacting with the grump, I might finally outgrow my silly attraction.

I think I may enjoy being Zach and Zoya's nanny.

I clear my throat, heat warming my cheeks. Am I really going to accept?

"Sorry, I didn't mean it." Declan closes his eyes, shaking his head. "It just felt good to have someone here whose presence they embraced. They chased all the other nannies away, but they seem to like you."

Oh. I slouch back beside him. I feel strangely deflated, but at the same time happy that Zoya and Zach accepted me.

"Maybe because they knew I'm here for a week only. Have you asked them why they didn't like the nannies?"

Declan whips his head to me. He looks like I just told him that the markets crashed—I assume that would shock him. After a long, weird pause, he sighs. "I'm failing at this parenting job."

"No, you're not." Our faces are so close to each other. I take his tumbler again to break the closeness. "I only have five days of experience, but it's hard."

"So fucking hard." He takes the glass before I have a chance to take a sip and downs the amber liquid.

I enjoyed sharing a drink with him. I should probably head out, but this rare moment of closeness with Declan has smoothed the frayed edges of my lonely soul. It shouldn't, and I don't understand why it does.

Besides my girlfriends, this is the first evening in over a year that I don't feel alone. Ironic, given that I'm sitting here with a man who seems to mostly avoid or ignore me.

Earlier, when his face was only inches from mine, and his gaze hugged me in exciting anticipation, I really thought he was going to kiss me.

He was probably just studying my crooked nose,

while naïve me thought that a man like Declan could ever want a girl like me.

When I saw him in the tux earlier, oozing power and sex appeal, I realized how unattainable he was. My body can tingle all it wants, but he's all man and dominance, and I'm just a girl with very little experience. I can't possibly attract him.

"You really never asked them?" I ask, because talking about his kids is safe territory. Also because I don't want to leave.

Perhaps it's the whiskey, but my legs feel heavy. Rooted beside him.

Also, I'm homeless. In the madness of adjusting to the childcare demands, I forgot to call Cora to arrange a sleepover.

While I was in the shower this morning, Mrs. Whitaker broke into my room and packed my things. Not a difficult task, since I only have one suitcase and a box of personal things I accumulated since I arrived.

Both are now stored in the closet in Declan's entry hall. I don't want him to see me dragging those out. I should have taken care of that earlier. Before the school run. What was I even doing?

"Every time a nanny left, I was overwhelmed. Between the search for a new one, juggling the schedule..." He looks at me now, and it's jarring.

His gaze is soft, and there is so much pain in his

expression. He really believes he's been failing as a father.

He shrugs. "I just assumed it's a phase."

"I'm sure the new nanny is really good."

"You're really good at this. I didn't even realize I should tell them they get a new teacher in Grade One. Fuck, I didn't even know they were attached to the current one."

"Declan." I sigh, wanting to give him a hug, to make him smile. Anything to make his anguish go away.

He makes a sound between a groan and a choke, like his name on my lips gives him pain. I guess I shouldn't be this familiar with him.

"After their mother left them, I just focused on handling it all, keeping them alive and safe, but mostly keeping myself sane. My work gives me sanity, so I tried to schedule my kids around my work. How pathetic is that?"

His admission puzzles me. This man who is so formidable—successful, accomplished, confident, and often aloof—offered me a glimpse of his softer side. A side that worries, that cares, that loves.

I wish he hadn't done that. I wish I could still pretend he is an arrogant bastard who doesn't even acknowledge my presence most of the time. And he is all of that, but now I see him in a different light.

I wish I didn't.

"You're here every morning and cook them breakfast. You could easily leave that to your housekeeper like many fathers in your position would do. And you try to be here every evening."

He looks at me with a raised eyebrow.

"Okay, you didn't manage this week, but your housekeeper told me that that's the exception, not the rule." I smile, and he looks away.

"Now you're just making me feel better."

"Don't be modest. It doesn't suit you." I throw his words back at him, and a rare but very real smile twitches his lips.

"Touché." He stands up. "I'm going to get a refill. Do you want one?"

"I'll share yours." The words are out before I can stop them. What's wrong with me?

He narrows his eyes but smirks. "Okay."

I fully expect him to come back with two glasses, but he doesn't. He takes a sip and passes me the glass, sitting beside me again.

I was surprised when he did it earlier. He could have just sent me home, but it felt like he needed company. God knows, I welcome some too. Especially if it comes with the side of his velvety timbre.

"I don't mean to pry, but where is their mother?" I take a generous sip and start coughing.

Declan takes the glass from me. "Careful there, Seagull."

"Seagull?" I chuckle.

"I wanted to say sailor, but that doesn't fit you at all."

"And a seagull does? They are like the rats of the ocean." I wrinkle my nose, but a part of me loves that he gave me a nickname. Okay, he used it once, but still.

"Have you ever watched them glide through the air? They have grace and lightness. You could be a seagull."

Has he just given me a compliment? A grin stretches across my face. "If you knew how many of your plates I broke this week, you would call me clumsy, not graceful."

He snorts. "Believe me, I know."

I gasp. "You do?"

He flinches but then shrugs. "I count my dishes; I'm a numbers man."

What? And weirdly enough, I could totally see him doing that. "Are you teasing me?"

He smirks.

"Wow, I didn't know you had it in you. Joking?"

He takes a sip. "I possess basic social skills."

I chuckle. "Basic? Basic social skills are hello, please, and thank you. You usually have a stick up your ass."

He gives me a mock gasp. "You break half of my dishes, and now you offend me?"

"I'm sorry." I can't stop grinning.

"It's just dishes, but perhaps fewer sharp shards around my children will be welcome." He hands me the whiskey.

I take a small sip, savoring the smooth heat of it. When I open my eyes, they meet with Declan's. He's been looking at me a lot tonight. It's unnerving. But not all that bad. Not at all.

"Still, I can't be called graceful." It was my father's second biggest regret.

First, that I wasn't a son, and then that I turned out less than a perfect female heir. Not that his standards were ever fair.

"Okay, you are loud and chatty, so you still can be a seagull."

I laugh. It doesn't escape me how he skillfully avoided my questions about his ex-wife, but I don't want to bring her up again. This lighter conversation is such a rare, unexpected occurrence, I want to revel in it longer.

"At least you didn't say my hair is almost as bad as what A Flock of Seagulls used to sport."

"A Flock of Seagulls?" He takes the glass, frowning.

"A band from the eighties."

"How would you know a band from the eighties? What are you, like twenty-two?" He swirls the liquid but doesn't drink.

I wonder how much he drank tonight. His breath is as intoxicating as the drink. Is that the reason he is more approachable tonight? Will he go back to being himself and pretend I don't exist next time he sees me at Saar's or Celeste's?

"I'm twenty-five, and I don't know the band, but you must remember the *Friends* episode."

"I've never watched it."

I pivot, not believing him. "You never watched that episode?" I scoot my legs under me, angling my body toward him.

His profile is exquisite. His jaw is veiled in dark stubble. Tonight he looks slightly older, with all the lines of exhaustion marring his forehead and the dark circles under his eyes. They make him look more alluring, too.

"I've never watched the show." He takes another sip and hands me the glass.

I ignore it. "What do you mean you've never watched the show?"

"I don't have time for television. It was never watched in my house growing up. I have a theater upstairs where I occasionally watch movies. And I have a TV in my office, but I only rarely watch the news." He shrugs.

"I thought you didn't have a TV so the kids don't watch until they're older. I grew up in a house where my great-grandmother's TV blared at full blast all the time. She refused hearing aids, so I feel like television has been the background of my childhood."

I loved hiding in her rooms growing up.

He studies me for a moment, and somehow it makes me feel bare. Why did I mention my nana? I never talk about my family, because that only opens me up to questions about my background. Questions I can't answer.

"Where are your glasses?"

I touch my face. Shit. Have I forgotten them... Where? When was the last time I had them on? I'm always so careful with them. "I must have left them in Zoya's room. Let me get them."

"I can grab them."

We both stand up at the same time, and my hip bumps him. I lose balance and almost fall back onto the sofa. Only I don't, because Declan wraps his arm around me. His effort to prevent my fall plasters me against his chest.

We freeze. Well, I kind of daze at him, immobile, but Declan goes rigid. He doesn't release me, though. It's like he doesn't know what to do with me.

"Like a true James Bond. You saved me." I try to lighten the tension, because Declan's posture isn't the only rigid thing. A bulge is growing in his pants, and I don't know what to do.

Having this effect on him thrills me, but with my limited experience, I don't quite know how to react in a way he'd welcome.

I might have inappropriate thoughts about him, but he is still my boss... Well, my client.

My words don't make him laugh. He steps back like I stung him, steadying me with his hands. "You should go, Lily."

His words are like a cold shower, sobering me. Reminding me who we are. That he might have indulged my presence, our conversation on a drunken Friday night, but that's all this is.

"Yes," I rasp.

"Let me get your glasses." He turns and practically runs upstairs.

The sooner I get out of here, the better. I have no idea how to handle this man. He must be attracted to me. Unless he has some disease causing spontaneous erection. I should google it.

I walk over to the wall of windows and rest my forehead against the cool surface. What am I doing?

Why does this man make me feel all these things? I'm hot and thrilled one moment. In awe of him at times. Annoyed with him a minute later. And completely inadequate most of the time.

Okay, it's time to behave like a well-adjusted adult and give up this unhealthy obsession with him.

It's not like there is any chance of anything happening between us, and I need to start acting normal around him. I wouldn't see him much after tonight, anyway.

When I hear him descending, I turn around, my back against the window. I fold my arms over my chest, because somehow it makes me stronger against him. Or protected from him. Regardless, I feel I stand taller.

"Don't lean on the glass," he scolds.

Fuck him. I roll my eyes, push off the glass, and snatch my glasses. "Good night, Declan."

I start toward the entrance, hoping he will just go back upstairs. I don't need him to witness my homelessness.

"Why are you wearing them?" His voice—that stupid voice—reaches me before I cross the room.

The question makes me pause, and I turn slowly, not sure if I'm frustrated or exhausted. "What do you mean?"

"Why do you wear your glasses? They are not prescription, and forgive me, but they are not really a fashion statement either."

His hands are in his pockets as he stands casually

in the middle of his kingdom, owning the air, owning the narrative, owning my dignity. And now, owning a small piece of my secret.

"It's none of your business," I snap and whip around.

"You look better without them," he says, and grunts like the words cause him pain.

*Just go away, for the love of God.* But I don't wait for him to leave anymore; I need to get out of here, and I no longer care if I add my current unresolved living situation to the list of humiliation this man has inspired.

Gripping the sleek handle, I yank the door of the closet, but it doesn't budge. I shake it again.

Declan's scent envelops me as he reaches from behind me and pushes at the wooden surface. The door clicks open.

Goddammit. I can't catch a break tonight.

His proximity sends shivers down my spine. *Stupid, treacherous body, we're leaving. Forever. Don't get any ideas.*

Stepping to the side, I pull the handle toward me to fully open the closet, and graze Declan's shoulder in the process.

Graze is a diplomatic way to put it; I pretty much hit him with his door. As a thank you for helping me open it. And for not having me fired this week. *Good job, Lily.*

He doesn't flinch or acknowledge the attack. I'm mildly aware of my irrational agitation, but him finding out my glasses are fake... What if he snoops around to see what else is fake?

He wouldn't. He doesn't have time. Nor does he care enough about me. But still, it was a close call. I need to be more careful.

"What is that?" he asks as I haul my suitcase and box from the closet.

I sigh, closing my eyes briefly. It has been the longest night ever, and its ending negates all the pleasant parts. "I robbed you, obviously."

He frowns. "Okay. Hopefully nothing I would miss."

Is he cracking jokes now? I try to load the box on top of my suitcase, but it keeps sliding. By now I have tears in my eyes, the effort to get out of here frustrating me.

"Let me help you." He picks up the box. "Can I get my driver to take you somewhere?"

Jesus. My mind scrambles for a reasonable way out. Unfortunately, it settles on verbal diarrhea as my best shot at saving my dignity. I snatch the box from him.

"My landlady threw me out, and I was busy with the kids and forgot to arrange a weekend stay with Cora... I should have called her. Also, you're too busy to be helping me with this... I don't want to be a burden... I should have moved my things to Cora's this afternoon, and I didn't, and now it's late. And I just really want to leave. This is not your problem... I'm fine. I'm really fine—"

"Lily." His voice is a warning, and I halt. "Are you telling me you have nowhere to go?"

I nod, heat scorching my cheeks. The stupid glasses slide from my nose, but my hands are full. I'm painfully aware I must look deranged after my confession.

He snatches the box from me, tackling it effortlessly under his arm and grabbing my suitcase in his other hand. "You'll stay here tonight."

It's not a polite offer. It's a decision he made for me. He doesn't even wait to see if I follow as he carries my things.

Sighing, I decide not to argue. It's not like I have other choices. As much as I hate not having choices, I got myself into this mess.

I'll set my alarm for five and get out of here before they are up.

With that solution in mind, I trudge after Declan upstairs. He opens the door of a luxurious guest room and puts my things down.

"There is an en-suite bathroom. You should have everything you need here, but if not, you know your way around the house."

"Thank you. You really didn't have to..." *Okay, shut up now, Lily.*

He looks at me deadpan. "Good night, Seagull."

He rasps the nickname like it pains him, but somehow, his using it makes everything just marginally better. Like everything is okay, even though the night has been full of weird twists and turns.

I watch him leave, allowing myself one last time to ogle his solid, lean behind, and a smile almost returns to my face.

It dies when he reaches the door and, without turning, issues an ominous warning. "Lock your door, Lily."

# Chapter 7

## *Declan*

*Lock your door, Lily?*

What the actual fuck?

Well, Lily, you are staying in the house of a creep who has filthy thoughts about you. But he's a decent man, and he warned you. Kill. Me. Now.

Rooted to the ground in front of her room, I wait for the click of the lock, but only silence follows in the few beats while I try to gather my wits.

I fail miserably, because instead of crossing the floor to my bedroom, I pull out my phone and log into my security system.

Yeah, I'm officially a stalker. And my poor, innocent victim is probably regretting that she helped me out this week.

Lily sits on the bed, staring at the door. I look back,

like the solid wooden plain is transparent, before I tiptoe away. Rational much tonight?

Why is she so still? I must have freaked her out after I completely lost my mind. I came home hoping to reclaim my sanity with her gone forever.

Instead, I spent the evening squashed beside her on the sofa—if she files a harassment claim, I wouldn't even be surprised—and then I offered her a room.

What is wrong with me? Can I even blame it on tonight's whiskey?

I should lock my door and throw the key out of the window. Fuck.

Okay, I couldn't let her go out there in the middle of the night with everything she owns under her arms. Is that everything she owns? I need to pay her more. *She's not your employee, asshole.*

At least I was sane enough to put her in the spare room, as far away from me as possible. It doesn't do much for me, because my pants are tenting, and the primitive part of my brain is suggesting I go over there and declare my confusing feelings to her.

Thank God there are more mature, logical parts of my brain that rule my life, so I don't end up being interrogated by the police. That would play into Kendra's cards.

Fuck. My ex-wife. The custody battle threat. It

was nice to forget about that little clusterfuck for an hour while talking to Lily.

She stands up and starts pacing. Only then do I realize I've been doing the same. Two people caged.

Me with an insane pull toward my young, no-longer nanny.

Her? Probably scared to shut her eyes and considering fleeing this place. She should.

I march to my closet and shed my clothes, before going into my bathroom and stepping under the rainfall of my shower. The arctic-cold water sobers me up—literally and figuratively.

Lily will be gone tomorrow, and I can go back to my routine. Hopefully the new nanny stays long enough to bring some peace and order to this house before the kids start their summer school.

I will return to my latent ignorance of Lily during any future meetings. I've been good at that. Only she's no longer just an enigmatic beauty.

She is a real person who made me smile. Who cared for my kids, and they took her in like no one else before.

A real, intriguing woman, who made me feel tonight like I may not be failing my kids completely.

Who is delightful company, bringing lightness into my life. Something I haven't experienced in the longest time.

A real woman who broke several dishes in her five short days here... Fuck, that was a close call. I almost admitted I've been watching her.

Who wears non-prescription, unattractive glasses. It was just a mindless tic to put her glasses on... It's a weird accessory to have, but even weirder was her need to flee after I asked her about it.

She's hiding something, and to my chagrin, it only makes her even more intriguing.

But yeah, ignoring her from now on won't be as easy as before, but with the summer coming, I might get lucky and not see her for months.

Good. Everything will be okay. Maybe I'll go on a few dates, just to get her out of my mind. I cringe at the idea as I wrap the towel around my waist.

I would miss her grace and lightness. Even her noisiness, giggles, and chattiness. My Seagull.

No, not mine. Fuck. She's eleven years younger. She has her life in front of her. I might be a selfish bastard, but I'm not going to ruin that for her.

Done. Tomorrow, this is over.

I check the feed and see a small form under the blankets of the guest bed. My mind immediately starts forming a new fantasy, but I shut it down before it has a chance to bloom.

I turn off the app and pull on my pajama pants.

Sliding into my bed, I fold my hands under my head and close my eyes.

In some strange—and very unfortunate—way, this week was one of the most eventful in a long while. If I didn't have good, legitimate reasons to resist the temptations, it could have been quite an exciting week as well.

But any chance for joy left with Kendra. I stare at the ceiling while I think about resolving her third reappearance in my life. The first two cost me a lot of money.

They would have resulted in a lot of emotional damage for the kids if they remembered: The first time, she pretended at the revival of her maternal instincts. The second time, I paid her off before she could get near them.

It's not like they won't be dealing with the abandonment issues as it is, but I won't allow anyone to add real memories to those mental scars. Over my dead body.

She left them when they were only three months old. Who does that? She should have been automatically erased from their birth certificates. And if I wasn't up to my neck trying to figure out how to survive her betrayal and protect the babies, I would have made that happen.

We had a day nurse and a night nurse back then. I

used to pay for a housekeeper, a cook, and a shopping assistant. I could have been home more, but my busy schedule doesn't compare with her decision. 'This life is not for me,' as she put it.

And there goes my sleep. Thinking about my evil ex does that, with a hundred percent reliability.

Those first months when the babies were newborn, I spent a lot of time blaming myself. For sure, there is a responsibility I will carry for the rest of my life, but at least my therapist helped me see things for what they are.

My guilt trip wasn't what Zoya and Zach needed from me.

I sit up and walk to the bathroom to have a drink of water. I shouldn't have had that last whiskey. But sharing a glass with Lily was irresistible. Forbidden fruit. My demise.

I gulp down a glassful, and before I think about it, I leave my bedroom. To check on the kids.

To check on my daughter and my son who are sleeping peacefully, not realizing what a creep their father is.

Lily is only a few feet away. She is at my house. Sleeping, and equally unaware of my perverted mind.

Zoya sleeps, splayed across her bed. The girl travels around the mattress while she sleeps. A grin pulls at my lips. Is it horrible that seeing my children sleep is one of my favorite parenting moments?

I peek into Zach's room. My son has his hands behind his head, frowning even in his sleep. I read somewhere that newborn mammals resemble their fathers the most right after birth, to make sure he sticks around to protect them.

Zach is a mini version of me, and has been growing into that resemblance with an alarming dedication. It makes me proud, and marginally concerned for him.

Checking on my kids usually brings me serenity after a busy day. Tonight, the looming danger from their mother, and the sleeping beauty down the hall, take up my mental space, and any hope for calm disappears.

I'm about to return to my room when a sound stops me. Is Zoya crying? I glance back, but she is fast asleep.

Another sob reaches me, followed by a whimper. From the direction of the guest room.

Fuck. Is Lily crying? Did I make her cry?

*It's none of your business*, I tell myself while I stay still.

"No." A muffled cry presses against the silence.

My legs move before I even fully comprehend what the sound is. After two knocks—insistent but careful not to wake my kids—I turn the doorknob as another strangled cry seeps through the air.

I turn the handle, cursing myself for telling her to lock it. But the door gives way easily. She didn't lock it. *She didn't.*

"Lily, I'm coming in." Adrenaline pumps through my veins.

The lamp beside the bed is on, and I immediately see Lily thrashing on the bed, chanting, "No, please, no."

Fuck. A nightmare. I approach her gingerly. My kids usually wake up from their bad dreams. Should I wake her? Or is that a bad thing? No, that's more dangerous with sleepwalkers. Or?

In a millisecond, my mind also offers other useless trains of thought before I finally put my hands on her bare shoulders. "Lily, wake up. It's just a dream. Lily."

A wail leaves her small body before she lunges at me, and piercing pain sears through my arm.

"Oh my God." Lily stares at me, eyes wide. "Declan?" Her face fills with horror.

My head spins a little; it's like the adrenaline is pumping and wearing off at the same time. A strange, wet warmth spreads down my arm. My mind scrambles to catch up with my body's signals.

The burn. The throb. The pulsing sting.

"Jesus Christ," I hiss, instinctively gripping my biceps. The pain is hot enough to make my vision blur for a beat.

*A Convenient Secret*

"Declan—oh my God—oh no, no, no!" Lily's voice rises, breathless and panicked, as she scrambles back against the headboard, her hands flying up to cover her mouth.

Her eyes dart from my arm to my face and back again, wide and glassy with horror. "I didn't... I didn't know—it was—oh no, no, no... Are you okay? I... Oh God, you're bleeding."

Bleeding? I glance down. My hand is slick, crimson seeping down my forearm. The sight of the blood feels surreal, like I'm watching someone else's arm. What the hell just happened?

"Shit," I mutter, pressing my palm harder against a wound I can't explain. "What's going on?"

Her hands fly to her hair, yanking it into fists as she stammers, "I-I didn't mean to—I swear to God... I thought... I thought you were—I-I'm so sorry... So, so sorry... Oh no, Declan, you're hurt... What do I do? What do I do?"

"Just stop talking," I snap.

She plasters her hand over her mouth, shaking. Fuck. Despite the sudden onset of nausea and a mother-fucking level of pain, I feel guilty about scaring her.

"The kids are sleeping." My voice is hoarse, caught somewhere between a warning and disbelief. I don't know if it's the blood loss or her rambling, but the pieces don't fit.

"I didn't know it was you!" she cries, her words tripping over each other. "I-I was having a dream—no, a nightmare... And then I woke up, and you were there, and I thought... Oh God! I didn't mean to... I just... I'm so sorry, Declan!"

Her voice breaks at my name, her hands trembling as she fumbles toward me like she wants to help, but is too afraid to touch me.

The bed creaks under her shifting weight, and for a moment she's just staring at me, her mouth opening and closing like she's trying to find the right words to undo whatever just happened.

The pain throbs again, cutting through my haze. I take a step back, blood still seeping through my fingers. "But—" My words stall as my gaze lands on the bed.

A knife. A small, gleaming blade glints in the lamplight, its edge stained dark red.

I exhale sharply, a bitter laugh escaping despite myself. "You stabbed me?"

# Chapter 8

## *Lily*

I gasp, my hand flying back to my mouth. "No... Yes. I mean, yes, but not on purpose! I'm so sorry... I didn't mean to... I... You need a doctor. Do you need stitches? I think you need stitches. I'm such an idiot. I'm so, so sorry."

Fuck. I'm babbling again, my voice high-pitched and breathless as I try to make sense of the chaos.

"Pull yourself together. I don't want the kids to find us like this." Declan glares at me, blood dripping down his arm. "You sleep with a knife?"

I freeze, my face turning the richest crimson known to man, I'm sure. "Yes."

I don't know how my voice comes out in an audible volume, but the war in his eyes suggests he's fighting the next question. Or ten. How am I going to explain this? He will file a police report and then—

Declan sways, and a pang of guilt hits me. I'm so selfish. I can worry about myself later. I scramble out of the bed and run to get a towel from the bathroom.

Declan sits on the edge of the bed when I return.

"Here. You need to apply pressure on it." I press the towel against his arm.

The wound just above his elbow is ugly, but doesn't look deep. Thank God. *And now you're a doctor, Lily?* "Let me call nine-one-one."

He glares at me, which I take as his acquiescence, and I grab my phone from the nightstand. After I make the call, I chance a look at him. He's still glaring. And who could blame him?

"Jesus Christ," he mutters and looks away, shaking his head.

"I'm sorry," I whisper.

"You mentioned that a few times," he growls. "If I need stitches, you will stay here with the kids."

"Of course, of course, anything you need. Do you want me to call Cormac, or Saar? Or your mother?" What or who can make him feel better? "Do you need water? Or maybe whiskey? Or I can—"

"Just shut up, Lily." His voice is exhausted, but not necessarily mad. But then he is probably in shock.

I stay quiet, my hands shaking and my chest heaving. Jesus. The last thing this poor man needs right now is my panic attack.

*A Convenient Secret*

The silence stretches, heavily descending on me. I didn't expect to fall asleep in Declan's house. But having him intercept my nightmare is... Well, a nightmare.

I fidget, stepping from one foot to the other. When I chance a glance at Declan, my jaw drops, and despite the gory situation—because there is something seriously wrong with me—my pussy clenches.

During the chaos earlier, I didn't notice he was shirtless. Which only speaks to the volume of my shock. But now I can't take my eyes off the planes of muscles that form the masterpiece of his torso.

He's the ultimate package—broad shoulders, sinewy chest, multi-pack abs—all covered in olive skin with a dusting of dark chest hair. And currently some blood.

I should be ashamed, mortified, worried, guilty, and regretful. I feel a potent cocktail of those emotions. What I definitely shouldn't feel is lust. And yet, here we are.

I've always known my childhood and early adulthood couldn't possibly lead to well-adjusted behavior, but this is the worst timing ever for any depravity. Jesus.

"Do you want me to get you a shirt?"

He groans and looks up at the ceiling, probably searching for the strength not to strangle me. Then he stands up and sways a bit again. Of course, I cross all the boundaries and jump to help him.

He angles his body to avoid me, I think, and takes a few steps toward the door. "Make sure the kids are not concerned when they wake up if I'm not here yet. Tell them I cut myself and I went to see the doctor, but do not scare them. Don't go into details, for fuck's sake."

I nod, like he can see me with his back to me. "Where are you going?"

"I'll wait downstairs for the ambulance. Stay up here," he says through his teeth and leaves.

> I stabbed Declan.

CORA

> Took you long enough (laughing emoji)

SAAR

> I was going to write the same.

CORA

> Have you heard from Cal yet?

SAAR

> We're here in the hospital. No baby yet.

> Declan might join you soon.

*A Convenient Secret*

SAAR

I thought today was your last day.

> It was an accident. I don't know what to do.

CORA

Fuck, Lily, you are not joking?

SAAR

Of course she is.

> I have to go. I'll fill you in later.

"Lily, you'we still hewe!" Zoya jumps from her bed right into my lap.

My limbs scream in protest after sitting up the rest of the awful night in the armchair in Zoya's room.

I didn't follow Declan downstairs, but I heard the murmur when the paramedics arrived. They weren't here long, but everything after the nightmare has felt like an eternity.

Zoya yawns and snuggles against me, and my eyes mist. The bone-weary exhaustion is almost physically painful now.

I will my mind to linger on this one beautiful, innocent moment, but when I close my eyes, layers of different nightmares of the past, not so recent and very recent, form a knot in my stomach.

The knot tightens when Zoya's small voice seeps through my consciousness. "Awe you still ouw nanny?"

Most definitely not.

"I stayed tonight because your dad needed to take care of something." Panic whooshes through me again, and the need to tell Zoya way more than she should hear, or I should ever share, is strong.

"But he was hewe last night. We awe going to chase pigeons. He pwomised." She looks at me with her large brown eyes, her bottom lip quivering.

"He will come soon. He might need to rest for a moment, but he will spend the weekend with you." I don't know that, but if Zoya starts crying I won't be able to keep it together.

She nods and settles her head on my chest. I wrap my arms around her, stroking her back. The motion gives me a sense of peace. Like she is my lifeboat. And yes, there is a storm awaiting me, but for now, I'm safe.

"Can we make Fwench toast?"

Oh, shit. "Do you know how to make it?"

"Suwe." She slides down from my lap. "Zach, wake up; we awe making Fwench toasts."

Turns out the kids don't know how to make French toast, and neither do I. I pull out a video on my phone, and we watch it together.

"You don't know how to cook, do you?" Zach asks,

matter-of-fact, hands in the pockets of a flannel housecoat more suitable for a senior than a child.

Being judged by this little dude is as effective as his father's glower. I want to shrivel. "I know plenty." I try to sound breezy. "Like how to use a microwave. And... how to open cereal boxes. That counts, right?"

Zoya giggles and turns off the video. "It looks easy," she says with confidence, holding a whisk like it's a magic wand.

Perched on the counter, she swings her tiny legs back and forth, her fluffy slippers discarded.

Zach watches me with a mixture of suspicion and something close to disdain. The weight of his gaze is not helping the tornado of thoughts swirling in my head.

"Easy peasy." I force a smile. My voice sounds strained even to me. "Piece of cake. We've got this."

We do not have this. I have never used a whisk.

My stomach churns, but not from hunger. I can't even imagine eating. But I need to create a normal, fun morning for these kids. I owe them that, at least.

Why can't I do anything in the kitchen? I check my notifications, hoping for some sort of update. Nothing. Just the same blank screen mocking me.

I pull my gaze away and try to focus on the task at hand. "Okay." I clasp my hands together. "Let me get toast from the pantry."

I open the door behind me, right beside the cleaning closet. I immediately see myself with Declan standing there while I retrieved the vacuum.

He was affected by me then, but I believed it wasn't about me but rather his need. But then, last night, when he asked me to lock my door? There was something carnal behind it. Like he couldn't control himself, so he asked me to do it.

That was what my overactive imagination offered, anyway. I didn't lock it. And I would lie if I didn't imagine him coming to check on me. That fantasy turned out very differently in real life.

I should have locked it. He wouldn't be in the hospital now.

Sighing, I step into the pantry, looking for toast. What I find floods me with a strange feeling of homesickness. I stare at the shelf full of Spinelli pasta and sauces, memories rushing through my mind.

"What's taking so long?" Zoya bumps into me from behind. "Oh. You can't find the toast?" She sneaks around me and reaches for the bag with the white bread.

"You guys like Spinelli pasta for sure," I mumble.

"It's the best." She looks at me like I come from another planet, and don't know the obvious.

"It is the best." I close the door quickly, lowering my forehead to the wooden surface.

*A Convenient Secret*

It must be my lack of sleep and last night's adrenaline that stirs this weird melancholy. I shut it all down, just like I learned to do when I left home.

I turn to the twins with a smile. "Step one: crack the eggs. Who wants to try?"

Zoya eagerly raises her hand. "Me! Me!"

Her enthusiasm brings a smile to my face despite everything. "Great." I hand her an egg. "Just... be gentle." Or maybe it requires strength? It looked easy in the video.

She smashes the egg against the rim of the bowl with the subtlety of a wrecking ball. Half the shell crumbles into the bowl, the yolk barely surviving the assault. The other half plops to the counter.

"Oops." She giggles.

"Maybe we should order breakfast." Zach narrows his eyes.

Zoya wipes her hands on her pink pajamas. "Fwom that waffles place." She bounces, the cooking project forgotten.

Their father makes their breakfast almost every single day, and here I am, responsible for his absence and failing to recreate their normal morning.

"It's okay. We can make our own breakfast," I say quickly, fishing out shards of eggshell with my fingers.

"Why are you even here?" Zach asks bluntly, his serious tone cutting through Zoya's giggles.

I pause, my fingers midair with a piece of eggshell on them.

"Stop it, Zach. We like Lily, wemembew." Zoya swipes hair from her face, and now there is egg gluing her tresses.

Zach glowers, and there is so much of Declan in that expression I avert my eyes.

My phone continues to mock me from the counter. The clock does as well. It's six-fifteen in the morning. My fatigue presses against my eyes.

"I'm just helping your daddy while he can't be here, Zach."

"Why is he not here?" Zach demands, and Zoya turns her curious eyes to me.

*Do not scare them.*

"Your dad had a minor cut and needed to see a doctor, but he will be back any minute now."

"He cut himself when shaving?" Zoya asks, seemingly unperturbed by the fact her father needed to see a doctor.

"And then you will go?" Zach asks, but it sounds like a demand.

We got along this past week, but I was right: his acceptance extended to the limited time frame of my stay with them.

It breaks my heart a little, but this is not the time or

the place. Certainly not the circumstances to win him over.

I'll be gone in an hour. Probably forever banished from this house.

"Yes, Zach, I'll go." His rejection stings more than I would have expected. I force yet another smile this morning. "Let's focus on making the best French toast ever."

I look at the counter. Shit. Somehow, while I talked to Zach, Zoya attempted to crack a few more eggs. Eyeing the egg massacre, I bite back a sigh and dip my fingers into the bowl, fishing out all the shells.

"Step two is adding milk." Zoya yanks open the fridge door and takes out the carton.

"I'll do it." Zach snatches it from her.

I turn to wash my hands.

"Zach," Zoya screams as drops wet my ankles.

I turn so quickly I get dizzy. Zach stands, smirking at me, the cartoon in his hand turned upside down, milk seeping quickly across the tiles.

He really is unhappy with me still being here. Is this what chased all the nannies away? I know this is deliberate behavior. I experienced this boy at his best.

He might be overly serious for a six-year-old, but he is also fiercely protective of his sister, funny, and smart. He is not a bully.

The gleam in his eyes right now suggests otherwise,

but I decide to believe my intuition. If he's trying to rile me up, he'll be surprised.

"Zach, did you miss the bowl?" The cheer in my voice is forced but sounds genuine.

He drops the carton. More droplets land on my feet. "I'm not hungry. I'll be in my room."

"Daddy," Zoya cheers, and Zach and I turn.

Declan glowers from the dining room, but his expression softens as Zoya runs to hug him. Her bare feet splash through the milk.

Declan squats to hug her. "Careful, my arm hurts a little."

"How did you cut youwself?" Zoya wraps her arms around his neck and kisses his cheek. My ovaries decide this is a good time to shimmy.

Declan's eyes find mine, and now I understand the expression, 'Please, ground, swallow me,' because that's exactly what I need to happen right now.

"I was a bit clumsy, sweetheart." He stands up.

Still in his pajama pants and wearing a black T-shirt, he sports a large sterile patch above his elbow. Some blood—far less than last night—and a yellow disinfectant stain his arm.

His gaze lands on the milk puddle. "What happened here, Zach?"

"We wewe making French toasts," Zoya chirps.

"Zach?" Declan prompts with authority.

"It was an accident," I blurt out, and Zach's eyes whip to me.

Declan sighs. "I guess we will have to order breakfast this morning."

Zach studies me for a moment, and then he smirks. "That's what I suggested."

"Awe we going to the park still?" Zoya asks, her bottom lip already sporting her famous manipulative pout.

"I'll order the breakfast and have a shower. After we eat, we go to the park," Declan tells his kids while he stares at me.

I have been on the receiving end of his glower, but this stare is new.

He's eyeing me with curiosity, his eyes lined with exhaustion, but also with a similar softness to that he shows his kids.

I must be hallucinating, the lack of sleep and last night's trauma playing tricks on me.

"Can Lily come with us?" Zoya bounces around him.

I hold my breath, wracking my brain for some excuse.

Declan sighs heavily. "Sure." He doesn't look at me anymore. "Let's go upstairs."

The twins file out of the kitchen. Avoiding my eyes, Declan walks to the fridge, stepping around the milk puddle. He opens the door and gets a bottle of water.

My heart hammers in my chest, but I find my voice, however small. "How are you feeling?"

He gulps down his water and leaves the kitchen without another word, or a glance my way.

# Chapter 9

## *Declan*

The more I try to avoid Lily, the more present she is in my life. I couldn't refuse Zoya's request. They will have a zombie father as it is after the fucked-up night I had.

I ended up with six stitches only, and I paid for a private room to have a nap, to regroup. I snuck around because somewhere in the same hospital, my business partner was having a baby.

There is a slim chance that the events of last night could become an anecdote we would all laugh at, but that time is not here yet.

After a power nap—something I mastered as a father—I called my driver and returned home. Home where Lily is still present, and my kitchen is in disarray.

And as soon as my gaze latched onto hers, I wasn't

sure how to proceed. On one side, there is the need to distance myself—for her sake and for mine. On the other hand, there must be a reason she sleeps armed to evoke a sense of safety.

Why is that? The question has been looping in my mind, and as much as I try, I can't park it. I should be furious—or at least alarmed. And I am, but it's not about me. My concern lies with the woman I want to erase from my life.

A futile effort.

Lily isn't erasable.

Lily isn't forgettable.

Lily isn't ignorable.

Though the last one I've come as close to perfecting as possible. And I leaned into it all day today.

I poured my attention into my children, going about our habitual Saturday activities as if it was just a usual Saturday. Like Lily wasn't here with us.

Okay, Zoya wasn't ignoring her. It was I who carried that badge proudly. And Zach mirrored my behavior.

Somehow, overnight, he seems to have changed his attitude toward Lily. He treats her like any other nanny. They didn't hear my arrival this morning, but I saw his little stunt.

Lily and Zoya meander in front of us, chatting and

eating ice cream. Lily has been guarded and quieter than usual, stealing curious glances at me. To her credit, however, she is focused on the kids.

Well, on Zoya, who is animatedly explaining something, drops of her ice cream flickering around as she gesticulates with joy, holding the small plastic spoon.

Lily's face equally expressive, she listens and oohs and ahs like my six-year-old daughter is telling her something incredibly riveting. She may be, I guess.

"Do you want to tell me about the milk incident?" I ask Zach. My arm throbs, but I don't want to take painkillers. I don't want to be high around my kids.

"Accident, Dad." Zach scoops a small dollop of his ice cream.

"I saw." I veer us toward a bench when I see Lily and Zoya sit on another one.

Zach sighs but doesn't say anything.

"I thought you liked Lily as your nanny." I angle myself so I don't see said nanny, because, for this conversation I don't want to be distracted.

"That was before." Zach's jaw is set.

"Before what?"

"When she was with us for one week only." He basketballs his uneaten cup into a garbage bin.

"I don't understand."

Zoya chats two benches away from us. Even

without seeing her, I'm viscerally aware of Lily's presence.

"I don't want a nanny." Zach folds his arm.

"Zach, I have a demanding job, and I do my best to spend as much of my time with you as possible—"

"I know that," he interrupts.

"When I'm not around, we need help. You're a smart boy and a great brother, but you seem to misbehave on purpose to drive the nannies away. Why?"

He stares at the ground, and then shifts his eyes to peek at me.

"You're not in trouble, buddy. I just want to understand, so we can find a solution." I pat his shoulders.

"You won't get mad?"

I frown. "I won't get mad." I break my rule of never promising that.

As a parent, I learned that coercing that promise from me usually leads to something that makes me mad.

"If we have no nanny, Mommy might return. She would know we need her."

His words cause another stab wound. Unlike the one in my arm, this one spreads pain through my heart. A wave of hopelessness mingles with regret and anger. At Kendra. At me. At this situation.

*Have you asked them why they didn't like the nannies?* Fuck, why hadn't I asked sooner?

I pull Zach closer to me. "Your mom..." I peter out, unsure how to continue this conversation. I'm absolutely unequipped for it.

I knew it would come one day. That my vague response about their mother having to live far, far away wouldn't cut it forever.

I'm not ready to address it now. Not on a day when I'm running on coffee and pain.

I look at Zach, who is staring at me with eyes full of hope and curiosity. And trust. So much fucking trust.

"Zach, if your mom could be with you, she would, I promise." That's not a lie. I'm just not ready to burden him with the reason why she can't. "But her presence is absolutely unattached to you having a nanny. Even if your mother was around, you would have one."

He frowns, contemplating. "Really?"

"Don't your classmates have nannies?"

"They do."

"I'm sure many of them have both parents."

He nods.

"See. Your nanny is there to help us with a crucial task, the most important task, to care for you when I can't be around."

We sit in silence, Zach processing. I glance at the other half of our small group. Lily is squatting and tying Zoya's shoe while my daughter keeps talking.

To an outsider, she may look like her mother. My kids would be lucky to have a mom like Lily.

"Why can't Mommy be with us?" Zach's words interrupt my unhelpful line of thought.

Give it to my son to investigate all the details. Seriously, like father like son is too literal with him.

Zoya springs from the bench and starts running.

I sigh. "It's complicated."

"Zoya." Zach launches forward and rushes to his sister who whimpers on the ground. When did she fall?

I eat the distance between us, Lily already examining Zoya's knee. I squat beside the three of them.

Zoya is sniffling while Zach keeps patting her shoulder. Her knee is scratched, but it's nothing serious.

"Daddy," she sobs, at least partially for effect if I know my drama-queen daughter.

Lily pulls a water bottle from the kid's backpack and pours a little on the scratch. "Now it's clean, and will heal soon."

"I don't think I can walk," Zoya acts up.

"Could you walk for lunch if it was pizza?" I ask.

The excitement in her eyes betrays her, but she stifles it. "I think so," she whimpers.

"Oh, come on, Zoya." Zach grips her hand and pulls her up. "I'll help you walk." He pulls her forward, rolling his eyes.

"Not so fast," Zoya protests, but it doesn't take long before she skips forward with her brother in the direction of our occasional-treat restaurant two blocks from the park.

I'm relieved Zach's questions about his mother and the knee scratch are forgotten, at least for the time being.

But now I'm left beside Lily. The hair on my neck stands on end, her scent immediately sparking an electrical current through my body.

We walk in silence, both of us watching the kids in front of us. The tension lingers. The silence is loaded with my stupid need. And the unanswered questions about last night.

I wish we had met under different circumstances. But that's a useless line of thinking, so I quash it, and with the gentleman I am—not—I pick up my pace.

Unfortunately, Lily keeps up regardless, so the torture walk continues.

"How is your arm?" She breaks the silence, slightly out of breath.

On impulse, I slow down a bit. "I'm fine," I growl.

There must be a way to scare her away. To break her streak of kindness. To get rid of her.

The idea makes me want to vomit.

My brush-off does the trick, and she doesn't try to make conversation. I pack the rest of the day with activities, exhausting the kids and myself way too much. All because I'm trying to delay our return.

Once we're back home, I need to decide what to do with Lily. We need to have a conversation about last night. If she needs protection, I will help her.

As much as I want her out of my life, I couldn't forgive myself if something happened to her.

And a woman who sleeps with a knife is expecting danger.

* * *

I carry Zoya to her bed. She's half asleep as I help her change into clean pajamas. Her hair is sticky, her face is soiled with food and ice cream, but fuck the rules. It's only seven, but the last thing I need is for her to get all riled up during the bedtime routine.

"Good night, sweetheart." I kiss her forehead. Okay, she needs a shower, but we can burn the sheets tomorrow.

"This was a pewfect day, Daddy," she murmurs. "I wish Lily would stay."

The vice around my heart tightens.

I find Zach standing in his pajamas in the doorway connecting their rooms. "It's early. Can I still play for a bit?"

I ruffle his hair and walk with him to his bed. "Sure. Do you want me to read with you?"

"No, you go talk to Lily and ask her if she wants to stay."

Fuck. My. Life.

We sit on the edge of his bed. "Zach, Lily has a different job."

"People change jobs. Ms. Corrine's husband was a teacher like her, and now he's working in a theater." His logic is sound.

"Okay, I'll ask her if she wants, and can stay." Have I just lied to my son? God, when I ask her, I really hope she says no.

"Good, hopefully she can stay."

Again. Fuck. My. Life. I make an unidentifiable sound of commitment. "I don't know if she can."

"Just like Mommy." He sighs, and something dies inside me.

"Zach, I don't think I know how to explain it to you, but your mom loves you. Not everyone shows their love the same way. And she... Well, her love is strong from afar." And now I've definitely lied to my son.

"Okay. Is that one of those things that kids my age don't understand? Because I understand way more than other kids in school. I know all the planets. Zoya doesn't. You can explain things to me." He shrugs.

I nod. "I know I can, buddy. But even at my age, this is one of the things I don't understand."

He frowns, and then extends his arms in a rare display of affection. I pull him into an embrace, needing it more than him.

"It's okay, Dad, we will figure it out together. Or maybe, one day, Mom will explain it to us."

Am I making a mistake by fighting Kendra on this? Keeping her away from the twins? The two times I gave her a chance, she bailed on them. I will protect them with my life, if needed, against another abandonment.

"Good night. Don't stay up too long." I turn to Zach before I leave his room. He nods, his focus already on the airplane he's swooshing through the air.

I trudge over to my office where Lily is waiting for me. The door is ajar, and I take a moment to organize my thoughts.

She stands in front of my library, craning her head to inspect the books on the higher shelves.

In her jean shorts and a long-sleeved yellow blouse, she looks out of place in the dark room. She pads farther along, stopping at the antique solid-wood table that used to belong to my grandfather, and then my father.

She inspects an old photograph, and then another one. Tucking her hair behind the ear, she tilts her head

*A Convenient Secret*

here and there, studying the scattered papers on the wooden surface.

While order reigns everywhere in my life, my hobby is the only place where unfinished and unopened prevail. I like it that way.

I take a deep breath and walk inside.

Lily whips around, putting her hands behind her back like I caught her snooping.

"I've never been here before," she blurts out, verbal expulsion her go-to when she's frazzled.

I put my hands in the pockets of my slacks. Fuck, my arm hurts. "This is where I fire nannies."

Her eyes widen before she catches my poor attempt at lightening the mood. "It's good I'm not your nanny then." She smiles.

I wish she wouldn't. Her smiles are like bullets, killing me slowly.

"Kids would disagree."

"Zoya maybe." She chuckles humorlessly, shifting from one foot to the other.

Several feet separate us—with my desk to my side and the old table behind her, there is nothing between us. Only unresolved issues—some real and some in my head—and pent-up energy.

"Zach has just asked me to inquire if you would stay." I'm a grown-up man; I can put my stupid temptations into a vault—along with the messy feelings I don't dare name—and put my kids first.

"He did?"

"Would you?" In my mind, I'm already planning a new schedule that will minimize our interactions.

Her forehead creases. "You would want me to?"

"I think it would be best for Zoya and Zach."

She nods. "I would have to quit my job."

"If you're willing to start on Monday, I will take care of things with Summit Solutions."

She thinks for what feels like an eternity, and then she nods. "Okay."

A boulder drops from my shoulders, immediately replaced with imaginary shackles. Let's hope I survive this. And after last night, I mean it literally.

I look around my office. My tidy desk, my messy antique table, my organized books. All of it usually gives me a sense of order. It doesn't seem to work tonight.

"I asked." Not the conversation I thought I would have with her. My new nanny. My new permanent nanny. Fuck.

"Asked?" She frowns, and her glasses slide down her nose.

"I asked Zach why he hates all the nannies."

Her lips form an O. My cock thinks it's an invitation. Fuck.

"It's not my place to ask, but—" Lily starts.

"You're going to ask anyway," I groan, and she startles.

She must think I'm upset with her, when the reality is way more prosaic and tragic.

I'm upset with myself. For my lack of control. For what she does to me. For all the forbidden feelings.

She stares at me, her eyes pleading for way more than an explanation of my nanny issues. For forgiveness. For anything. She must have been on pins and needles all day, waiting for this conversation. About last night.

Fuck. I thought by ignoring her I'd be doing us both a favor, but today she needed an update. Feeling like a complete asshole, I answer her unfinished questions. "They believed that without a nanny, their mother would come back."

Lily whimpers, her hand flying to her mouth, pain palpable in her expression. Again, I hate her a little for that. For her compassion. Something I don't deserve. The kids do, but her reaction only reminds me of how quickly she built a connection with them.

Yeah, I definitely hate her for that. Because she can't stay.

Can she? Isn't it me who is robbing everyone here? She doesn't even know I want to get rid of her because I can't control my primitive emotions. Fuck. And haven't I offered her the job, anyway? What the fuck is wrong with me?

"How is your arm?" She changes the subject.

She asked about Kendra last night, and I avoided the answer. She understands a lot about my family dynamics. All in the span of one week.

She understands I'm not ready to share that fucked-up story. I respect her for that. And hate her a little. Why does she have to be so perfect?

"It's fine," I grumble.

She takes a few steps closer. "Will you press charges?"

"No." I don't have to think about that one.

An audible sigh of relief leaves her. Was she worried about that all day? Fuck. I can't catch a break around her. A world-class asshole—the one thing I'm not failing at.

"Thank you," she whispers.

I nod curtly. "But you need to tell me why you sleep with a knife."

She meets my eyes, a war brewing in them. "It's New York. It's normal to have protection."

"Mace in your bag, sure, but you slept with a knife in my home."

She accepted I'm not ready to talk about Kendra. Shouldn't I extend the same understanding to her? If she confides in me, we would remove another layer of boundaries. Not a good idea.

"It's a habit," she insists.

"Goddammit, Lily, you stabbed me. Don't you think you owe me an explanation?"

I must have taken a step or two toward her without realizing, because her scent hits me, spreading through me like a potent drug.

"You barged into my room." She pokes at my chest.

"I told you to lock the fucking door." Fuck. No control or common sense around this woman.

She takes another step, and now we are way past personal space. "And why? Tell me, Declan, why did I need to lock my door in your perfectly safe house?"

I glare at her, my nostrils flaring. Her chest heaves, her cheeks tinted pink, her eyes sparkling.

She is so close, and so beautiful. Like an angel of revenge, upset with me, fiercely protecting her secret and not knowing how much she's challenging my restraint.

Something inside me snaps. "Fuck it."

I cup her nape, yank her closer, and leaning in, I fuse my lips with hers. A soft gasp escapes her, but she immediately wraps her arms around my neck and parts her lips.

Somewhere on the periphery of my mind, the voice

of reason suggests something about stopping, but I squash that suggestion.

My tongue darts out, and I explore her sweet mouth. I wasn't prepared for this... I fantasized about this woman, but the reality exceeds any dream.

She tastes like forbidden fruit, like sin and innocence. Kissing Lily is like nothing I've ever experienced.

Kissing has always been something I considered a necessary part of a physical relationship.

Never have I thought a kiss could feel like this.

Essential. Lifesaving. Vital.

At almost thirty-seven, I finally understand what being weak at the knees means. Because I may hold this woman, but I need her supporting me even more than she does.

I angle her head slightly, feral with the need for a closer connection, for better access, to take from her all she would give in this moment of insanity.

Lily receives my attack with such eagerness that within a few moments I'm practically fucking her mouth with my tongue. Her body flush against mine, I revel in the feel of her.

She moans into my mouth, and my cock twitches. I walk her backward, my mouth fused with her sweet lips the whole time. We don't need air as the world fades away and it's just us.

She yelps when she hits the table, giggling.

It's the lovely, innocent sound that reminds me of where we are. Who we are. I jump away from her like she's just burned me.

"We can't..." I shake my head like I could erase the last few minutes from my memory. From her memory.

"Why?" she asks, her lips swollen and so inviting. And now I know their taste, so I look away.

Raking my hand through my hair, I retreat to the other side of the room. What have I done? "You, me, us... I can't."

"Why?" she repeats, a genuine confusion in her tone.

I turn to her, and I wish I hadn't. She looks just-kissed—by me—and if that doesn't make me feel like I have a claim on her. Like she could be mine... Fuck, the complication of it hits me with a dose of icy reality.

"Because you're not erasable, Seagull."

# Chapter 10

## *Lily*

Declan carries my luggage to the elevator while I trudge behind him. We shared silence before. An awkward one, a comfortable one, an annoyed one. This silence is new. It's heavy and horrible. It's worse than him ignoring me.

*You're not erasable, Seagull.*

What does that even mean?

He kissed me. He was the one who leaned in and took my lips. And yes, I gave willingly, because why not? I've been lusting after this man for months. And *he* kissed *me*. Why do I feel like the guilty party here?

*You're not erasable, Seagull.*

I want to push for an explanation, but Declan found his old grumpy personality, and the thermostat was readjusted—everything between us cold and impersonal.

I feel discarded, disposable, and quite frankly, stupid. In my naïveté, I leaned into that kiss. Not only because that was the best kiss I've ever had—and how am I going to forget that—but because it felt so real.

It felt like Declan has been feeling at least a fraction of the attraction that has been haunting me. Like he really wanted to kiss me, and perhaps even had thought about it. Maybe not as much as me, but he had.

Just wishful thinking. He regretted the kiss.

"My driver is waiting for you downstairs. He will take you to your friend."

He puts the box on top of my suitcase. Of course when he does it, the stupid box stays put, unlike last night. Jesus, was it only last night?

"Declan, I don't understand what just happened." Maybe I should let it go. People kiss and regret it, but how am I going to work for him if this hangs above our heads?

He bows his head, sighing like I'm testing his patience. "Lily—"

"It certainly feels like I'm erasable."

He whips his gaze to me so fast, I almost falter. He takes a step closer, and my heart jumps to my throat. It's like a predator zoomed in on me, and if I was smart, I would run.

He is so close again that I can almost taste his lips, his breath fanning my face. There is a fight behind his eyes; I'm just not sure if I'm the adversary or the casualty of his battle. I'm definitely the reason.

I wouldn't say I fear him at this moment, but it feels like pushing him further is not a good idea.

"In another lifetime, under different circumstances, I'd bend you over my desk and have my way with you until your pussy would milk my cock dry. You wouldn't be able to walk after I'd be done with you, and yet you'd beg me for more."

My heart hammers so loudly, I'm not sure if he really said those words. Nobody has ever spoken to me like this. I'm mortified and aroused at the same time. What? Aroused? I didn't know dirty talk—dirty threats were this hot. Jesus.

He must be consuming all the oxygen, because I can't breathe. Heat cruises through my body.

I'm in way over my head here, but I still find my voice. "And yet..." I challenge him.

He hovers over me for a few more breaths before the elevator dings open. Saved by the bell, I guess.

"I'm not going to deprive my kids of a good nanny because of a moment of a poor judgment. It won't happen again."

**SAAR**

Amelie Clementine van den Linden was born this morning. Both my beautiful niece and her mommy are doing well. Cal is annoyingly happy.

**CORA**

Congratulations. Pictures, please.

> That's amazing. I can't wait to meet the little girl.

**SAAR**

I only had a peek, but she is the most beautiful baby.

**CELESTE**

She is. Thank you, guys.

> How are you feeling?

**CELESTE**

Tired, elated, scared. Full of love.

**CORA**

You got this. Can we stop by tonight for a moment?

**CELESTE**

If Daddy Bulldog lets you in. He's been protecting my rest (eye-roll emoji).

**SAAR**

Please don't call my brother Daddy in front of me.

*A Convenient Secret*

Something heavy and hot is crushing my chest. I try to turn, and needles push into my skin before the weight disappears.

Cora's cats mew at me in unison and saunter away from the sofa. I stayed at my friend's place last night, and clearly her cats, Pitt and Clooney, thought they had a new bed.

I can't believe I fell asleep at all, but I guess after the previous sleepless night my body just shut down for survival reasons.

I told Cora about Mrs. Whitaker's sneaky eviction, and I told her a very stripped-down version of the stabbing accident. Since, in my panic, I confessed about it in our friends' group, I couldn't avoid that one.

I didn't tell her that Declan officially hired me. That for a moment there it made me happy, because who knew that childcare was something that fulfills me? It's not like I would ever do what I had been preparing for my entire life. That life is only a shadow from my past.

At one point, I still believed my exile would be temporary, but eighteen months down the line I accepted that nothing would change. This is my life now. I'm a nanny for two beautiful kids.

My excitement died with that kiss.

My pussy clenches at the recollection, and for a moment I allow myself to relive it without letting the uncomfortable aftermath taint the memory. It was the hottest kiss.

I haven't kissed many men.

Scratch that. I have only kissed boys in school. Kissing a real man, who devoured me with an intensity that made my ovaries dance a victory dance, is a novel experience.

And what an experience! I bite my lip, trying to recall the savage attack. My hand immediately traces the swell of my breast and travels lower, under the waistband of my panties.

I'm soaked. Just thinking about his tongue, his lips, his possessive grip and expert swirls and thrusts can get me off. But just in case... I slide my finger toward my clit. Circling around the sensitive spot, I moan.

The sound is indecently loud in Cora's empty apartment. I should stop, but that kiss got me all riled up, and I need to release this tension. Or perhaps the buildup started months ago when I first heard Declan's voice.

That voice.

My arousal escalates so quickly that a few minutes in, I come. My moan is long and guttural. My release is satisfying somewhat on the physical level, but completely unsatisfactory because it isn't him drawing it from me.

Him.

*A Convenient Secret*

Fuck. Declan is my new boss. In the light of day, it was smart that he put a stop to everything. And while my rational mind kind of agrees he made the right choice, the girl in me is hurting.

He didn't want to even explore this because he needs me as his nanny. I'm just his nanny, and he wouldn't fuck that up.

Screw him. He's just my employer from now on. At least his kids are great. And they are the ones I will dedicate my time to.

When he asked me to stay and work for him, I deliberated for a moment, but in the end I decided to push my attraction to the side. Perhaps a mistake.

I pad to the kitchen and get a glass of water when I notice a note.

*Help yourself to some breakfast and come over to the bistro. Cora*

I take out milk and cereal and pull out my phone to search for an apartment. An hour later, I'm so discouraged by my prospects, I decide to take a shower and get out of here.

I'm about to enter Cora's bistro when my phone pings.

DECLAN

I took care of your job at Summit Solutions. They are looking for an apartment for you closer to my place, so you don't have a long commute.

Efficient as ever. An unexpected pang of anger sweeps through me. Mr. Almighty taking care of the poor homeless girl? Fuck him. Before I think better of it, I reply.

> I don't need your help.

The three dots dance around.

**DECLAN**
> Are you sure?

Bastard.

I turn off my phone, plaster a smile on my face, and enter the bistro. The air conditioning breezes a bit of sanity into me, and I regret the bratty message a bit. Maybe taking the job was the worst idea.

"Hey." Cora waves from behind the counter where she is talking to her employee, Sanjay.

I make my way to our usual table. Cora's bistro is quaint, and right now almost all the tables are occupied. She took over her father's business, and has been barely keeping it afloat.

There are so many things she could implement to grow it, but I'm careful with my advice. My friends believe I moved to NYC to become an actress. I can't blow my cover, even though I trust these women. It's too risky.

It makes me feel like the worst person at the same time, so I took over the bistro's social media. A little help with marketing was the least I could do. Especially after Cora gave me a job when I first arrived.

I sit in my usual place and watch the sweltering streets. This little table where I regularly meet with my three friends feels like home. As strange as it is after losing everything, I didn't expect to feel safe. Ever. And yet, here is where I do.

"Check your phone. Celeste sent pictures." Cora puts two cups of cappuccino down and sits beside me.

I don't particularly want to see if Declan responded.

"My phone is dead," I lie. "Show me." I rub my hands in glee, banishing the thought of Declan. And failing. The man is already etched in my mind.

"What did I miss?" Saar shows up. "Isn't my niece adorable?" She plops down across from us and waves at Sanjay, who already knows her usual order.

"She's adorable." I admire the wrinkled newborn.

"I know Zoya and Zach are my niece and nephew by marriage, but Amelie feels a little more mine. Is that a horrible thing to say?" Saar scrunches her nose.

"No, it's not," I argue. "Amelie is your brother's and your best friend's. As you said, Zoya and Zach came into your life as Corm's family. It doesn't mean you don't love them."

"I adore them." She purses her lips. "In small doses."

"They are amazing kids," I defend them, surprised by the strong need to do so.

"Yes, they are." Saar takes her latte from Sanjay. "You would know. You spent the entire week with them, and stabbed my brother-in-law. He had it coming probably."

Cora snorts.

"It was an accident. Long story." I wave my hand. "Talking about Zoya and Zach, I accepted a permanent position as their nanny."

Both friends look at me with surprise.

"You didn't tell me that last night," Cora says.

"Last night?" Saar asks.

"Oh, yeah, on top of everything else, I'm homeless at the moment."

I quickly fill Saar in.

"I didn't know you were renting a room only. Is Declan's nanny a live-in position?" she asks.

"No. And I did a brief search this morning and..." I sigh.

"Something will come up." Cora pats my hand.

"Declan will help you out, I'm sure," Saar reassures me.

He will help, and drive me crazy in the process, but I don't share that with my friends. "He kissed me."

*A Convenient Secret*

For the second time today, my friends look at me with surprise. Only this time, it's more with shock.

"Is that why you stabbed him?" Saar asks.

And she's not even kidding. I feel strangely indignant on his behalf. I shouldn't, but I do.

"Of course not. I actually enjoyed the kiss."

"Isn't there some sort of a code? Don't fuck your nanny?" Cora asks.

"We didn't..." I look around, blush heating my cheeks. "He remembered *the code* and stopped."

"On some weird level, this makes Declan almost more human." Saar grins.

"Is it going to be awkward now when you work for him?" Cora asks.

I blow out a long breath and lean back in my chair. "I don't know, but he is not home much, so we really only meet for a few minutes in the morning and in the evening."

"You enjoyed the kiss." Cora pokes me in the ribs. It's not a question; it's a statement.

What gave my feelings away? Do I have a large sign on my forehead that says I have a crush on Declan Quinn, and that I've never been kissed like that?

"It was okay," I deflect, heat now spreading from my face down my neck. Has the air conditioning stopped working?

"Just okay? By the level of blush, I'm almost

tempted to ask for X-rated details, but since Declan is my brother-in-law, I'll try to forget about the whole thing." Saar makes a face like she's just swallowed a lemon.

"He probably did already." I sigh.

"Lils?" Cora probes, empathy lacing her voice.

I groan. "Okay, I find him attractive and I enjoyed the kiss. But that doesn't mean anything because I work for him, and because he regretted the moment of poor judgment, as he called it."

Saar reaches her hand over and squeezes mine. "I'm sorry, but I think it's for the best. What got you to take the job, anyway?"

I shrug. "I enjoyed my week with the twins way more than I enjoy my current job. And they accepted me after so many nannies failed. They deserve some stability."

"As long as you don't get hurt because you have the hots for their father," Cora says, her words spreading another wave of heat down my body.

"Declan is not a good idea, Lils." Saar stirs the foam in her drink. "He is dedicated to those kids after their mother abandoned them. He has no room for a relationship, even a casual one."

"When did his wife leave?" Cora asks.

Saar's face contorts with pain. "First time, when they were three or four months."

Jesus. "First time?"

"She came back briefly when they were three, and decided yet again that motherhood is not for her." Saar shakes her head slowly, as if the movement can make the statement more comprehensible.

"That's horrible." Cora's hand flies to her heart, while mine is breaking for the twins. And for Declan.

"And that's the reason Declan doesn't let women close," Saar says. "The wounds Kendra left are ones that can't be healed. He protects his heart and his twins fiercely. I mean, the man hires an escort for each event, and probably takes care of his needs in the Velvet Room."

"The sex club? Not even casual hookups?" Cora asks.

"I don't know for sure, but Corm believes his brother just gave up on intimacy." Saar looks at me. "Lils, protect yourself against that kind of pain. You deserve better, and more than he can ever offer."

\* \* \*

The man is good, I'll give him that. If I thought he ignored me before, he is now bringing his A-game. It's like I don't exist. Like that moment in his office two weeks ago truly was a moment of poor judgment that he erased as quickly as he changes his tie.

That kiss really meant nothing to him. With Saar's warning on top of everything, I should be cured.

I'm not.

I'm stealing glances at him every chance I get. There are only fleeting moments. My favorite are the mornings when I arrive.

Instead of trying to forget about the kiss, like Declan did, the memory has been running on a loop in my mind. And to make things worse, I've taken to watching him every morning, as if that could in any way help me move on from this unrequited... What? Infatuation?

I stay in the shadows before entering the kitchen and watch him preparing breakfast for his kids. I feel like I'm secretly intruding on their sacred, special moments, but I can't help myself.

To my disappointment—I mean luckily—he's been fully dressed every morning, unlike that first time.

He dances around the kitchen with proficiency, and chats with the kids about their day and schedule.

Some days he looks tired, showing up out of duty more than enthusiasm, going through the motions because it's on his calendar, but he always shows up, and I admire him for that.

I also admire the way his sinewy body moves, his muscles bulging as he flips pancakes. Or when he opens the fridge.

I have it bad for him.

"Would you like a pancake, Lily?" His voice pours over me with its chocolate-like decadence, and a dose of shock.

Shit. He knows I've been lurking?

"Good morning." I trip into the kitchen, steadying myself on the counter.

"Good mowning." Zoya swings the fork with a syrup-coated pancake in the air.

"Morning," Zach grumbles.

"Pancake?" Declan growls at me. Is he annoyed?

Why on earth I find him attractive is beyond me. Perhaps if we spend more time together, my feelings will settle.

"No, thank you." I don't look at him.

I'm embarrassed he caught me snooping. Also, I haven't looked him in the eyes since the night of the kiss, and I really don't want to do that. His intense gaze always robs me of my sanity. Even more than his voice.

"Thank you for breakfast, Dad." Zach slides down and ambles away, deep in thought. I should investigate what's going on.

"Ready, Zoya?" I smile.

"These wewe pewfect, Daddy. Thank you. Awe you coming with me, Lily?" She bounces to the floor and skips around. The girl is always in motion.

"I need to talk to Lily," Declan says. "Go get your things, sweetheart."

Fuck.

Zoya rushes away, and we're left alone in the kitchen. My shoulders stiffen, and I start collecting the dishes after the kids. Anything to avoid him.

"I'm working from home today, so I can spend time with the kids before the function tonight."

I open the dishwasher and put the plates in. "Okay." Why is my voice high-pitched?

"Are you still okay to stay longer tonight? I'm not sure how long I'll be, so feel free to stay in the guest room. I don't want you to travel across town only to come back a few hours later."

"Okay." I move a fruit bowl and continue looking for things to do that keep me in motion, and without a direct need to look at him.

"Have you found a new apartment yet?"

In my periphery, I see him leaning against the kitchen counter casually, and suddenly I'm really pissed that he unsettles me this much. That, somehow, he reduces me to a bundle of anxiety and nerves and lust, and then he mocks me with his nonchalant attitude.

"I don't see how that is any of your business." I fold my arms across my chest and glare at him.

First tactical mistake. There was a good reason for

avoiding his gaze. His eyes hold mine before they drop to my cleavage. Second mistake, but I refuse to drop my arms because his eyes roam.

"I can help you with your living situation. Don't be stubborn, Lily."

He pushes off the counter. At the same time I step forward, ready to storm out of the kitchen. The unfortunate result is that now he's blocked my path, and his scent has vaccinated me against reasonable behavior.

So instead of protecting boundaries, I poke at his chest with my finger. "Perhaps that's who I am. Stubborn and erasable."

He spins me around, my back hitting the island where he cages me with his hands on each side of me. He lowers his face to mine, so close I forget to breathe. An unfortunate but common occurrence around my boss.

"I tried to give you space, little Seagull, but you keep taunting me, with your morning spying, with your lingering scent when I come back home. Don't mistake my restraint for lack of desire. I fucking want you, Lily. I want you so much that my cock is hard just knowing you exist. I want to discover what's under those flimsy, indecent shorts of yours."

He lowers his forehead to mine, and I almost whimper, overwhelmed with a series of physical reactions that can't be healthy. My heart skips a beat, my stomach twists, my skin bursts into flame, and my brain explodes. What's happening in my panties is plain mortifying.

I try to look away, but he grips my jaw, not too hard, but enough to coax my chin up. "But I hold back, because one of us needs to be responsible. I hold back, because not only would it be a bad idea, but by now, I'm pretty sure you wouldn't survive if I got my hands on you."

As if to prove his point, his erection pokes into my stomach, and fuck, he may be right. I wouldn't survive him. Not just physically. I'm not ready for his intensity. I don't think I can match it.

"So don't test me, little Seagull, for both our sakes."

# Chapter 11

## *Lily*

I gape at him, my heart pumping in my temples.

"Lily?" Zoya's voice carries through the house from somewhere on this floor.

Declan jerks away, and I rush out of the kitchen like my ass is on fire.

"I think Zach needs youw help." Zoya hikes her backpack on her small shoulder.

I frown, willing my pulse to normalize. "Okay, your dad is still in the kitchen. Go help him while I go to Zach, and then we leave. Do you have everything?"

She nods and skips across the room toward the kitchen. If I don't get a chance to compose myself after... whatever that was, he can also deal with real life after his declaration. Threat? Warning?

*I'm pretty sure you wouldn't survive if I got my hands on you.*

But what a way to go. *Stop it, you little slut.*

Still shaken, and with an irregular heartbeat, I take two steps at a time and find Zach standing by his dresser, his soccer jersey in his hands.

"What's going on, Zach? We need to leave."

"I hate soccer." He turns and challenges me with a raised chin. Like he's already prepared his arguments and dares me to point out the benefits of soccer.

"Okay." I squat beside him, taking the jersey away from him. "Did something happen at the practice?"

"No. I'm even decent at it. Well, I'm good at everything." He shrugs. He's not wrong, but overly confident for a six-year-old. It's adorable, and a bit worrying. "I just don't like it."

"Did you tell your dad?"

He looks at me with horror. "I can't tell him. He expects me to be good at sports."

Oh boy. He's probably right, but surely not at all costs.

"Zach, he wants you to be happy first and foremost. If soccer isn't your thing, you may take up another sport; I'm sure your dad wouldn't force you to play soccer."

"I don't want to disappoint him." He glowers at me like I'm not understanding what's going on.

Frankly, his father has just seared my brain, so I may be a bit slow.

"Zach, between you and me, I'll let you skip today's practice. It would be our secret, but only if you promise to talk to your dad about this."

He eyes me for a moment, and I can practically hear him thinking.

When he doesn't respond, I continue. "I don't know how your dad will feel about you quitting soccer, but I'm sure you can't disappoint him. Ever."

"I'm not so sure, but I'll talk to him if you let me skip today." He extends his hand to shake on it in a very adult way.

I take it and give it a serious shake, hoping that playing hooky at the soccer won't get us both in trouble.

We get downstairs. Zoya waits for us, but I don't see Declan anywhere.

"Ready?" I usher the kids to the elevator.

"Daddy said you'll sleep hewe tonight." Zoya skips around the car as we descend.

"Where is Dad going?" Zach asks.

"He has a date." Zoya beams.

Motherfucker.

I drop the kids off and send the driver away. I need to walk off this energy. What the actual fuck? He cages me in the kitchen with his dirty declarations while he has a date tonight?

Not that I have any claims on him. He made it clear nothing would happen between us, but still, he can't say he's pining after me and then go on a date.

I'm so pissed, I march down the street like a mad woman. What an asshole. I'm so disappointed, I want to return to his house and tell him what I think about his stupid restraint.

*One of us needs to be responsible.*

Patronizing bastard. He wants me, he said. I should take some solace in that. At least my infatuation hasn't been one-sided.

I don't even know what I'm so pissed about.

It's good he has a date. Isn't it? He promised—no, he threatened—not to act on his attraction toward me, so he should move on. We both should.

But he hasn't dated in years, so why now?

To hurt me? And he dared ask me to sleep over. Though if he is his usual self, that date is doomed anyway.

I pause.

Does he want me to hear him fucking another woman? Oh my God. What game is he playing?

Why did he even tell Zoya about having a date? If I know his daughter, he'll be investigated thoroughly tomorrow.

Someone bumps into me, swearing. Our sweaty skins brush, and I shiver. Summer in New York can be really gross.

I enter a coffee shop and get myself an extra-large iced latte with double syrup, because I need to wrap my nerves in a bit of sugar. Or a lot, so I order a donut as well.

Deciding to enjoy the fridge-like conditions of the indoors, I find a seat and try to enjoy my sweetness overdose.

The kitchen scene keeps replaying in my mind. His words and his presence. The dominance when he spun me around. The burning touch when he forced me to look at him. His heaving chest. His rigid jawline. The scorching heat in his eyes.

The outline of his cock.

Yeah, I wouldn't survive him. His aggressive behavior should have concerned me. Scared me. And it did, but in a thrilling way. What's wrong with me?

His declaration should have quashed my lust. And it did the opposite. It aroused my curiosity, and ignited an even stronger yearning. Before, I thought I was the only one in this, but now I know he is just better at hiding his feelings.

I slurp my drink, watching the pedestrians trudging about in the heat of Manhattan. It may be the cool coffee, or his date, or just the insanity of it all, but as I calm down, I recognize he has a point.

His kids come first, and the two of us, even for a casual fling—and I'm not sure I'm that kind of a girl—is not a good idea.

The nanny code and all. I don't want to lose this job. I don't want things between us to get awkward. I laugh at that. They couldn't be more awkward, even if we tried.

Suddenly, unexpectedly, it dawns on me how selfish I've been. I should have never accepted the job. What if my past comes calling after all? I'll just be another person to abandon those kids. Jesus.

The thought makes me more miserable than Declan's stupid date. What was I thinking?

Spending time at the house with Zoya and Zach has felt like home. I let my guard down.

I push the donut away, deflated. I planned to search for an apartment during my free time today, but my mind is misfiring in all different directions, so I decide to visit Celeste.

I send her a quick message, and she begs me to come.

The penthouse is eerily silent when I step out of the elevator into Celeste's vast living room, which looks over Central Park only half a block from Declan's vantage point.

My friend lounges on the sofa and puts her finger to her lips, her eyes pleading desperately to stay silent.

As I approach her with caution, I realize a bassinet is beside her, Amelie sleeping peacefully.

Gingerly, I slide down to sit on the floor close to Celeste, with the best view of the sleeping infant.

"How are you?" I mouth.

"Exhausted." Celeste yawns.

"Can I help with something?"

"Just don't wake her up."

I smile and pat Celeste's knee. "Close your eyes. I'll watch her."

"Thank you," she whispers, her eyes already closed.

I scoot closer and put my hand on Amelie's chest. Drawing from her innocent calm, I instantly feel better about everything.

Funnily enough, I never had time to consider if and when I wanted to be a mother; and now, in a span of several weeks, I've grown to discover how much joy and love I've found around children.

Will I ever be able to settle down and have my own family? When I arrived in New York, I was sure that anything that normal probably wasn't in the cards anytime soon.

Not in my situation.

To cope, I decided to stop thinking about the

future. To stay in the present. It may take years before I can go back to my former life, so what's the point? I just need to bide my time before I can return to my roots.

But if it takes years? Am I strong enough to put my life on hold? Am I ready to just wait and live like a hermit?

I pushed those thoughts so deep inside. Why are they resurfacing now? *Because you realized you're the next person to abandon those kids.*

Celeste stirs. "Are you crying?"

I reach for my cheek and wipe a tear. "It's from joy," I lie. "She's beautiful."

"How are you?" Celeste slouches a bit, and we huddle around the bassinet. "I need some adult conversation."

I sigh. "Where to begin..." I purse my lips. "Cora's sofa is killing my back. And don't tell her, but her cats are super mean."

Celeste lets out a muffled giggle. "They are, aren't they?"

"I think they are taking revenge for their names." Having a whispered conversation is strange, but not in a bad way. It gives my frazzled, confused, upset mind the pause it needs.

"Also, Zach confessed today that he hates soccer, so I allowed him to skip the practice."

Celeste rolls her eyes. "Let's hope you won't get caught, rebel nanny."

We stifle our laugh, our shoulders shaking.

"But why would Declan force him to play if he doesn't like it?" I ask.

"I don't know him well enough, but Cal tells me Declan's need for control is non-negotiable, and he is not very flexible. It might be because, as a single father, he has so much to juggle. I assume he signed up Zach for soccer, whatever the motivation, but making a change to his well-established schedule is hard, so he doesn't question if said schedule makes sense."

"Wow, for not knowing the guy, this is quite insightful." Is Declan clinging to things the way they are because he fears that changing one piece would break the puzzle? "And if you're right, it's sad."

"Believe me, until Amelie, I never realized a routine is such an important part of keeping sane." She shrugs with a tired smile. "As a future—a very near future—nanny employer, I must advise you: don't let the kids skip the schedule. Talk to Declan about it. He may not even know he's forcing his son into something."

I nod. "Have you met Declan? It's not that easy to talk to him."

"Oh please, you can handle it."

"Thank you for the vote of confidence." I roll my eyes, slouching a bit.

"Hey, don't be modest. When we accepted you into our fold, you were a disaster. You're the only person I know that can burn iced coffee. Wherever you came from, you were shielded from basic survival skills, and yet you survived."

I stare at my friend. I never realized she deduced so much from my guarded behavior. "Just because I'm shit in the kitchen—" I start protecting my cover.

"The point is, you can handle yourself in any situation. Talk to Declan about Zach. One thing my marriage taught me is that open communication is the key to a successful relationship."

If she only knew how open Declan was this morning in the kitchen.

The housekeeper has a day off, so I return to the penthouse, ready to chill and collect my thoughts. It's only when I step from the elevator that I recall Declan is working from home.

Shit. I almost spin around to leave when he saunters from the kitchen with a coffee mug. He glances at me and pauses.

Our gazes collide, and it's almost like some strange

truce descends on us. Like we got tired of the dance and avoidance. Or maybe it's just me.

"Kids delivered okay?" he asks.

I nod.

He opens his mouth. Is he going to talk about what happened in the kitchen? But then, to my relief and disappointment, he bows his head curtly and goes upstairs.

I let out a breath I didn't know I was holding and slouch against the wall. A part of me wishes he didn't tell me all those things this morning.

An equally persistent, darker part of me—I didn't even know I have this side—is reveling in his brief loss of control. I did that to him. It's a heady feeling.

But as I sit on the sofa, enjoying the view, the rational me comes through. He is right, this attraction has no chance of blossoming.

I work for him. My past is holding me back. His children need stability. He doesn't want to pursue it, and I need to respect that. Even though I want to throw tantrums.

Declan doesn't come downstairs for lunch. Thankfully. I put crackers and cheese on a small plate and decide to sit outside before I have to leave to pick up the kids.

I balance my water and the plate in one hand, jutting out my hip as I reach for the handle. Everything tumbles to the ground when a shrill, piercing wail stabs my ears.

The silence shatters with unforgiving intensity. The high-pitched screech I prayed to never hear again reverberates off the walls, its urgent rhythmic blare demanding attention.

I freeze, paralyzed as the fear overtakes my body, along with the relentless sound drilling into my skull.

## Chapter 12

### *Declan*

"Are we still waiting for Cal?" Corm asks, rocking in his office chair.

"Yes, we need him for this conversation." Roxy doesn't even look up, typing.

"Why are you working from home, Declan?" Xander pops something in his mouth. Does he always eat?

"Has your nanny quit on you again?" Corm teases, knowing full well, if that were the case, he would have heard it from Saar already.

"That would be a shame. Isn't she into knife-play?" Xander stuffs his face again.

How does he even know about the incident? How is it that in a company that deals in confidential information, and one that keeps so many corporate and financial secrets, our personal lives seem to be common knowledge?

"Fuck you," I spit and glare, knowing that the effect is muted by the screen.

"Come on, that was funny." Corm snorts.

He wasn't laughing when his sleeping in the office to avoid Saar became the topic of the water-cooler conversation.

"Am I laughing?" I growl.

"What did I miss?" Cal's face appears on the screen, and he looks like he hasn't showered, shaved, or changed his shirt in weeks.

"Dick comparing," Roxy mutters.

"We were discussing how Declan got stabbed by his nanny." Xander's shit-eating grin fills the screen.

"Oh, I thought that was a secret." Cal looks confused.

He knows as well? Fuck.

"Perhaps we can proceed with the actual point of this call." I tap my fingers on the table, my eyes gliding to my phone where the downstairs security feed shows Lily preparing a snack.

Yeah, I'm that fucker who tells her I'm exercising my common sense and restraint, and then I continue to cyberstalk her.

When she didn't come immediately after the school drop-off, I worried for a moment that I might have scared away the first suitable nanny I'd had in years.

Fuck.

As much as I try, I barely hang onto my control around the woman. I adjusted my schedule to cross paths with her as little as possible. It wasn't enough. Just the knowledge that she's been here every day continues to feed my fantasies.

I couldn't get her out of my system even if I tried.

"Declan?" Corm's voice snaps me back to the meeting.

"Is the nanny playing with the knife again?" Xander snickers.

"You fucking mention her again, and I swear to God you will be the one needing stitches." Second time today I exhibit a lack of control.

I've never threatened one of my colleagues. Xander has been testing me, but I've never stooped to his level of razzing. Nor have I ever taken his bait. Fuck.

The silence on the line is loud, hammering in my temples with a relentless pulse.

"Okay, now, when the informal part of the agenda is over—and thank God for that—" Roxy's voice carries an unwarranted amount of cheer. "Let's talk about the London office before I'm forced to send you all into a timeout."

A wailing siren rips through the house.

"For fuck's sake." Corm sighs.

Shit. I forgot about the planned fire drill. "Sorry, it'll go off in a minute."

I glance at my phone and, fuck—

Ripping my headphones off, I disconnect the call without any explanation and run out of my office. I skid down the stairs, almost tripping over my own feet.

The sight in front of me is heart-attack-inducing, even though I don't understand what's going on.

Lily is shaking on the floor, covering her ears, her entire body curled in on itself. Shards of glass glitter in the afternoon light, water pooling across the floor.

I take this in in a second, still unsure what the hell I'm looking at.

The fire alarm keeps blaring overhead. "Lily," I yell.

No reaction. Not even a flinch. She is rocking back and forth. I want to approach her, but the scar on my arm proves she may act on instinct.

I don't mind getting hurt, but what if she hurts herself? If she moves, she may get cut.

Fuck, I hate being useless, powerless. "Lily!" My voice is sharp, cutting through the noise, but she continues acting like she's in the middle of a goddamn war zone.

I take a step closer, glass crunching under my soles.

I crouch, trying to catch her gaze. Fuck. My pulse

skyrockets and then drops as I will myself to stop panicking and focus.

Lily's eyes are unfocused, wild, her chest rising and falling too fast. She's somewhere else. Not here. Not in the present.

I force my hands to stay at my sides, even though every instinct screams at me to reach for her, to shake her out of whatever Hell she's trapped in.

"Lily," I say again, softer this time, controlled. "You're okay. It's just the drill alarm. It's not real."

She doesn't move, doesn't blink. Her fingers dig into her scalp like she's trying to claw herself out of her own head.

Instinct sharpens my focus. I need to get her out of this. I reach for her hands first, gently prying them away from her ears. The second my fingers touch her skin, she jerks violently, her breathing ragged.

"Hey, it's me," I say, my voice firm but steady. "You're safe. It's just a drill. That's all."

Her lips part like she wants to speak, but all that comes out is a fractured gasp. Her shoulders heave with each breath, her pupils so blown out her eyes look nearly black.

I should have turned the damn alarm off before coming down here.

"There is no fire?" she finally whispers, her voice hoarse, barely audible over the wailing siren.

"No fire. Let me turn the sound off." But I don't move yet. She still looks like she's seconds from shattering into as many pieces as the glass surrounding her.

Instead, I shift. "Look at me."

She struggles, her gaze flickering, but she does. Barely.

"Breathe with me," I say. "In." I exaggerate the inhaling, slow and deep, holding it for a second before letting it out in a controlled exhalation. "Now you."

Her first attempt is shaky, uneven, but it's something.

"Again," I say. "Nice and slow."

Another breath. Still choppy, but better. The shaking of her hands is less violent.

I nod, reinforcing the progress. "Good. Keep going."

Three more breaths and she's still tense, but she's here. With me.

I glance at the broken glass, irritation spiking at the thought of her sitting in the middle of it. "Can you move?"

She blinks, looking down like she's noticing the mess for the first time. "I-I don't know."

Before she can panic again, I shift forward and slide an arm beneath her legs, the other behind her back.

"There is no fire?" Her voice wobbles as I lift her.

"No fire, baby. Relax. I've got you." I keep my voice even, but my grip firm.

She's stiff at first, but after a moment she curls into my chest, her hands gripping my shirt like she's anchoring herself.

At least the fucking alarm is off finally. I carry her upstairs and lower her on to the bed in her room. Well, the guest room technically, but ever since that one time she slept here, I started referring to it as Lily's room.

Her breathing is more even now, but she looks wrecked—like she's been pulled out of deep water and still isn't sure if she's drowning.

"Can I get you anything?" I ask, and hesitate; I'm not ready to leave her alone.

"I'm fine," she whispers, though her voice cracks. She's not fine.

"Let me get you a glass of water. Stay put." I stride to the bathroom.

When I return with a full glass, she has her knees drawn up to her chest, her arms wrapped around her legs, fingers twisting into the fabric of her sleeves.

She takes the water from me, avoiding my gaze. She gulps down the whole thing and puts the glass on the nightstand. "I thought there was a fire."

"And your reaction was to stay put and not move?"

She flinches, her lips pressing together.

I exhale through my nose, forcing patience. "Lily."

She closes her eyes for a beat, then opens them again. "I don't want to talk about it." Her jaw clenches, but she's still pale, her hands still trembling slightly in her lap.

"We don't have to talk about it now, but we will."

I'm not letting this one go. This may not be the time, but I still don't understand why she sleeps with a knife. And whatever just happened, it was more than panic. That was intense fear. And I want to know why.

She scrambles from the bed, her movements still wobbly. "I need to go pick up Zach."

She must be still disoriented.

"Zach has his soccer practice today."

The sigh that escapes her is almost a groan or a whimper. Is she hurt? Did I miss something? There was broken glass. I skim my gaze down her body, her naked legs, her white T-shirt. She doesn't seem hurt.

"He doesn't have soccer today." She stands up and stumbles.

I grip her elbow, steadying her. "Lily, I think you need to rest. Zach quite definitely has soccer." Gently, I push her to sit at the edge of the bed.

"Not today," she repeats, tears gleaming in her eyes.

"Was it canceled? I didn't get notified—"

"Declan, let me just do my job. Thank you for

helping me before. I'm sorry I panicked, and even more sorry you had to witness that. I'm perfectly fine."

"I call bullshit. Rest, and I'll pick up the kids. You just had a..." Shit, I don't know how to name it. "Just rest."

"Just don't be mad at him," she blurts before I reach the door.

"At Zach?" I frown. "Explain." It's a command that is perhaps a bit too harsh, given what she's just gone through.

But when it comes to my kids, I struggle to maintain reason at times. Especially when I am clearly in the dark.

Kendra kept me in the dark about her real feelings and motivations. I don't allow anyone else to do that.

Lily flinches, her face veiled with fatigue, but as the fighter she is, she pushes to stand. "He doesn't want to play soccer, so I allowed him to skip today's practice until he talks to you. But before you get mad, be mad at me. I should have discussed it with you first, but this morning, I... well, after this morning—"

"Enough."

She startles, but when she blabbers from anxiety, there is no other way to snap her out of it.

At the same time, I'm unreasonably grateful for her current word expulsion, because at least it gives me hope she's feeling better.

"Declan—"

"Lily, please, just fucking be a good girl and rest. I will respect your unwarranted promise to my son, but just fucking stop talking and stay put."

I march out of her room and barrel into my office. Snatching my phone, I call my driver. I text my assistant to cancel my afternoon calls. I wanted to spend time with the kids today, after all.

I have seven missed calls from Cormac and three from Roxy. Shit. I completely forgot I bailed in the middle of our call.

As I dash downstairs, I dial my brother to prevent myself from checking on Lily.

"What the fuck? Is everyone okay?" Corm answers after the first ring.

If only I knew. "Yes, it was just a drill alarm, but Lily didn't know and got scared."

He hums like there is more to that information. Fucker with his sixth sense.

"Did you agree on the next steps?" I focus on business while getting into the elevator.

"While we still hope you'll change your mind and move to London for a year, for now we approved a change in the budget to account for an outside hire. Roxy is working with the recruiter to bring us names to vet."

"Good, because I'm not moving." I get to the

underground garage and nod to my driver before sliding onto the backseat of my Escalade.

"It's a shame, but I understand."

"Thank you."

"So what's with you and Lily?"

# Chapter 13

## *Declan*

I freeze. "What do you mean?"

"You dropping the call without explanation to rush and help her during a false alarm comes to mind."

"It was a real alarm drill, and she thought there was a fire. Your point?"

"No point. You'll tell me when you're ready."

I groan, resting my head on the backrest of my seat. "I don't know. As much as I try to stay away from her, I... I don't know. I need to get laid, I guess."

"Look, bro, I'm the first one to cheer your attempt to get out there finally, but don't complicate things. She is my wife's friend, and your nanny."

"I know." I sigh. "I swear, I'm going to take one of the divorcees' offers tonight. Is Saar coming with you?"

He snorts. "Is the Earth turning?"

For the first time since my brother settled down, a pang of envy rakes through me. Like he has something I will never have. Something I didn't even know I may still want.

* * *

"Zach, you committed to your team, and when you skip the practice, you let them down."

We sit on his bed, me still in my tux, arriving from the stupid function at ten. I bailed on the event pretty much after the first hour.

Corm laughed at me, barely stopping himself from making a nanny comment.

Xander held his tongue this time. There was business to be dealt with and people to schmooze, but I needed to be back home.

I found Zach still playing with his airplane.

He nods, not looking at me. "I won't do it again."

Sighing, I put my arm on his shoulder. "I understand Lily allowed you to skip the practice—"

"Don't be mad at her. She told me I need to talk to you."

As if I could be mad at Lily. And yet I'm agitated by her presence, constantly. "And she was right. So you don't feel like playing anymore?"

He leans forward, bracing himself with his elbows

on his thighs. After what feels like half an hour of silent deliberation, he sighs. "I'll play, Dad. I just didn't feel like it today. I'm sorry."

"Zach, sometimes I don't feel like doing something. Life is full of instances when we would rather skip things, but we don't always have the luxury to do so."

"Okay."

"When you commit to something, people rely on you, buddy. You need to rise to the responsibility, respect their time, and not let them down."

He nods. "Can I play now?"

I ruffle his hair. "It's a school night. You should get some rest."

Helping him to climb under his covers, I kiss his forehead. "Good night."

"I love you, Dad."

Those words break and mend my heart every single time. "I love you, too, buddy."

By the time I get next door, Zoya is fast asleep. I watch her for a moment before I leave the room, yanking my tie loose.

Movement to my right grabs my attention. Lily is coming up the stairs wearing pink pajama pants and an oversized hoodie. She looks like a college student in that getup, and my depraved cock awakens.

I glare at her like it's her fault she stirs up the animal side of me.

"How was your date?" she asks.

"What?"

She rolls her eyes. She fucking rolls her eyes at me. "Never mind."

"Has Zoya made up a date again?" I groan.

My daughter watched some stupid—and certainly age-inappropriate—romantic comedy at Saar's and decided a date would make me happy.

"Good night." Lily turns toward her room.

"Can we talk?" Without waiting, I start toward my office.

She sighs and follows. I walk to my desk and lean against it as I undo the top buttons of my shirt. Pulling the bow tie off, I put it in my pocket.

Lily enters and stays by the door. I've half a mind to eat the distance between us and fuck her against the door, her legs around my waist while her tits bounce in her large sweatshirt.

"Why doesn't it surprise me you were in a debate club?" I chuckle.

She frowns. "What?"

I nod toward her and tap my chest to where her Stanford Debate Club logo is.

Puzzled, she looks at her jumper. "Oh, it's not mine." She shakes her head. "I mean, I was more of a cheerleader."

Why do I again feel like she's hiding something? "What happened today, Lily?"

"I would prefer not to talk about it. As I said, I'm sorry you had to witness that."

I put my hands into my pockets because, at this point, I need any form of restraint when around her.

"I want to be sure you can take care of my kids if something like this happens again." Not my proudest argument, but fuck, her secrecy pushes my buttons. More than her allure.

Her gaze flashes with anger, igniting a blush all over her face. "Really? You're going to pull the safety of your kids card? That's a low blow even for you."

What does she mean, even for me? "You're giving me no choice. You seem to have PTSD. You sleep with a knife." As usual, I don't even realize before I cross the room to stand in front of her.

"I was trapped in a room during a fire. Happy now?" She pants, and I'm not sure if it's a reaction to her confession or to my sudden closeness.

"Fuck. I'm sorry." I guess it doesn't explain everything, but seeing the glimmer in her eyes, I feel like an asshole.

At the same time, something awakens in me, and I have an overwhelming need to protect her.

"Is that all?" She gives me her bratty look, her chin high.

I'm a reasonable man. A man who prides himself on the level of control I exude. A man who speaks only when he has something to contribute.

None of those familiar attributes count when Lily is in my vicinity. With her, I'm a man who loses any sense of propriety or reason.

"It's not all. Let's talk about Zach. You're not authorized to change his schedule, let alone let him ditch."

"He wasn't ditching. I allowed him to take a break. I encouraged him to talk to you."

"I've just talked to him, and he will continue playing soccer." My voice is unreasonably vehement. I'm not even sure why I'm arguing with her.

She jerks her head back. "He will?"

"Of course he will. He needed to be reminded of his commitment."

She fucking rolls her eyes at me again. "Really? Did you ask him what he would like to do instead? Have you ever asked him what he wants to do? Or did you just schedule all the activities to keep them busy? To fill their time the way it suits you."

"Don't you dare challenge my parenting! You know nothing about our circumstances."

"Don't I? Because, sometimes, it feels like you make decisions to ease your burden. A selfish decision without considering their wishes."

"You judge me? You've been here for three weeks, and you know better how to run my family?"

"Your family doesn't need to be run. They need to be seen. They need to be heard. They need to know they can come to you when they have a problem."

We glare at each other, panting. This seems to already be a wearily familiar situation. Her sweatshirt brushes my shirt. Her eyes glare with frustration.

The same frustration that is running through my veins. I want to strangle her, punish her, kiss her senseless.

"Just don't encourage my son to skip his obligations," I grit out through a clenched jaw, hoping we can both step away from this.

"Did you know Zach didn't want to talk to you about soccer because he didn't want to disappoint you?"

If she slapped me, it would sting less. I grind my teeth, my hands shaking. "Fuck."

I step away, turning my back to her. I hang my head, my world crumbling again as another failure joins the rest of my inadequacies.

A warm hand connects with my skin through my shirt, and I shudder. Lily's touch on my back is comforting, like I've just learned to breathe again.

"Declan," she whispers, her voice full of compassion. Compassion I don't deserve.

"I'm trying my best." I hate how whiny that admission sounds.

"And your kids love you and respect you. They want to be like you. Especially Zach. Just make sure he still remains himself. That he knows you respect his choices."

I don't ever want her to remove her hand from my back. It's like she is recharging my batteries, uploading a new operating system, and making sure I can function for a bit longer.

"Thank you." I turn slowly, even though it means I'm losing her touch.

Her smile hits me like an arrow to my heart. I just yelled at her, and she comforted me in return.

"Lily—"

"It's okay, Declan. I understand where I made the mistake. I promise to be a good girl."

We freeze. She didn't aim for a double entendre, but fuck if she didn't just awaken the beast in me. She must realize the slip, because heat rushes to her cheeks, and her eyes pop out.

I should just ignore it, glance over her slip-up, but my cock has different ideas. He wants a good girl.

I move closer, pushing away all thoughts of propriety. A distant inner voice warns me. I can't afford to lose another nanny. Especially not one my kids have accepted. One that complements my family in the best ways. But I tune out that fucker as if Lily is the only woman in the world.

And for a brief second, I allow myself to believe she is.

Because for me, she is the only woman.

I step forward, and she steps back, her back hitting the door. I don't allow her any personal space, the suggestion of her body under her clothes enough for me to lose my mind.

"You want to be a good girl for me, little Seagull?"

Her eyes widen, mixed with innocence and curiosity. It's such a turn-on.

My hand skims her rib cage through the thick cotton of the sweatshirt, slowly brushing the swell of her breast up to her neck. I wrap my fingers around that delicate column. Not squeezing—just needing to feel her pulse flutter.

What I find is an erratic beat. For a moment I worry I scared her, but her eyes tell a different story.

And then she nods, licking her lips, and I stifle a groan.

"You're not a good girl though, Lily. Far from it. Just this morning, we agreed to keep our distance." I trace her chin with my thumb.

"Are you referring to your monologue? Because I didn't agree to anything." She bites her lips, stripping me of my last bit of restraint.

Grinding against her, I fuse my lips with hers.

She moans and wraps her leg around mine. Fuck. She should stop this. I should stop this.

To the soundtrack of those thoughts, I thrust my tongue into her beautiful mouth. Holding her leg in place, I reluctantly leave her throat and move my hand down, skimming her breast again, wishing I had the patience to spend more time there.

But I resisted this temptation for too long, so I go straight for her waistband. Lily cups my nape, pulling me closer, our bodies flush.

I groan when I dip my hand inside her pants. "You've been walking around with a bare pussy, little Seagull? You're just determined to drive me insane."

"Maybe," she says, so sweetly I almost come in my pants.

My fingers graze her between her thighs, and she moans. "Fuck, I need this sweet pussy."

"I thought one of us needed to be responsible," she taunts me.

"Do you want me to stop?" I ask, but at the same time I circle her sensitive bud, and she arches into me.

"God, no, Declan, don't stop. Please don't stop."

"Tell me what you want, baby." I massage her clit, my cock painfully straining against my pants.

She looks at me with so much desire and trust in

her eyes, I almost bolt, sure I don't deserve her. But I'm too far gone to do the noble thing.

I seize her lips, not allowing either of us to lean into reason.

The voice of reason comes from outside the door. "Daddy!"

# Chapter 14

## *Lily*

CELESTE

Caleb hired two day nurses and a night nurse, a nutritionist and a dog walker.

SAAR

Jesus.

CORA

I didn't know you had a dog.

CELESTE

We don't.

SAAR

Is it for Amelie's future dog (laughing emoji)?

> It takes a village to raise a child.

CELESTE

I don't like this village.

CORA

Typical man, trying to help without asking how.

@Celeste at least you get more sleep.

SAAR

I'll talk to him.

CELESTE

I'll talk to him. But first I have people to fire.

SAAR

Should I prepare our guest room?

He won't throw her out with the baby.

CORA

(laughing emoji) I'm sure she meant for Cal.

\* \* \*

Turning off my alarm, I stretch my arms over my head, a smile spreading across my face. I slept like a baby, the memory of Declan's fingers grazing between my legs forming into a full, three-dimensional, high-definition wet dream.

I take a quick shower and put on fresh clothes. I wish I'd packed something more sexy. Teasing Declan Quinn and making him snap is fucking empowering. The power I seem to have over him is a new uncharted feeling for me, but it is damn good.

And scary.

I don't quite know how to handle the man, and my head spins at the thought of his hands on me, his mouth on my lips.

I lose myself in him, feral with need and curious to explore more. More of his body, but also more about mine.

I'm a twenty-five-year-old woman, and I'm only now embracing my sexuality. Having the chance to discover it with Declan seems like winning some imaginary orgasm lottery.

His fingers only brushed my embarrassingly wet pussy, and I know that an orgasm caused by Declan would be life-altering.

The chemistry and heat between us are undeniably unique. Not that I have much to compare to, but I don't think it's normal to feel like this.

The outline of his erection scared me a little. How on earth is he going to fit that thing inside me? That wasn't an average cock. Fuck, I'm so unprepared for this.

Clad in a simple white T-shirt and a short, black, A-shaped skirt, I venture out, ready to ogle Declan as he prepares breakfast.

"Fuck," his voice comes from his bedroom.

"Money in the jaw," Zoya calls from her room before she skips into the hallway.

Declan appears in his doorway, and my steps falter. He's bare-chested, only a towel around his waist, and the sight has me pushing my thighs together. I should have taken care of my need last night, when he left me all riled up after we got interrupted.

Now I'm going to have to walk around with this lustful desire all day. What was I thinking?

Our eyes meet, and even imprisoned in his gaze, I'm painfully aware of his glistening skin, and every single bulge and dip around his sinewy shoulders and chest.

I'm so distracted, I don't even realize he's glaring at me. Is he pissed? His enamel is certainly taking a toll, his jaw working.

"Good morning." I find my most cheerful voice.

His gaze drops to his daughter. "Zoya, I'm running late. Zach," he calls.

Zach comes out. "Morning."

"Take your sister downstairs. Today we're having cereal. You're in charge." His tone doesn't leave room for negotiations.

"Why is he in chawge?" Zoya puts her hands on her hips.

"Zoya," Declan warns.

"Oh boy, Daddy is in a mood." She sasses him with a dramatic eye roll, and I want to high-five her.

Both kids make a beeline for the stairs.

"Slow down." I glance at Declan and turn to follow the kids.

"Lily," his voice booms behind. "A word."

Filled with anticipation, I almost skip across the floor like Zoya. *Pull yourself together.*

When I reach his door, I realize he already walked in. If this was a romance novel, he would shut the door and pin me against it.

In the reality of Declan's dark soul, he's already putting on his shirt. I falter. I've never been here.

His room is large, luxurious, and airy, with white curtains billowing around the glass walls. It's in such contrast to his personality.

In the middle, the bed looks larger than king-sized, the white bedding so at odds with the man.

The sheets are crumpled, and I can't help but think about his body rolling in them… With me if possible.

There is a freestanding mirror in the corner, and I see him in its reflection, moving about his walk-in closet. Unfortunately he already shed the towel, his ass clad in briefs as he puts on his pants.

"Have you found an apartment yet?"

His question throws me. I didn't expect this topic. I thought he would set the rules for us fooling around, or the exact opposite: go back to insisting the two of us are not an option.

He slides his arms into his shirt, the muscles bulging.

"Lily?" he urges, his tone showing about as much patience as a toddler in a toy store, ready to throw a tantrum.

What was the question? I look away, hoping to find my wits.

"No," I say, hating that the morning starts with me admitting how my life is not at all under control. In such stark contrast with his.

"My housekeeper just called. She needs to leave for a few weeks; her mother is sick." He buttons his shirt. "Would you be available to stay with us for about three weeks to help me run the household?"

"You want me to move in?" I enunciate each word, like saying it slowly will make the situation easier.

He walks out, and without looking at me he marches to the mirror to tie his tie.

"I understand it's an inconvenience, but if you get additional responsibilities, it makes sense you stay here with us."

Is that his way of making sure we have more alone time together?

"Sure. I'll bring over my things—"

"Don't worry about it. You're doing us a favor; the least I can do is take care of your things." He straightens the knot and walks back to his closet.

Us? Who is *us* in this equation?

"Just send my driver over." He walks out again, putting on his suit jacket.

Damn, the man can wear a suit. I lick my lips. He comes to me, and again, with his gaze-avoiding superpower, he reaches above me. My breath catches, but I immediately feel like an idiot when he pushes the door open.

So this is how it's going to be? Let's just go back to the Ice Age.

I take a deep breath and grip his arm. A current zaps through us, and he jerks away, his gaze finally landing on me.

"Declan, we should talk—"

"No, we shouldn't."

I huff. "I would like to talk about it."

"There is nothing to talk about, Lily. I apologize for my lack of control. But if Zoya's interruption taught us something... I'm not available."

So he got scared again. I step closer, frustration zipping through me. This man is infuriating. "And yet you can't control yourself around me."

He closes his eyes briefly on a deep sigh. "Let's keep this professional."

"Just like last night?" I challenge. I want to rile him up, so he finally gets his head out of the gutter.

"Lily," he warns. "We both know this is for the best."

"I don't know that."

He turns, his steps long and fast approaching the staircase. "Don't be a brat; you're just proving my point."

His words are like a slap. This is how he sees me? A brat? I rush behind him, but I'm forced to push my anger aside. He effectively dismisses me, moving the conversation to the topic of the children.

"You don't need to take over all housekeeping responsibility, of course, but if you can manage the meals... You know how to cook?"

It's beyond frustrating to talk to his back. But fuck, I'm not letting him win this round.

"Of course," I lie as we enter the kitchen.

Zach cocks his head, but doesn't say anything.

"When I said squares, I didn't mean they need to be geometrically correct." Cora rises to her tiptoes as if she can get a better view of the cutting board over the screen.

"You could have said small pieces then." The knife slides, grazing my finger. "Shit." I put it between my lips.

## A Convenient Secret

"Did you nick yourself? I should have just cooked meals for you. You're a danger to yourself in the kitchen." Cora walks around her kitchen in the bistro with ease, probably finishing her fourth order while she tries to coach me on FaceTime.

Moving in with Declan has been quite torturous. The man exhibits such a level of control that I almost admire him.

Or he turned off any attraction he might have harbored. After another two weeks of an awkward—at least for me—cohabitation, I'm wondering if it was all just in my head.

It doesn't matter, because Declan is not going to pursue anything with me. And even if there was a chance of anything—and my pussy weeps at the idea—he would probably switch it off again easily.

That only exposes me to getting hurt. He's really doing us a favor. After a week of sulking, and another week of getting my lust under control, I realized we need to find a new flow to our relationship.

I'll serve a delicious homemade meal, and we will talk. Bury the imaginary hatchet. He may not want to fuck me, but I can't work for him if he treats me like I'm invisible.

At least the kids have been amazing. Tiring and challenging, but definitely rewarding. We've had so much fun together.

Another positive thing was to discover the freezer was fully stocked with homemade meals. God bless the housekeeper, because I've been slaying my new responsibility. Okay, except for a few burned meals and broken dishes, but I'm getting better.

That last streak of luck unfortunately ran out, and after two nights of takeout, I need to provide the family with a homemade meal.

"Remind me again why you are trying to cook for a man who's been ignoring you?" Cora looks at the camera, deadpan. All the while, she is chopping carrots at the speed of a ninja. How?

"To prove a point." I manage to slice off another small piece of chicken breast without skinning myself.

"Are we adding arsenic to the sauce?" It's concerning how excited she sounds about the prospect.

I snort. "No. We're not. I tried to stab him, remember? He's immortal."

She laughs. "He's an asshole."

"That too." A part of me wants to defend him, but I need to focus on yielding this knife without losing a finger.

"So," Cora starts, and it's that kind of prolonged *so* that leads to uncomfortable topics. I look at the camera. "What point are you making, Lils?"

"That I'm not scared of his large dick." Shit. Where did that come from?

"Oh my God, I have to bleach my ears now. I don't want to think of Declan's dick when I see him next."

"It's the only thing I think about," I murmur, and return to slicing.

"Oh, Lils." Cora picks up her phone to move it closer to her face, like she can comfort me better that way.

"No, no, don't feel sorry for me. I'm a cliché. Nanny who fell in lust with her employer."

"Seduce him and quit."

I giggle. "What do you think the meal is for?" Is it? I want to confront his abhorrent behavior, not to get naked with him. I mean, I want the latter, but I can exhibit the same control he does. I'm not forcing myself on him.

"I was joking." Cora's worried face fills the screen. "You would get hurt. Unless I don't know you at all, you're not a casual kind of girl."

I check on Zach and Zoya, who are both fast asleep. Lingering in the doorway, I enjoy the moment of peace. It was a difficult evening, because Zoya had a meltdown and Zach refused to finish his Math worksheet from the summer school.

At least they enjoyed my chicken fajitas. After we added ketchup. A lot of ketchup to give them taste.

I'm tired, but still vibrating with nervous energy. Because, of course, on a night I want to showcase to Declan I can be professional, and that he doesn't have to avoid me, he doesn't even show up.

Something must have come up, because he doesn't miss the kids' bedtime if he can prevent it. For all his aloof assholeness and controlling tendencies, his schedule always benefits the twins.

Zoya smiles in her sleep, and a wave of affection hits me. I don't know how I fell in love with these two perfect little humans so quickly.

I make my way downstairs and pour myself a glass of wine. So very adult of me. I smile to myself. It's a warm evening, so I decide to enjoy the chilled rosé on the terrace.

The city doesn't sleep down below, and I cherish the bustling sounds with closed eyes. I've always loved the noise of a busy town. It makes me feel like I'm not alone. Like I'm an extension of something bigger.

It's the reason I picked New York as my new home. For a city lover, there is no better place to live than here.

"My sinful nanny," Declan's voice snaps me out of my reverie, and I spill my wine over my hand.

"Jesus, you startled me. I didn't hear you." I move the glass to my other hand and shake off the drops.

"Sorry." He sways a little. He is in his shirt and his dress pants only. No tie, no jacket. "Those are the least sexy pajama pants."

Despite the words, his voice is like molten chocolate, but the cadence is off. He stares at me, and again I wonder if demanding he pays me some reasonable, professional attention is such a good idea. He takes a few unsteady steps.

"Are you drunk?"

He falls into a lounger beside me. "Don't worry. I'll behave."

"That's not very comforting," I murmur, and put my glass on a stool beside me.

He rolls to his side. "Would you like me not to behave, little Seagull?"

The fervent desire lacing his voice has a direct line to my core. *This is alcohol talking,* I remind myself.

"Let me make you some coffee." I stand up. "Have you eaten anything?"

"I don't think so." He stretches his arm. "Don't leave."

I sigh. Okay, this is not how I planned this evening. "I'll be right back."

I fix him a plate of leftover fajitas and a double

espresso. Placing everything on a tray with a bottle of water, I carefully bring everything outside.

He swings his muscular legs and pushes himself to sit. I place the tray beside him and sit across from him. The two loungers are close enough that, somehow, I end up sitting practically between his legs.

Declan gulps down the entire bottle and picks up the plate. He eyes the contents. "We ran out of the frozen meals?" He lifts a fajita and balances it above the plate before he shoves half of it into his mouth.

He knew about the frozen dishes? Jesus. The man knows everything. Also, why is it sexy to see him eating with his hands? The perfect, always-composed man is wolfing down his food. It's like watching porn.

"Jesus, this is quite horrible." Despite his comment, he takes another bite.

"Careful there with all the compliments. First my pajamas, now the results of my kitchen slavery?" I nudge his leg with mine before I twist to stretch on the sun bed.

He laughs, and it startles me. He smirked, chuckled, and almost grinned before, but laughter? What was he drinking tonight?

"I miss talking to you, Seagull."

Oh, my poor heart. "We kind of talked only once, I think."

"And it left a lasting impact." He puts the plate on

the ground and downs the coffee before he mirrors me and lies back, the recliner propped up to admire the view.

Well, wasn't that my mission tonight? To find a friendly modus operandi. "We can talk. Just because you believe we can't fuck—"

"Jesus," he spatters. "Lily, don't mention fucking because I will lose it again."

"And we wouldn't want that," I say sarcastically.

He whips his head to me, glaring, but there is softness beneath it. "Lily, Lily, Lily, you're so young, and I'm an old fart with two kids."

I snort. "You're not that old."

He turns back and seems to watch the skyline for a moment. "I certainly feel that way."

I wholeheartedly disagree, but the sentiment in his voice is heavy with bone-deep fatigue. He feels old because he doesn't let himself relax for a moment. Always working, always fathering, and nothing in between. My chest constricts with compassion.

"Look, Declan, I'm not going to force you to give in to our mutual attraction, but you don't have to go to the opposite extreme. We can still talk. You can treat me like a person."

He sighs. "I'm sorry I've been such an ass."

"A rare moment of self-reflection. Do continue." I pretend to perk-up, teasing him.

His eyes find mine, and he glares, but it's not his usual grade of asshole. "Don't push it. And don't cook anymore. Call Summit Solutions and get a chef organized, before you burn down the kitchen."

I sigh. "I really wanted to learn—"

"You're pretty perfect without cooking."

That shuts me up.

His praise sprouts goose bumps all over my skin. Perhaps he is right, and we can't have a middle ground when his compliments make me all wet. Not good.

We sit in companionable silence, with the background of the sounds of the city. He stands up and walks to a small cooler. Pulling out two bottles of water, he gives me one and gulps the other.

Leaving me behind, he walks to the massive stone balustrade that lines the entire terrace. He moves with more confidence, sobered up.

The idea of aiding him with my mediocre meal and coffee... The idea of taking care of him warms me inside, spreading feelings I shouldn't have. He was definitely right to keep his distance.

Leaning back, he puts his hands in his pockets and crosses his ankles.

Fuck, a casual Declan in the middle of his kingdom is a sight for... Not a sight for his nanny. *Keep it professional, you ho.*

"How were the kids tonight?"

Good, that's the safe zone for us. "Zoya had a meltdown, probably just tired after her swimming class. Zach said the Math worksheet is an insult to his intelligence. Now they are sleeping peacefully."

His expression softens, and a smile tugs at his lips. "They are great kids."

"They are wonderful." I recall the heart-squeezing moment from earlier when watching Zoya.

His jaw ticks, and the smile disappears, replaced with a deep line on his forehead. "I can't have her fuck them up."

"Who?"

He looks at me, pain seeping through his gaze. "Their mother."

I wait for a moment to see if he elaborates, holding his gaze to let him know I'm here to listen.

He opens his mouth a few times before he turns his back to me. I'm pretty sure the moment of almost sharing is gone.

"I don't think I ever truly loved her. She fit my five-year plan and, as much as I hate to admit it, she tricked me." He watches the city for a moment, rolling the water bottle around the stony surface of the balustrade.

"She got married again and has money now. She wants shared custody." His words float out into the night sky, descending on the city as if they were any other chatter of the night.

"But she abandoned them."

I can't sit anymore. It feels frivolous to sit during this topic.

"Twice." He snorts.

"You can't be sure she is serious this time. Poor babies."

I move to stand beside him. What kind of a cruel woman would just test to see if she enjoys motherhood and then bail? Twice? It certainly puts my mother's absence into a much more favorable light. Jesus.

"Oh, I don't trust her. She had her chances, but she is now taking this to court, and it's not my decision. I should have erased her from their birth certificate the first time she came for a payout."

"What do you mean?"

He chuckles humorlessly. "Usually, her sudden awakening of motherly genes happens around the time she needs money."

"That's horrible. You have to pay to keep your kids safe from a woman who uses them for her own gain."

"Pretty fucked-up, isn't it?" He leans on his elbows.

"No court would ever side with her." I don't know the legal system well enough to make such a statement. And I know common sense is not always what wins.

"She has a stable household now, and enough money to prove she is a fit parent. No court would give her Zoya and Zach full-time, but they might allow visitation rights. Courts tend to side with mothers. And then what? A year later she will ask for some days, and... And then one day she changes her mind, and they will remember." He turns to me, his eyes full of desperation and anger. "This time, they will remember she abandoned them. Yet again."

"Declan..." I reach to squeeze his arm. It feels like such a pointless gesture, but I'm at a loss for words or actions of comfort.

"What if she's changed?" He sighs. "What if I'd be depriving them of their mother?"

My heart breaks a little for this beautiful family. "She proved the opposite. I don't know the woman, but I can imagine she had all the resources to have all the help in the world. Regardless of how unhappy she could have been, she made a choice, and those kids should not pay any more for her choices. Even if she feels it was a mistake. Which I doubt, because she doesn't have it in her if she managed to leave them in the first place. That's not something she could just turn on."

I realize I have no authority to judge her, but I do anyway.

"You fight for them like a mama bear." He reaches to push my glasses up my nose, and I shiver.

"I love them, Declan." It might be ridiculous, but it's true.

"You truly are perfect."

The familiar charged tension sneaks between us, and I scramble to move us out of that territory. "Just remember my fajitas."

He chuckles and leans back on the balustrade. "My lawyer believes I have a better chance of fighting her if I am married."

"Why?"

"He thinks she will use my workaholism, and the fact that the twins are with nannies most of their day, against me."

"That's preposterous."

"If I believed in the fairness of courts, I wouldn't be drinking tonight."

The idea of him getting married, of bringing another woman to meet the kids, swipes through me with an unwarranted surge of jealousy.

"I'll marry you."

## Chapter 15

### *Declan*

**D**on't accept. Don't fucking accept.

Lily looks sick. Her eyes widen like she is as shocked as me by her words.

Don't accept. Just don't fucking accept. But I don't seem to find the words, and she is gaping at me, and by the looks of it, mortified.

I can't even blame it on the half bottle of whiskey I polished off at the office after the meeting with my lawyer. Her horrendous excuse for food and coffee sobered me up.

With gargantuan effort and self-discipline, I stayed away from her for weeks again. I have even stayed away from the security footage. Almost. Like a junkie, I had a few lapses.

I keep reminding myself that I'm too old for her. Though based on the number of inappropriately timed erections every time I think about her, that argument seems ridiculous. I've turned into a teenager.

All my noble attempts went down the drain the minute I came home drunk and my legs led me to her like she was a magnet, charged to attract me.

She looked so beautiful in the flickering lights on my terrace. The sight hit me with a sense of possessiveness, with the need to claim her.

But somehow, we both resisted and behaved, achieving a new reluctant level in our co-habitation. Our fucked-up relationship unfulfilled.

She opens her mouth, and to prevent her from another word vomit, I interfere. "Why?" My brain was about to refuse her gently, but my mouth completely disconnects from reason.

Her eyes flash in surprise, and then she looks at the nighttime city as if the answer is written somewhere there.

"I need money." She doesn't look at me.

"You need money?" I repeat her words, because it seems like a trap. Or a lie. Or my head refuses to accept that this woman I think I know, whom I invited to my home and let care for my kids, may offer something for her personal gain. The scenario is too bitterly familiar.

At the end of the day, I don't really know her. Do I? She is hot, and good with my kids, but she is hiding things.

Can I go through with this? It will solve an issue for me. And not much will change.

"Yes. We can help each other." She lifts her chin. It's an attempt to display confidence, but her gaze is still unfocused, darting around.

I should just shut this down. "Why?" I parrot instead.

"I just told you."

"Why would you want to help me?" Just fucking refuse the idea finally, you jackass.

"I love Zach and Zoya." Okay, I believe that. "And I need money. Look, it's not my proudest moment to be in my situation... But we will all benefit... And look at your brother and Saar, or Cal and Celeste: they fake-married and..."

She trails off, probably realizing that those two couples are now happily married.

"You're blabbering again." She flinches, but I take her hand. "Fuck, Lily, I'm tempted to agree, but it's insanity. We already have a complicated relationship."

"So you'd prefer to bring a stranger to live with your children?"

Fuck, when she puts it like that... Having a sham marriage with a woman who already takes care of my kids would make the most sense. I told my lawyer to find a different strategy. But maybe it's that simple... That's preposterous.

"How much?" I'm not sure why I'm investigating that. I'm not going to go through with this, am I?

"How much?" She frowns.

"You said you're doing it for money." I study her. Even in the shadows of the dimly-lit terrace, I see her cheeks darken with a blush.

"Ten thousand," she blurts out.

"What do you need ten K for?" It doesn't feel like a high enough sum to bother. But perhaps my expectations have been skewed by Kendra's demands.

"That's none of your business. And stop interrogating me. I thought I was helping you, not subjecting myself to scrutiny."

I close my eyes, a part of me wishing I could open them to possibilities where she was mine, truly mine. An equally strong part reminds me I need to backpedal from this.

Herein lies the problem, though. If last month taught me anything, there is no backpedaling from Lily.

I look up, hoping for some interference from the universe, but my eyes land on the upper level where the two most important people of my life sleep soundly, unaware of the potential threat of their mother breaking their hearts.

"Nobody can know about this. Especially not the

twins." Have I just made a decision? Am I accepting this insane plan?

"How would that work?"

"The lawyer will protect the kids at all costs. They won't be subjected to testifying. He's getting Kendra to agree to that stipulation. She will, because it wouldn't help her case for a cooperation. She would accept to establish her goodwill. So the worst that could happen is a visit from social services."

"So I'll just remain your live-in nanny, but on paper you look like you have a stable home."

"Pretty much." Fuck, why are we discussing these details?

"And you give me ten thousand," she reminds me, and a part of me resents her for that.

I have no right to wish she would do it for free. I have no right to expect her to do it, period. And yet here I am, resenting her a bit for it.

She looks out, pinning her gaze to the flickering skyscrapers beyond the park. The lights twinkle playfully on her beautiful face, illuminating her cheekbones and that beautifully slanted nose. She's a vision.

Her chest rises and falls, but otherwise, she is perfectly still in the background of the nightlife.

And in that moment, I know I'm about to make the worst mistake of my life.

* * *

"It looks like you finally have a nanny who survived." Roxy crosses her legs, trying to engage me in idle chatter while we wait for the rest of the team in Corm's office.

Apparently, timely arrival at our regularly scheduled partners' meetings is no longer expected.

I tap my fingers on the armrests. "Zach and Zoya like her." Not as much as me. I banish the thought as quickly as it appears.

"Good, finally a responsible nanny."

Neither of us is responsible, if the courthouse appointment in two days is any indication.

I glare at Roxy, hoping to stop her from talking, even though I know she is immune to any and all intimidating tactics.

"I can't say I missed this office." Cal saunters in ten minutes late, but I don't point that out since he saved me from Roxy's interogation.

"Sorry I'm late." Corm files in before Cal even takes a seat. "Where is Xander?"

"I'm here, gentlemen." He walks in like the world revolves around him. At least he isn't in his sweaty gym clothes, or slurping a kid's beverage.

"I got new projections for London, with an addition of five years' salaries and bonuses for the manager." I hand out folders to each of them.

"That's a mil we could have saved." Xander throws the sheets at the table.

"Don't be a dick, X." Cal, who usually sides with Xander, surprises me with his defense.

"It's not a saving if it's a necessary expense that should have been in the original projections." Corm backs me up as well.

For some reason, the two men stepping in to defend plan B makes me feel like a bigger failure. Like everyone has to come up with a story to fit my narrative.

Would it be so bad to move? What? Where did that thought come from? As if there weren't enough wild circumstances in my life currently.

"Okay, it would cut into initially projected profits, but it still makes the venture interesting." Xander raises his arms in surrender.

"Look, you guys can play nice." Roxy grins. "I knew the sedative I added to the water would tame you in the end."

"It leaves more testosterone for you, Roxy," Xander deadpans.

"I can smell it... The beautiful payout from the sexual harassment suit." She flips him the bird.

"Okay, let's move on." Corm takes control of the meeting.

We spend another half hour discussing the most pressing accounts, and I forget about my fake soon-to-be wife. Work has always saved me from my fucked-up personal life.

"Okay, who are you two taking to the gala on Friday?" Corm addresses me and Xander. "If we can, let's not have paid escorts joining us..." He peters out, the hypocrite.

"So it was acceptable when it was your only option?" Xander scoffs.

"We need to grow up. Just a few months ago we almost lost a large account because my morals were questioned. Besides, it would be nice if my wife had someone to talk to. Is Celeste coming?"

"Things are a bit chaotic at the moment, but that's the plan." Cal closes his tablet.

"If Celeste and Saar are coming, why don't I take Saar's friend, the ginger one?" Xander stands up, moving to the door.

"Cora?" Corm frowns.

"A friend for your wife to talk to." Xander shrugs.

"Okay, I'll talk to Saar to invite her. Why don't you bring Lily, then?" He turns to me.

"She minds my kids when I have to spend evenings with you clowns, dressing up and schmoozing like doing business in a boardroom isn't reasonable anymore." I walk out of there, suddenly itching to yank my tie off.

I lean on my elbows, grateful for the large desk between us. Lily, sitting on the other side, crosses one elegant leg over the other. Again in the stupid pajama pants. I hate that pink monstrosity. It makes her feel even younger.

My home office has always been a place where I decompress, where I find distraction or ground myself after a shitty day.

There were many of those right after Kendra left for the first time. I wanted to drown myself in whiskey, but I had the babies to take care of. So I'd come here and heal... or rather seal off whatever was left of my soul.

After Kendra entered and left our lives the second time, I used to come here to wallow in my own stupidity. Eventually I buried myself in work and my hobby, and this room became my sanctuary. My man cave. My space.

It's been a place to hide from the children, to recharge, to enjoy myself.

Tonight, it's a place of peace and discomfort

mingling and trying to get attention from my conscience.

My conscience checked out gradually between the day I saw Lily for the first time and tonight.

I'm not a good man. There is no doubt in my mind that I'm taking advantage of this young woman. Yet I can't stop myself.

Ever since I made the decision on the terrace downstairs when she suggested her outrageously stupid proposal, there is nothing that can prevent me from moving forward.

I'm aware she's doing it for money, and I resent her for that. Not enough to stop. I won't stop anymore. Lily will be mine.

She reads the paperwork, her gaze fixing on some passages and skimming through others. Sometimes she scrunches her nose as if considering. Some paragraphs cause her lips to purse to the side.

She's hauntingly perfect, like an antique statue, but also too fluid, too real, too breathtaking in her imperfection.

She turns the page and arches her eyebrows, and I itch to round the desk to see what part of the contract she is reading.

The gentle slope of her shoulders moves with every breath. The delicate column of her throat bobs with every swallow.

She could be a timeless masterpiece; only she is alive, shifting, breathing, untamed. I don't move, afraid to break the spell, and grateful for this moment.

I didn't expect her to plow through the prenup with such dedication. She does; she studies it with the concentration of a person who understands what they are reading. Fuck, I haven't even read the fine print.

A new level of respect for her blooms inside me, as if I needed more reasons to admire her. It also makes me question what the hell I am doing. I don't know who this woman is. Clearly she's someone who knows she shouldn't sign a contract without reading it.

Does it even matter? It's a fake marriage, after all. I trust her with my children, and that will have to do for now.

I'm ashamed to admit I'm surprised she's this diligent. But the fact that she is... The fact she took off her fake glasses to read it in detail, makes me hard. But then what's new in her presence?

Finally, she gets to the last page. Her chest moves with a deep breath in and a long breath out before she picks up a pen and leans in. Her hand hovers above the signature line, and I hold my breath.

She hesitates. She is going to do the right thing. I'm fucked. I can't have her recant now. I don't have a plan B. I don't fucking want a plan B. I clench my fists.

Will she take more money?

Can I sweeten the deal for her somehow?

What the hell is wrong with me?

The pen connects with the page, and she scribbles her signature. "It's done."

A boulder dislodges from my chest. I wait for regret to settle in, but it doesn't arrive. An unexpected wave of elation sweeps through me, and I grip the armrests to prevent myself from pouncing.

She closes the folder and pushes it toward me. Her eyes dart around the office like she's not sure what to do next. I'm not sure what to do next. Offer her whiskey? Shake hands?

Probably without thinking, she picks up a spreadsheet I was evaluating before.

She studies it like she knows what it is. I should be concerned with the confidentiality of the information, but I enjoy watching her way more.

As if she caught herself suddenly, she drops the paper. "Sorry... I-I-I don't know why I picked it up."

"It's okay."

"Is that your client's?"

"It's a company our client wants to acquire."

"Will you report them?"

I frown. "What do you mean?"

She leans forward, and now I have a close-up look at her cleavage. Jesus.

She points to a line in the spreadsheet. "They

reported two separate accounts for operational costs, but the line items are practically identical. Same vendors, same amounts, just shuffled around under different categories."

How did I miss that? How did she catch it?

"I didn't know you studied accounting." Who is this woman? Hasn't she barely finished college?

Her cheeks warm with that pink shade that colors her tawny skin so often. "I'm not just a pretty face."

"Obviously."

She jumps up like I zapped her with an electric current.

A part of me hopes she will leave, but instead she meanders around the office. She is wearing a shawl-like cardigan instead of a sweatshirt tonight. As she reaches for a book, the fabric slips from her shoulder, revealing a thin strap of a tank top.

My cock doesn't twitch; it fucking grows hard like she's just stripped in front of me. I stifle a groan.

She frowns, looking at me over her shoulder. "Are you okay?"

I guess I didn't stifle that groan. I want to walk over and push the flimsy cardigan up her shoulder, but how many times can she see my erection before she realizes she is not safe with me?

"I'm good. You?" My conversation skills are top game tonight.

"I'm strangely calm, given that I just got myself a fiancé, no ring. In two days I'll have a husband, no wedding. I was technically the one who proposed... I'm living every girl's dream." She giggles, pulling her garment up and wrapping it around her torso. "Besides, I'm probably committing a felony, and I'll be a divorcee before the age of twenty-six."

This woman wants to save my children from their unstable, narcissistic mother, and in return I crush her dreams. Fuck. "I'm sorry."

It's not a lie. I vow to make sure she doesn't regret this, to improve her life in every possible way. Because I truly am sorry for her sacrifice.

Not enough to do the right thing.

"Oh, don't be. I'm getting a dashing, rich husband out of it." She winks. It's sexy as hell.

*Do the right thing, asshole.* I pick up the papers. "Do you want me to shred this?"

"Jesus, Declan, chill. We're doing it for the kids, and it's just a formality. I was kidding. I have plenty of time to get my fairy-tale wedding. And knowing I helped you protect your twins makes me feel invincible, and grateful. Like I'm a good person."

The idea of someone else giving her the fairy-tale wedding makes me see red, but I push that irrational burst to the side. "You are a good person."

She snorts. "I wish that was true. What is all of this?" She points to the large table with my research.

She is skillfully redirecting the conversation from herself, and I play along, because I'm not ready to find out why she would claim not to be a good person. There will be time for that later. Or perhaps not. Perhaps she'll leave my life soon, and this will only be a memory.

A painfully tantalizing snapshot in time.

"Research for a family tree."

She looks at the mess on the table with renewed curiosity. "Your family tree?"

"No. Mine has been done by my grandfather. Genealogy was his passion. I used to help him, and somehow it grew into my hobby as well. That is actually his table. My father enjoyed piecing family histories together too. Now they're both gone, and I moved the table here. I do most of my research online, but I like that connection with Grandpa and Dad."

She smiles at me with a gaze full of fascination. "This is the only messy surface in your house. I like it."

"It's not messy. It's an organized chaos."

She tilts her head to the side, still smiling at me, like everything I'm saying is interesting. Fuck, she is killing me. It's one thing when she is drawing— unknowingly—my darkest desires from me, but stroking my vain ego... How will I survive this vixen?

"So whose tree is this?" She picks up an old black-and-white photo and studies it.

"A woman from Miami. I take on projects for others, since our family has been charted several branches wide."

"That is so cool. You help these people uncover their stories."

I stand up and walk over, my dick finally half-mast only. I step into her private space and revel in her quickened breath. She turns to me, dropping the photo.

I tuck a strand behind her ear. "I can research your tree."

Something akin to panic flashes through her eyes. "No, thank you." She turns away. "I should go and let you do... your thing... The kids are up early... I better get some rest—"

She is blabbering again. What spooked her? "Lily—"

My phone vibrates, loudly dancing on my desk.

"Good night, Declan." She sneaks out of the office.

I'm about to follow her and demand answers, but one glance at my flashing screen stops me in my tracks.

I look at the door where Lily disappeared and pick up my phone to kill the call. Instead, I click on the green icon to answer, not yet knowing the call will kill my chance at happiness.

"Kendra."

# Chapter 16

## *Lily*

SAAR

Looks like we're all going to the fancy event together.

CELESTE

I'm not sure I can leave Amelie.

CORA

Come on. I haven't been at such a glam event for ages.

Scratch that. Ever. You have to come, Celeste.

SAAR

I had stylists scheduled to come to your house @Celeste.

> What are you talking about?

CELESTE

Declan didn't tell you?

> ???

> **SAAR**
> Jesus, one of these days I'll strangle the man.
>
> **CORA**
> This chat would be admissible as evidence, you know that?
>
> Nobody is killing anybody. Where are you going together again?

My phone rings.

"Hey Saar. What's going on?" I pop a grape and climb on the stool at the kitchen island.

"I can't believe Declan didn't fill you in. How can you live with that man? At least his kids are adorable."

If she only knew that I not only live here, I married the man. I want to tell her just to enjoy her reaction.

"Fill me in." I chuckle, but it comes out strangled.

I know she can't read my thoughts, but keeping something this big from my friends? It should come easy because I've kept other things from them. It doesn't come easy.

I want to pretend it's not a big deal, but frankly, the enormity of my deal with Declan only dawned on me when my account beeped with a new balance, and he gave me a copy of our marriage certificate. What was I thinking?

The idea of bringing someone temporary into Zoya

and Zach's life was just heartbreaking. As if I wasn't temporary. Jesus. What was I thinking?

I'm in no position to act as someone's wife.

The night when I signed the prenup, I came close to breaking my cover. Just like with the forgotten glasses, I commented on the spreadsheet, and he questioned me again. And then he offered to do my family tree, and I bolted.

What was I thinking?

Now I'm married to the man when I'm not even able to live beside him without dropping my guard.

"There is a gala, and the boys decided to take the four of us. I mean, obviously I go with Corm, and Celeste with Cal. But Xander agreed to invite Cora, so I guess they went with it, and you are left to be Declan's plus one."

"How lovely." I close my eyes. I'm going out with my new husband.

"Shit. I didn't mean it like that. You can officially go with Xander if you want. The point is, the four of us are going to the party of the year together. The men will do their business, but we can have a lot of fun. Car is picking you up in half an hour."

I slide down and walk to the window, like I can see the vehicle approaching from here. "What? I don't have a dress... and I have to pick up the kids... and we can't both leave them—"

"Lily, chill, babe; Declan is taking care of the kids. I think Dorothy is coming over to stay with them. All I know is, I'm in charge of styling, and I sent the car to pick you up. Dress has been arranged."

The fact that everything is arranged sounds like Declan. The not keeping me in the loop is weird, but also not unexpected from him.

"Okay."

"Yes!" Saar cheers. "We'll have so much fun."

"Where is the car taking me?"

"To Celeste. Since she has separation anxiety and has to breastfeed, we will do all the preparations at her place."

"I can walk over."

"Or you can let me treat you like a queen. Just be downstairs in fifteen."

We hang up, and I text Declan.

> A gala you forgot to mention?

DECLAN
> Sorry. Saar will take care of you. Mom is watching the kids. I'll pick them up.

Annoyingly efficient as ever. Since we signed the prenup four days ago, we have been living in a new state of collaboration. Almost like we're partners in crime, so we no longer tiptoe around each other.

It's this weird state of co-parenting. We focus on children because none of us wants to think about the unresolved tension. Or I focus on children because, for all I know, Declan doesn't seem interested in me anymore.

One good thing that came out of this new arrangement is that he isn't ignoring me.

He is not exactly going out of his way to spend time with me, but the ice has melted. Which is also a new challenge because now, when I'm not mad at his abhorrent behavior, I have more time to ogle him.

This morning, I ran into him when he finished his workout, all sweaty in a tight T-shirt and workout shorts, and I think I had a micro-orgasm just from the sight. This is not going to be easy.

I either seduce him, or die from being horny.

* * *

"I wish I was going." Mia, Celeste's teenage stepdaughter, throws herself on her bed.

"Two more years, and I'm sure your dad will take you," Saar says.

She rolls her eyes. "I doubt that. He will always take Celeste."

"Then I'll take you to the best and most fabulous event of the season." Saar sits on the edge. She has rollers in her hair and wears a pink robe that she got for all of us, like we are a bridal party.

We're in Mia's room because it's the only room available for all the things Saar had people wheel in: several racks of gowns, cases with accessories, and all the styling products.

It's actually fun, but also unnerving. Can I go to a large event like this and avoid photographers?

"You need to shed the glasses," Saar says. "Do you ever wear contacts?"

Can I risk it? Can I go to an event as myself? I mean, the glasses aren't a mask, but along with the haircut and hair color, they have helped me to blend in and become invisible.

"There is no time to get you chic prescription glasses, Lils." Celeste switches Amelie to her other breast and looks up, so the stylist can apply mascara to her lashes.

"I don't know..." I trail my fingers over the silk and velvet of the gowns.

"But we do," Cora offers from her seat, where someone is taming her curls into an intricate updo.

"Okay." I sigh. "I have contacts in my purse," I lie.

Saar claps and comes over. "This one is yours." She pulls out a deep purple gown.

It's stunning. Exactly my color, but when I see the

sleeveless style, sweat trickles down my back. Shit. How do I get out of this one?

Saar narrows her eyes, but she hangs the dress back before picking up another one. It's a similar color, slightly deeper purple, and I immediately love it, a smile stretching across my face.

The gown is simple, but it exudes elegance and grace. The fitted bodice cinches at the waist, highlighting the silhouette, while the long, voluminous bishop sleeves add a touch of drama with their billowy fabric. The flowing skirt cascades to the floor. The off-the-shoulder neckline adds a romantic charm.

"I love it."

Saar studies me for a moment, and then smiles like a Cheshire cat. "Interesting."

Now it's my turn to frown. "You don't like it?"

"I thought the first one was perfect for you, but Declan said the long-sleeved one was more acceptable."

Heat spreads through my skin, and I swallow several questions, trying to figure out which one I can say out loud.

"Declan chose Lily's dress?" Cora asks one of my questions.

Saar hikes her shoulder. "The least he can do is buy her a dress. She's been running his household and taking care of his kids. And now she has to spend her night off with him."

"Did Xander buy my dress?" Cora asks, clearly accepting Saar's explanation.

Saar snorts. "He's covering the cost of the rental at least."

"Okay, I'm ready for you." The stylist turns to me as Celeste vacates her chair.

"You look gorgeous," I tell my nursing friend, and sit gingerly.

"What would you like—" The stylist runs her hand through my hair.

"The cut is horrendous, but if we fix that it will be too short again. Why don't you do a sleek-back style?" Saar jumps in with suggestions, both her hands pulling my hair away from my face.

"That's a good idea; that way, we can smooth out the uneven parts. I would recommend natural makeup because the dress and the hair would be a statement, and we don't want to overdo it."

"Yes, let's keep it simple," I say quickly. I don't want to make a statement. I want to blend in.

"Just trust me." The woman smiles at me.

The murmur of the chitchat fades into the background as I get prepped and pampered. I want to relax into the fun of it all, but my mind is spinning.

Declan buying my dress is one thing, and even if I

accepted Saar's explanation, there still lies another question. He bought a dress with sleeves for me. How does he know?

The other night my cardigan slipped a bit, but I covered myself fast enough. Is it just his observation skills? Because I'm wearing long sleeves, he assumed that's my style?

"Lils? What do you say?" Cora's voice penetrates my reeling mind.

The stylist steps to the side, so I can peer over to where my friend stands. Cora's ginger hair is tamed into intricate braids, and she is wearing a black dress that suits her like a second skin. "You look... Wow, just wow."

"This beauty is wasted in your bistro." Saar hands her a glass of bubbly and then offers me one.

"I'll have a sip, too, but don't tell Cal." Celeste bounces Amelie and takes a sip from Saar's drink.

"You know what I realized?" Cora says. "We've been out clubbing, but never with all of us. This is the first time we're going out together. And in style." She shimmies.

We all raise our glasses and drink. This is as normal as my life has gotten in the last year. I'm surrounded by women who love me and bring joy to my life.

I'm going to allow myself to have fun tonight. I'm not going to let my complicated past or my unresolved present, including my infuriating fake husband, rule me for a few hours.

"You keep this for retouches during the night." The stylist hands me a tube of lipstick.

"Okay, Lils, let me help you into this gown." Saar lays the purple dress on the bed. "I forgot to tell you to bring a strapless bra, damn it."

"It's okay, I'll go bra-less."

I hadn't even realized that Mia left with Amelie. The stylists are packing up and ready to leave, and my three friends, dressed and dolled up to the nines, are all staring at me. Expecting me to strip and put on my dress.

"Lils, the men are waiting downstairs already." Saar opens the door so everyone but us can file out.

My heart hammers and my cheeks burn as I look at the gown. Earlier, I donned the robe while I was in the bathroom, but how would I explain dragging the gown in there?

"Do you need some privacy?" Celeste takes my hand. "You can get dressed in the closet." She picks up my dress and hangs it in the walk-in just as the last rack of gowns disappears. She closes the door gently, and I exhale the breath I was holding.

I hurry to put the gown on, and when I step out of the closet, all three of my friends gasp. I straighten the skirt, feeling self-conscious.

I used to play dress-up with my friends, spending all Saturdays roaming the stores and getting fitted for dresses. Where is that carefree girl now?

I banish the melancholy quickly. I didn't get this far to get homesick.

Twirling, I laugh. "Let's get this party started."

Caleb and Celeste's penthouse has the design of a loft, both levels overlooking Central Park, connected by a glass staircase.

"Oh my, it looks like a James Bond convention." Saar smirks.

The four men, founders of Merged, stand downstairs. Dressed in tuxedos, they are all handsome in their own way. Unlike our lively chitchat upstairs, each of them is on the phone.

Caleb types furiously, sitting on the sofa. Xander is leaning against the backrest beside him, his gaze buried in his device.

Corm is talking on the phone in one corner by the windows, and Declan is swiping his screen by the staircase.

"Are they mad at each other?" Cora leans forward, examining the scene.

"No, just workaholics." Celeste rolls her eyes.

I slide my sweaty hands into the well-disguised pockets of my flowing skirt, admiring my fake husband.

I've seen him in a tux a few times, but every time

threatens my vital functions. I clench my thighs, my heart rate spikes, my lungs can't fill with oxygen, and my body overheats.

"I left the lipstick," I remember, and dash back to Mia's room.

I snatch the tube, and glimpse myself in the mirror. I look... I look like me. It's a strange feeling to see the woman I used to be blending with the woman I became. I'm not sure if I'm ready to examine it.

Maybe I should make something up and stay here. Help with Amelie, or... Before I can chicken out completely, I rush from the room to join the others.

My friends are downstairs already. I pause at the top, gingerly putting one foot forward. I gather my skirt and commence my descent.

If I expected an approving look or a glimpse of surprise... If I expected that romance novel moment when he looks up and sees her dressed up... that time-arresting, heart-stopping moment of uncensored admiration, I would have been bitterly disappointed.

Declan doesn't lift his gaze from his phone.

The night turns out fantastically. While the men work the room, the four of us share laughter and a few drinks, and when I don't think about my aloof fake husband, I finally taste freedom I haven't felt in a long while.

We gossip about other guests and giggle like schoolgirls, gaining us judging looks from older New York socialites.

Saar bids money on ridiculous items in a silent auction. The gala is extravagant, and everyone is pulling out checkbooks without a second thought. It warms my heart, because the proceeds go to a children's hospital.

"If I don't go home or pump soon, this gown will be sporting a new design in my breast region." Celeste cups her boobs, scrunching her face.

A couple beside us at the bar scrambles to the side, as if being in our company could give them a disease.

"Don't go yet." I wrap my arm through Celeste's.

Saar downs her drink and raises her arms, shimmying to the music. "We all need to stay and protect Cora." She points toward the dance floor.

Cora is twirling around in Xander's arms, laughing.

"I'm sure she can protect herself." Celeste snorts and checks her breasts again.

"I would love to hear her when she tells him off," I muse.

"Do you think he invited her because he wants to..." Celeste arches her eyebrow.

"I think Xander always wants to, and with anyone," Saar says.

"I still don't think she needs our protection," Celeste says.

"I agree. Are you going to pump? I need to go to the bathroom." I look at Celeste.

"I'm going to find Caleb and head home."

"Party pooper." Saar pouts and puts her glass to her lips.

A large hand stops her. "May I have a dance, Mrs. Quinn?" Corm takes the drink away from her.

She beams at him before they both saunter to the dance floor.

As I turn to find the bathroom, a solid wall presses against me from behind.

"You look ravishing tonight." Declan's breath fans my neck as he leans in to whisper in my ear.

A full-body shiver rakes through me. His heat. His scent. His voice. That fucking voice will be the end of me.

*No one can know.*

We're covered by a group of men, hidden from view, but still...

"How would you know? You haven't even looked at me." I want to face him, but he snakes his arm around my waist and holds me in place.

My heart rate goes haywire. The possessive move is everything I ever wanted, but what the hell?

"I have looked at only you all night, Seagull."

"Hardly." I hope he hears the figurative eye roll in my voice. Okay, the wine perhaps speaks a bit too.

"Don't be a brat. You spent most of the night chatting and drinking with the girls. You laughed at the comedian's performance, and had to wipe your eyes when he made that lame joke about polar bears—"

"That was funny," I protest, all the while trying to comprehend what he is saying. Has he really paid so much attention to me?

"No, it wasn't."

I chuckle. "One could never accuse you of a sense of humor."

His large hand skims my rib cage, stopping just below the swell of my breasts. A soft groan escapes him, and I realize I leaned into him.

"Perhaps, but you can't accuse me of not seeing you."

"Why from afar?" My voice is just a breath.

It's strange talking when my back is to him, but I welcome it at the same time. Like I can hide my reactions. Though I'm sure he feels my goose bumps and my shudders, just like I feel his hardness.

"Two reasons."

"Care to share?"

"If I got close to you, I would have ripped this dress off and done things to you, Lily, that are not noble, nor appropriate."

My breath hitches. It's a good thing his arm is wrapped around me because my knees buckle. "That's one. What is the second reason?"

"There are still traces of a decent man in my darkened soul. Traces that stop me from destroying you. You're so young and vibrant, and seeing you today with your friends... I shouldn't tie you to me and my baggage."

I make to step forward, and he loosens the grip, so I can turn and look at him. It's like facing a storm head-on. "Shouldn't?"

He traces my cheek. I feel the brush of his touch down in my panties.

"You think I didn't even look at you tonight?" He utters a disbelieving chuckle, shaking his head. "Tonight or any other day, I see you. I see you... humming a song while you tidy the kitchen. Reading to my kids and laughing with them... How you stifle your yawns so you can read one more page of your book... The way your eyes sparkle with curiosity every time you discover something new... Or how they retreat to the past you hide... Or how you tag on your sleeves just before you start spitting out words of anxiety... How you always see a glass half full. I fucking can't unsee you, little Seagull, and I'm over trying."

And there goes my poor heart. "You're done trying?" A grin tugs at my lips.

"Unless you stop me." The intensity of his gaze is scorching, imploring, lethal.

I don't want him to stop... but his attention is almost too much. "You barely looked at me for months, and now I put on a pretty dress and you..." He what? What does it even mean he's done trying? "It makes you shallow," I tease, trying to insert some lightness.

He gives me his signature look, which is a mixture of boredom and annoyance. "You married me for money." He deadpans.

I giggle. "Fair enough. We are both shallow."

We stare at each other for a moment, my entire body awakened by his closeness and attention.

I remember my earlier need. "I need to go to the lady's room."

He nods and steps to the side, but as I step forward, he follows. "Are you coming with me?"

"Yes."

"You can't follow me to the toilets."

"I can, but no worries; I'll wait for you outside."

I narrow my eyes. Who is this man? What is happening now? "You will wait for me in front of the bathroom?"

"Is something wrong with your ears? Was the music too loud?"

"Oh, no, no, you don't get to be an asshole again."

He stops, frowning. "Again?"

I scoff. "Whatever."

Pushing the door open, I enter the bathroom and leave him outside. Okay, so he's done trying to stay away? While I welcome the idea, there is no need to walk me to pee. Jesus.

When I exit, I find him leaning against the wall. The sight is arresting. No matter how many times I've ogled him, he still makes my stomach quiver.

He looks up from his phone. "We have to go."

"Has something happened with the kids?"

He almost smiles at that. "I love that your first concern is my children. But they are not home."

"Where are they?"

"They are spending the weekend at my mother's. Let's go." He snatches my hand and practically drags me toward the exit.

"What's going on, Declan?" I halt.

He lets out a low growl. "I cannot pretend any longer. I told you I'm done trying. Are you coming home with me, Lily?"

If I didn't know any better, I would think there was fear in his eyes. Like my answer is a matter of life and death. Like he needs me.

"Yes," I whisper.

"Thank fucking God." He moves again, a man on a mission.

The butterflies in my stomach flutter, my heart beats erratically like a spooked horse, my brain is misfiring like a drunken monkey... All a fucking zoo of reactions.

"Wait, the kids are away for the entire weekend? Did you plan this?"

Instead of answering, he grins at me.

The Declan Grump Quinn actually grins at me. I barely survived him when he was guarded, but this lighter version of him?

God help me.

# Chapter 17

## *Lily*

My back hits the elevator mirror, Declan's tongue exploring my mouth while his hands seem to be everywhere at once.

Well, on my ass now as he lifts me. I wrap my legs around him, the skirt tangled between us. We barely talked during the ride from the gala. I was getting worried he was having second thoughts.

By the time we pulled into the underground, I was practically vibrating with need, and a latent fear he may have changed his mind.

Now, I'm wondering if this was also a part of his plan. To rile me up. If history taught us anything, his ignorance is an aphrodisiac for me.

"The things I want to do to you, little Seagull." He sinks his teeth into the sensitive skin of my neck.

I arch my back, grinding into him. "I can't wait."

"Do you have plans this weekend?" He murmurs against my skin, grazing around my exposed clavicle, licking and nipping around the deep neckline of my dress.

"Why?" I grip his hair like it helps me balance.

His hips pin me against the cold mirror to free his hands. He expertly awakens every cell in my body with his insistent touch.

"Cancel them. I need time with you." He hits a button, and the elevator jerks and halts as he seizes my lips again, trailing his hand up my thigh. He squeezes my ass cheek. "I need to use your pussy. To punish it for teasing me all this time. I need you to use my cock, and scream my name until this entire city knows you're well taken care of."

Oh my God. I already deduced that all the words he saves by giving people short answers come to life during sex. But the level of Declan Quinn's dirty talk catches me off-guard.

His words thrill me and scare me at the same time. Well, not scare, but—

"Declan—" I try to push him, but moving a brick wall would be easier. "Declan."

He abandons my cleavage and looks up. Fuck, he is breathtaking. His hair in disarray, traces of my lipstick smeared around his lips. But it's his eyes that squeeze at my heart. The uncensored, inhibited need in them.

"I need to tell you something." I bite my lower lip. Am I going to kill the mood?

He straightens, lowering his forehead to mine. "Nothing is easy with you, Seagull," he murmurs—no longer his usual annoyed snap, but rather a sigh of resignation.

"I...I..." I grip his collar. To steady myself, or to prevent him from leaving? I look up and see us in the mirrored ceiling.

What a sight—my legs around his waist, both of us dressed up; we look like we're from a glamor photoshoot. "I'm all for your plans, but I think... And I hope you won't change your mind... It's not a big deal—"

He snatches my jaw, forcing me to look at him. "No blabbering, Seagull."

"Right. I've only been with one man... A boy, back at the end of high school. And we dated only for a few months, so what I'm trying to say... I'm not very experienced."

Heat burns my cheeks, and I want to look away, because for some reason, my admission embarrasses me. And I don't want to see his disappointment.

"Fuck, Lily, can you be any more perfect?"

He captures my lips in a bruising kiss like he can't help himself or hold back anymore.

He lowers me slowly, never disconnecting his lips from mine. When my feet touch the floor, I almost collapse from all the sensations this man is eliciting with his hands, lips, and tongue.

We're only making out, and I'm already at the brink of an orgasm, so worked up I can't stand. I reach for the control panel, ready to get the party to the bedroom finally, but Declan snatches my wrist.

"Not yet," he growls, and drops to his knees.

Before my brain fully reacts to what's happening, Declan has my dress bunched up at my waist. "Too much fucking fabric. Hold it."

What the hell is he—? I squeal as he hoists my right leg over his shoulders, practically lifting me effortlessly. I stop breathing when he buries his nose between my legs, taking a long, languid inhale.

"Fuuuck," he utters reverently, while I regret not having a shower at Celeste's.

"We don't have—"

"Relax, baby, I need to taste this pussy now. I have been waiting for months. Hold on."

Months? But I don't have time to contemplate that because he lets go of my behind, expecting me to... well, hold on.

I balance on one foot as this large man grips the crotch panel of my panties and yanks. The fabric snaps.

"Have you just ripped off my underwear?" I don't

know if I should berate him or reward him. Again, not even second base yet, and I'm about to come.

He doesn't bother to heed my question and spreads my folds, humming with appreciation.

It only takes me half a second to throw away my inhibition as he swipes his tongue slowly, circling at my entrance and back to my clit.

The moan that rips out of me is animalistic, coming from somewhere deep where my desire has been hibernating without my even knowing.

"Atta girl, give me all your sounds."

Declan sucks and licks, testing my reactions and getting to know my body better than I do. And like a good girl, I give him all the sounds.

Not that I have a choice; they spill out of me freely as this man eats me like I'm the only meal he's ever had.

I lose myself completely under his expert ministrations, thrashing and gripping his hair, pushing him away and closer at the same time. Not that I could move the man, but the assault of sensations is too much.

My orgasm comes so suddenly, I scream and cry and laugh at the same time. "Declan." I clamp my thighs so tight, I may give him a headache.

He doesn't let up, and continues swirling his

tongue, prolonging my pleasure. When he slides my leg slowly to the ground, I'm sure I'm going to pass out.

He stands up and scoops me into his arms in one swift move, seemingly unaffected by what has happened. Bar the steel rod poking into me.

Spent and dazed, I lower my head to his chest. He shifts a bit and pushes the button. The elevator hums to life, and we ride up.

"That was..." I sigh, contentment spreading through me.

"First thing on the agenda. I've been fantasizing about your taste for way too long. I might need another taste as soon as we're up."

As the hormones settle, a blush creeps into my cheeks. "Maybe I should shower first."

He glowers. "You, little Seagull, taste like heaven."

I roll my eyes. "What's next? Poetry? Who even are you?"

His expression shifts, turning serious. "Your husband."

\* \* \*

The flickering lights of the city are mesmerizing tonight. The door to the terrace clicks, and I turn.

Declan, who has shed his jacket and bow tie, saunters in with a glass of whiskey. It's a hot night, but the breeze is refreshing, giving me a needed break before Declan moves to whatever is next on that agenda of his.

As if he knew I needed a breather, he carried me out here as soon as we stepped out of the elevator. I ride that thing with the kids... Jesus, my face will be permanently red.

He puts the glass on a small table, crooks his finger, and beckons me to him.

"The dress needs to go," he orders.

"You want me to take it off here?"

"I can do it for you. You can't be cold."

"I'm not... and I know we're very high, but what if someone hears us?"

"That's the point, Seagull; shrill away." He winks. He fucking winks.

A playful Declan. I won't survive tonight.

I stop in front of him, and he reaches for the zipper on my side. How does he even know where the zipper is?

I realize this man is probably a few steps ahead of me. And always will be. It's a threatening concept for someone who is trying to outrun her past.

He turned on all the lights here, the faux candles flickering in the dark. He whips me around, my back to his chest. Slipping his hand through my neckline, he grazes my nipple and then cups my breast almost painfully.

With the other arm on my waist, I'm completely trapped in his embrace. He lets out a groan as he brushes his thumb over my very alert nipple.

"I need to fuck these tits." He nips at my earlobe.

The combination of his words, his voice, and his breath sends a shiver down my spine. Who am I kidding? I've been trembling since he stepped behind me at the gala.

"You need to fuck, period. This situation has to be painful." Sliding my hand behind me, I cup his erection and revel in his groan as he lowers his head on my shoulder, barely hanging onto his control.

"Anything to do with you has been painful." He plays mindlessly with my nipple, but lets go of my waist and covers my hand over his erection. "Agonizingly unraveling. You make me weak, and I don't even fight it anymore, little Seagull."

I rest my head on his shoulder. "You didn't even know I existed a few weeks back."

He chuckles and twirls me around, locking his eyes with mine. "Have you ever checked the log at work? I've been paying a retainer at Summit Solutions for years, but the frequency of my calls increased at one point. Ask me when."

His words give my heart rate a jolt, but I don't let it bloom. "When your wife left and you needed more help?"

"Ask me when, Lily," he growls.

"When?"

"When you first answered the fucking phone. It was your voice."

The flickering lights, the city's murmur, the summer heat and humidity, it all fades away. My heart, my mind, my soul zoom in on this moment, on his words.

My voice?

I grip his shirt and pull him to me, fusing my lips with his in a desperate kiss, trying to comprehend his declaration and erase it at the same time, the rolling feelings almost too overwhelming.

Declan holds me close, moaning into my mouth. Our bodies flush, I still feel like I'm not close enough, clawing at him, desperate for more. For closer. For deeper.

He slides the sleeves of my dress down while he kisses me. His hand falters as it grazes the skin under my elbow.

The uneven skin, a patchwork of raised and smooth textures, where the burn once seared deep. He pulls away, the dress pooling at my waist.

I shiver as if the temperature dipped suddenly. He looks at the ugly scar covering my forearm and part of my torso, a network of faint lines and ridges, like a landscape forever marked by fire, a quiet testament to pain endured and never forgotten.

He stills and stares at it.

In that moment, I know.

My body still tingles with desire, making my skin hot and cold at the same time.

But my heart and mind already know that the moment is over.

He sees the damage. He will see me damaged. He will focus on all the broken pieces.

In the last attempt to change the outcome of tonight, to return it to what it could be... I cup his face, forcing his gaze away from the scars.

I plead with my eyes... desperately hoping he didn't really see it in the low light. The ugly reminder of my past.

I plead... no, I dare him to stay in the moment. To let us have this moment without the inevitable gory story. Just this one moment when my past doesn't invade the first good thing that's happened to me in the longest time.

Something dark passes through his eyes, his breath ragged.

His gaze on me is too much, penetrating the hidden crevices of my consciousness, reading me like he is trying to comprehend the story I don't want to share. Not tonight. Not like this.

His eyes on me burn... No longer with that delicious temptation and need from earlier. They burn with unanswered questions, even with my own guilt for keeping things from him.

With everything unspoken and hidden. With my lies. And my secrets.

And then, when I'm sure it's all over before it even started, he lifts my arm and starts kissing the scarred tissue with the same reverence he kissed my lips, my cleavage, my pussy. Like it's a part of me, equally beautiful to him.

My breath hitches as I swallow a sob. His gaze keeps me prisoner as he turns my arm in his hand, planting kisses over my ugly skin.

"Declan—" The whisper sounds indecently loud after the moment of holding my breath, and the stillness of his discovery.

"Tell me you need this as much as I do." His hoarse voice is my undoing. It's nourishing in a familiar way, but also new, filled with desperation.

"I need this," I whisper, and Declan yanks my dress down along with the scraps of my panties. He cups my nape and pulls me in for a kiss.

He's taller and stronger, but somehow my naked body molds into his, the fabric of his shirt soft on my marred skin.

Reaching for his belt, I fidget with the buckle, and

then with the zipper, unable to get the job done while he kisses me frantically like I'm his oxygen.

I'm about to push his pants down, but he steps back and sits on the lounger, pulling me with him to straddle him. His hot mouth finds my nipple, grazing it with his teeth and then soothing it with his tongue.

I arch into him, wanting more of this. More of him. More of us.

He switches to my other breast, and I quiver. His large hands roam my back. I can get lost in this man.

He sucks with fervent dedication. I didn't even realize my nipples were so sensitive, but I'm wild with arousal, grinding my hips, desperately seeking friction.

"So responsive. Such a good little Seagull."

His words spark little detonations all over my body. "Declan..."

"Yes?" A hint of teasing laces his question. "Tell me what you need."

Nothing has happened yet, and I'm dizzy, just putty in his arms. "I want you."

"You need to be more specific. What part of me does your sweet pussy want?"

Oh, shit. I like how he talks dirty to me, and I-I thought such thoughts and played such fantasies in my head, but I can't voice them. I'm not a prude, but... Am I a prude? I don't have enough experience to know who I am sexually.

With one hand he cups my cheek, languidly dragging his thumb over my bottom lip. His other hand is doing the same to one of my nipples while his gaze holds me hostage.

"Come on, Lily, you're thinking it." A lazy smirk stretches on his face as he watches my reaction.

My breath comes out shallow and fast, heat coloring my cheeks. Is he not going to proceed if I don't say it? Oh my God.

I cover my face, embarrassed. Not by his words, but by my inability to play the game on his level.

Declan pries my hands away from my face. I close my eyes. Because yeah, I'm really mature tonight.

But this man is way out of my scope of reference. No amount of porn could have prepared me for the intimacy that sprouted so effortlessly between us.

"Look at me, Lily." He growls the command with an edge of finality, and I snap my eyes open. The bastard is smirking wider. "Let me help you." He moves my hand over his erection. "This is how much I need you. This is what you do to me. I need my cock buried deep inside you. I need to fuck you so you come so hard, you won't be able to walk."

He starts moving my hand over his hardness, letting out a guttural moan. I really do this to him. It's more my curiosity than lust, but I pull out my hand from below his and peel the waistband of his briefs down.

His cock springs free, and Declan leans back on his elbows to let me discover more of him. But instead I freeze, and swallow a gasp.

"This will never fit."

He chuckles and lies down, pulling me with him. My pussy is now perched over his length, and the friction is delicious.

"We will make it fit, Seagull." He shuffles and pulls out a condom from his pocket, handing it to me.

I rip off the wrapper and take my time sheathing him. His cock is scary large, but it's beautiful. Never have I thought I would call someone's penis beautiful, but here we are. I slowly roll the condom down, and Declan hisses.

The sound of his hunger boosts my confidence, and I lower myself so his cock rests between my folds. I gyrate my hips, his erection creating a delicious build-up.

His belt buckle pokes my thigh, and I shift a bit before leaning forward to unbutton his shirt. "I need to see your collarbone."

He raises his eyebrows. "Your dirty-talk game needs some work."

I chuckle, opening his shirt. Humming with contentment, I trail my hands over his ridiculously defined pecs and chest. Leaning forward, I kiss his collarbone. "I can't explain it, but your collarbone is sexy."

He laughs. He laughs, and the sound is so precious, I almost forget what we are doing. He kisses me and then lifts my hips. "My collarbone is honored, but this boner needs you."

I take his cock into my hand and align it at my entrance, but then hesitate. Fuck, it really is huge.

"Seagull, you're in charge. We can go slowly, but you need to trust me." He brushes my clit with his thumb and my pelvis trembles, then relaxes. Before I realize, his tip is inside me, stretching me.

The sight of our connection is mesmerizing, and it spurs me forward. I sink deeper, and this time the burn ignites between my thighs, and while it's not too bad, it is uncomfortable.

"You're killing me here, Lily. Your pussy is so tight. So perfect." Every word is laced with restraint, like he's holding something volatile inside. God, I want to unravel him. That need almost takes my mind from the pain. Almost.

I need to get out of my head. This man knows what he's doing, and I want this. "Declan..." I pant. "I need you to be in charge."

His gaze darkens, and he stills completely. "Are

you sure? Because I'm barely hanging onto my control here, and—"

"Take me, Declan. Make me scream your name." The king of control is losing it, and the thought injects confidence into my veins.

"Fuck, Lily. I warned you."

He grips my hips and thrusts up at the same time as he jerks me down, impaling me on his cock.

I cry out, but I don't even have time to adjust or to contemplate how full I am, and he starts moving. His hands firm on my hips, he controls the tempo, grinding his jaw. And while he said he won't be able to control himself, I can see he's still taking it easy on me.

A part of me wants to provoke him to let go, but let's keep it for the next time, because right now I'm so deliciously filled, I can't cope with anything else.

He circles his thumb around my clit, and I relax enough for the pain to turn into a heady sensation, and before I realize I start bouncing, chasing my own orgasm.

"Atta, girl. Ride my cock, little Seagull."

His hands freed, he reaches for my tits and kneads and pinches and toys with them. My knees go weak; I don't even know where the energy to move comes from.

"Declan, I'm going to—"

I yelp, my head spinning because he flips us over,

and I'm on all fours now. He yanks my hips up. He slams into me from behind so hard, my face deep-dives into the mattress. "Not yet," he warns.

Jesus. As if I could... All thoughts leave my mind, because he sets such a punishing tempo I hang on for dear life. Declan rams into me without mercy, and fuck, I love it.

He builds me up again so fast, I clench around him just to cope with the overwhelming force of everything —his body, my arousal, his words.

"Please," I chant, not even sure what I'm pleading.

He snakes his arm around me and pinches my clit, and I clench around him on instinct. "Come for me, Lily. Milk me dry."

The wave of complete oblivion takes me by surprise, and I scream something unintelligible. Declan doesn't stop his thrusts, prolonging my orgasm while I go numb with pleasure.

I'm boneless in his arms when he halts and groans, while his cock jerks inside me as he finds his own release. He collapses on top of me, hovering on his elbows.

"Confession," he pants, planting kisses on my shoulders.

"I'm pretty sure you fried my brain, so say whatever you want." I kiss his biceps, because that's about the range of movement I can muster.

"I was hoping one time would be enough to get you out of my system."

I bite his biceps. "You were also hoping you could resist this, so I guess when it comes to the two of us, our preconceptions are wrong."

Somehow, he flips us again. The lounger isn't wide enough, so he arranges me on top of him and kisses my crown. "Thank God for that. This might be the only time in my life I'm fucking glad I lost control."

## Chapter 18

## *Declan*

"Let the city hear you, Lily. Come for me."

Her hands are on the banister as I'm taking her from behind, practically holding her up, her body used and spent.

Maybe I'm too hard on her. I should have taken her to my bed and let her rest after the first time.

But I'm a weak man when it comes to her. I gave her a break for all of ten minutes before I had to bury myself in her again.

No control. No fucking control.

I was half-hard all evening watching her in that stupid dress, and restraining myself from either pouncing on her or punching every fucking asshole who ogled her.

When I arranged the weekend at my mom's for the kids, I told myself it was to get some time to catch up on work and on the genealogy project. I kept telling that to myself, hoping I would believe it.

I failed miserably, and when I saw her coming down in that dress, all made up, no longer hiding, I knew, without a shadow of a doubt, she would be mine this weekend.

I had to pretend to stare at my phone because I wanted to grab her hand and drag her out of Cal's house and straight to my bed.

And still, the fool that I am, I was telling myself it's only for this one time. She is so young, innocent, so vibrant... But that story got old too quickly. I needed to have her. Her warmth calls to me like she is the only fire on Earth.

It's not enough to have her here in secret. It's not.

I have tried my best to resist her, to do right by her. But I'm done. Lily is mine, and I will do anything to keep her. And everything to make it up to her.

"You take me so well, baby."

The blush on her face when I asked her to speak up about her desires... Fuck, her confession that she's only been with one man... It made me even harder instantly. Like I could be her one and only.

Like I could offer her that. I can't. But I'm unable to stop anymore. I'll have to find a way.

"Declan, Declan, Dec..." she chants, and my name

on her lips does it for me, and I unload, my release so strong I almost drop to the ground.

Instead, I scoop her to me and turn to lean on the cold, stone balustrade. She fidgets to wrap her arms around my waist and rest her head contentedly on my chest. And in my mind, I can see us like this every day, all the days far into the future.

I banish the thought immediately, because it's a silly, orgasm-induced fantasy. One that could never happen. If nothing else, then on account of my kids. It's not like I would want to get rid of them every weekend.

I may want Lily, but how available am I really?

Depressed by this line of thoughts, I discard the condom unceremoniously on the ground and pick her up bridal-style before I walk inside.

"Where are we going?" She smiles at me, her just-fucked, flushed face and swollen lips already rushing blood to my cock.

"Bedroom. I'm pretty sure they heard you in Brooklyn." I carry her up the stairs.

Her eyes widen, and she covers her mouth, but then she catches herself and swats at me. "It's all your fault. I might have a sore throat tomorrow."

A pang of guilt grips me. "I went too hard on you." I kick the door to my bedroom open.

"I loved it." She beams at me, and I almost drop her

from the sheer overwhelment. This woman will be the death of me.

"You're trouble." I put her down gently in my bathroom.

She looks down and bites her lip. "I didn't disappoint you? I mean...I know you're used to women who are... and I hope you..."

Fuck, the way she sways between bursts of confidence and bouts of self-doubt is infuriating. But also so raw and real. The fact she doesn't pretend in front of me. Doesn't act. She just is.

All her smiles, giggles, verbal diarrhea, chin-ups, and lost gazes. All of her. So fucking genuine.

I step into her space and take her face into my hands, lowering my lips to hers. I don't take her mouth like before, desperate for a connection, feeding my own desires.

I kiss her to tell her how perfect she is. How much I respect and admire her. How grateful I am for her role in my life.

She snakes her hands around my waist, wrapping herself tighter around me. The quiet intimacy of our kiss is almost scary, opening my chest wide, making me vulnerable and exposed. But also making me whole and invincible.

It's a strange feeling. Like I want to bring the stars to her feet and protect her at all costs. At the same time, I know, at this moment, that whatever happens tomorrow, my life will never be the same.

That everything led to this moment, when a girl who offered to marry me became my wife. Whether she's ready for it or not.

"What was that for?" she asks me, breathless.

"You can't ever disappoint me, Lily."

All her muscles tense in my embrace, and something akin to fear flashes through her face. Fuck, I'm scaring her with my premature declarations.

"Your pussy fits perfectly around my cock," I add, to make my words less severe for her.

A smile tugs at her lips. "I will get better at this."

"At your dirty talk? Yeah, we need to work on that." I walk to the shower and turn the water on, testing the temperature with my hand.

Lily comes and kisses my back. I bow my head, the stream beating down my shoulders. I want to make her see how much she already means to me, but I need to remember who we are. She's a decade-younger woman, who needed money and helped me out.

Yes, the chemistry is off the charts between us, but for her, it's probably just that. Getting experience with an older man. Something she can get out of this period in her life before she moves on.

"I want to be the woman you deserve." She puts her hands on my shoulders.

*When it comes to the two of us, our preconceptions are wrong.*

And here she is proving that theory right. "Lily," I grit out, and turn to face her.

Beads of water roll down her face and her body, and she looks so fragile and strong at the same time, my chest expands with blissful pain.

"Don't worry, I understand nobody can know about us, and that 'us' may last this weekend only, but you make me feel beautiful, cared for. You make me feel safe, and I haven't felt safe for a very long time. I want to reciprocate."

She reaches between us and grips my cock. I should stop her. I should tell her she means more to me than sex. I should be as brave as she is and tell her how she makes me feel.

Instead, I drop to my knees and kiss her between her thighs, and then I trail kisses up her torso, over the scarred tissue. "You're beautiful."

She whimpers. "Declan."

My name was on her lips before she gripped my cock, but this time it grips my heart. "Let me take care of you." The words scrape my throat like sandpaper.

"Declan," she sighs, her voice cracking the same way mine is.

I stand up and cup her face. "But you can never be the woman I deserve."

Her eyebrows pull together, creasing her forehead. She swallows visibly, and her bottom lip trembles slightly before she presses it into a firm line. "I see," she rasps.

I kiss her forehead. "No, you don't. I could never deserve you, little Seagull. I already told you, I'm not a good man."

She smiles, and the clouds over the conversation lift immediately. "I think you're a good man, Declan Quinn. But maybe we can be bad for each other and enjoy the hell out of it."

And as much as I wanted to give her a break and let her rest, I pounce, lifting her. Her back hits the wall, and she laughs.

But that beautiful sound morphs into a moan when I reach between us and push one finger into her tight pussy.

"You have quite some stamina for an older man."

Lily takes a bite of a sandwich I made for her, because her attempt failed. Did she grow up in a house without a kitchen? How she survived this long is beyond me.

"I'm not old." I elbow her and lean in to have a bite.

"Hey." She turns to protect her food. "Wasn't that your key argument against this?"

I smear mayo on a slice of bread to make my own late dinner. "The argument was you're too young."

She watches me making my food, munching contentedly. "Sometimes I feel very old."

"I feel like I'm a hundred most days. Maybe I needed your youth to forget that."

Her eyes sparkle with mischief. "That must be it. A confetti fight?"

I laugh. I laughed so much tonight, it will last me for the rest of my days. I don't even know if I ever laughed before Lily came into my life.

"A pillow fight?" she teases. With her hair mussed, sitting naked in my kitchen, she is so fucking sexy, I want to freeze the moment.

"I can spank you. That would be a good game." I put my sandwich down, and her eyes flash with something that looks like excitement. Fuck me.

"Maybe not tonight, but I'll get there." She takes my glass of whiskey and wets her lips, watching me through her lashes, a slight blush coloring her cheeks.

How did I get this lucky? Her curiosity is such a fucking turn-on. But it doesn't strip me of my guilt. "Are you very sore?"

"A little." She slides down and takes her plate to

the dishwasher. She slams it against a bowl and the plate cracks. "Shit." She jumps back.

I'm grabbing her hand immediately. "Did you cut yourself?" I fucking train daily, but my heart is not ready for these spikes.

"No. It just split in two." She giggles, showing me the two broken parts of the plate. "I'm sorry. I keep destroying your kitchen."

"Sometimes I wonder if those glasses don't need real lenses." I shake my head.

She looks away, her eyes darting around, before she decides not to respond and goes to discard the plate.

I close the dishwasher and take my whiskey. I wish she trusted me with her secret. Her fake glasses. Her scars.

Seemingly lost in her thoughts, she steps to the window wall. I join her, passing her the glass, and she takes a sip. I like this sharing whiskey with her. I love it.

"I like sharing whiskey with you," she says, and something dislodges in my chest.

We watch the city in silence, sipping the amber liquid.

"I don't want to ruin the moment, but when you said you feel safe with me..." I start, and she sighs. It's a heavy sigh, and I want to make it lighter for her.

The need is strong. I have never felt such a strong need to protect any other person besides my children.

When she doesn't speak, I push because the not knowing is killing me. "The day of the fire drill, you said you... Are the scars from that time?"

"Yes. There was a fire in our house, and my cousin locked me in my room so I couldn't escape."

Before I realize, my fist punches the window, and Lily jumps away. The rage blurs the edges of my mind. "Where is he?"

"Declan." She steps away, pleading.

"Is he in prison?" I demand, trying and failing to keep the onslaught of feelings under control.

"It doesn't matter. Stop it."

"Is he in prison? What's his name?"

Lily shakes her head, stepping farther from me. "Stop."

I step closer to her. "Give me his name, Lily."

She puts her hand on my chest, and the warmth of her palm once again clears the fury-induced fog, and my mind clears slightly. I'm hit with the sight of her face, anxious but defiant.

"Is he the reason you sleep with a knife?" I reign in my tone, because the last thing I want is to scare her. What is it with this woman that I barely hang onto my control?

She nods, and I swear, turning away because I need to punch something one more time. Or more.

"You said I make you feel safe." I don't remember

the last time I raised my voice. "How can I keep you safe if you don't tell me what the danger is? How can I help you?"

"Right now, the only danger is your anger fucking up this perfect night. You're helping me... You gave me a home. You made me feel beautiful tonight; instead of focusing on my scars, you worshiped my body. I haven't felt this whole for months, years even. You made me feel whole tonight, so please just drop it. Don't ruin tonight."

I can practically feel the vein popping in my temple, but her words penetrate the rage enough for me to see how my reaction is not going to get us anywhere.

I hang my head and take a deep breath in, trying to tame my raging heart. "I'm sorry. Just the idea of someone hurting you..." My voice cracks.

Lily reaches out, wrapping her small hand around mine. "It's very chivalrous of you, but let's focus on here and now. I know I'm safe here. And the sex is pretty good, too."

I snort, pulling her to me. "I think it's time for that spanking. Pretty good is a lame description."

She palms my cheek. "I might need a further show and tell to find a more appropriate one."

"I thought you were sore."

She blushes again, biting her lower lip, and fuck if I

don't love that look on her. "Maybe I can get on my knees."

She yelps as I lift her, throwing her over my shoulder.

"Where are we going?"

"I'm taking you to my bedroom and never letting you out, Seagull." I slap her ass.

* * *

I startle awake and turn to check the clock. It's nine. Where are the kids? The movement beside me grounds me immediately, and I relax back.

When was the last time I slept in on the weekend? Not that we slept much. Lily murmurs something in her sleep and smiles.

She's smiling in her sleep, and shallow me takes credit for it. She looks so peaceful, her face looking even younger, more innocent.

I reach out to stroke her cheek, unable to help myself. She sighs and turns away slightly. The cover slips from her shoulder, exposing her tits. I stifle a groan, considering how to wake her up.

She lets out a soft snore. I should let her rest. Besides, there is something I need to do. I slide out of the bed, careful not to wake her, find a clean pair of briefs, and make my way to my office.

Checking my phone, I find several photos my mom sent me three hours ago. Based on the angle and the quality of composition, I suspect Zoya took the pics of all three of them preparing breakfast.

Fuck, I miss them. If it wasn't for the woman in the next room, I would have gone to pick them up already.

Instead, I allow myself one selfish weekend with the woman who makes me feel powerful and powerless all at the same time.

I boot up my computer and find Lily's file I got from Summit Solutions. Pulling out her data, I start to search.

An hour later, I lean back in my chair, my eyes and mind straining to understand. As someone who's been piecing people's lineages together, I'm quite well-equipped in searching for relatives, especially with a history as recent as Lily's.

But all of my usual publicly accessible sources come back empty. I follow my process, my curiosity piquing, trying to discover Lily's family tree. A mother, a father, siblings, an old census record...

Except there's nothing.

Not nothing in the way that makes sense—missing records aren't uncommon. But this isn't that. This is a dead end, so perfectly constructed it's almost like someone built a wall where her past should be.

I rub my fingers over my jaw, narrowing my eyes at

the screen. I'm used to tracing lineages back centuries. Give me a name and a country, and I can usually uncover more details than a person even knows about their own history.

But Lily?

Lily Thorne is a ghost.

Her social security number checks out, which means on paper she exists. But everything else feels... off.

No rental history under her name. No paper trail. No traces of childhood school records, no medical history—none of the usual documentation that would back up a life lived.

I drum my fingers against the desk.

Did she change her name? Is she running from something? From someone? Who the fuck is this cousin who would leave her in a burning house? Not just leave her, but lock her in?

I brought her to my house; I trust her with my children. I fucking married her. I mean, I married a stranger, a woman I didn't know, but I didn't appreciate just how much I didn't know about her.

"Here you are?" She saunters in, smiling sleepily.

She is wearing my white button-down, only one button done up, exposing her legs. It covers all the little secrets beneath the fabric, and I almost forget about her big secret.

"You should only wear my shirt." I click out of all the tabs, so only my desktop shows on the screen, my kids grinning at me from a pic on my background.

"Are you working?" She rounds the desk and sits in my lap, wrapping her arms around me.

"No, I was looking for your cousin." I watch her face closely.

She tenses and moves to stand, but I tighten my grip on her.

She sighs. "Declan, I don't want you to search for him. Nothing good can come out of it. I don't want to confront that part of my life. Can you accept that?"

My instincts scream at me to trust her. But the evidence behind her on my computer raises questions. Do I have the right to ask them?

I tuck a strand behind her ear. "I'll try."

She brushes her lips against mine gently. "He bullied me for a very long time. The night of the fire was the last straw for me to pack up and leave that toxic environment. I came to New York and used my money to get into therapy, so I didn't succumb to the ghost of his assaults. And I met Celeste, Saar, and Cora and created a life here. And then I met you, so a part of me is grateful for the previous experience, because without it, we wouldn't be here."

Fuck. Can she be any more perfect? I still want to find and destroy the bully. I still have a lot of questions, but she confided in me, and I need to create a safe space for her to share more. I'm painfully aware I don't deserve her trust.

"Thank you for sharing that with me." I stroke her cheek.

She hugs me tight, holding me strongly like she fears I may disappear.

"I don't want you to worry about it anymore. I'm fine. Or getting there." Her warm breath fans my shoulder.

Stroking her back, I bury my face in the crook of her neck, inhaling the essence of her. "I'll try. I'll focus on family trees that I was actually asked to create."

She shifts, and my dick gets ideas. "It's a really nerdy hobby, but somehow it's sexy on you, Declan Quinn."

"Nerdy? My amateur sleuthing gets me ladies," I taunt her.

She glances down. "I thought it was your monstrous cock."

"I would appreciate a bit more awe and appreciation in your tone."

She laughs. "I'm eternally grateful that your cock fills my pussy so well." She widens her eyes like her words surprised her.

"Look, you're already improving your sex talk." I kiss her.

"I need to get better to compete with all your sleuthing-skill admirers." She grins.

I cup her nape and pull her to me, resting my forehead against hers. "Actually, there hasn't been anyone in probably the last two years, maybe longer."

"Can you be any more perfect?" She sighs, throwing my compliment back at me.

If only she knew how imperfect I am. I vow to let go of her secrets, because if she discovers mine, she will run.

# Chapter 19

## *Lily*

**CORA**

You all disappeared on me last night.

**SAAR**

You seemed under the spell of Xander.

**CORA**

Don't be ridiculous.

> Sorry, but I'm sure you had fun.

**CORA**

You left like a ghost too.

**SAAR**

I'm guessing we have my grumpy brother-in-law to thank for that.

**CELESTE**

Lils, you didn't have to leave with him, we would have given you a ride.

> **SAAR**
> @Celeste, how is your dress?
>
> **CELESTE**
> Ruined by breast milk (sad face emoji)
>
> **CORA**
> How did I miss that?
>
> **SAAR**
> Xander

> Xander's distraction.

> **CELESTE**
> Xander's allure.
>
> **CORA**
> I'm leaving this chat.

"Is everything okay?" I ask as Declan walks into the kitchen, hanging up his phone with a sigh.

He is bare-chested in his gym shorts, sweat beading on his skin. The man must have been the model for all Renaissance sculptors. I love that I can ogle him freely now.

"Other than you being unattended in the kitchen?" He takes a bottle of water from the fridge.

I refrain from rolling my eyes. "I was hungry."

His gaze drops to the tub of ice cream and he raises his eyebrows. "Is that your breakfast?"

"I think it's been established I can't cook."

"You can't even make a sandwich."

"That's what I just said." I stab at the mango sorbet, but it's not very satisfying since it's still frozen.

"Making a sandwich is not cooking, Seagull." He chugs down his water. "It's been established you're a danger to yourself and others when in this part of the house."

I glare.

Declan shakes his head, smirking. "How do you like your eggs?"

Okay, sorbet for breakfast was my desperate attempt to pack some calories and replenish my energy after the man seriously dehydrated me last night. But eggs sound way more appetizing.

"Sunny side up." I close the tub, return it to the freezer, and lean against the counter.

The sun beams through the glass wall, making the morning bright and joyful. I've been smiling since I woke up. I can't help it.

I let my eyes roam across his shoulders and down his abs to the happy trail. Perfection. My gaze languidly moves back up, and I meet his twinkling eyes and his smirk.

"Would you like me to turn slowly for you?"

"I wouldn't mind that." I bite my lip.

Declan launches at me, and I squeal as he lifts me, whips us around, and sits me on the counter.

"What am I going to do with you, little Seagull?"

"Whatever it is, can it please start with breakfast?" My stomach growls to confirm my need.

He kisses me, slowly, reverently. "Okay, sit here and don't move."

"Let me help, or I will never learn." I wrap my arms around his neck, smiling.

He studies me and then sighs. "Fuck it, let's burn down the kitchen."

"Look at you being spontaneous." I giggle, sliding down. "And I'm not *that* useless."

"That remains to be seen," he mumbles, but opens the fridge to get eggs.

Five minutes later, and after seven failed attempts at breaking an egg into the pan without crushing shells into it, the kitchen is messy, and we're nowhere close to having breakfast.

But we are closer to each other. While Declan complains about the mess and keeps wiping the surface, he does it with lightness.

It's like last night wasn't about sex only. Like he allowed me in, just a bit, and he dropped his typical glower. He dropped some of the walls.

We're also literally closer, because even if I'm making the cooking impossible, Declan doesn't seem to be able to stop touching me—he kisses my shoulder, swats my ass, caresses my hip.

He steps behind me as I pick up another egg. I

almost moan at the feel of his warmth on my back. He snakes his arms around me and takes my hands into his.

"We will get it right this time." He guides my hand to the edge of the pan. "You crack it gently." His scent is distracting. "With your thumbs, you separate the two parts and let the egg drop."

He uses his thumbs to gently pry the shell apart, and the egg slides into the pan.

I bounce like it's my doing. "I did it."

"Yes, but we're running out of eggs for you to practice on, so let me finish it." I pout and Declan sighs. "You can make the toast."

"You really want to burn down the kitchen?" I tease.

He kisses my forehead. "I believe in you."

I heard him say the same to Zoya and Zach a few times. "Are you unleashing your inner daddy on me?"

As soon as the words are out, a jolt of electricity cruises through me. Declan's shorts bulge, and he looks at me like I'm his breakfast now.

The air between us zaps. I lick my lips. He moves the pan away from the heat. The thermostat in the house must have short-circuited, because it's so hot suddenly I want to fan myself.

And then my stomach growls so loudly, the moment is gone. I cover my face, chuckling.

"You will call me Daddy again after you eat."

Why is that so hot? Not just the request itself, or my desire to execute it, but the way he demanded. Not you *can* call me. You *will* call me Daddy.

"Sorry, I have to take this," Declan groans and answers his phone, walking over to the windows.

We showered after our breakfast and ended up back in his huge bed. Sated on food and orgasms, we've been talking and, to my surprise, cuddling.

If someone told me two days ago that Declan Quinn was a touchy-feely guy, I wouldn't believe it.

The afternoon sun shines through, making him just a shadow, but I still can't help admiring the outline. His broad back narrows in a perfect triangle to his hips and toned ass. I can stare at this man for the rest of my life and not get bored.

"I don't understand why you believe that listing the same arguments would change my mind. I'm done discussing this, Corm. I won't change my mind."

His shoulders tense, and he taps his fingers on his thigh. I don't know what's going on, but I feel like I shouldn't be listening. I slide from under the covers and pad over to the bathroom.

I drink water and wash my hands to busy myself

and give him privacy. When I look up, Declan is leaning against the door frame.

Our eyes meet in the mirror.

"Is everything okay?" I ask.

He steps toward me and hugs me from behind, burying his head in the crook of my neck. He doesn't speak. He doesn't move, but the weight of whatever is troubling him radiates from his body.

I lean my head against his, caressing his biceps. We look like a real couple in the mirror. Like two lovers who trust each other. Two people who support each other.

My heart beats faster, seeing the picture I see in the mirror. Not because it's a lie. But because of how much I wish it was the truth.

"Merged is opening an office in London." Declan's voice is rough with a tinge of resignation. He lifts his head, and our eyes lock in the mirror again.

The mention of London spikes my heart rate, but this is not about me.

"And you and Corm have some disagreement over that?"

He closes his eyes briefly and rubs his cheek against mine. He kisses me gently and looks back at me. "It's me against the three partners. They think I should lead the new branch for at least a year."

"Move to London?"

He nods.

"And you don't want to do that because of the kids? You don't want to uproot them?"

He straightens and steps around me to lean against the vanity. His back to the mirror, he pulls me to stand between his legs. "You get it." He runs his hands up and down my forearms.

God, I will miss his touch. The thought intrudes on the important conversation and ties a neat knot in my stomach. I push it away, because this man is confiding in me and I want to be present.

"I mean, I believe that living in a new country is a great experience, but there will be plenty of time for that later. They are little and need stability, especially in your circumstances."

Something akin to awe and relief settles in his expression. "You do get it. Corm's argument is that with the kids starting a new school in September, it's the best timing. The problem isn't just their stability—it's an important factor, of course."

"What else?"

He sighs. "I know I'm the best man for the job, but the idea of relocating, finding new schools, a new nanny... just the whole spiel feels exhausting. At least here my mother can help. Or even Corm and Saar. But there? I will be even busier than now, and I will again depend on strangers. I felt helpless and out of control for so long. I will never cross that line again."

"Those are all reasonable considerations. You value order, planning, and control in your life. You don't need to apologize for that."

He smiles, but it doesn't reach his eyes. "You really are perfect."

The words hit me hard, especially after the earlier thought about the temporary nature of our arrangement. I really didn't think this through.

What happens after he doesn't need a fake wife? Will I stay his nanny? This was less of an issue before this weekend. Now everything is confusing.

"Your kitchen would disagree."

He chuckles and kisses my forehead. "You really think I'm not making a mistake?"

"I think you have the means to relocate to London whenever you want, if you really want to, but you don't want to at the moment. It's your life, your decision. Besides, in your current situation, the whole proposition is mute." I cup his cheek. I guess I can't not touch him either.

He frowns. "What do you mean?"

"You're in the middle of a custody battle. I doubt Kendra would give you consent to take the kids abroad on vacation, let alone long-term."

His eyes shift down, his jaw ticking. He turns away

from me, bracing his arms on the sink. I guess mentioning Kendra triggers him.

I kiss his back. "Talking about kids, when are they coming back? I miss them."

"You do?" He turns, the cloud over his expression gone.

I nod. "I mean, I love the way you fill my time, but I still miss them. Maybe we can pick them up later today instead of tomorrow?"

I'm so attached to this little family already, it scares me.

He smiles, and from a man whose smiles are so rare, it just wraps me in a fantasy I decide to enjoy while it lasts.

"I think it's a great idea, little Seagull, but let me do some of that *filling of your time* first."

\* \* \*

"For the love of God, there is nothing between me and Xander. We had fun dancing. Period." Cora shakes her head, her hands huddled around her coffee mug. "It's not like I knew anyone else there to dance with. I'm not from your world."

She took a break after a busy lunch hour, and we've been teasing her relentlessly. I welcome the distraction because my mind is on Declan, and I need to start functioning without constantly thinking about him.

"Sorry, none of us besides Saar is from that world." Celeste smiles at her.

"Now I feel like an outsider," Saar huffs.

"That's not what I meant." Cora sighs. "I didn't know anyone else besides you at the gala, so Xander actually stepping up and treating me to a fun night was exactly what I needed after spending the last three years here."

"We need to take you out more often," Saar says.

"Also, you and him dancing was the most scandalous thing that happened." Celeste peeks into the stroller. "Beside my boobs leaking."

"That is pretty sad." Cora smirks.

"Where did you disappear to?" Saar turns to me.

My cheeks heat up. So much for trying to distract myself from Declan. "I was too tired."

"Declan was probably grateful to get out of there. He hates these things." Saar takes a bite of her wrap.

"I didn't fire the night nurse, and now I feel guilty about it." Celeste fortunately changes the topic.

"Because you didn't fire her? I'm sure she's grateful," Saar points out.

"Guilty about having her. About not being there for Amelie at night."

"I'm not an expert here, but I think you getting

better sleep allows you to be more present with her during the day," I say. "You can be a zombie with her twenty-four seven, or you can be a hundred percent with her for twelve hours."

"Wow, look at you, a nanny for a month and already such a pro." Saar pokes me. "Are you enjoying the job?"

"I do. I really do."

I'm also enjoying my boss very much, but I'm not ready to share that with them.

"I'm happy for you," says Cora.

"I met someone, and he's a bit older and more experienced than me," I blurt out, surprising everyone, including me.

"Whoa, and you're only telling us now." Saar drops the wrap and turns to me. "Spill the beans."

I chuckle. "There is nothing to say, but he's a dirty talker and he wants me to... Well, to talk, as well."

Cora tuts, and Celeste elbows her before turning to me. "And you don't feel comfortable doing that?"

"Oh, I'm uncomfortable, but only because it's so new, and I don't quite know what to say. But his talk feels good."

"You must have loved Declan's kiss," Cora says, wiggling her eyebrows.

Heat covers my cheeks. What? How does she know? "What are you talking about?"

I try to sound nonchalant while panic rises inside me. *No one can know about this.* I know he meant our pro forma marriage, but I'm still freaked out.

Cora shrugs, grinning. "If you found yourself another daddy."

Jesus. I look away, not sure how to respond.

Luckily, Celeste picks up the conversation. "Unlike an orgasm, you can't fake dirty talk. It needs to be genuine. Otherwise it kills the mood."

"Just voice what you're feeling when he's doing something right," Saar suggests.

"Yeah, praising him for his skills always works magic," Celeste says. "Or voicing what you want. Don't be shy."

"Your dick fills me so well," Saar whisper-moans.

"I can't wait for you to fill me," Cora whispers seductively. "Fuck me with your fingers and your cock."

"Or speak French to him." Celeste shrugs, smirking.

I look around, shocked by my friends' openness, but also inspired by it. When did I start believing sex was taboo, or something embarrassing?

Obviously it's not a formal party topic, but that doesn't mean I need to be shy about my needs. Especially with my friends. Or a partner I trust.

Sometimes, I wish my mother hadn't left when I

was a teenager. Or that I had a sister. But it's not like I'm with my family anymore. My family is here and now. And talking to them just made me feel more grounded in my own desires.

Maybe I can become a badass.

"Yuck, that's too specific to your bedroom, and for fuck's sake, I don't want to know you're having sex with my brother." Saar shivers.

"You know your niece was conceived—" Celeste starts.

"Stop it." Saar covers her ears. "Back to you, Lils; don't let any man make you feel like you have to do anything."

"But also, always speak up when you want or don't want something. Even when they are more experienced and dominant in the bedroom, you're in charge. It's your body." Celeste takes the whimpering Amelie from the stroller, and the baby settles immediately.

"I don't know why I feel so mortified to speak up." I look out of the window, replaying our weekend in my mind. With Declan, I feel safe, cherished, and feral with need, so why can't I cross this one line?

"Probably because you want to do it for him," Celeste says.

I frown. "But it is for him."

"But it needs to be for you as well. You need to

enjoy it; otherwise you're just faking it," Celeste explains.

"And let's hope you don't have to fake it with your new, more experienced lover." Cora wiggles her eyebrows.

"Where did you meet him?" Saar asks.

Oh, shit. "At Zach's soccer practice," I lie.

"You need to take me with you next time, so I can get myself a daddy." Cora snickers.

I chuckle, but my nerves twist it into a choking sound. I hate that I'm lying to my friends.

Can I share with my friends? The secrets seem to pile up in my life.

The conversation, though, made me feel strangely empowered. I've had very few choices in my life, and I've enjoyed my autonomy in the last few months. But let's face it, being in hiding, and with limited funds, it's not like I could have truly spread my wings.

Could I possibly find freedom for the first time in my life through my relationship with Declan? Will he push me in real life the same way he seems to challenge me in the bedroom?

Discovering and accepting what I need—what I want—is such an uncharted territory for someone whose life has been planned for them. Can I lean into that?

A smile plays on my face as I realize that, for the

first time in I don't know how long, I feel energized by something. By someone—Declan—of course, but also by the idea of growing into myself.

If only I could be the person I've become, and ignore who I am.

# Chapter 20

## *Lily*

"You need to be really gentle, Zoya," Saar says, lifting a smelly litter box to take it outside.

Saar started volunteering at the shelter after she quit her modeling career. To her husband's initial chagrin, it ended up with them owning an adorable kitten, and recently they adopted a traumatized dog.

I hover with the kids above a box with four tiny kittens. "You can pet them, but with your finger only. Super gently."

"Is Auntie cleaning kitty poop?" Zach, with his arms crossed over his chest, wrinkles his nose.

"Yes, she is preparing fresh litter for the cats." I smile, watching Zoya's attempts to be gentle.

"I think I'm a dog person," Zach says firmly, and walks down the long corridor lined with large cages.

"Once I'm finished here, we will take some of them for a walk, okay?" Saar comes back with the box.

"Lily, can we take these cute kittens home?" Zoya pulls at my sleeve.

"They're too young for that, and you'd need to talk to your dad about it, not me." I try to pull her toward the dogs, hoping that would take that pout off her face.

Her father will kill me if I add a pet to his overwhelming list of responsibilities. He would probably scowl at the added responsibility of having that conversation with Zoya.

The few days since the gala have passed in bliss, with me mostly being busy with the kids because Declan had to leave on an unexpected business trip. I thought the distance would dim the sparkle, but the man calls me every morning and every night like clockwork.

It's exhilarating and confusing. It deepens the intimacy between us, and I'm not sure if that's a good thing. It's like we jumped into this whirlpool of something that doesn't feel casual, but we're avoiding the complexity of our union.

"Okay, let's get the leashes," Saar announces, and Zoya skips behind her while Zach walks with his spine straight, eyeing everything with curious disinterest—an oxymoron to some, a perfectly mastered ability to this little man.

## A Convenient Secret

We get coffees on the way to the nearby dog run, and sit on a bench while the dogs and the kids run around. Or Zoya runs, and Zach roams behind like her bodyguard.

"You finally shed the ugly glasses." Saar nudges my shoulder.

Shit. "I guess I liked the contacts at the gala." I shrug, hating that I lie to my friend. Yet again.

"You looked great. You're such a beautiful woman, Lily. You need to own it."

"Thank you. I'll try."

"Are you okay?" She eyes me for a moment, but then returns her attention to the running dogs.

I sigh. "Have you ever kept a big secret from Corm?"

"I don't think so. Why?"

"I haven't been completely forward about my past with you and the girls, and sometimes, I feel like I'm lying to you."

"Lils, I figured there are things you're not ready to share. You came here to pursue an acting career was what you told Cora at first, but you never go for any auditions. I wondered if those glasses and hair were perhaps a disguise. The long sleeves in this heat are also not completely normal. And, yes, my ego demands you tell me what the story is, but then I respect that you're not ready to share. Or that you can't for whatever reason."

My eyes well up. "Thank you." I wipe a tear. "I didn't realize you're so observant. Do Celeste and Cora know?"

"Yeah, Celeste says we're crazy, but Cora and I, we have a bet running. She thinks you're in witness protection."

I gape at her. "For real?"

"Are you?"

"No." I chuckle nervously.

"You wouldn't be able to tell me, anyway. My money is on a murder."

In the midst of a sip, I almost spit out my coffee. "You think I murdered someone?" I whisper.

She shrugs, mischief in her eyes. "It's always the unsuspected ones."

I shake my head, grinning. "Your imagination is wild."

"Look, you came here, and you found your footing. Whatever you had to leave behind is in the past. You've showed up for us enough times for me to know you would tell us if you could."

"It's not that I don't trust you. But—"

"I know, Lils. Don't worry about it. I'm sure you won't bring danger to us. And I hope that if you do feel in danger, we've proved to you already that you can trust us."

"A million times over."

"You showed up and fit right in. I'm glad I have you in my life."

"You even drank the atrocious coffees I made at Cora's. I don't know why it's so hard to foam milk and prepare a latte."

She snorts. "I never drank them, and it really is not that hard."

I laugh, and then suddenly I just can't keep it all inside me. "My family is very controlling and set in their ways. There was a reason I had to leave..."

Perhaps it's the added secret about me and Declan, but suddenly I feel that if I don't share at least some of it, I will lose my mind.

Saar says nothing, waiting for me to either continue or to drop it. She would respect my choice, and it gives me courage.

"But it was only after I left and was forced to gain my independence that I realized how much I've been manipulated. How little choice I had growing up. How my path was decided for me, not by me. These past eighteen months have been such a great revelation. I learned so much about myself. And I met some amazing people."

Saar smiles at me. "Will you ever go back?"

"I don't know. A part of me is homesick, but I know that a lot will have to change. The newly discovered me wouldn't be able to return to the status quo. And the status quo is too ingrained in my family."

"Does your family know where you are?"

"No, and it has to stay that way."

"You have no contact with any of them?"

I shake my head. I miss my father terribly, but when it mattered he didn't choose me, so I'm not sure he would step up for me if I returned.

"Zoya." Zach's voice spurs us both up from the bench.

"Fuck," Saar curses, but I'm already running toward the kids.

And dogs.

Zoya is wrestling with a large Newfoundland.

"No." I try to stop Zach from rescuing his sister, but I'm too late, and his jerky move spooks a mongrel from Saar's shelter. The dog topples Zach to the ground.

Luckily, Saar interferes, and I focus on Zoya.

With my heart pounding, I grab Zoya's arm, ready to pull her to safety.

"Are you okay?" I gasp, keeping my panic at bay. For now.

Zoya giggles. *Giggles.*

The gigantic dog sprawled over her wags its tail

happily, its massive tongue lolling out as it licks her face with unrestrained enthusiasm.

"I'm cuddling!" Zoya announces, wrapping her tiny arms around the dog's thick neck like she's hugging a giant teddy bear. "His name is Mawshmallow, and he loves me!"

I blink. "You—you're cuddling?" Relief washes over me.

Zach groans dramatically from the ground. "I jumped in to save you," he grumbles, rubbing his elbow as he sits up.

Saar is already helping him, checking for any signs of an actual injury, but he looks more disgruntled than hurt.

Marshmallow's owner issues a command, and the dog rolls off Zoya who sits up. Her hands still wrapped in fluffy fur, she blinks at her brother. "Fwom what?"

"From that." Zach gestures to the Newfoundland, which is now rolling onto its back, paws in the air, letting Zoya scratch its belly.

"Mawshmallow is a good boy," Zoya insists, looking deeply offended on behalf of her new best friend.

Saar smirks, ruffling Zach's hair. "Your heroism is noted, kid. Maybe next time, check if the damsel actually needs rescuing first."

Zach looks from his sister to the dog, his face twisting in disgust. "You *wanted* to be on the ground?"

"I love the gwound." Zoya beams, hugging Marshmallow again as he lets out a happy huff. "It's the best place to snuggle."

Zach scowls. "You're impossible."

Zoya scrunches her nose at him. "I'm having fun."

Saar snorts, covering her mouth, and I bite my lip to keep from laughing as Zach mutters, "God help me."

Just then, Marshmallow stands up, shaking his giant body—and sends a wave of slobber straight into Zach's face.

Zach freezes. Slowly, painstakingly, he wipes his hand across his cheek, looking like he might re-evaluate every life decision he's made in his short life.

Zoya claps her hands. "That means he loves you, too!"

Zach glares at me. "We're never coming here again." He marches to the gate. "Thank you for inviting us, Auntie." He remembers his manners before he reaches the entrance to the enclosure and starts wiping the dust from his clothes.

I look at Saar, and we both turn so he doesn't see us laughing.

\* \* \*

"What happened to you?" Declan stops his descent from upstairs.

I didn't expect him to be home already, and the sight of him in his suit makes my stomach flutter. It's been only a few days, and I almost forgot how good the man looks. Or how drawn I am to him.

"Daddy, we walked the dogs." Zoya runs to him.

Even Zach moves with some enthusiasm to welcome his father. "I missed you, Dad."

He squats to hug his kids, kissing their cheeks. His eyes find me while the two snuggle against him.

The need to run and join them catches me unprepared. His set jaw and hardened gaze even more. I avert my eyes and pick up the backpacks to take them to the kitchen.

"What dogs? And why do you look like the dogs walked you?"

I grin at that while I enter the kitchen area.

"Don't even ask," Zach grumbles.

"I was cuddling Mawshmallow on the gwound, and Zach wanted to save me."

"And I regretted it," the little man points out.

"Okay, you can tell me the whole story later. Go to the bathroom, so you can have a proper bath. I'll be right there."

I busy myself emptying the children's bottles and still feel strangely uneasy about Declan's expression. Is he mad about the dogs? Has he changed his mind about us?

But we spoke this morning, so what has changed?

I feel him enter, and before I turn, he steps behind me, caging me against the counter. He turns off the water.

He doesn't say anything, just stands there for a beat before he lowers his mouth to my ear, and my entire body quivers.

With anticipation.

With recognition.

With need.

"I missed you," he practically groans, and cups me between my thighs.

"I missed you too." I match his groan with a mew, or some unidentifiable sound as he dips his fingers through the crotch of my shorts and sinks them between my folds. My knees buckle.

"Spread your legs," he whispers, the command in his tone igniting wild desire in every cell of my body.

"The kids," I warn, but stand as wide as I can, unable to deny him.

"They are loud enough for us to know their whereabouts in the house." He thrusts at least two fingers inside me. "So wet for me, Seagull. Such a good girl. Whose pussy is this?"

"Yours." I moan loudly as he crooks his fingers inside me, and immediately whimper when he stops moving.

"You will have to be quiet." He chokes out, barely hanging onto his control.

Stepping back, he pushes me between my shoulder blades, bending me over the counter to gain better access.

I bite my forearm to muffle the sounds. He's been at it for a minute and a half, and I'm almost there, completely mad with yearning.

With his other hand he kneads my tits, alternating, as his fingers move in and out without finesse.

It's not gentle or romantic. It's messy and crude. And I explode around his fingers in record time.

"It's nice to be home." He leans forward and kisses my cheek.

I'm going to rest on this counter for a moment, or a day, before I can move again.

Pulling his fingers out of me, a gush of my arousal leaks down my legs. What a mess. Jesus.

He brings his fingers to my lips and smears all around them. "Taste yourself, baby."

I dart out my tongue, and he shoves his fingers inside. Every time I think I've caught up on all my lack of experience, he surprises me.

I suck on my fingers, tilting my head so I can see his face. Full of reverence. Of hunger. Of yearning.

"Daddy, we awe waiting and I'm cold."

I freeze, but Declan seems unperturbed. "Lily is coming to help you."

Bastard.

He reaches for a paper towel and wipes my thighs quickly.

"Me?" I peel myself from the counter and stumble like a newborn lamb.

He points to his crotch and shrugs with a smirk. "I can't go there like this, obviously."

# Chapter 21

## *Declan*

Never had I realized what a cock blocker kids are.

It's been four days since I returned from Chicago, and we've fucked once. Once. I planned to *work* from home this week, but the housekeeper returned. Why do I even need a housekeeper?

I've half a mind to buy another condo in my building for booty calls.

But it's not even about having Lily naked in all possible ways. I miss talking to her. Between unexpected evening meltdowns, falling asleep while reading, and my work demands, we seem to miss each other.

"Are you listening to me?" Roxy taps her pen on her thigh.

I blink, and realize the other three partners are staring at me. "Why do we hold a meeting in my office?"

Roxy narrows her eyes, examining me for signs of a mental breakdown. "You called the meeting."

Shit. "Sorry, it's been a busy morning."

"Daydreaming?" Xander snorts, leaning against the closed door.

I don't even look at him. "I wanted to give you an update on my follow-up from Chicago. The company looks sound, but I have some concerns."

The company in question is a startup that our client, Baldo Cassinetti, wants to buy. A company that we would have bought for him if it wasn't for Lily's keen eye.

"What concerns?" Corm asks from his seat across from my desk.

"I've noticed irregularities in the bookkeeping, and I sent the files to our forensic accountant. He confirmed this morning that the company has been inflating its revenue streams. He also found discrepancies in their expense reporting."

"Fuck." Caleb puffs out air from his cheeks.

"Why didn't you tell us about your suspicions?" Xander throws his arms up in exaggeration.

Because my head has been elsewhere. Mostly in

## A Convenient Secret

my nether region. Because a part of me was more busy trying to figure out why Lily is this savvy with accounting practices. I came up empty-handed, which drives me crazy. Goddammit.

"You know Declan doesn't assume; he always backs up his claims with data," Corm says. Oh, yeah, I guess I still have a reputation for having things under control.

Xander bows his head, shaking it. "Sorry. This was such a good match. Okay, I'll call Cassinetti."

"Are we reporting them?" Caleb asks.

"Is it just creative accounting, or outright fraud?" Corm turns to me.

"I will need to dig deeper. But if it's just creative inflating of their value, we might use it for our advantage and save Cassinetti money."

"Okay." Corm stands. "Xander, talk to Cassinetti. Declan, you dig deeper, and Cal, you should look at their operations to make sure accounting is the only problem. I'll make a few calls to scout a plan B."

Everyone moves to leave.

"Actually, since you're all here," Roxy interrupts.

What now? I fucking want to talk to Lily.

"I have three candidates for the position to lead the London office. Plus the recruitment company suggested two names here in the States who might be interested in relocating. How do you want to proceed?" Roxy looks from me to Corm.

"I don't have time to vet people." Corm shrugs. "Declan will do it."

"Are you kidding me?" I stand up and walk around the table.

All four of us stand in a semicircle, glaring at each other.

Roxy smirks from the corner. "While I enjoy the standoff, I think you should partner up on this one."

We turn to her in unison.

She shrugs. "As charming as you are, gentlemen, if Declan meets the candidates alone, then the three of you would meet with the most promising one afterward. If you do it one by one, it will take ages. If you do it together, you will gang up on them. And in my humble opinion..." She purses her lips, and looks up like she's considering her next words. "In my experience, rather, the more of you together, the less—"

"Don't finish that sentence, Roxy, because I will cut it from your paycheck," Corm growls. "But you're right. In the name of a speedy process, Declan and Xander will do the first round. I will only meet with the final choice."

"I guess my opinion doesn't matter," Caleb grumbles.

"More time with the baby." Corm laughs and saunters out.

I return to my table, grateful to be finally alone. No such luck. Caleb stands in the doorway and closes it. *Come on in, fucker, I have no work. Or other needs.*

"How did you do it?" he asks.

"You need to be more specific." I sigh.

"You had two babies at the same time. How did you cope? I'm fucking exhausted. And worried all the time, and when I'm home I fucking hate all the chaos, so I come here, and I miss them and want to go right back. Sometimes I come here to hide. I fucking hate that, too."

"Good news or bad news first?"

"Does anybody ever want to hear the good first?"

I snort. "The feeling of worry will never go away. Also, the chaos, get fucking used to it."

His jaw ticks. "What's the good one?"

"Amelie will move out in about eighteen years."

"Fuck you, Quinn."

I chuckle. "At the end of the day, amid all that chaos and exhaustion, worry, and that all-consuming need to protect them, you have someone to love. You have someone who loves you unconditionally. You have a daughter."

The corner of his lips curls up. "Amelie is pretty awesome."

"My advice: book a hotel and have a twelve-hour sleep. Then, with an actually functioning brain, decide how to navigate this and devise a schedule that works for you. Two, three days here—the rest, work from home."

"Sleep and scheduling is your answer?"

"Yes. Anything to keep your sanity. Now go away." I turn to my computer.

"I don't think I can go to a hotel and leave Celeste alone." He opens the door.

"Well, Kendra used to do it several times a week while I listened to the night nurse consoling my kids." A wave of rage swipes through me at that time in my life.

"That's fucked-up." Caleb finally leaves.

I close my eyes for a moment, expecting the dark memories to resurface. But what I see in my mind is the smiling woman who landed in my life by accident, and already feels like my safe harbor.

I open the security camera on my computer. I haven't spied on Lily since before the gala, but I can't help myself.

A few clicks, and I find her in her room. Perched on the pillows against the headboard, she's reading in her bed.

Before reason can stop me, I dial her number.

She smiles and answers. Even that small action makes my cock twitch.

"Good afternoon, Mr. Quinn," she says, her voice sultry.

"You can call me sir," I tease.

"Or Daddy?"

I groan. "I will put that mouth of yours to good use the first opportunity I have."

"Those have been scarce lately." She sighs and slides down, sprawling across the bed. She stretches languidly, and I groan again. "Are you okay?"

"No."

She sits up immediately. "What's wrong?" Her genuine concern constricts my chest.

"I miss you."

She plops back down, chuckling. "You saw me this morning, and will see me again in four hours."

"Okay, let me be specific. I miss your pussy."

She shifts a bit, crossing her legs as if she's clenching her thighs together. Or I'm projecting. Regardless, my cock is at half-mast already.

"Would you be a good girl and touch yourself for me, Seagull?"

Her breathing hitches and becomes labored. She doesn't answer.

"Lily?"

"Okay," she breathes. "Will you touch yourself as well?"

She's perfect.

"Wishing it was your hand." I go to lock the door, and when I come back Lily's hand is in her panties, her skirt bunched up around her waist. Fuck.

I unzip my pants and pull out my heavy, angry cock, already leaking pre-cum.

"Where are you?" she asks.

"In my office. I locked the door, and I'm in my chair." I give myself three pulls before I spit on my hand. Why don't I have lube in my office?

"Don't you want to know where I am?"

Fuck. I stop moving and close my eyes for a moment. Am I so far gone in lust that I was going to... Fuck.

"Lily." I clear my throat. "Look up into the corner above your door."

This might be the end of us. What was I thinking? Lily entered my house, and my control collapsed, and with it went my moral compass.

She follows my instructions, and it fucking feels like she looks at me. Her eyes widen, and she sits up.

"Are you watching me?"

I wish I could decipher what emotion is behind her question. Furious? Scared? Excited?

"Yes." I hold my breath.

She narrows her eyes, and it feels like a lifetime before she speaks. "Have you watched me before?"

Okay, I'm leaning toward furious. Better than scared. I think. "Yes."

"Doing what?"

"Only wandering around the house. I would never—"

"Refer to a minute ago. I practically caught you."

"Lily, I—"

"Don't... Just don't. I need to digest this."

The line goes dead. Fuck.

She paces back and forth, and I start packing my things, almost forgetting that my cock is hanging out. I have to go home and talk to her.

Explain. Somehow. How? Apologize. Grovel. Flowers. I need flowers.

What the fuck? I haven't bought her flowers ever, and now I'm going to use them so she looks at my fucked-up actions more favorably? The whole idea feels insulting.

I zip up, and I'm about to turn the monitor off, but the image pushes me back to my chair. Lily is back on her bed, spreading her legs, angled toward the camera.

"Seagull," I groan and turn the feed off. Good punishment, knowing she is getting herself off.

My phone vibrates in my pocket. "Lily." I breathe out.

"Are you still watching?"

Again, I can't detect the tone behind her question. "I've just turned it off."

She remains silent for a beat, and I feel like I will explode from tension, the unresolved energy cruising through me like a series of electric shocks.

"Turn it back on."

The entire world pauses, including my breathing. "Lily, you don't—"

"Do as I say." Her command brings everything to high definition.

Fuck, that was hot. I turn the monitor on and bring the app back to the screen. "It's on."

"I'm all wet for you, Declan," she breathes into the phone, and drops it to the bed. "And mad. Really mad at you, but you're going to make me come over that line so I can work through my anger." She must be on speaker now. Both her hands roam up her thighs.

"Of course, baby."

"But you can't touch yourself. This is for me." She peels off her panties.

"How do you know—"

"Promise me." She opens her legs, and my cock pushes against my zipper painfully.

"I promise," I grit out.

She hums contentedly. "I need this, Declan."

I close my eyes and take a deep breath in. "Can you spread wider for me?"

She scoots her heels closer to her ass and opens her knees.

I grip the armrests.

"Touch yourself, give your clit attention. You're so fucking beautiful, Lily."

Her hand inches between her thighs, and the moan that comes out of her when she massages herself is almost my undoing.

"How does it feel?" I rasp.

"So good," she mews.

The sound has me groaning again. "Does your pussy need to be filled? Is it quivering with that need?" The words scratch my throat, barely passing through.

"Yes. I want you to fill me."

"Imagine it's my hand, Seagull—where would you want it?"

She thrusts her fingers inside herself, and her back arches off the bed.

Fuuuuuuuuck.

I stand up, hoping a few paces back and forth will help my throbbing situation.

"Declan," Lily breathes out, her voice both wanton and innocent. So vulnerable, and yet so beautifully strong.

"My other hand would be squeezing those beautiful tits of yours. Give your nipples some love." I sit back down, unable to move anymore.

She keeps fucking her hand and reaches to squeeze her breast through her T-shirt. She groans and pinches her nipple between her fingers.

"Tell me how you feel, baby." I don't even recognize my voice. I lean back, spreading my legs, but that gives me no relief.

"It's not enough. Your monstrous cock ruined this for me," she whimpers.

And while I want her to find her release, the idea that she needs me now to get there makes me grow a few inches. Figuratively, but also painfully real behind my zipper. I groan again.

"Fuck it." Lily sits up and reaches for her drawer. She takes something out.

Flipping to all fours, she juts her ass up as she shoves a fucking dildo into herself.

"Fuck, Lily, you're killing me here."

She rides the toy, and I reach into my pants. Not to break my word, just to give myself a squeeze. It only makes things worse, but I promised, so now I suffer.

"You should see yourself, Lily. Finish for me."

"I-am-I-am-close."

"That's my girl. Turn to me. I want to see your face."

She shuffles around and leans back on her haunches, thrusting up and down while she looks into the camera.

She cries out, closing her eyes. Her head falls back, the pleasure raking through her body. She's always been beautiful to me, but in this moment... I fucking screenshot the beauty.

The toy falls from her hands, and she collapses to the mattress, a smile lingering on her face.

\* \* \*

Beethoven's *Für Elise* echoes around the house when I arrive. Zach has soccer and Zoya has ballet, so Lily must be with one of them. I came early to surprise them when they returned home. Did I get the days wrong?

I drop the keys and enter the living room to find Lily and Zach behind the piano. I stop in my tracks, first hit by the sight of her. She's smiling and nodding to the rhythm.

The sun bathes the room, illuminating her face as she's looking at my son with pride and affection. The image gets stuck in my throat, making it difficult to swallow.

But it's Zach's perfect, flawless rendition of the

classic that shocks me even more. My son plays the piano?

Instead of soccer?

Behind my back?

I'm hit with so many conflicting emotions, I clench my fists. While the music reverberates around the room, the prevailing one is pride. He's really good.

Zach hits the last notes, and Lily claps. "This was really good. I'm so proud of you, young man."

"I agree, it was really good," I say.

"Dad." Zach scrambles to stand up, his eyes wide.

"You're home early." Lily moves to stand in front of Zach. Not covering him, but clearly getting ready to protect him.

I want to kiss the hell out of her for that.

But does she really think he needs protecting? From me?

"It was amazing, buddy. I didn't know you played. Who taught you?" I cross the room and sit on the vacated piano bench, patting it for him to sit as well.

In the periphery, I see Lily pulling at her sleeves, stepping back, and then returning to stay close.

"Lily taught me. Are you mad?" Zach looks at me, the initial guilt in his eyes gone, replaced by a challenge.

"I'm not mad that you are this good at playing the

piano. It's extraordinary that you managed this at such a young age, and in such a short time."

His face lights up, but then he remembers the circumstances, and his shoulders sag. "But you're mad I skipped the practice."

"I'm not mad at you, Zach. But we will need to address your training absence with your coach. Why don't you go to your room while I talk to Lily, and when Zoya comes home we'll go for sushi."

His eyes widen with excitement. "But it's not a sushi night."

Don't I know it? "We can still go." I ruffle his hair.

"Cool." He gives me a quick hug and leaves.

I stand up, and Lily steps back. Is she afraid of me?

"Dad," Zach calls from the stairs, "don't be mad at Lily. She really is an excellent piano teacher."

"Good to know." I wait for him to turn the corner before I look back at her.

There is fire in her eyes. "Before you talk to him about his responsibility to his team, or not giving up, please hear me out."

I fold my arms. "I'm listening."

She jerks her head, blinking a few times like she didn't expect me to let her talk. Then she squares her shoulders. She is still pulling at her sleeves, though.

"He is really good, and he enjoys it... Unlike soccer. I don't think his talent and interest should be ignored... And why does he have to play soccer? Is it some sort of stereotypical, macho thing? Because I think—"

"Stop blabbering, because I will take you over my knee."

Her eyes widen. "You heard him play."

"Yes, I did, and I agree he's really good. But he is my son, and you decided that going behind my back and skipping his soccer practice is a good thing. You should have talked to me."

"And you would have said that soccer is on the schedule, and it's responsible to do it."

"It is responsible to finish what you started."

"I agree. And it's also healthy and responsible to accept when it's time to let something go. To make room for something new. Let me ask you, is this really about him being responsible and acting with integrity toward the team, or is it about your convenience? You drew up his schedule to fit yours, and the idea of changing it is unacceptable to you."

I step closer to her, crowding her. Her back hits the piano. "You know nothing about the past six years when I was trying to figure out how to do this."

"I can only imagine how hard that was, and it will be for a while, but sticking to your set routine sometimes makes you miss other things in life. You need predictability, I get it. But life is not always predictable."

She touches my ribs, the warmth of her palm burning through my shirt.

That simple gesture almost clears the contradiction in my head. Almost. I open my mouth, but she's not done.

"And what difference does it make to your schedule if he's at soccer or practicing piano? Not much changes for you. Only your son will be happier."

I seize her lips. She stiffens for a beat before she opens up for me. I kiss her to punish her, and to reward her at the same time. I kiss her to punish me. I kiss her because I'm not good with words.

I kiss her because I want to. Because she is mine. Well, I want her to be mine.

"Declan..." she breathes. "Zach is upstairs."

Reluctantly, I step back. "I don't like that you went behind my back."

"I'm sorry I did. I thought that if you heard him play, you would understand—"

"I understand." I nod, not yet ready to acknowledge her accusation about my convenience driving my decisions about the kids. "You still shouldn't have done this behind my back."

"Hello, kettle?" She deadpans and looks up at one of the cameras.

I sigh, closing my eyes briefly. "That's—"

"Don't say that's different. My secret brought joy to your child, and I didn't believe he had a chance to practice if we talked to you."

I sigh. "My secret brought you joy today."

"My vibrator brought me that joy." She folds her arms. "Joy that is still tainted because you invaded my privacy—"

I cup the back of her neck. "It was wrong. But the need behind it was—is—real. I can't help myself around you. You've stripped me of control, of reason, of sanity. I know it's not an excuse, but I need you to understand I've never acted like this before. And a part of me isn't even sorry, because the need to own you, to own every minute of your day is all-consuming."

She stares at me wide-eyed. She's going to bolt now, but the thought doesn't stop me.

I continue, "I recognize that invading your privacy is the lowest of the low, and you don't deserve that. I'm sorry, Lily. I will never do it again."

She licks her lips, her chest heaving. She hasn't stormed out yet, and I don't think I would let her. Fuck, now I'm not only a stalker, but a kidnapper?

"I will never do it again," I repeat when the storm behind her eyes continues, but she doesn't say anything.

A blush covers her face and neck. She swallows and takes a deep breath in. I brace for the end of us.

"I'm not sure if I want you to stop."

Out of all the things she could have said. "Seagull?"

"I'm mad at you, but the idea of you watching me arouses me. Is that wrong?" She looks away. Is she embarrassed?

"At the risk of repeating myself, can you be any more perfect?" I lower my lips to hers. "It's not wrong. Not at all."

"It was wrong that you were doing it without my consent."

"I know. I'm sorry."

"Does it arouse you, watching me sit around?"

"Your existence arouses me. I'm walking around half-hard like a teenager most of the time. Watching you gives me a sense of... I don't know; maybe it's my need for control that takes over. I haven't watched you since the gala night though, but I missed you today. Today, you aroused me. Painfully so."

"But today I gave you a show." She smiles, the wanton confidence fusing with her blushing innocence.

"And what a show it was. Maybe we just discovered our kink." I tuck a loose strand behind her ear.

Her hair is long enough now to be in a short ponytail. I like it off her face. I like her without the fake glasses.

"What are we doing, Declan?"

"Being happy."

In that moment, I want to plan my future with this woman, hoping she can forgive all my deceit as easily as she did this time. And blissfully unaware that the end of us is lurking around the corner.

# Chapter 22

## *Lily*

> I spoke up and it felt really good.

CELESTE

What are we talking about?

SAAR

I think the soccer dad.

CORA

Good for you, Lils. No more uncomfortable?

> Still. But also liberating. I love you all. Thank you.

SAAR

It took sex-related advice for you to realize we're the best?

> Exactly (laughing evil emoji)

CORA

I need a man!!!

> **CELESTE**
>
> I'm sure there is a soccer practice somewhere near you (winking emoji).

"Working?" I lean against the door frame of Declan's office.

The sushi outing was a success, with both kids tired out and sleeping as soon as their heads hit their pillows.

But that's only part of it. After our disagreement, and after all I'd learned about myself today, spending time with Declan, Zoya, and Zach at a casual restaurant felt like... like family.

Like these three people are my closest. Like I can see my future with them, even though I don't think it's possible.

This afternoon, when Declan defended the soccer against the piano, I stood up to him. I haven't done that in the longest time. Without knowing, he encourages me to speak up.

It may have started in the bedroom, or it may have come from sheer frustration, but I know it also came from trust, and safety.

It's like I've grown into myself, shedding the past trauma—not yet all of it—and leaning into my new phase in life.

I didn't know how long I'd be suspended in this limbo of my current life. Not being able to step into my future because my past would catch up and derail me.

Here, with Declan and his family, it feels like an independent path may be possible. It's probably just a naïve fantasy, but it makes me more alive than I've been... ever.

It also makes me want to cherish every moment. I was expecting Declan to sneak into my room, but when he didn't... I came to find him.

"Sorry, I was waiting for the kids to fall asleep, and I lost track of time. This woman's line is obvious for four generations, and then I keep hitting a wall. There are three potential people who could have been her paternal ancestors."

"You know you don't need to impress me with your sleuthing skills." Closing the door, I walk over to the corner and sit on a wing chair. I'm wearing a short, silky nightgown. Nothing else.

I sit un-lady-like at first, my legs wide, before I cross my legs elegantly.

"Seagull," he groans.

"Yes?" I smile, batting my lashes innocently.

He pushes his chair and rounds the desk, but then he stops, studying me from afar. Oh, the need in his eyes makes me so wet, I worry he will need to reupholster his chair. Shit. I hope it's not an antique.

He's wearing a black T-shirt that hugs his muscles like a second skin, and flannel, checkered pajama pants. How can I be this attracted to someone? It baffles me.

"Have you forgotten your underwear?" he rasps, folding his arms across his chest.

I smile. "No, I haven't forgotten."

He narrows his eyes. "You planned this."

"Kind of a spur-of-the-moment decision. Like the unplanned sushi night." I lick my lips. "Who knew you could be spontaneous?"

"I blame that on you," he rasps.

His pants tent, and it gives me confidence. "I always wanted to be fucked against bookshelves. Like that library scene in *Atonement*."

He probably doesn't know the movie.

He groans. "Tell me more about it."

It's a challenge. He doesn't necessarily want the scene description; he wants me to express myself about my desires. I didn't understand why he pushed that at first, but I'm grateful now.

He respects my boundaries—minus the cyber-watching—but he also pushes them, and that's liberating. So I lick my lips and smile coyly.

He's clenching his fists, and I love the reaction. I make an exaggerated spectacle of re-crossing my legs.

"He lifts her leg to the ladder." I lick my lips. "She

is pinned against the shelves behind her. And the camera shows this detail when he thrusts in..." I swallow, suddenly parched, my arousal pooling between my thighs.

"A detail?" Declan rasps, his pupils large, making his eyes even darker than usual.

I swallow again. "He weaves his fingers through hers and holds her arm up, above her head."

It's a minor detail that makes the entire scene more intimate. Like their connection is beyond the act itself.

"And she tells him she loves him," he murmurs.

Shit. I didn't plan on going there, and I didn't know he'd watched the movie. And why would he remember that part?

I stand up, panicked, and glance at the door like I'm scouting exit routes. Am I? I guess my newfound confidence has its limits.

Declan must have the same thought because he lunges at me, whipping us around. "I don't have a ladder." He holds my hands behind me, walking me backward.

"Oh..." This man keeps reducing me to monosyllables. An achievement given my tendency to blabber.

My back hits the bookshelves.

Declan hooks his foot on a stool beside the shelf and drags it closer. He lifts me and thrusts his hips forward, pinning me, while he guides my foot to the chair. "This will have to do."

He raises both my hands above my head, imprisoning my wrists in his large hand. I'm completely at his mercy. I guess that's what I wanted.

"Tell me exactly what you want, little Seagull." His whisper is almost threatening. In response, my body quivers with desire.

With his leg, he pushes my knee farther up, spreading me wider. Without warning, he pushes two fingers inside me. The stretch is nothing compared to his cock, but he already learned the perfect angle.

The moan that leaves me is desperate and impatient.

"So wet for me. So ready. What is it you would like to do against my library, Seagull? And think well, because unlike in the movie, we won't get interrupted. Nobody can save you."

His words should scare me. I've been threatened before, but I recognize there is a promise behind his threat. A promise that will only bring me pleasure.

Now would be the time to remind him we can indeed be interrupted, but I can't find the reason. It dissolves into nothing when this man has his hands on me.

"I want you to fuck me with your fingers. I want to come all over your hand."

"That's a good girl." He inserts another finger.

I'm wild with need, but I think my inability to move heightens my arousal. I yank my hands, trying to free them.

He tuts. "You thought you could come here teasing me and not bear the consequences?"

"I came here to be fucked," I quip.

"And I'm more than happy to oblige, little Seagull." He seizes my lips in a bruising kiss. "You thought you could drive me wild getting yourself off with that pathetic vibrator of yours? As if this pussy didn't belong to me."

He moves with urgency, hitting the right spot. I practically hang suspended from his large palm, my leg all wobbly on the stool. I find purchase on the shelf with my other foot, my thigh leaning over Declan's.

The man is strong. I bite his shoulder to stifle my moans while he fucks me relentlessly with his hand.

"Whose pussy is this?" he growls, crooking his fingers.

"Yours," I pant, and a freight train of an orgasm rams through me, jerking through every fiber of my body.

Declan lets go of my wrists, and my arms fall to his shoulders. He snakes his hand under my ass, and I instinctively wrap my legs around him.

Spent in his arms, I kiss his jaw, his neck, his collarbone, the L word on the tip of my tongue.

But as much as I'm ready to speak up more around him, I don't think he's ready to go there. I don't think I'm ready to bear the consequences of such a declaration.

"I need to be inside you, Lily."

"I need you inside me."

"I need to get the condom from the bedroom."

The idea of him leaving me here all vulnerable, even for a brief second, feels unbearable. It's irrational, but my hormone-laced mind can't cope with the idea. "Don't. I'm clean."

He tilts his head to look at me. "Me too. Are you sure?"

"I want to feel you. I'm on the shot."

He narrows his eyes. "Fuck, Lily. What am I going to do with you?"

He reaches between us, and in one swift move, my back is pressed against the shelves again, and his cock stretches my inner walls, drawing a moan from me.

He covers my mouth with his hand. "You have to be quiet, Seagull." His speech is labored. "Eyes on me."

The books rattle as he rams into me, holding my gaze. With his hand across my mouth, I'm barely getting any oxygen, and all my senses heighten, completely immersed in this moment.

In this man.

In our connection.

Declan doesn't let up, relentlessly chasing our release while he doesn't look away once. It's unnerving and exhilarating at the same time. It's like he fucks me with his cock but is making love to me with his eyes.

The intimacy sizzles, scaring me, but also deepening our bond.

"Who do you belong to, Lily?" he grits out, barely hanging onto his control.

"You," I mumble into his hand.

I know it's only bedroom talk, but my entire being wishes it was the truth. That he would claim me outside of our little cocoon.

"We'll go for ice cream to celebrate the end of school," I announce as we're finishing family dinner.

The weather has eased up in the last few days, breathing reasonable temperatures through sizzling Manhattan. The breeze is so pleasant that I set up our meal on the terrace.

"I have good news, Zach," Declan says, putting his hand on my thigh under the table.

Zach looks up, his eyes twinkling with excitement. "Yes?"

"I talked to your coach, and he understands you will be pursuing other interests."

Zach smiles. "Thank you, Dad."

"I also got you a few lessons with the best piano teacher in New York."

"Dope," he exclaims, but then looks at me like he's seeking permission.

I pierce the strawberry in my salad, trying to calm my heart. "It's a great opportunity for you, Zach. Besides, I can't teach you more." I lean over the table. "Don't tell anyone, but you're already better than me," I fake-whisper to him.

My eyes meet Declan's. A smile lingers on his face as he squeezes my thigh.

Ever since the library, something shifted between us. It's been a week, and we haven't talked about it, but it's undeniable.

Declan has been coming home earlier. He's done a few school pickups with me, so we can spend the afternoon with the kids. Stolen looks, touches and kisses are the norm now. I don't know how long we can pretend.

He's insisted on unplanned family outings, ignoring the color-coded system on his fridge door.

He worked from home for two days this week, though all his *work* occurred in my bed. Not that I'm complaining.

It's moments like these when the longing rattles

through me, unwilling to stay put. The need to reach out and squeeze his shoulder, to hold his hand, to kiss him is growing stronger every day.

But I take what I can get at present. And a family dinner on this luxurious terrace is one of those moments I will cherish forever.

"I can't wait. I'm going to be the best," Zach boasts. "Can I go to my room and call Grandma about it? I will be back for dessert." He's already standing up.

"Can I go to my woom, too?" Zoya asks.

She's been really quiet today. "You haven't eaten much. Are you okay, sweetheart?" I reach to touch her forehead.

"What about that ice cream?" Declan puts his fork down.

"I'm not in the mood fow ice cweam." She slides down and shuffles away, following her brother.

Declan swipes the linen napkin from his lap. Before he stands up, he looks at me. Like we're a team. Like he wants my opinion.

"Go talk to her, and I'll tidy up."

"Leave it and come with me. Let's talk to her together." He extends his hand, and I let him pull me up.

We climb the stairs in silence, and he brushes his hand against mine, squeezing my pinkie.

"I hope she's not coming down with anything," I say.

"Let's find out." He moves his hand on the small of my back as he leads me to her room. While my mind is full of worry, my body tingles with excitement.

"Hey, sweetheart, we came to check if you're okay." He knocks on Zoya's open door.

She sits up cross-legged on her bed, her shoulders slouched. Declan sits beside her, and I stay, leaning against the door.

She looks at me, and then at Declan. "Lily says there is nothing wwong with me, but I think she's twying to be nice."

What is she talking about? And the fact that a six-year-old knows about pretending makes me mad at the world, and sad at the same time. When did she lose her innocence?

Declan glances at me, and then leans toward his daughter. "I think Lily is an honest person, and she would not lie to you."

And there goes my heart, the reminder of my lack of honesty squeezing my stomach. I need to talk to him. I need to tell him everything. He deserves to know.

"Yeah, that sounds like hew." Zoya smiles, but it doesn't reach her eyes. What has wiped that beautiful, always-present grin from her face?

Declan opens his arms, and Zoya crawls into his

embrace. "I agree with Lily; there is nothing wrong with you."

She sighs. "Why can't I say 'w'?"

Declan looks at me like a deer in headlights. I cross the room and sit beside them. "Love, sometimes it takes longer."

She purses her lips, contemplating before she says, "Zach can say it."

Declan sighs, pulling her tighter. He kisses her forehead.

"Do you know when he started walking?" I ask.

Declan raises his eyebrow.

"No." She shakes her head.

"When he was fourteen months old. Four months after you. Today, you are both pretty good at walking. No one can tell when you started." I wink at her.

Declan stares at me.

Zoya perks up. "I was first?" She looks at her dad with expectation.

"It's not a competition, sweetheart." He kisses her forehead. "But if your tongue doesn't obey you by the time Grade One starts, we will take you to a specialist."

"What's a specialist?" She looks from Declan to me.

"Someone that is so good at saying R, they can teach you." I smile at her.

Her eyes widen. "Can we go now?"

"Not right now, sweetheart, but we can make an appointment."

"Tomowow?"

"Sure." He nods. "Let's get ready for the ice cream outing."

* * *

I take a sip of whiskey, leaning against the banister and looking at the flickering city.

"I think I had too much ice cream." Declan joins me.

I chuckle. "Yeah, you definitely did. Are they sleeping?"

"Yes, and I'm exhausted and vibrating with sugar at the same time." He takes away my glass and sips.

"I'm tired, too. It was an eventful day. I haven't felt lonely since I started living here." I take the drink back.

"Kids will do that." He sighs, his elbow touching mine.

"I like it. I like living here with you. It scares me how quickly it's started feeling like home," I confess.

He watches me for a moment, a content almost-smile lingering on his lips.

"Earlier tonight with Zoya, how did you know when they started walking?" He leans in and kisses my shoulder.

"The albums beside the pictures in the dining room—there is one with their firsts. Who made it?"

"My mother. I'm glad you were there when I talked to her. Sometimes I'm so focused on things to do that I forget how to connect with them."

"Don't be so hard on yourself. You made Zach very happy today, and you spoiled them at that ice cream parlor. I wonder, who even are you lately? So reckless and spontaneous." I poke him with my elbow, grinning.

"I can show you reckless and spontaneous and bend you over this banister." Delicious darkness laces his voice.

"Been there, done that," I tease, and he slaps my ass.

Our eyes lock. "We're a good team," Declan says.

"We are." The grin I've been carrying lately may split my face.

His expression grows serious, and he straightens. I follow, turning to face him. Declan tucks a strand behind my ear. "We need to tell the kids."

"That we're a good team? I think they know."

"About us."

And my grin falters. We're a good team, but the admission is tainted. With my secret. With our secret. With the strange circumstances of this union.

"Are you sure?" I ask stupidly, because a part of me

hopes he will wave his hand and say he was just kidding.

"Yes. I want everyone to know."

Jesus. My heart hammers loudly, drowning the rest of the city noise. "I don't know if it's a good idea."

"Why not? I can't pretend with you, Lily. I cannot lie to my children that you're just my nanny—"

"But I am your nanny."

"That's not the point. I'm not saying it's without complications, but you are way more than my nanny. You can't deny that."

It breaks my heart how much trust he has in me. It hurts that I can't be completely honest with him.

I need to tell him who I am, but I don't want all of that to come crashing down on this blissful bubble. Not yet. I need to protect the three of them. Not until I'm sure it's safe.

"Jesus, Declan, you pretended I didn't exist for months. I'm sure you can do a little more pretending."

He frowns. "I thought we were on the same page." The disappointment in his voice stabs me in my chest.

"What is it you want to tell them, Declan? That we're dating? Or that we're married?" I challenge him, because offense is my best defense.

He bows his head. "We will tell them that we're dating."

"Then let's wait until the divorce." The words sound foreign to me.

Declan steps into my space, his nostrils flaring. "I am. Not. Divorcing. You."

Oh, my poor heart. Oxygen doesn't reach my lungs. I can't avoid the truth anymore. He deserves the full story. Then he can decide. Then he will probably divorce me immediately, just to protect his family. I would.

A part of me wants to beg him to give us more time. To allow us to enjoy what we have without my burden spoiling everything. But I can see the hurt on his face. I can't do that to him.

"I have to tell you—"

"Daddy, I can't sleep," Zoya whines, rubbing her eyes by the door.

# Chapter 23

## *Lily*

CELESTE

I need some adult conversation.

SAAR

And I need to know about Lily's dirty talker.

> Lady doesn't tell.

CORA

Lady did ask, so lady owes us some scoop.

> Not much to tell.

SAAR

That sounds like there is something to tell.

CELESTE

Let's find out in person.

> CORA
> Can't wait to see you.

"Thank you very much." I scoop the bouquet from the concierge. The elevator closes, and I carry the flowers into the living room.

Setting them on the table, I pull out the card.

*From Declan*

I chuckle. Efficient as ever. After our unfinished conversation last night, I guess he's pulling out all the stops to get what he wants. I don't think I ever got flowers before. Not from a man.

My mind wanders to my father. The thought shocks me. Not that I don't think of him daily. Or read something about the family in the news, but I've learned to disassociate from that.

He never gave me flowers either. Why does it make me sad, suddenly? Jesus. I banish the sentiment.

I inhale the scent of the red roses and look into the corner. Is Declan watching me? Does he know the bouquet was delivered?

My phone pings.

> DECLAN
> You like them?

A shiver runs through me, and I smile at the camera.

> It's not my birthday.

DECLAN
I know.

> Why the flowers, then?

DECLAN
Just because.

Just because.

I'm going to tell him everything tonight. It might break us—the obligations, the implications—but as I stared at the ceiling last night, unable to sleep, another scenario occurred to me.

One where Declan will accept the reality and help us navigate it together. Because as I confessed last night, I haven't felt lonely since I moved in with Declan. And hopefully, that means I don't have to carry the burden alone.

If Declan is trusting me with his family, welcoming me into it, I can trust him with the drama that comes with mine.

With that cautious determination, I make my way to the bistro.

Celeste waves at me. She is moving the stroller back and forth, smiling.

Cora comes from the back. "Here you are."

"Is Saar coming?" I whisper, leaning over the sleeping baby.

"She's late as always," Celeste says.

"I'm here." Saar rushes around the tables and sits down.

"Why does it feel like we haven't seen each other for ages?" Cora sighs.

"You're not joining us?" I sit beside Saar.

"I need to finish prepping for tomorrow." She swipes loose hair from her glistening cheek.

"Where is the cook you hired?" Saar looks toward the kitchen.

"He quit this morning." Cora plops down beside Celeste, a line of concern splitting her forehead.

"Shit. I'm sorry. Can I help?" I offer.

"Stay away from my kitchen." Cora snorts.

I act indignant. "I will have you know that I can now make sunny-side-up eggs. Okay, I can get them into the pan perfectly. I'm still mastering the scooping out of the pan part."

"So, really, what you're serving is a mess of runny yolk with a potentially fried egg white?" Saar smirks.

"It tastes the same." I fight a smile. "I can call my friend at Summit Solutions and see if they can source you a new one quickly."

"I can't afford to pay for a fancy concierge service.

Or a chef from their database." Cora waves at Sanjay, her server, circling her finger above our table. He nods and starts prepping our coffees, already familiar with our usuals.

"It would be my treat. I broke enough dishes here." I shrug.

"Look at you. I didn't know the nanny position was so lucrative," Cora teases.

Shit. I don't want to tell them I took Declan's ten thousand. The money sits in my account, so this would be a good cause. I was going to donate it, anyway.

"Declan pays a retainer he hardly uses, so really it's paid for already." I turn to coo over the baby, because talking about Declan makes me feel hot all over.

*When you first answered the fucking phone. It was your voice.*

He was into my voice as much as I was into his. How is this my life?

"Talking about Declan, is he the dirty talker?" Saar asks, and I literally stop breathing.

"What?" Cora laughs.

I swallow. I shake the stroller, or rather my hands shake, rattling the stroller. I desperately try to remember how to breathe.

"Why would you say that? Is he the soccer dad?" Celeste looks at me, causing more heat to spread across my cheeks.

Have they known all along? Did Declan say something to his brother?

Has he decided to tell people without discussing it with me? Or finishing the conversation from last night?

*I am. Not. Divorcing. You.*

I turn slowly to Saar. "Yeah, why would you say that?" I go for casual, but it comes out as a squeal. Or maybe only to my panicked ears.

Saar narrows her eyes at me, like my reaction is an epiphany, but then she shrugs. "I'm joking... but have you seen the story?"

"What story?" Cora asks.

There is a story about me and Declan? Where? How public is it?

Saar pulls out her tablet, swipes through, and sets it in the middle of the table.

*New nanny snatches the unattainable Declan Quinn.*

I read the headline several times. It doesn't change the meaning. It only blurs in front of my eyes, constricting my chest.

"Wow, I know I saw you, but you looked really good at the gala." Celeste turns the tablet toward herself and scrolls through the pictures, like my appearance was the point here.

"Let me see it." I snatch it from her.

There are several pics from the gala, and then more of me at school pickup, another one in front of Zoya's ballet school. There are even two or three shots of the kids when we went to the park.

"This is horrible," I whisper.

"It's just gossip. Don't worry about it," Celeste says.

"Fucking vultures. And they dare to photograph the kids. I hate them." Saar pats my back.

Jesus. The children. I've been so shocked and absorbed by the implication of my photographs roaming the internet, I didn't realize the further ramifications.

Of course, everyone else sees the gossip. If they only knew how much truth is in that story.

And, of course, everyone else is outraged about the invasion of privacy. And I am, too—seeing Declan's innocent kids all over some trashy website is disturbing. And so unfair to them.

What they don't see is that my face is all over the internet. Everyone now knows I live in Manhattan. Everyone can track me down. But not everyone will be looking.

My family will.

"Are you okay?" Cora asks.

I shake my head. I need to talk to Declan. Zoya has a ballet recital at her ballet summer school this afternoon, but there won't be an opportunity there. Maybe I can go to his work before that?

"Lils?" Saar urges.

"Why did they even pursue this?" I ask, as if that was relevant.

"They had pics from the gala and decided to fabricate the story around it." Saar shrugs.

I know that. I lived that before. But this time, I can't be discovered. I'm not ready to face my family. Not when things with Declan seem so... promising.

I can't bring danger to his door. I need to prepare him for that first.

"There were other couples there," I point out. It's like finding the reason behind the piece will give me an anchor.

"Like boring married people?" Celeste rolls her eyes. "We are not clickbait anymore. Unless there is cheating."

"Xander was there with Cora." Again, what am I trying to prove? I must have suffered a stroke or something.

"He wasn't looking at me like that." She turns the tablet back to me.

The event didn't allow photographers inside the venue, but there were plenty of them in front of it.

The first photo is of me talking to Celeste while Declan looks at me. The admiration in his eyes is undeniable. He is not ogling me. With that gaze, he is owning me. Claiming me.

Jesus. And, of course, someone snatched that one.

The burden of all the secrets crushes my lungs. I can't do this.

"We've been sleeping together." Some of the shackles dislodge from my stomach. "We don't want people to know. Not yet." I drop the tablet.

"So it's, like, serious?" Celeste speaks first.

I shrug. "Yes. Maybe. I don't know. There is a lot we need to unpack first. I'm sorry I didn't tell you... But with the kids... And with everything else... I—"

"Hey, hey." Saar wraps her arm around my shoulder and squeezes. "You don't owe us anything. You would have told us at some point."

"I'm not sure how I feel about knowing Declan talks dirty." Cora scrunches up her nose.

"Let's pretend it was someone else." Celeste picks up Amelie to feed her.

"Thank you for understanding. I'm such a cliché." I chuckle humorlessly.

I try—and fail—to ignore the fact that I'm yet again not telling the whole truth. Because we're not just lovers. He is not just my employer. We're married.

I should have never married him. It only layers more complexity over my life, our lives, at the moment. What was I thinking?

Not that I don't want to be his wife. Oh my God, I do want to be his wife. I need to talk to him and explain everything. With these pictures, my secret may be out soon, and I need to own the narrative.

"I better go. Zoya has a recital." I stand up.

"She invited me too. Let me call my car." Saar joins me in saying goodbyes.

"Don't worry about it," Celeste whispers. I put my hand on Amelie's back, the warmth of the newborn giving me unwarranted peace.

We get into Saar's car. "So you and Declan. Maybe we'll be sisters-in-law." She winks, smirking.

*We already are.* I smile at her, hoping my internal conundrum doesn't show.

"The pictures..." she starts. "They put you in danger?"

The cars honk and move like molasses through the Manhattan traffic. "Let's hope not." I sigh.

Living in my cocoon here, the danger became distant—still lurking around the edges of my mind, but somehow removed, residing in my head only, well-guarded. A memory. A secret. But now?

The kids. Declan. What I wanted to prevent seems to come crashing in on my little bubble. Did I really believe I could disconnect from my past this easily?

"If my family finds me, it will be difficult," I add.

"I respect that you have reasons not to share, but

now my niece and nephew are involved, and Corm's brother... They are my family, so please promise me that you will ask for help if needed."

I reach out to squeeze her hand. "Thank you. I will explain everything soon. I trust you, Saar. I've been quiet because I felt that the more people know, the easier my family can find me. I wanted to protect everyone."

"Are you in the Mafia?" she whispers, like somebody can hear us.

I snort. And it feels good to feel some mirth after the turmoil. "You really have a wild imagination. I'm sure some of my family is morally dark gray, but nothing organized."

"That sounds ominous."

"That was put diplomatically." It feels good to talk to someone. "I would tell you more, but Declan deserves to know first."

She smiles at me. "Fair enough. Before Corm, I would be offended, but now having someone who is always my first for everything, I understand."

Is Declan my first? Will he want to stay my first when he knows who I am?

The man doesn't want any complications. Will he accept mine?

## Chapter 24

## *Lily*

"Lily, Auntie!" Zoya runs to us. "I have to go backstage now. Whewe is Daddy?"

I squat to kiss her cheek, and she wraps her little arms around my neck. It's an automatic gesture, but in my current state it brings tears to my eyes.

"He's on his way. You go to your group and focus on the performance. I can't wait to see you on that stage."

She gives me a wet kiss. "I have a feeling it's going to blow evewybody's mind." She winks at me and hops away.

I chuckle. That girl won't get lost in this world. With her confidence and her loving family, she will slay.

Saar looks from the hopping Zoya to me. "I'm pretty sure we'll be sisters-in-law."

I sigh.

She pokes me, smirking. "What? That girl adores you. And you're sleeping with her father," she whispers. "I see a happily-ever-after."

"Saar." We both turn. "Lily." Declan's mom smiles at us, Zach walking behind her, frowning.

"Dorothy, were you spending a day with this young gentleman?" Saar hugs her mother-in-law.

"And what a delight it was, wasn't it, Zach?"

He bows his head briefly, the same way his father does. "We went for high tea and an art auction."

I blink. "Wow. Did you have a good time?"

"Some pieces there..." He sighs. "I don't think something that looks like someone spilled ketchup on it should cost a million dollars." He shrugs, putting one hand in the pocket of his pants. "And now I have to finish the day here."

"Zachary," Dorothy warns.

"You don't want to see your sister's recital?" Saar asks.

"I'm not inclined to support her after that disastrous day at the dog run."

I bite my lip so as not to laugh. "Zach, she's your sister, and you might have different interests, but as a gentleman and as a good brother..." I squat down in front of him. "I know Zoya would appreciate your support."

"Please take your seats. We're about to start," someone announces.

"Go get us seats; I'll wait for Declan." I send the group ahead.

I won't have time to tell him everything now, but I want to see him at least. It's like seeing him, even with all the secrets hovering above us, would make everything instantly better.

And it does.

He rushes inside the hall, and it's like lightning strikes me. My body is buzzing immediately, but it's my heart that swells. The lump that lodged in my throat when I saw the article loosens just slightly.

Dressed to the nines as always, he looks like a movie star in his gray pin-striped suit. Even hurrying, he immediately commands the room.

The lines on his forehead smooth when he sees me.

"I'm sorry I'm late." He extends his hand, but stops himself like he just remembered he's greeting his nanny.

"You're right on time. Saar, Zach, and your mom are inside already."

"Thank you for waiting for me."

We stand there and grin at each other like idiots.

Everything will be okay. With his adoring gaze on me, we will face everything.

And perhaps everything is not as bad as I inflated it in my head. People leave their past behind them all the time.

\* \* \*

I sneak out to an alcove just off the atrium where all the parents and kids celebrate the recital.

Leaning against the cold, white wall, I let the sun bathe my face through the arched window. Just a short breather to organize my thoughts.

The presumed benefit of running away and assuming a new identity was that I'd never have to think about a scenario when my new life would collide with my past one.

I knew that I would either start anew, or be forced to return to the old. With Declan and the kids in the picture, I need to find a combination.

But how? Declan puts his kids first. As he should. He loves his perfectly organized, planned life.

"Penny for your thoughts." His voice washes over me, soothing my aching soul.

"How did you find me?" I smile.

He steps closer, the alcove hiding us. "I'm drawn to you like a moth to a flame." He lowers his lips to my temple. "But we should go back, before I pin you against this window and make sure that you walk around with my cum all over your thighs."

My knees buckle. How does he do it? "I need to talk to you," I utter, before I lose the nerves.

"I know we need to talk. I'm sorry I pushed last night. Of course we can do things on your timeline. I'll wait if you're not ready." He strokes my cheek.

Oh fuck, if that was the only cloud above our heads. "Declan, there was an article—"

He puts a finger on my lips. "Don't worry about that. My lawyer served them a cease-and-desist order already. It will be down by the end of the day."

Could it be that easy? I may not be discovered after all. That would make things easier, or not. I don't know anymore. I need to explain the situation to him.

"Don't worry about it, Seagull." He kisses my forehead. "Let's go back and try to get out of here as quickly as possible."

He leads me back to the atrium, his hand on the small of my back. Until he drops it when we join the mingling crowd. I want him to keep it there. And he made it clear he wants to keep it there, but I stopped him.

I stopped him, because I wasn't brave enough to tell him my story earlier.

Tonight.

The determination grows strong inside me suddenly. I don't want to hide anymore.

That thought thrills and scares me, but the courage floods my veins.

Tonight.

I will bury Lily Thorne, or the hidden parts of me.

Tonight.

The atrium hums with polite chatter as parents mingle. I stay close to Declan as we find the twins and Saar.

"Yes, Zoya, you were exceptionally good on that stage." Despite his words, Zach looks unimpressed.

"Try to kill her with kindness, little dude." Saar ruffles his hair. "Ah, here you are." She turns to us.

"Thank you for staying with them," Declan says, looking equally unimpressed at his son.

Is he kinder to me only? I spent so much time with him alone that I forgot about the aloof, grumpy version of him. It became only one layer of this man for me.

I guess that one is still available to the rest of the world. For some reason, it makes me grin.

"If you don't mind, I'm going to dash now." She turns to Zoya. "You stole the show, girl."

As soon as she leaves, the twins go to get a juice refill. Someone approaches Declan, who steps closer to me while he engages in a polite conversation.

My eyes roam the room, and I feel the weight of

judgment. People are staring at me. Or at Declan. Or at us. Do people read the trashy pages?

Declan concludes his conversation and turns to me. "Ready to leave?"

A tall, perfectly put-together woman approaches, blond hair swept into a sleek chignon, a designer clutch tucked beneath one arm.

"Declan." The voice is smooth, practiced, and edged with just enough artificial sweetness to set my teeth on edge.

She places a manicured hand lightly on Declan's forearm as if she has every right to touch him.

I don't like her. Acid coils in my stomach, my gaze glued to those sharp, red nails.

Declan's jaw tightens almost imperceptibly, his posture stiff but polite. "Margot."

She smiles or purses her lips; I'm not sure which. She gives me the briefest once-over before she dismisses my existence entirely.

"I was hoping I'd see you here." She juts her chin forward like she is taking a selfie. "I have a box at the Met tomorrow night. I thought you might enjoy the performance. Just us, of course."

Declan inhales sharply through his nose. "I'm afraid I have plans."

She leans closer. "Cancel them," she purrs.

He doesn't even blink. "No."

I suppress a smirk.

Margot recovers quickly with a faux laugh. "Come on, Declan. The children are old enough to have an evening without you hovering." Her voice dips, turning honeyed. "And you could use a break. A little fun."

I'm standing right here, for fuck's sake. I have no public claim on him, but get a room. Or not. No rooms for her and Declan.

But some decency. Who arranges their dates openly in front of others?

Declan's shoulders tense, and this time, when he speaks, his voice cools by a few degrees. "I don't need a break from my children."

Margot waves a dismissive hand. "Of course not, but I imagine you could use a break from... everything else." Her gaze flicks to me again—this time lingering just long enough to feel like a deliberate slight.

Declan straightens, his expression carefully neutral. "Margot, this is Lily Thorne."

Margot offers a tight, insincere smile, but doesn't extend a hand. "Ah. The nanny."

I've dealt with small-minded people all my life. I open my mouth, but Declan gets there first.

"No," he says, his voice firm, final. "She's not the nanny."

Margot blinks, finally caught off-guard. "Oh?"

Declan puts his hand on the small of my back. "Lily is with me."

There's a beat of silence. A charged, palpable pause. Oh shit. I wish I could celebrate this public display of his intentions triumphantly. And a part of me indulges in the feeling. If only things were so easy.

Margot's lips tighten at the corners, her carefully maintained poise slipping just enough for me to see the irritation flash behind her eyes.

"Well," she says, forcing another smile. "That's... unexpected."

I arch a brow. "Is it?" I say sweetly.

Declan's lips twitch, just barely, and I know I've won this round.

Margot's nostrils flare before she turns sharply on her heels and disappears into the sea of parents.

I try not to roll my eyes, feeling the circle of mothers' eyes on me. When I glance up, I'm met with an amused expression. Declan is watching me, clearly not concerned about the crowds.

His lips twitch. "You're jealous."

I scoff. "Am not."

His expression turns downright pleased. "You didn't like her touching me."

"I didn't like her existing," I grumble.

Declan chuckles, low and knowing, before leaning

in, his breath warm against my ear. "You have nothing to worry about, Seagull."

A shiver runs down my spine, and I don't even bother pretending it's from the air conditioning.

Declan pulls back, his hand on my lower back again as he steers me toward the lemonade station. "Now, let's find the twins before you start plotting Margot's disappearance."

I lift my chin. "You assume I haven't already."

He chuckles. "Let's save the kids from sugar poisoning and get out of here."

"Has your mom left?"

He groans. "Right, we need to weave through this crowd to find her as well."

"Daddy," Zoya calls out, and we both relax, finding her with Zach and Dorothy.

All of us file out of the room, and that sense of belonging that has been growing inside me for weeks now blossoms as I look at our little unit.

A family I never thought I would find.

"Where is your car, Mom?" Declan asks as he opens the doors of his, watching the twins climb in.

"It will be here any moment." She bends to wave at the kids. "Zoya, you were phenomenal. I can't wait for our vacation."

"Bye, Gwanny." Zoya sends her an air kiss.

"I'm glad you could come." Declan gives his mother a peck on her cheek.

"I wouldn't miss it."

"It was nice to see you, again, Dorothy." I step toward the open door.

"Actually, Lily, can I have a word?" Dorothy stops me.

Declan frowns. "What's going on?"

"Just get in and wait a moment. I won't keep her long." Dorothy weaves her arm through mine.

Declan hesitates, but after a moment gets into his car.

His mother smiles at me. "We don't have much time, my dear, but I wanted to ask you for an explanation."

What's going on? Can I survive more pressure today? "An explanation?"

"Not to me, but Declan deserves to know."

She knows? What does she know? It's a good thing she has her arm through mine, because I might just collapse right here. *Think, Lily, think.*

"I have a dear friend in London, Lady Beatrice Fitzpatrick..." She pauses, expecting the name to be familiar.

And it is very familiar.

Dorothy knows who I am.

When I remain silent, she continues, "You see, I

showed Beatrice pictures from that gala. Those were the newest photos of my boys."

I let things go too far. But also, we let things go too far. This woman—Declan's mother, Zoya and Zach's grandmother—doesn't know we are married.

Not that after the exposé, and Declan's not-so-subtle "she's with me", Manhattan society won't assume we're a couple.

But married? In secret? Behind everyone's back? As a business transaction?

I left my previous life because I didn't want to let my father down. And I'm doing just that in this life.

"I will talk to him." I want to explain myself, and at the same time run away from this conversation.

"Thank you. I don't know why you're hiding who you truly are, and it's none of my business. But my son and my grandchildren are my business, so please, don't keep secrets from Declan. He's been burned by a woman before, and I see how he looks at you. He looks at you like you're his second chance. Are you?"

I swallow again, tears rimming around my eyes. God, I want to be his only chance. He is mine for sure.

"Just tell him who you are, Liliana Spinelli." She studies me for a moment and then perks up, letting go of the heaviness of the conversation. "Ah, there's my car." She kisses both my cheeks like we're best friends and leaves.

The heaviness of the conversation stays behind. I stare at her disappearing car, mourning the simple life of Lily Thorne. Desperately wishing she wasn't the heiress who, once discovered, would need to return to her heritage or fight to stay away. Let's hope Declan is ready to fight along with me.

*I felt helpless and out of control for so long. I will never cross that line again.*

## Chapter 25

### *Declan*

"Good morning." Lily comes to the kitchen, looking like a ghost, her voice raspy. "You slept like the dead beside Zoya when I came to find you."

"Good morning." I peek behind her into the room beyond. Coast is clear, so I kiss her crown. "Yeah, I can't believe I slept in there all night. Sorry."

"It's okay." She starts the coffee machine. Is she just sleepy, or is something off?

I lean beside her, tucking the messy hair behind her ear. I need to touch her all the time; it's like my next breath depends on it. "Zoya was overexcited about the recital, so it took a while to calm her down."

"I didn't sleep much." She reaches for her portable cup and fills it with coffee.

"Are you still worried about that article? It's been taken down."

She opens her mouth to say something.

"I'm weady." Zoya barrels into the room. "Good mowning, Lily."

My daughter wraps her arms around Lily's legs.

For the first time in ages, I feel like this is a real home. All thanks to the woman in front of me.

She has secrets, and we need to discuss how we will announce this relationship to the kids and everyone else. But there is no doubt in my mind I want her by my side.

I want to shout it from the rooftops, but my kids were abandoned before, so a carefully thought-out plan is a must. I can't throw a curveball into their lives, especially not now when things are going so well.

"Good morning, sweetheart. Are you excited about your camp?" Lily bends to kiss Zoya.

"It's an outdoor activities camp; what is exciting about that?" Zach enters, scowling.

"You can survive some fresh air for three days," I say.

"Besides, today is your first real piano lesson," Lily reminds him.

That gets us an almost smile out of him. "Perhaps I should stay home and practice. Outdoor camp just sounds dirty."

## A Convenient Secret

Zoya rolls her eyes. "Jeez, bwo, live a little." She takes Lily's hand. "Let's go."

"Go call the elevator while I put the cover on my coffee." Lily frees herself from Zoya's clutches, and the twins leave the kitchen.

"I guess my daughter now speaks like a true New Yorker." I snort and kiss Lily's cheek. "What did my mom want yesterday? You were awfully quiet on the ride home."

"She just wanted to confirm some details about the kids' schedule." She busies herself with her mug, missing the ridges to screw the cap on.

"Let me." I take it from her and fix the lid on. A blush covers her cheeks. God, she's adorable. "Here you go. I'll see you at one."

"At one?"

"The luncheon for my mother's charity? Did you forget?"

"You really want me to go with you?"

"Of course."

"But people would—"

"I don't care about that. Saar and Celeste are coming too. I don't want to go to these tedious functions alone anymore."

"But you shouldn't go there with your nanny."

"Do you want me to invite Margot?" I tease.

Lily huffs. "Don't you dare."

I laugh. Fuck, it's refreshing to laugh in the morning.

"I have to go drop the kids, Declan, but we need to talk about us before we do these public appearances."

"And we will. It's not like I'm going to announce that you're my wife. I'll just sit beside you through some boring speeches." I lean in, relishing the shiver that rakes through her. "Maybe finger-fuck you under the table."

She moans. "Maybe we can ask Saar if the twins can have a sleepover tonight, so we can talk?"

"If there are no kids to interrupt us, I have better ideas than talking."

"Declan," she warns, glaring at me.

"I was expecting a more enthusiastic reaction. But okay, let's see if Saar risks traumatizing her precious pets and takes on the kids. Maybe we can take them for an early supper and then drop them off."

"Good, I'll arrange it with her. We will talk first, though."

Something definitely feels off. She brings sunshine into every day and every conversation, but right now she seems on edge.

Is she going to try to delay our announcement? Does she want to continue the secret? "Are you okay?"

She closes her eyes briefly. "I need to tell you who I am."

Finally. It cost me a lot of effort to stay away from sleuthing her past. On some level, I needed her to tell me. To trust me enough.

She finally trusts me enough. Something grows in my chest. But I hesitate when I see her tortured expression.

"I don't care who you were, Lily. I know who you are now, to me, to my kids. That's what matters."

She smiles; it's a shy smile that doesn't reach her eyes. "Okay, we will talk tonight and turn a new page."

"We've been waiting fow ages," Zoya calls from the entrance.

\* \* \*

"Both candidates look good on paper. I was impressed by both of them." Corm rounds his desk and joins the rest of us in his seating area.

My eyes land on the oversized photograph of Saar, and I realize I don't find it ridiculous. I would plaster my entire office with images of Lily.

She is one of a kind.

She is mine.

The worry in her eyes this morning gutted me. I don't want her to have secrets, and I fear I won't understand. It's not like she's a murderer. Is she?

Fuck, I should have pushed sooner. At this point,

I'm so far gone with this woman she could be a visitor from outer space and I would just shrug.

"Okay, I'm going to be the asshole who says it, but I think we should hire the guy." Xander clicks his pen, grating on my nerves.

"On account of being equally qualified as Ms. Drake, the female candidate?" If looks could kill, Roxy would be arrested for murder now.

Xander doesn't even flinch. "Unfortunately, yes. I don't like it, but it's the reality."

"You make me sick." She stands up. "I don't mind working in a boy's club. I can laugh off a lot of your *innocent* comments because I'm snarky and sarcastic myself, and I take it all as team banter. Never have I felt like just a woman among you. But I don't want to listen to this conversation. You disappoint me." She reaches the door.

"Don't be dramatic, Roxy. Please sit down," Corm says, his tone almost gentle but the demand behind it undeniable.

"Or what?" She glares at him.

"Or we will not have minutes from this meeting, and you won't be able to sue us for discrimination." He shrugs.

She narrows her eyes. "You *are* discriminating!"

"We're putting the company's interests first," Cal argues.

"Then we should hire Vivienne Drake," I chime in, and all heads turn to me. "She would not require a sign-in bonus, and she is available sooner."

"Roxy, please, don't take it the wrong way; I'm just raising a point to consider." Xander holds his arm toward Roxy like he wants to physically stop her from speaking. "And if she gets pregnant in a month or two, we will go through this again? Risk the stability?"

"For the youngest member of this team, you're about as progressive on this issue as an ashtray in a maternity ward," I grumble.

Seriously, I can't believe we're having this conversation.

"Or as in a boardroom where a woman is only taking notes," Roxy deadpans, but at least she sits back down.

"Oh, come on, so now you demand we hire the woman and make her a partner." Caleb snorts.

"Roxy, what these idiots are so *eloquently* trying to consider is that we can't afford to hire someone if they won't give it their all for the next three years." Corm leans forward, looking at Roxy with a kind of softness I have rarely seen in his eyes.

Roxy crosses one leg over the other and mirrors his pose, before she sticks her pen into the high bun on her head. "What you're saying is that you can't risk hiring a woman because what if she gets pregnant. Then hire the man. Hopefully he won't get hit by a truck tomorrow, or overdoses before he starts. Or—"

"Okay, you made your point." Corm stops her with his hand raised.

"We have the fundraiser to attend; why don't we sleep on it and vote tomorrow?" Cal stands up, buttoning his jacket.

"I suggest Roxy votes with us," Xander says, and we all turn to him, Roxy perhaps the most surprised.

"Only partners have voting privileges." I stand up. I get Roxy's point, but rules are to be obeyed.

"Maybe we can include her to make sure the female perspective is included." Xander pushes off the sofa.

"You're an idiot. Her point was that gender shouldn't be any part of this consideration." I walk to the door.

"Are we driving together?" Corm asks.

"I'm picking up Celeste at home, so we'll meet there." Cal heads for the door.

"I have a stop to make, and would like your help," I tell my brother.

"Okay, downstairs in five?" Corm turns to check his phone.

"Sure, I'll go by myself," Xander whines.

I get to my office, and unfortunately he follows. "I made an ass of myself."

"A rare moment of self-reflection?" I snort and lean against my desk.

"But I'm right; there is a threat."

"I don't think a woman having a child is a threat. Unless you're an emperor ready to usurp someone's throne. In that case, having an heir matters."

"Are you suggesting my view is medieval?" He chuckles.

"Outdated at the least. Enough chitchat; get out of my office." I round my desk to get my valet, ready to get out of here.

"What, do you have a jerk-off session scheduled?"

"Fuck you, X."

"You're warming up to me; only the closest call me X," he mocks.

"Get the fuck out of here."

## Chapter 26

### *Declan*

"What are we doing here?" Corm complains as we enter the jewelry store.

"Buying a ring." I shrug, a part of me wanting my brother there and a part dreading the explanation. Maybe I should have come alone.

"A ring?" Corm's eyebrows shoot up as the glass door swings shut behind us.

The store is all polished marble and hushed elegance. The lighting is deliberately soft, casting a glow over the displays of diamonds and gemstones—nothing too harsh, nothing too loud.

"Do you have a hearing problem?"

Corm snorts. "Did you knock someone up? Is that why I'm here?"

I sigh. "No."

He nods solemnly. "Then you're being blackmailed."

"Fuck you. You're such an idiot."

He smirks, unfazed. "I'm just trying to narrow it down. I didn't know you were even seeing someone."

"The ring is for Lily," I blurt out.

"That seems excessive for a babysitter." Corm peruses the displays.

"Don't be a dickhead; I'm trying to tell you that Lily and I..." Now is where it gets complicated, because I don't necessarily want to tell him I married her already. But calling her my girlfriend isn't right either.

"You hooked up?"

"Don't call it that."

"Jesus, talking to you is like pulling teeth. Is this a consolation gift, so she understands that it was a one-time thing?"

Where does his mind go? "It's not a one-time thing. I'm serious about her."

He cocks his head. "Isn't she like half your age?"

"Fuck you, Corm. She's ten years younger. But, to my surprise, it doesn't seem to matter to her."

"At least she can keep up with your kids, old man." He smirks.

A sales associate approaches, immaculately put together in a sleek black dress and with a sharp smile.

"Mr. Quinn, welcome. My name is Claire. We've prepared a selection for you. Would you like to step this way?"

Corm gives me a sideways glance as we follow her to a private consultation area—a glass-topped table surrounded by plush chairs, discreetly tucked away from the main showroom.

"So you made an appointment? Damn. You really are serious about her."

I drop into a chair and ignore him.

Claire sets a velvet tray in front of me and lifts the cover with a flourish, revealing an array of engagement rings. They're... fine. Elegant, classic, and completely unhelpful.

Corm scratches his jaw. "So what are we thinking here? Something small and subtle? Or are we going full-on 'I own a sports team' levels of obnoxiousness?"

"Something in between."

He gestures vaguely at the tray. "Then congratulations, you've got fifty versions of that right here."

I exhale slowly, studying the rings. A few have sleek, modern bands; others have intricate detailing. Some are massive, others more understated.

None of them says Lily.

Claire clears her throat delicately. "Do you have any preferences? Style, setting, gemstone shape?"

Corm leans in conspiratorially. "Do you sell rings

that come with a cheat sheet? I don't think my brother knows if it's an engagement ring or just an 'I like you very much' ring, or perhaps a 'please don't leave—I can't look for another nanny' ring."

I shoot him a look. "You're not helping."

"I'm not the one who invited me."

Claire keeps her professional smile intact. "Does she wear jewelry often?"

"She doesn't like anything too... much," I say after a beat. "Something classic. Timeless. But not boring."

Claire nods, already flipping through another tray of rings. "Perhaps an oval cut? Or something with a hidden halo? Elegant but understated."

She places a ring in front of me—a delicate platinum band with an oval-cut diamond, the setting clean and modern, but not over-the-top. It catches the light in a way that reminds me of Lily's eyes when she laughs.

"This one."

"You sure? You barely looked at the others," Corm asks.

"I don't need to."

His smirk fades slightly. Not much, but enough for me to notice. "Damn. You're really in it, huh? It doesn't surprise me actually."

"It doesn't?"

"I mean the woman stabbed you, and you didn't even fire or report her; you hired her permanently.

She is great with your kids, and you stared at her like she was your lunch at the gala. You also almost ripped Xander's head off when he teased you about her."

Fuck, all of that happened before we even slept together. Tonight, I'm not giving up. We're fucking announcing everything to everyone tomorrow.

I pay for the ring and put the box in my pocket.

I search for any signs of heaviness in my chest. But with the ring weighing in my pocket, I only feel lighter.

\* \* \*

"Here they are," Saar exclaims as we enter the foyer. Cal and Celeste are beside her, but I ignore them and approach Lily.

"Hello to you, too," Saar says sarcastically, while I pull Lily to the side.

"You look wonderful." My eyes roam down the simple black dress that hugs her body, leaving me desperate to peel away the layers and taste her.

"I got more flowers today." A smile lingers on her face. "Why?"

"Just because." I itch to touch her, painfully aware of the room full of people.

"Just because." She repeats the words like they are a secret promise.

Not exactly the words, but our own language to use in the meantime while we're finding our way.

It's like our whiskey-sharing ritual.

The sounds, the people, the surroundings cease to exist as I stare into her eyes, and resist the urge to bend her over backward and kiss her. Soon.

"I better talk to Saar about tonight," she says hurriedly and starts to leave, but then she stops. "Do you think they will be okay with her?"

Her concern is like an arrow to my heart. I fucking love this woman. "They will be fine, Seagull. We need an uninterrupted talk."

Suddenly, that conversation seems like a nuisance. I want to claim her, right here, right now. I want to tell her how I feel about her. I want to be with her. I want—I need—everyone to know she's mine. And I'm hers.

She smiles. "Okay."

I mingle with my partners before we are all ushered into the dining room.

"Where is Xander?" Cal asks as we get to our table.

"He should be here any moment." Corm moves the chair for Saar to sit.

We eat appetizers and talk—something I always considered quite tedious, but with Lily by my side, the occasion is pleasant. There are people I respect around this table; I just never had much interest in finding out more about them.

Well, I know my brother, of course, but I've been involved so much in my own personal drama, I've never cared to indulge others.

Yet Lily does it so effortlessly, she pulls me into her chatty world.

"Cora," Lily exclaims as they serve the main dish.

I turn to see the redhead rushing to the table with Xander in tow.

"What are you doing here?" Saar grins. "This is wonderful."

Cora shrugs. "This guy reimbursed me for keeping my bistro closed, and I came here with him."

Everyone looks at Xander. "This wasn't something I expected you to share."

"I'm excited to be catered to instead of serving others for a day. You did me a favor." She grins at him and sits down. "Thank you." She shrugs her shoulders, grinning at the server who put a plate in front of her.

"Never had I thought I'd see a day when Xander pays for his plus one." Corm smirks.

"Yeah, that used to be yours and Declan's thing," Caleb says.

"Fuck off." I glare at him, and squeeze Lily's thigh under the table.

"Don't worry, Lily, ever since you showed up he's been acting more human." Corm leans in, his voice hushed with a knowing edge. "It seems you're good for the twins and for him."

Motherfucker.

Lily looks from me to him and back. Immediately, she guesses I shared with him. She glares at me for a moment, pursing her lips, but it looks more like she is trying hard not to grin.

"I'm going to the lady's room." Celeste stands up.

"I'll join you." Lily puts her napkin down.

"Where did the two of you go before this?" Saar asks.

"Jewelry store." Corm doesn't miss the opportunity to mess with me.

Saar looks from me to him, puzzled.

"Yeah, just wait for your present." I smile at Saar, giving Corm the I-can-return-the-favor-brother look.

Saar's eyes widen. "Oh, you know the way to my heart," she teases, rubbing Corm's arm. "What did you get me?"

He glowers at me before he takes her hand, kissing it. "It's a surprise."

Celeste and Lily return, and my attention moves from my brother. Lily's face is white as she keeps looking over her shoulder.

"Are you okay?" I help her to her seat.

Her eyes dart around before she gives me a

distracted smile and then shakes her head. "It's nothing. I thought I saw someone."

I look around for... I don't know what.

Whoever she thinks she saw changed her demeanor; her eyes are roaming around with something akin to fear in them. Her shoulders are tense, and her jaw is set so rigid it must hurt.

An urge to wrap her in my arms is overwhelming. I'm about to drag her out of here when she puts her hand on my thigh.

Seeking comfort? Or calming me down?

I cover her hand with mine, and she exhales a long breath, giving me a quick smile before she turns to the table.

"Since this circle is quite tight, and I know I can explicitly trust most people here and hopefully, by extension, all of you..." She takes another fortifying breath.

"What's going on, Lils?" Saar frowns.

"You might hear things about me soon. The photos of me, the public appearances... Anyway, I want you to know the basic story before it gets out of control." Her hand quivers in mine.

"Lily," I utter, not knowing what's going on but wanting to help somehow.

She gives me another tight smile. "I came to New York to hide from my family." She speaks softly, but with confidence. "My family runs a successful business, and it became a point of competition between my father and his half-sister.

"All the business affairs are under my father's control. After my brother had a fatal accident, my father essentially lost his heir. Enter the spare. I was only seventeen at the time, and I dropped everything to step up."

The table is absolutely silent, everyone listening to her story, our meals untouched. For them, it's a tale of her past.

For me... I'm waiting to see how it connects to her scars. How it connects to our future.

She shakes her head like she needs to clear her thoughts. "I'm making it sound like a sacrifice. It wasn't. I was interested in the family business, and to be honest, my brother's tragedy was an opportunity for me, as bad as it sounds.

"I wouldn't get that opportunity otherwise. Maybe some position within the company, but not a CEO gig. Anyway, I was enrolled in an MBA, and I started working for my father, being groomed to take over, and—"

I squeeze her hand to ground her. She's blabbering again. The gesture gives her pause, and she smiles at me, flips her palm, and weaves her fingers through mine.

*A Convenient Secret*

"Obviously, that didn't sit well with my aunt, and the intrigues, very common in my family, escalated. It got to the point when I felt my life was in danger. It sounds dramatic, but where I come from, appearances matter, but behind the scenes, all gloves were off."

"That's horrible." Concern mars Celeste's face.

"You're so brave." Saar reaches over Corm to rub Lily's shoulder. "Do you think they might have seen the pictures and know where you are? You are safe with us."

It's my job to comfort her. I wish I could hug her and tell her everything will be okay, but I need to respect her need to talk things through about us first.

As much as I'd like to snatch the mic and sing it to everyone, in the meantime I squeeze her hand.

"Jesus, I thought my family was a nightmare." Cora lets out the air from her cheeks.

"I told you now because I trust you. I told you because you know me as Lily Thorne, and I hope you will continue to see me as her—"

"Ladies and gentlemen, thank you all for coming." My mother's voice descends upon the room, and everyone's attention turns to the podium. The worst timing ever.

"That's why the article upset you so much," I whisper. "I'm sorry. I didn't realize it scared you."

Her cousin almost got her killed. She must have

been terrified that he would come after her since the piece came out. I had it taken down, and I thought that was it, but I never even thought... Fuck, I'm failing her already.

She smiles at me, and I see the courage and adoration in her eyes, and it's almost my undoing. Fuck the audience; I take her hand and kiss it gently, my mother's speech in the background reminding me to behave. "I won't let anything happen to you."

She nods. "I know."

Her silent endorsement sets the final piece of my broken heart into its place, mending me.

We turn to listen to my mother, but I don't hear anything. I lean in and whisper in Lily's ear. "So what is your real name?"

It's not like she could be anything but Lily to me.

She turns, her breath warm by my ear. "My full name is Lady Liliana Catherine Spinelli."

The name sounds fucking aristocratic. It takes me a moment to compute... because she is fucking nobility. "The Spinelli food empire?" I stare at her incredulously.

She nods.

The woman beside me comes from one of the richest families in the world. I try to digest the information. She's richer than me. Fuck, that's refreshing. But that's not what bothers me.

## A Convenient Secret

While everyone listens to my mother, I watch the beautiful profile of my wife. My wife. It hits me. Which is bothersome.

She took ten grand from me to marry me. It makes no sense.

The ring burns in my pocket.

I really don't know her at all.

Applause erupts as my mother announces the sum this event raised, and a sea of waiters in white gloves floods the room to serve us coffee and dessert.

"I'm sorry. I need some fresh air." I drop the napkin on the table, pushing my chair back.

"Dude, it's sweltering hot there," Xander comments.

"Declan," Lily's voice soothes over me, but I have so much pent-up energy, I can't stay here.

I bolt for the door to the outdoor patio, open it, and rush outside. Fuck, Xander was right. The humidity sticks to my shirt as I try to find a shaded area.

If I wished for some privacy to collect my thoughts, I went in the wrong direction. The staff opens the three sets of double doors, and the guests file out to continue their chatter.

Corm finds me. "What's going on?"

"Nothing. I just needed a moment. Where is everyone?"

"We're here," Saar says.

All of my colleagues join the circle, along with their partners.

My eyes find Lily's.

She looks lost.

I feel lost.

It's like there is a gap between us that I don't quite know how to bridge.

I want to step closer and tell her she is safe with me. Tell her I love her and everything will be okay. Tell her we will defy her family, even though I don't yet understand what that entails.

I hate being in the dark.

But I can't move. For whatever reason, I just can't.

The group breaks into private conversation, and we stare at each other.

Our conversation can't happen here.

I can sense she is waiting for me to make the move. The laughter, the heat, the crowd all become unbearable, when the only thing we need is to be alone and find each other again. Under these new circumstances.

*Yes, fucker, snap out of it and take her home.*

"I need to get some water," Lily announces and turns, shaking her head.

I move to follow her, but stop in my tracks.

"Nice ass on her," a voice muses beside me, thick with a British accent.

My eyes flick to the offender. "What did you just say?"

But he doesn't get to answer because I draw my arm back and my knuckles connect with his jaw, sending him backward. I lounge at him, but someone's arms stop me.

"Declan," Corm warns.

On the periphery of my blurred vision, I recognize that the party stopped around us, all eyes on us.

"Don't you fucking so much as look at my wife."

"Your wife?" The idiot scoffs, wiping blood from his lip.

"Yes, my wife." I try to shake Corm's arms from me. "If you value your life—"

"That's enough." Corm tries to stop me from making a public threat.

I finally shake my brother off, but I feel the presence of my colleagues ready to interfere.

"Who the fuck do you think you are?" I adjust my cuffs to give the illusion I'm composed, but I'm not sure I'm done punching him.

"Her fiancé."

# Chapter 27

## *Lily*

Declan launches at Timothy, who staggers backward. Corm, Cal and Xander grab Declan, trying to pull him away, and other guests in suits intervene.

"Get the fuck out of my sight while you can." Declan tries to break free.

"You're gonna pay for this," Tim snarls, shaking off the other men. He adjusts his jacket and walks away.

Oh my God. I should have insisted on leaving the minute I thought I saw Tim. Just a glimpse on my way to the bathroom. I should have trusted it. But I thought it was just a trick of my imagination from all the pressure.

"Your wife?" Corm asks, and I snap my head to face him.

Declan is shaking his hand, avoiding everyone's eyes. But he must nod, or there is some secret communication that passes between the brothers.

Corm looks at me, then at Saar, who raises her arms in surrender, shaking her head to confirm it's the first time she's heard this.

"Why the fuck did we shop for a ring then?" Corm turns back to his brother.

Ring? Declan's gaze finds me. There is war behind his eyes. A dangerous war that threatens to rebuild the barricades he used to hide behind.

I step closer, unsure where we stand but unwilling to continue this public display. Declan stretches out his hand to stop me, and something inside me dies.

He pulls a small velvet box from his pocket. "You can fucking have the ring." He pushes it into his brother's hands.

"What's going on?" Declan's mother shows up, and her two sons straighten up a bit.

She looks from one to the other. Jesus, out of all the places, this had to happen at her event. As if the situation needed a bit more drama.

"Nothing. I'm leaving." Declan strides away, but stops and snatches my hand. "*We* are leaving."

I can barely keep up with him as he drags me away from the onlookers. We cross the dining room amid several curious gazes from other guests.

*A Convenient Secret*

I try to smile at them, but then I give up and bow my head. We don't look like we're leaving. It looks more like he's kidnapping me.

"Declan," I plead when we turn the corner, heading toward the main exit.

"Not now," he snaps. "Not yet."

The wait for the car takes the longest five minutes of my life. Each moment moves slowly, wrapped in tension. Declan paces a bit, then he stands beside me. Not touching me. Then he paces a bit more.

I want to say something, but I think it's best to let him work through his rage first. I should have told him everything earlier.

I thought at first our union was temporary. And then a cowardly part of me thought it would never get to this. That was naïve.

But at the end of the day, I was worried about his reaction. It looks like that worry was warranted.

Declan halts and whips around to look at me. He opens his mouth, and then shakes his head like he's changed his mind. He remains silent.

The car finally comes. Declan opens the door for me, and as I step closer he puts one hand on the small of my back, and the other one on the door opening to protect my head.

I cherish that small gesture even more, given the current temperature of our relationship.

"Mr. Quinn, is it true you secretly married Liliana Spinelli?" someone calls out.

I turn to see who it is, but I'm immediately blinded by several flashes. Declan swears under his breath and steps behind me, his back to the quickly growing group of paparazzi.

I slide into the car, and he follows quickly after. The flashes continue to blink as the car tries to merge into the traffic.

Driving in this car for several weeks now, I never realized how large it truly is. Declan watches the streets, pressed against the door, as far from me as possible.

I can't stand it. Yes, I should—could—have told him sooner, but I don't deserve to be treated like a contagious disease.

"Say something," I urge.

He turns to me, his gaze blazing with all sorts of emotions. And while their range may be quite wide, I desperately search for affection.

"You know what I liked about you when you first crashed into my life? That raw honesty about you... In a way, you challenged me as a parent, but also praised me. That honesty in admitting when you felt vulnerable or out of scope. Your honesty in admitting the mix-up with my nanny. Honesty..."

I swallow, pain searing my throat. "You knew there

was more behind the fake glasses. But it doesn't matter. I'm sorry I didn't get a chance to tell you sooner."

"And then you went and told the entire group. Only because of the pictures, so I can't be sure you would have even tried to tell me."

I see his point. Maybe it wasn't the best course of action to explain it at the table. But it felt safe. "I told you this morning I wanted to tell you."

"Why did you marry me?"

Okay, that's not what I expected. "To help you with the custody battle."

"Just like that?" he snarls.

*Don't do this*, I sigh inwardly. "Just because."

He flinches. "But you asked for ten thousand."

"I can return the money," I say, annoyed because this is the last issue we need to discuss. Why is this so important to him?

"That's not the point. If you wanted to just help, why did you put a price on it?"

"I didn't put a price on it. I offered to help you, but you asked for a reason, and I blurted it out without thinking. You wouldn't have accepted the help otherwise."

"Why did you want to help me?"

"Why are you pushing this, Declan? I wanted to help... just because."

He flinches again, and stares at me for what feels

like several lifetimes. "That asshole claimed to be your fiancé. Who even is he?"

Jesus. I didn't hear that. That's why he's so upset. He has no clue whom he punched.

"Timothy Spinelli," I say, and Declan frowns. "My cousin."

His jaw tenses, and he pushes the intercom. "Turn the car around. We're going back."

"What? Why? What are you doing?" I scoot closer to grip his biceps like that can stop the car from turning.

"I'm going to finish him." He looks at my hand on his arm. "Fuck, I almost left you there with him," he murmurs.

He did? Shit.

"Declan, please, let's just go home. Don't give him a reason to come after you."

He looks at me, and it's like he sees me for the first time since the fight. His eyes search my face for something. I hope he finds affection, and a plea.

"You don't believe I can protect you." His words are like a splash of cold water, my skin erupting with goose bumps.

It's a statement. Not a question. He says it with finality. Incredulity. Hurt.

"I told you already that I feel safe with you."

"But you didn't tell me about the real threat. You didn't trust me with that information."

"For the first time in my life, I was living on my own terms, and a part of me wanted to protect that. I worried you would dig into it deeper, and my family would discover me. Tell me I was wrong."

"That man almost killed you. He should be in jail, not causing more trouble for you." He grabs my shoulders as if he wants to shake me. But he just holds onto me, his hands trembling, his jaw ticking.

I need to divert him from this rage. It's blinding him to what's important here.

"You got a ring for me?" I divert.

He glowers at me and drops his hands. Not the best diversion, I guess.

"It doesn't matter. Apparently you're already engaged. To your cousin."

"I'm not engaged." I want to slap him out of this unproductive ire. "But I'm married. To *you*."

"To help me with my kids," he scoffs, turning away from me.

I clutch his shoulder, stopping his retreat. "Why are you really upset, Declan?"

"You didn't trust me with your secret. You don't trust me now with your safety." His control finally snaps. That's progress.

"I wanted to protect you—"

"That's my fucking job."

"Is it? Because I don't think it applies to fake wives." Not my finest moment, but the man is pushing all my buttons.

"Lily." Warning rings in his voice.

"I wanted to protect you from the deadly family politics of my kin because I care about you, and I care about your kids."

"And how would telling me the whole story put us in jeopardy?"

"I don't know," I admit, unsure about everything. "I guess I wasn't really considering the scenarios. I lived in fear for months, so I got used to the idea of protecting my story."

"You should have trusted me."

"Yeah, it feels like it... Based on your reaction now, returning to do I don't know what to Tim. You were searching for him after you saw my scars. Can you look me in the eye and tell me that you would have just listened to my story and resisted your urge to right the wrong?"

He glares at me, his nostrils flaring as he clenches his fists.

"That's what I thought." I scoot back to the door on my side. Maybe we need a bit of space. The idea guts me. I hold his gaze, the car feeling really large. "Even now, when I need you to stick by my side and make me believe that everything will be alright, you're waging some personal vendetta."

He glares at me, his nostrils flaring. After the longest staring contest, he punches the intercom. "Change of plans. Take us home."

Round one done. I'm not sure who won, though. It feels like we both lost.

"We need to pick up the kids from the camp," I murmur.

"Fuck."

* * *

"...And then we planted twees. Did you know they awe just this tiny?" Zoya holds her hands a foot apart. "And it takes yeaws fow them to gwow?" She chats away, all hyped up from the day of activities.

The car stops at an intersection, and there is a tiny part of me that just wants to jump out and find another city, job, or friends. Start anew. Yet again. But the easy way out seems even more painful.

"Did you have a good time, Zach?" Declan asks.

"It wasn't as bad as I feared." Zach almost sounds excited.

"And now a sleepovew at Auntie Saaw. Lily, do you think the kitten will be sleeping again?"

I'm pretty sure Saar locks the cat in her bedroom to protect her from Zoya's not-so-gentle handling. "I don't know. She's one sleepy cat."

"Yeah, pwetty bowing."

"Okay, Zach, we will drop you here for your lesson, and Auntie will come to pick you up later." Declan steps out and leaves with his son.

Zoya continues chatting away while I try to follow, but my mind wanders in several directions. I want to be alone with Declan, finally, and not even talk—just let him hold me. I hope he will want to.

Declan comes back, sliding beside me.

"Why awe you sad, Lily?"

Oh God, I guess I'm wearing my feelings on my sleeve. "I'm a bit sad, but I'll get better. In fact, I'm already happier knowing you had a great time at the camp."

Declan's hand touches mine on the seat between us, hidden from Zoya's view.

I look at him, and he hooks his pinkie with mine. I give him a tentative smile, and he gives me a slight nod.

It's like in the sea of misinformation, secrets, and lies, with two tiny gestures we reached a truce, and hope blooms inside me.

We drive in silence. On one side, Zoya is dozing

off, tired from all the activities, and on the other side, Declan holds my hand. And for a moment, I imagine that this is our life. That there are no threats and no past. Just us, here and now.

The minute the car stops, Zoya jolts up. "We awe hewe." She rushes from the car, running across the driveway to the entrance.

Saar opens the door. "Zoya!" She opens her arms.

We stay for a moment of idle chatter in the kitchen while Corm carries Zoya around on his shoulders, and she giggles.

"Okay, let's go," Declan says, while Corm gallops out to the patio.

"So, you two got married?" Saar asks, before I have a chance to catch up with Declan.

"Not like you and Corm." I shake my head, tired of the layers and layers of explanations my life needs.

"My marriage started unconventionally too." She puts her arm around my shoulder as we walk outside.

"Declan is set in his ways; this is a lot for him to digest." I watch as he opens the car door but doesn't get in, waiting for me. Always the gentleman.

"He will adjust."

"Let's hope." It's like after all this time with him, I feel dreadfully lonely again.

She smiles and wraps me in a hug. "I'm sorry about everything today."

I lean into her embrace, because I can use all the friendship energy available. "Thank you."

* * *

The car turns into the ramp for the underground garage, and two men jump in front of it, jolting us to a stop. Several others swarm around us, cameras clicking.

"Jesus." Declan pushes the button. "Drive over them."

Our car proceeds slowly, but after a certain point they would be trespassing, so we enter the garage.

"I'm sorry," I say as he helps me to get out.

"Stop that, Lily. You have nothing to be sorry about. I just wish I was better prepared for all this shit."

His rage came from that place deeply encoded in him, the place that craves control. That needs it to survive. This caught him off-guard. At least he's not mad at me. I hope.

We enter the penthouse in silence, and Declan goes to the alcohol cabinet immediately. Not sure what to do, I remain at the base of the stairs.

With one glass of whiskey in his hand, he walks to the wall of windows and stares out for a moment.

I take a few steps toward him, my heart galloping,

my stomach constricted. He turns and locks me in his gaze. It's familiar, and strangely alien.

He walks toward me, slowly, like he isn't sure if he wants to get closer. Like he's deliberating how wide the gap between us should remain.

But at least he doesn't stop until he gets to me. After taking a sip of his drink, he hands it to me.

A hesitant wave of relief floods me as I take the whiskey and let the liquid swirl around my tongue. It's sweet and spicy, and the taste will forever remind me of us.

He takes the glass from me and puts it on the coffee table. "Let's start with this."

Pulling me into his arms, he lowers his lips to mine. The kiss is languid, painfully gentle, but also insistent. It's healing and reverent, and I welcome it with equal relish.

My head spins with the pure emotional charge, so poignant, so unexpected, so right. Declan sighs and holds me tighter, before he leads me to the sofa and picks up the whiskey again.

We sit beside each other and take a small sip each.

"Why did he say he is your fiancé?"

"My grandmother isn't a good woman. My grandpa lost his first wife when my father was born. He married again and had a daughter. Daddy's stepsister always believed she deserves more, and Granny was equally thirsty for the Spinelli fortune.

"When my grandfather passed, Granny announced my engagement to my stepcousin, Timothy. My dad took her side."

Declan swears, clenching his fist.

"Or rather he begged me to do it, because it would cease the internal fighting and ensure that I could protect the family legacy. So I agreed. He was a broken man after he lost my brother. And a part of me thought this was something my brother would have never been able to do. To marry our cousin."

I take another sip and give Declan the glass, chancing a glance at him. He fell for Lily Thorne, not Liliana Spinelli, the heir to a rotten dynasty. Is he going to see me as one of them?

"Why is his name Spinelli?"

"He was born out of wedlock, and we never knew who his father was. In my circle, it gave him a bastard label. I guess it might have contributed to his personality."

He takes my hand and brushes it with his lips. "Go on."

"Timothy has always been a bully. A useless, lazy asshole, who spent a fortune but never contributed. His abuse was mostly verbal, and I was used to it. It didn't impact me, so I believed I could handle him.

"It was when he hit me the first time that I realized it would only escalate from there. I was going to break the engagement, so he locked me in the room and set it on fire."

Declan's leg bounces, his fists now in a white-knuckle grip. I place my hand on the vibrating leg, and he stops tapping it.

"I got out, but I knew he wouldn't stop until he got what he wanted: the entire inheritance and me out of the way. I went to my dad, and he said I should endure it while he tries to collect evidence about Tim's wrongdoing."

Declan's leg starts bouncing again.

"I couldn't. I couldn't do it. So I decided to disappear. I was hoping Tim would fuck up enough to end up in jail or something. Or my father would find enough evidence to act on it. I believed that good would prevail. At least, for now, the company is still led by my father."

Declan takes a generous sip and goes to refill the glass. I'm not sure if it's because he needs another drink or to walk off the pent-up energy.

He comes back, carrying the bottle. He pours us another glass and hands it to me.

"So, now you know what kind of crazy I come from." I try to sound jovial, but it comes out flat.

I yelp as Declan scoops me up and sets me in his lap. "I'm sorry for everything they did to you, Lily."

"My grandfather was a great man. Spinelli Food was a work of love for him. The brand represented family, people coming together over a meal. I love that about the company, but for the longest time now, it's been mostly just marketing spiel. The Spinellis as a family play their part as upstanding citizens and pillars of the community while stabbing each other in the back. Only Dad makes sure the Spinelli brand is protected."

"Your father should have protected you. Not the fucking brand." Declan takes a sip.

"I know you can't possibly understand this, but one of the reasons I didn't tell you is because I wanted to protect the brand. I knew you would force a confrontation with Tim. He and his mother would use any excuse to further propel the inside wars within the company. It would only blow up Dad's careful balancing act of keeping the company in the right hands."

He contemplates my words for a moment. "I think I understand. I disagree, but I understand." He sighs. "What's going to happen now?"

"We can hope Tim will pack up and go home—which is wishful thinking. I'm pretty sure he'll stay to feed the media frenzy."

"I'll hire security."

"I never wanted to bring this to your door."

"You apologize one more time and I will have you over my knee."

Jesus. There is something wrong with me, because despite the dreadful day and the gloomy conversation, his words arouse me. "Yes, sir."

Holding me tight, he leans forward and puts the whiskey down. He barely reclines back before he seizes my lips again.

We kiss, this time with more urgency, before he cuts the kiss short.

"Besides media, what else can we expect?" His need to plan and control wins over the passion.

"I will have to call my father and explain my lengthy absence."

"Maybe we can take the twins to visit London, and you can talk to him in person."

I wrap my arms around his neck. "Can you be any more perfect?"

"That's my line, Seagull."

"It's a good line."

We stare at each other, the tension melting slightly, the need for more closeness growing. I know the next few days, perhaps weeks, will bring a lot of pressure, that Declan doesn't quite understand what it means to step into my world, but for now, I take the closeness.

Because if he stands by my side, we can conquer the world.

I hope.

"I thought I'd be telling the kids about us and announcing our relationship to everyone. Now that option has been taken away from us."

"I'm sor—" I cover my mouth, remembering his warning. No more apologies.

He takes my hand and kisses my knuckles. "I bought you a ring."

It's like we circled back to the conversation from earlier in the car, which feels like a lifetime ago.

"I thought you bought it for Corm," I tease, still hurt about the way I found out about his plans. Plans that he abandoned too quickly.

He reaches into his pocket and pulls out the velvet box. "I got it back." He flicks it open.

A beautiful, gentle solitaire sits on an intricate band. I love it. "It's beautiful."

"I know we've done things backwards, so before we sort that out, I want to give it to you as a commitment ring." He takes it out and pauses just before sliding it on. "I hope you'll accept it."

I nod, trying to keep the tears at bay.

"I didn't think I would ever allow anyone close again. Give them the power to break me. But you, my little Seagull... I stood no chance the minute you crashed into my life. I love you, Lily." He slides the ring on my finger.

I sniffle. "I love you, too."

He cups my neck and pulls me in for a kiss. This third one is scorching, desperate, all-consuming. It's like all his kisses, fresh with need, and wild with want.

The frustration of the day takes over, and the kiss turns into a frenzy of roaming hands, possessive touches, and a hunger for release.

Bunching the tight skirt up to my hips, I straddle him, his erection pressing between us. I fiddle with his belt while he undoes my zipper and yanks the top of the dress down, attacking my nipples.

I arch my back, moaning, forgetting what I was doing. He groans and pulls my bra cups down, not bothering to unclasp it.

"I need to be inside you," he murmurs against my skin.

Dazed, I hear his words but don't quite capture the meaning, my mind and all my senses focused on his tongue on my skin, his warm hands supporting my back, the taste of whiskey and the smell of him. The feel of his hard cock between us.

Oh yes, that. I return to my task and finally free him, wrapping my small hand around him. Declan lets out a savage sound.

"Now, Lily, your pussy around my cock. Now."

His loss of control is like an aphrodisiac. I don't even care if I'm ready for him. I'm probably soaking his pants anyway. I lift my hips, and he guides himself to my entrance.

I sink in slowly, languidly, taking every inch of him, relishing the feel of him. "Take me, Declan. I need to scream your name. I need to forget everything. Make me get lost in you."

He groans, grips my hips, and starts bouncing me up and down. "Your pussy takes me so well, little Seagull."

"Harder," I pant. It's like the deeper he gets, the more of him I need.

Declan flips us around. "Hands on the backrest."

I grip the sofa as he lifts my hips and enters me from behind, and I almost fly over the backrest.

"I said hold on." He thrusts. "I'm going to punish you for not telling me sooner. For not trusting me."

I'm so close, I can barely hear him.

He grabs my hair, pulling me closer. "Why, Lily, why couldn't you explain sooner?"

As if we didn't just talk about it, his need to gain control over the situation, which is already out of our hands, feeds all his insecurities.

"I didn't need a savior," I yell out in frustration.

"You're mine, Lily, mine." His delicious assault picks up, his grip on my hair almost painful, making the entire experience deeper. "Do you understand?" he roars.

"Yes, yes, I'm yours."

We chase our release, unaware of the heartbreak to come.

## Chapter 28

## *Declan*

"I need them out of my fucking street," I yell at my lawyer. "I can't get out of my own building without being harassed."

Lily comes into the kitchen and scowls at me. Fuck, the kids may come down any minute, and I'm out of control.

"Okay." I nod, listening to the same lame bullshit the lawyer has been spinning since this shit started.

Out of control.

That's what the past week has been like. It doesn't matter what we do or where we go, the news about the lost heiress follows us relentlessly.

The speculations about our marriage have topped all the other gossip. To make matters worse, Lily's father is refusing to take her call.

I wish I could whisk her to London and help her

deal with all that shit. I hate the man for failing to protect her, but she still seems to feel some sort of allegiance to him. As a father, I can only wish Zoya and Zach would give me such grace when I fuck up.

We should have left for London already, but Lily didn't want to interrupt the twins' camp. I don't understand how she manages to continue as if our lives are normal. At least we're leaving tomorrow. Finally, away from this madness.

If no reporter finds out we are in London.

Hopefully, by the time we're back, the interest here will have died down.

I hang up and reach for Lily, kissing her crown and holding her, not only for her comfort but for mine. "I don't know what to do."

The admission makes me feel even weaker, but sharing my weakness with Lily doesn't seem like the end of the world. It brings a sense of ease.

"I grew up being chased by paps every time something happened with our business or with my family, and believe me, my family loves scandals. It doesn't get better, but it's easier to deal with once you accept it as a part of your life."

"That's not the life I want for my children," I scoff.

"Of course not." She looks away, nodding, her hand on my heart.

## A Convenient Secret

Fuck. This is exactly the life we will have now, isn't it? I don't have a choice in the matter.

"They will move to a new story soon, and we will be fine." I say the words like she's the one who needs reassurance. Fuck, the last time I felt this helpless was when Kendra left.

Only this time, I stand to lose way more if I don't get a grip.

"The kids want to go to chase the pigeons—"

"No way," I protest.

"Maybe we can go, let them take a few pics, and they will leave us alone? Chasing pigeons is the least juicy scoop they can get."

"I'm not letting them take photos of my kids." I turn and pace to the window, running my hand through my hair.

"They are doing it anyway, Declan." Her hand touches my back, the tension melting just a little under her warmth. "The summer camp had to call the police twice. It's not going to stop until they get what they want. Let them get the photos, so we can enjoy a semi-normal day, and then issue a cease and desist. They will give up eventually."

The fucking helplessness is like a poison, gripping me in a vice-like hold. I turn to face her. "Thank God we're leaving tomorrow."

Lily winces.

Fuck. I feared she was too young for me, yet here we are and she's acting with way more calm and perspective. "Sorry, baby, I'm just on edge."

She wraps her arms around my waist. "Let's pretend to have a normal day in the park."

I nod. "Okay, but we'll leave with the car to drive us to the other side, so hopefully we can sneak in without the vultures downstairs following us." The plan gives me a sense of direction while I'm still completely lost in the mayhem.

"Good. Let me get the twins ready."

"Daddy, is Lily your giwlfwiend now?" Zoya skips beside me, holding my hand, the ice cream dripping down her hand.

Oh fuck. "Something like that," I evade. "She loves you very much, and we will be taking care of you together."

"I like that." She licks her ice cream, the situation uncomplicated through her innocent eyes. I wish it was that easy.

Zach is explaining to Lily something about his piano lesson, and she's listening with the same attention she always bestows on everyone. Only I see her eyes dart around, ready to protect him from the prying questions and cameras.

This outing has always been peaceful. It's been a routine that we all loved. Normal.

Instead, there's now a bodyguard a few steps behind us, scanning the sidewalk. I inherited a lot of money, and I made even more myself. I'm a rich man with two children, and yet I've led a fairly normal life.

My name was mentioned in the business pages a few times. I regularly attend high-profile events. It's not like I'm completely new to living in the public eye. But this level of madness is something I thought was only for celebrities.

We catch up with Lily and Zach. Lily gives me a tense smile, and helps Zoya clean up before the twins take off to run around.

We find a bench and watch them for a moment. Zoya chases the pigeons while Zach explores the area, careful as always.

"It's good for them to have a normal kind of Saturday," I admit, and take Lily's hand in mine, keeping them in between us in case someone is snatching pictures.

"Maybe I'll wear the fake glasses again in London. I can even dye my hair to make sure we can explore the city without interruption."

She's trying to make it easier for me and my family.

I love her for that, but it deepens my sense of helplessness.

It's like, with her newly claimed status, there is this new lifestyle to manage, a new reality to fit into, and as much as I'm trying, I don't know where my place is.

I want to talk to Lily about it, but she has so much to adjust to, I don't want to burden her with my vulnerabilities.

She seems to be better at navigating it all, at protecting us, at knowing what to do. It's like she dove deep into the new circumstances, and I'm still looking for the fucking oxygen mask. How long before she swims away?

"Perhaps sunglasses that actually suit you would work better." My attempt at joking is pathetic.

"Declan, if you prefer to stay here with the kids and take them to the Hamptons, I can go talk to my father."

"I'm not leaving you to deal with them alone. Or to face your cousin. Out of the question."

She sighs. "I will have security."

"I'm not discussing this, Lily. We all go."

We still haven't talked about what happens after she speaks with her father. He still needs his successor. How will that work when she lives here?

"Do you want to return to London and work with your father again?"

"Declan, I love you, and I love Zoya and Zach. That's my priority. A lot can be achieved long-distance. It's just a question of figuring out how we will make it work."

Her words calm the storm within me a bit. They also add another layer of fear. She's considering options to return to the business. She's a Spinelli after all. But what if that's not possible? "You think he will agree to such an arrangement?"

"I don't know, but there is no point stressing about all probable outcomes until I speak with him."

"The uncertainty is driving me crazy," I admit.

"I know. Just don't give up on us, and we will find the way."

"Fuck, I wish I could kiss you."

"As soon as I tell my father the truth about us, you can kiss the hell out of me. You'll finally make the front page, handsome." She winks.

I snort. "That has been my life's ambition."

She chuckles. Maybe we can try to find some normal amid this madness.

"Please don't tell him the whole truth about us."

"You think he wouldn't like that I took money from you to marry you to help with your custody battle?" She pokes me with her elbow.

"Shit. Don't tell him we're married."

"I'll tell him we're engaged."

"Shouldn't I ask him for your hand in marriage first?" Fuck, I married an aristocrat.

"My father is an earl, and technically I live in a kingdom, but we've moved into the twenty-first century."

She's so beautiful, her crooked nose pronounced on her young, smooth face, the sunshine playing on her hair.

"I just want to do right by you, Seagull."

She watches the kids, but her profile lights up with a smile. "You can never do wrong by me, Declan."

"Why is your accent American?" How have I not thought about this?

"My mother is American. I spent my childhood in Chicago. That's another piece of juicy gossip. My mother ran away with me when my father took a mistress."

"But she returned to England? How long were you here?"

"We were here for three years. We returned to my father as soon as the money ran out. And I came back for two years in high school, before my brother died. Mom had left us by then. I guess my ability to speak without a British accent was the best part of my ridiculous disguise."

"You were beautiful even with that weird haircut and ugly glasses."

"I was trying to be invisible."

"And yet I noticed you the first time we met."

She whips her head to me. "It wasn't my voice?"

"I didn't know the two were the same person until later. I saw you at Caleb's vow renewal, and I couldn't unsee you again."

"I was totally into your voice. At Cal and Celeste's party, I realized you were the voice, and I couldn't believe it. I can't believe you noticed me there. You were so disinterested in everything."

"I was very interested in you."

She smiles at me, and I relish the moment of normal we've achieved. Maybe we can do this.

The twins join us. Zoya is sweaty with messed-up hair, Zach with his hands in his pockets and an unimpressed expression.

"Why do we have him?" Zoya tugs at my sleeve, gesturing at the large man in a suit.

I exhale slowly, keeping my voice steady. "To keep us safe."

Zach scoffs. "From what?"

I sigh, rubbing a hand down my face. "From people who don't know how to mind their own business."

"What does mind youw own business mean? I don't have any business." Zoya shrugs.

Lily stands up and takes her hand. "Imagine your friend is whispering to someone, and you keep asking,

'What are you talking about?' If they say, 'Mind your own business,' it means they don't want to share, and that's okay—because it's not something you need to know."

Zoya puts her other hand into mine, and we head toward our building with Zach striding beside us.

Zoya swings my hand back and forth. "Those guys with the camewas... they don't mind theiw business."

I nod. "Exactly."

"But why awe they taking pictuwes of us?"

I hate that she even has to ask, the temporary peace of our outing evaporating rapidly.

Lily takes this one, her voice light but firm. "Because some people love gossip more than minding their own business."

Zoya considers that, then shrugs. "Gwanny said gossiping is bad."

"Granny is right, sweetheart, but not everyone understands that." I grab Zach's hand to cross the street.

As we reach our block, my stomach knots.

They're already waiting. I should have called the car again. I got lulled by the surface peace.

A small crowd of paparazzi loiters near the entrance of my building, cameras slung around their necks, their hushed murmurs turning to alert whispers the second they see us.

## A Convenient Secret

The building added security, and the two concierge clerks keep the group out of the immediate vicinity of the building's property. It's not enough.

My jaw tightens. Zach slides his hand into mine. "Stay close," I murmur to Lily, who has picked Zoya up.

With my hand firmly on my wife's back, we advance. Our bodyguard steps forward, moving ahead of us to clear the path.

The second we get within range, the shouting starts.

"Mr. Quinn! Declan! Is it true you secretly married your nanny?"

"Lily, how long have you been hiding here?"

"Are you leaving the country? Is the marriage real?"

The sidewalk turns into a chaotic mess as we weave our way through the blinding flashes and overlapping voices.

"Daddy?" Zoya's voice is small.

I hate this.

We keep walking, heads down, bodies close together, following the bodyguard in front of us, clearing the way.

We're almost at the carpet that lines the entrance to my building when someone pushes forward.

I don't see who. I don't see what happens.

I more feel than see Lily stumbling and losing her balance. She tumbles to the ground, Zoya's small body trapped under her.

Someone jostles against me, and Zach's hand rips from mine. I crouch to help Lily and Zoya out. The shouts quieten down as people around us realize what has happened.

"Are you okay?" I scoop Zoya up, and the bodyguard reaches for her. "Take her inside," I order. "We'll be right there, honey."

My daughter nods, her eyes wide, but I block that out. Lily is standing up already.

"Dad," the scream reverberates through the chaos as the footsteps of those fleeing the scene echo around me.

"Zach," Lily shouts, and as I turn, she already drops to the ground beside my wailing son.

I'm on my knees a second later, grabbing his small frame, my hands skimming over his body. Panic. Adrenaline. Rage.

His face is scrunched in pain, his left wrist swelling.

He's hurt.

I turn to the few paparazzi who stayed behind, my voice a roar of fury. "Back the fuck up!"

The security from the building rushes out, the photographers stepping backward.

Lily cradles Zach, murmuring soft reassurances while tears streak down his cheeks, his tiny body trembling.

Is he going into shock?

I don't think. I scoop him into my arms, holding him close. "I've got you, buddy. I've got you."

Lily scrambles to her feet, and I try to usher her in front of me, more with my body language than anything else.

Someone dares to snap a picture, a few flashes blurring my vision. We reach the entrance and finally enter the lobby.

The eerie silence is interrupted only by the sobs of my children.

I check if I have my family with me. Zoya stands frozen beside the bodyguard, her face pale. Lily nods that she's okay, but I see her limping to hug my daughter.

"Dad," Zach whimpers.

"We need to get to the hospital." I turn to the bodyguard and pass him my son. "Get them to the car. I'm right behind you."

"Declan." Lily's voice almost penetrates the rage in my head with a beacon of reason. Almost.

"Daddy," Zoya whines.

"Dad," Zach whimpers.

"I'm coming." But instead, I turn to open the door

again, and the shutters click. Fucking assholes. "If any of you so much as breathe near my family again, I will destroy you."

My hand itches to throw a few punches so they have something to report, but I have my family to focus on.

## Chapter 29

*Lily*

"We should have never gone to the park," Declan growls as we get into the waiting car. He doesn't look at me, but I know that right now, in this moment, he's blaming me.

He's blinded by rage and worry, but if I'm honest, I shouldn't have suggested the outing. I was really hoping that we could defy the odds and coexist with the sensation-thirsty reporters.

Zoya is clinging to me while Zach, nestled in Declan's lap, his lips pursed, puts on a brave face. His wrist is huge, and I try to be strong for all of them, but tears stream down my cheeks, regardless.

This just proved that living in secret was safer for everyone. In my wildest dreams, I couldn't have imagined that the kids would suffer this much.

Declan doesn't look at me. His chin rests on Zach's head as he stares into empty space. The silence in the car is coiling around my frayed nerves. My chest hurts as the emotions coat my throat, making it difficult to swallow.

Declan calls his mom who is on the board of the hospital, and once we arrive we're immediately ushered into a private wing.

We move swiftly through the eerily quiet hallways, our steps on the pristine white floors almost obnoxiously squeaky.

A nurse shows us the exam room, and Declan turns to me. "Stay with Zoya." His voice is flat, his face unreadable.

I nod, swallowing down the ache in my chest as I squat beside Zoya, who buries her face in my neck. Her little fingers clutch my sleeve, her breath warm against my skin.

"Will he be okay?" Zoya's usually boisterous voice is small.

"Yes, he might need a cast, but I'm sure he will be okay. Are you okay?"

"They didn't mind theiw business." She sighs.

"They didn't." I kiss her crown.

"If he gets a cast, can he still fly to London?" She looks at me with those huge, curious eyes.

## A Convenient Secret

Shit. I didn't even think of that. "Let's see what the doctor says first."

Declan wheels Zach out of the exam room. "He needs an X-ray," he explains, his voice on edge, his jaw rigid.

"Zach." Zoya rushes to her brother.

"Don't worry, Zoya, I'm fine," Zach says, wincing a bit. Like his father, he's already learning to bear pain in silence.

"I want a chaiw like that." Zoya looks at her father.

"Stay with Lily, Zoya," Declan says. "Zach needs the chair now." He veers to follow a nurse.

Letting out a shaky breath, my heart breaks for both of them as I watch Declan's broad shoulders disappear down the hall.

"Do you want a chocolate bar?" I turn to Zoya.

"We should get one fow Zach and Daddy."

"Great idea."

As I take her hand, my phone rings. "Give me a moment, sweetheart."

I answer, and my aunt's sharp voice sends chills down my spine. "You can congratulate yourself, Liliana; you've really done it now."

"I really don't have time to talk." I close my eyes briefly, turning to the window.

"Your antics gave your father a heart attack," she says.

The hospital air suddenly feels too thick, too sterile, pressing in on me from all sides.

I can't move.

I can't breathe.

I force myself to respond. "Is he... alive?"

"Yes, he's strong as a bull," she says, her tone carrying a hint of disappointment. The breath I finally suck in is shallow and painful.

This can't be happening. Not now. "Thank you for letting me know." I end the call, my hands shaking as I shove them into the pocket of my summer dress.

The double doors swing open, and Declan steps back. "He's getting his cast. Where is Zoya?"

I whip around. "Zoya?" I say, uselessly.

"Where is she?" Declan roars.

"I took a phone call... She must be somewhere here..." I dash down the corridor, opening the doors.

"You were supposed to watch her," Declan accuses me.

This is too much. I reach the corner, and my heart almost bursts out of my chest. "Zoya."

"I found the chocolate baws." She waves at me, standing in front of a vending machine.

Declan passes me, rushing to her. "You can't wander off like this."

"We wanted to get tweats fow you, Daddy."

Her adorable innocence breaks something inside

me, and I lean against the wall, tears rolling down my cheeks.

For Zach. For Zoya. For my father.

For Declan. For us.

I sense their approach, and I quickly wipe away the tears.

"We got one fow you, Lily." My precious girl hands me a bar.

"Thank you." My voice cracks.

Declan's gaze flicks at me. He sighs and stops, not too close, not touching me.

"My father is in the hospital. He had a heart attack," I whisper.

"Fuck," he murmurs.

"Money in the jaw," Zoya chimes. "Whewe is Zach?"

Declan takes her hand and heads toward the exam room. I follow him, my mind blank. It's like a freight train ran over me, leaving me completely flat. Exhausted by everything, the emotional turmoil of the past few hours is taking its toll.

I search for sadness, anger, frustration, but I'm only numb. Hollow. Declan was barely holding it together this past week, and I guess he reached his limit. I wish I could fight for us.

But this is not the time. He needs to be here for his children. Zach is hurt; they are both shaken up after the incident. This is where he needs to be, and suddenly, I don't feel like I belong.

The double door opens yet again, and the nurse wheels Zach in. He looks groggy, but gives us a curt nod. That's almost like a smile for the little dude.

"How are you, Zach?" I try to smile, ignoring my ripped heart.

"I got a cast," he says with a sense of pride, like it's his battlefield trophy, but his voice is tired too.

They show us to a room and help Zach settle in the bed. Zoya hangs from the edge, on her belly, examining his cast, her legs dangling.

"A word," Declan says, not even looking at me. "We'll be right back," he tells the kids.

Stepping outside, I place my foot on the floor gingerly as if it could explode at any moment.

"The jet is ready to leave at ten tomorrow. Just take it."

It takes me a second to process what he means.

The jet?

Declan puts his hands into his pockets, his voice clipped, professional—like he's giving instructions to a business associate. "Just say goodbye to the kids before you go."

I stare at him, waiting for something.

A flicker of hesitation.

A crack in his armor.

A sign that he doesn't want me to leave.

But there's nothing.

He doesn't even look at me.

"Declan."

"What do you want me to say? You need to go and be with your father. I need to be with my son. With both my kids who went through a fucked-up, unnecessary experience today."

"What about us?" My voice cracks. Somewhere in the background of my tired mind, I recognize this is just the circumstances and his rage talking.

But his icy demeanor hurts. The mask is up. The wall is erected. The armor is fully in place. There is no space for more variables in his life.

He needs control, and I wreaked chaos on his carefully planned life. And to his credit, he tried to adjust.

"I need to talk to Zach's doctor. Go say goodbye to the kids." He turns and leaves me there standing, my heart shattered.

There is no point in trying to stop him. He's made up his mind. At least, in the current state of said mind.

But I need to see my father before it's too late, so I take a deep breath and return to the room.

I sit on the bed, patting Zach's leg. "Are you in pain?"

"Not much," he says bravely.

"Whewe is Daddy?" Zoya looks over her shoulder at the door.

Poor babies, they had quite a scare. Suddenly, one emotion overpowers the numb feeling of loss and heartbreak, and I get so angry at the reporters, I have to stand up and walk to the window to breathe through the outrage.

"He went to talk to the doctor, to see when we can go home."

Home. I hope it still is my home.

Returning to the bed, my barely found composure cracks a little when I glimpse the bodyguard through the glass pane in the door. I didn't even notice him earlier, but of course he's here. He'll become a permanent fixture to protect this family.

All because of me.

"I need to tell you something." My voice quivers.

They both look at me, their eyes full of trust.

I force a smile. "I have to go away for a little while."

Zach tenses, and his fingers running over the cast freeze. I see the wheels turning in his head, processing. He looks away, his jaw tense. I can practically see how he withdraws.

"For how long?" His voice is cautious, controlled, like he already knows he won't like the answer.

I inhale through my nose, blinking against the sting in my eyes. "I don't know, sweetheart."

"You can't go!" Zoya's voice is high-pitched, frantic, her small hands gripping the fabric of my dress like she can hold me in place. "You live with us now."

Oh, my poor heart.

Zach looks at me, but there is no warmth in his eyes. "Are you coming back?"

Before I can answer, his sister's tiny body collides into my side, nearly knocking me over. I press a kiss into Zoya's hair, my throat so tight I can barely breathe. "My daddy is sick. And I have to go help him."

Zoya sniffs loudly, hiccupping. "But why can't someone else help him? You awe helping us."

I squeeze her, my arms wrapping tight around her tiny frame. "Because sometimes, when you love someone, you have to be there for them. Just like your daddy is always here for you."

Zach watches me closely. I can see the way his mind is working through it, trying to find the cracks in my explanation.

"And you can't help him from here?" His voice is quiet but sharp.

At least he doesn't repeat his previous question. I can't lie to them, but I can't promise them I'll be back. If their father doesn't want me back? For the first time, I grasp the enormity of potentially losing them.

I shake my head, brushing his dark hair back from his forehead. "Not this time."

His lips press into a hard line, and I see it—the walls going up. "People always leave," he mutters.

The words crack through me like an icicle, shattering me into pieces.

I grip his small shoulders, forcing him to meet my gaze. "Not everyone. Your dad? He will always be here. And me?" I brush my fingers through Zoya's hair. "I will always love you, no matter where I am."

Zoya's tiny fingers tighten on the fabric of my skirt, her voice trembling. "I don't want you to go."

Neither do I.

"I know it's not fair, but I need you both to be brave, okay?"

Zoya sniffles, wiping at her eyes. "Okay, I'll be bwave fow you. I hope youw dad gets bettew soon, so you can come back."

"You both need to be brave for your daddy, and take good care of him."

Hopefully, my plea gives these little angels some reassurance. That in my absence, their dad still has them.

"Hopefully your dad gets better before I get my cast down," Zach says, and I barely keep it together.

Declan returns and Zoya runs to him. He scoops her up, closing his eyes, holding her close. I'm grateful he has them to comfort him. I'm mad at him for pushing me away, but I don't think I can get through to him now.

"Zach, you will need to stay here tonight. They need to make sure your wrist doesn't swell under the cast. It's just a precaution." He sits at the bed, Zoya snuggled in his lap.

"Okay," Zach says, his voice shaking slightly.

"I can stay with him," I offer.

"I'll stay." Declan doesn't look at me.

"Okay, Zoya and I will make you breakfast when you arrive tomorrow," I say, hopeful that this turn of events will force us to stay together, and Declan will realize he's acting out of frustration and fear.

"Actually, I called my mom. Zoya can stay with her." He stands up, still holding Zoya. He kisses her cheeks, still avoiding my eyes.

It feels like it's been ages since he treated me like this. Like I don't exist.

*I noticed you.*

He said that to me, but it feels like I'm invisible to him now. He doesn't even want me to stay with his daughter.

"Maybe you can take her over there?" He finally looks at me. It's like he is staring over me, the gaze I grew to love, to cherish, to provoke, gone.

"Of course."

As I leave with Zoya, I wonder if *of course* are the last words I will ever tell him.

* * *

Zoya chats in the car, but I only hear half of it, my mind returning to the hospital. *You need to go be with your father. I need to be with my son. With both my kids.*

That may be true, but it's not a finality. I need to visit my father, but I want to be with Declan and his kids. I love Zach and Zoya like they are mine.

He may push me away now, but I know he doesn't mean that. Does he? This is a horrible situation we are currently in. Instead of leaning into me, he's pushed me away. I'm not going to let him.

I'll delay my flight by a few hours and wait for him, so we can talk, and I can show him we are stronger than this. Because I hope we are. I believe we are.

I just hope I'm not the only one fighting for us.

"It's going to be okay." Zoya snuggles closer to me.

I hug her little body tightly, drawing strength from her. "Zach will recover quickly."

"But evewything else, too."

My heart gallops so fast, it may just escape my chest. What did she pick up on? How do I explain?

She tilts her head to look at me. "Youw daddy will be okay, and you will come back."

Jesus. "Sweetheart, you know how you were really sad on the last day because your teacher will no longer be your teacher? I told you the new teacher will be equally nice, and you said I can't know that?"

She nods, her lower lip quivering.

"This is similar. I don't know what's going to happen, but it doesn't matter what happens; you have a very special space in my heart, and that will never change. I know that."

"I will be bwave fow you and fow Daddy."

It sucks that she needs to be. It sucks that I am who I am, and her brother is in the hospital because of that.

It sucks that her father experienced so much turmoil in his life already that another blow has him doubting everything.

It sucks that I have to leave.

Dorothy welcomes us with a concerned smile. At least her residence isn't surrounded by reporters.

"Zoya, love, there are fresh cookies in the kitchen."

"Yummie." Zoya hugs my legs one last time and skips away.

"How is Zach?" Dorothy asks.

"He's good. Very brave. His wrist is broken though, so he's got a cast."

"I guess you're postponing the trip? What a shame;

the change of scenery would help you all. At least the story will die down in the meantime. I suspect Declan is suing everyone."

"He's focusing on Zach now." I evade her question, because if I tell her I'm leaving alone, I may just start crying.

"I'm so glad those kids have you in their lives now." She takes my hand. I guess I'll start crying regardless. "Thank God all that dreadful business with Kendra is behind us."

Behind us? "What do you mean? I didn't know the hearing had already happened."

"There was no hearing. I thought Declan told you that he settled out of court. But I guess that was shortly after you started working for him, so he wouldn't share that."

"He settled?" I repeat like a parrot, because it doesn't make sense. Shortly after I started working for him? I think my exhausted mind makes little sense of anything anymore.

"Yes, she gave up her parental rights finally. She was always after his money only. Some women should not be allowed to have children."

I mumble something unintelligible and leave in a hurry. I can't handle another goodbye with Zoya. And I need to replay Dorothy's words to comprehend them.

She lives only three blocks from the penthouse, so I

decide to walk. Why didn't he tell me Kendra settled? When I told him he couldn't move to England for work because of the custody battle, he flinched.

I thought it was because he didn't think of that argument. Was I wrong? Was it because that argument was void?

Did he really settle shortly after I started working for him? Why the marriage then?

All the unanswered questions swirl in my head. There is something that doesn't add up. But one thing is clear.

Declan kept something from me. Just like I kept something from him. And in light of his secret, his reaction to mine feels like another betrayal.

People keep things to themselves for a reason. What was his reason? It hurts that he would do that.

What hurts even more is that my marriage—however fake—suddenly feels like everything in my life as Liliana Spinelli. My relationship with Declan suddenly feels like that world.

Secrets and lies.

# Chapter 30

## *Lily*

SAAR

How are you doing, Lily?

CELESTE

I heard about Zach. What a nightmare.

CORA

Do you need anything? How is Zach?

> Broken wrist. My father had a heart attack.

SAAR

Shit. Is he?

> He's in the hospital. I'm leaving today.

CELESTE

What about Declan?

> Make sure he's okay.

> **CORA**
> You're not coming back?
>
> **SAAR**
> Lily?
>
> **CELESTE**
> What's going on?

I watch the coffee drip into the small cup, the black liquid forming brown foam. I need this coffee more than I need oxygen right now.

I haven't slept all night. I packed my suitcase, and I tried to get a bit of a shuteye, but sleep eluded me.

My head is throbbing. My eyes burn. My feet hurt from all the pacing. But it's all just a mild discomfort compared to the searing, gaping wound in my heart.

Yes, I don't know the facts, but the feeling is there. That feeling of clipped wings, of depending on someone's whims, of conditional freedom is all too familiar. It's what I grew up with. It's the world of manipulation I know too well.

Could he have known all along who I was? Did he marry me for my money and status? The idea is preposterous, but my exhausted mind offers it anyway. Along with other useless explanations that get my head spinning.

The rich, inviting aroma hits my nostrils as I take a sip, the warm liquid spreading through my aching body and soul. I glimpse the camera in the corner. I'm sure he's not watching me, but I flip him the bird anyway.

How dare he blame me for not telling him sooner. How dare he dismiss me last night like I'm just his nanny.

There are some remains of a decently functional logic trying to penetrate my frayed mind. It tells me I'm overreacting. That is the only reason I'm still here.

There must be an explanation I don't see, because I'm stunned by the revelation, yesterday's events, the lack of sleep.

How much can someone endure before they break? I think I'm dangerously close to my limit.

The elevator door swooshes open. They are here. Keys drop. Declan sighs. Footsteps disappear, probably into the soft carpet. Is he alone?

I walk out into the living room. He's standing by the windows. The man I fell for, broad shoulders, alluring presence, casual stance with his hand in his pocket.

"Where is Zach?" Has something happened? My heart, which has suffered several marathons in the last twenty-four hours, somehow endures another adrenaline spike.

Declan whips around, his rigid expression softening as he lays his eyes on me. "You're here." It sounds like relief. "We went to pick up Zoya, but Mom lured him in with cookies. They are staying there this morning."

He eats the distance between us, opening his arms. "Thank God you're still here."

I raise my arm to stop him and take a step back. "Don't."

He stops. Closing his eyes briefly, he takes a fortifying breath. "Lily, I'm so sorry. I was under a lot of pressure. The minute you left, I regretted everything. You needed me as much as I needed you, and I..."

I swallow a sob. This was the conversation I was hoping for when I left the hospital last night.

"Zach was in pain, and I was livid about the way it all went down. Such an unnecessary accident. And I wanted to carry his pain if I could. That was my focus. But I should have been there for all of us. I'm sorry."

This time, the sob doesn't stay jailed inside me. Declan's face constricts painfully, and he steps forward. "Seagull."

"When did Kendra give up her parental rights?"

Something dark flashes through his expression. "Does it matter?"

"After you blamed me for keeping my secret and not trusting you with it, I think it matters."

"Lily, don't do this—"

"Answer my question."

"It seems like you already know," he evades.

That's the worst-case scenario. He doesn't tell me the whole truth, not even now.

"Why did you marry me?" Jesus. Didn't he ask me the same a week ago? We both entered this arrangement on a pretense. It's all been as fake as it gets.

His jaw ticks, his hands curled into fists. He lets out a long breath, and then locks his eyes with mine.

It's the gaze that kept me prisoner every time he bestowed it on me. This time, it's laced with pain and desperation.

It's an odd feeling to see a man larger than life pleading. What is he pleading?

"Why did you marry me, Declan?" Somewhere deep in my heart, I know the reason. I'm just not sure if that makes the lie better or worse.

"Just because," he croaks.

I close my eyes, trying to draw oxygen into my lungs. "Don't you dare say that. All my life I have been manipulated, my agency taken away by people who should have loved me. I was told what to do. How to behave. Coerced to fit expectations. I felt safe and free here. And you just…"

"Lily, I was trying to resist you for so long, and then you looked at me with those bewitching eyes of yours, and you offered to marry me. Perhaps I was already in love with you, but I couldn't stop."

"When did you settle?" I don't even know why I need to know.

"She called the night you signed the prenup. I met her the next day."

"So before the wedding?"

He nods.

"You say you couldn't resist me, so you wanted to own me? To control me? You might have reasons that are more noble than Tim's or my father's, but at the end of the day, you just caged me because it suited you."

It could have been wrong actions, good intentions, but why did he hide it? A part of me desperately wants to see his motivations in a different light, but I need to stand up for myself.

"You're wrong. Don't you dare compare me to people who only hurt you. I love you." The vein on his temple swells.

"Really? You do? You watched me through the security cameras. That's not love. You had so many opportunities to tell me about Kendra settling and you didn't. You love me on your own terms. Blame me for not trusting you, but do you really trust me?"

"Lily, don't—"

"No, Declan, you don't. As you said, I have my father to take care of, and you have your family. We need to be on two different continents. But perhaps we were on two different continents figuratively from the beginning. Maybe you were right to resist me. You should have listened to that gut feeling."

"What about Zoya and Zach?" His voice is hoarse with desperation.

"Talking about manipulation," I scoff. "I can't believe you would drag them into this. I love those children, and it breaks my heart that I'm another person to leave them. That guilt and regret are like nothing I've ever experienced. But I'm not going to be the only one to carry that blame. This one we will share."

I can't look at him anymore. He's a broken man, and I want to hug him and make him feel better.

But I have tried to do things better for my mom and then for my father, for the company, for everyone else.

It almost cost me my life in the end. The scars on my body are a daily reminder of that. I deserve more than that.

I turn and walk to the elevator. Snatching my suitcase, I press the call button. A glutton for pain, I chance a look back.

Declan stands in the middle of his vast living room. The summer sun blazes through the windows despite the morning hour, illuminating the beautiful space with brightness. The man in the middle of it looks like a shadow.

He stares at me, but he doesn't move, frozen in his

own personal nightmare. Or unwilling to fight for us. With me gone, he can over-schedule his life again into a sense of control.

A part of me hopes he will stop me. It's like I've reached the limit of agony, and my body and mind scream for a break.

But Declan doesn't say anything. He watches me until the elevator door closes, but his broken expression haunts me long after.

The expression of a broken man who has lived through loss before.

I hold it together while in the car. I hold it together while the crew helps me settle on board. I hold it together to the point of absolute numbness.

I almost saw his side, but then he pulled out his kids. At that mastery of manipulation, something in me snapped.

Regardless of what went down, I don't think I will ever recover from this. I will never love like this again.

Declan's shattered expression is forever etched in my mind. Zach and Zoya's tears will torment me.

"Ms. Spinelli, Mrs. Quinn is on her way and asks us to hold the take-off. It will be another ten minutes. Can I get you anything?"

## A Convenient Secret

I frown. "Just water. Thank you."

Mrs. Quinn?

Is it Saar or Dorothy? The Quinns share this jet, but it makes no sense for any of them to join me. Fuck, I hope it's not Mr. Quinn. I can't handle more wounds.

A black Escalade pulls to a stop on the tarmac, and Saar and Cora get out. What? Both of them hurry up the stairs.

"Lils." Saar rushes to me and wraps me in an embrace. "We didn't want you to do this alone."

I sob.

"I'm sure we'll get to him on time. I read the *Guardian* online this morning, and there is no mention of anything," Cora says.

They are here because of my father. "I'm sure the family is keeping it hushed," I say, and the dam breaks, and I bawl.

They usher me to the long seat along the windows, each of my friends on one side of me, rubbing my back. I don't know how long I cry, but I keep at it until I'm so exhausted my body screams with pain.

"Declan and I—" I sob.

I can't utter the words, but my friends seem to grasp it, regardless.

"Let's take off, and you can tell us everything." Saar kisses my temple, squeezing my shoulders.

"Or whatever you feel comfortable with," Cora adds.

"You're really coming with me?"

"Of course," Cora says. "Celeste is sorry, but she couldn't leave Amelie."

"What about your bistro?" I sniffle.

"Sanjay can manage today, and I'm closed tomorrow anyway, and we'll figure it out afterward. This is where I want to be."

"And I prerecorded two episodes last week, so this is where I want to be," Saar says.

"Thank you. This is not where I want to be." I sniffle again, stupid tears doing whatever they want. "I married Declan to help him with his custody battle."

"But Kendra gave up her parental rights," Saar says.

"He forgot to mention that." I sigh and let my head fall back against the seat, heavy with sadness and fatigue.

"But why?" Cora asks. "Why did he need a wife?"

"To own me." I shrug and tell them my whole life story. From my choiceless childhood, my brother's death, my mother's absence, my parents' marriage of manipulation, my father's conditional attention, my engagement, my scars, the relationship with Declan.

It's cathartic just to retell it all. Through some parts I'm strangely detached, like they didn't happen to me.

Some parts I see differently than I used to. And through some parts, particularly the last few months with Declan, I ugly-cry, my heart breaking all over again.

At one point, the flight attendant enters and brings us breakfast, but leaves too quickly, probably horrified by my red face, swollen eyes, and runny nose.

My friends listen in silence, keeping a safe space for me to recount the details I kept to myself for so long. It's agonizing and cathartic at the same time.

"He was the voice?" Saar asks when I'm too exhausted to speak.

"It sounds like he was into you as well. Why else would he trick you into marriage?" Cora takes a bite of her toast.

"That's the point, though; he wanted me so he tricked me?" I force a sip of tea down my throat, the warm liquid soothing.

"I think you both were too emotional and exhausted for that conversation, though," Saar says.

She may be right. "Yeah, it's like all our traumas, fears, and habits collided under the pressure."

"Can you forgive him, though?" Cora asks.

"I think I can forgive him, but how am I to trust him? And that's not the only problem. We built a relationship on lies and secrets, and under pressure, we didn't stick together; we weren't able to bridge the gap."

"Or it's just a timing issue. If you didn't have to leave, you may have worked it out." Saar shrugs. "Relationships are hard, and yours is pretty new. Even if we forget about the secrets, you came into it craving autonomy, and he needs control. You had no room to find the compromise."

"So we were doomed from the beginning?" My lip quivers again.

"What I'm saying is that we need to dope you with painkillers and let you sleep first. Second, you need to assess the situation at home with your father. And then, after a day or two, if you feel like it, you call Declan." She smiles at me.

"But what if all the problems that bubbled up right now are really what will always break us apart? Something we will never overcome. Sometimes, love is not enough."

"Lils," Cora says. "You won't know until you give it a chance."

"Yes, if there were no children involved. We should have tested our chances before involving everyone else. I wouldn't be able to say goodbye to them one more time. And they can't have another person abandoning them."

Silence descends, only interrupted by the

monotonous humming of the plane. How did we get into this impossible situation?

But perhaps Saar is right; after a good sleep, I may see things differently.

I look at my friends and take each of their hands in mine, squeezing tight.

Eighteen months ago, I came to New York, scared and running, but also to find my independence. I found way more than that.

Today, I'm leaving to revisit my past life. Heartbroken, but with friends for life. Maybe I can survive this.

## Chapter 31

## *Declan*

"Liliana Spinelli became the interim CEO of Spinelli Holdings today." I raise my glass of vodka, talking to my empty home office.

I hate vodka, but whiskey doesn't taste good anymore. Not if I don't share it with Seagull.

Seven days, four hours, and—I check my watch—twenty-two minutes of misery.

I didn't stop her.

She didn't stay.

I declared my love. I married her because I wanted her, and it wasn't enough. I wasn't enough. Just like with Kendra.

"Fuck." I smash the glass against the door.

The audience in the sitcom on the screen laughs.

"It's not funny," I yell at the screen, because in my

drowning loneliness I talk to the empty room, or my TV.

Why couldn't she see I lied to be with her, not to manipulate her? I don't fucking know why I did it. Or why I didn't tell her sooner. After the security camera discovery, it didn't seem like a good time.

To be honest, the coward in me was hoping it wouldn't ever come up. I fucked up, and before I could fix it, she had to leave.

Would everything be different if she wasn't on the other side of the ocean? Or does the geographical distance bear no weight here?

Why did she have to fucking leave?

Even half-drunk most days, I still know that this time, I won't recover. After Kendra, I bounced into action.

This time is different. This time, the world shattered around me, and I just don't see how to pick up its pieces.

Not while I'm filled with regret, grief, anger, and such a fucking bleeding gap in my heart that I don't know how to breathe.

She's gone. And today's announcement about her stepping in to cover for her father confirms that she's not coming back.

I lean back in my chair, closing my eyes and lifting

my legs to my desk. I haven't slept in my bedroom since she left.

The door opens, and footsteps crush the shards of the vodka glass. I told the housekeeper not to let anyone come in here.

"Jesus." My brother's voice snaps my eyes open.

A mistake, because now I see he's not alone. Caleb, Xander, and Roxy follow him in. I'm firing my housekeeper.

"What are they doing here?" I ask Corm.

"Protecting our investment." Xander smirks.

"Fuck off." I drop my legs. "What do you want?"

"Where are your kids?" Caleb frowns.

"The Hamptons with my mother."

Corm hits the button and the shutters roll up, streaming daylight into my cave. I blink, the brightness upsetting my stomach.

"Why would you do that?" I complain like an idiot. Fuck, I hate this version of myself. I hate any version of myself that doesn't involve Lily. "What the hell do you want?"

Xander throws a folder on my desk. "We need you to sign the offer."

I frown, flipping the folder open. It's the job offer for the London job addressed to Vivienne Drake. "I see we went with the female candidate."

"Look, his observation skills are sharp," Caleb drawls.

"You could have signed and extended the offer without this unsolicited visit." I scribble the signature on the line.

"And miss this excursion to the life of the most pathetic man?" Xander snickers.

"Fuck you," I snarl, pushing the folder back toward him.

"Declan, you haven't shown up at work for a week," Corm says. "You're not answering your phone. I know you're alive only because Mom confirmed you call your kids once a day."

"You let your kids see you like that?" Caleb sounds scandalized.

"It's not a video call."

Yeah, I sunk so low that I ship my kids away so I can wallow. Only I didn't expect my heart wound would continue to fester for a week with no chance of improvement.

"It's time to take a shower," Roxy says.

"And grovel." Corm leans against the bookshelf. "Saar and Cora came back from London, and they are really pissed at you."

"They were in London?" They saw her; they talked to her. Fuck, I hate them.

"They left with Lily a week ago."

Jealousy coils up my spine, but I'm also happy she didn't need to face her former—and current—world alone.

"When was the last time you left this room?" Caleb swipes the glass shards by the door with the edge of his shoe.

"Why do you care?" I snarl.

"This conversation is really productive." Roxy sighs. "Declan, you either go get your woman, or you stop feeling sorry for yourself and return to society."

"In either case, please start with a shower." Xander picks up a photo from my research pile across the room.

"Don't touch anything." I stand up. The room swirls, so I lean against the desk. I fucking hate vodka.

"Look, man, I don't know what happened, but if this is the result, just go and talk to her," Corm says.

"After I hired her, you were the one telling me to stay away," I argue. "And now you think I should chase her?"

"Back then, I was talking about a sex-and-forget kind of a situation, you idiot. And yes, you let her go, so now, you chase her." Corm shakes his head.

"I didn't let her go. She fucking left." The words—or rather their volume—scratch my throat.

"The male brain is the biggest mystery to me,"

Roxy says. "But answer me one question, is she the one?"

"Does it matter? She left, and just took a job with Spinelli Holdings."

"Your point?" Corm scoffs. "She didn't marry her job, you idiot. She's still your wife. However that came about."

"She didn't want to stay." I stumble around. Where did I put the bottle? I need to numb this pain.

"Did you ask her to stay?" Caleb asks. Not helpful.

"I don't know anymore. She has to stay there. It's her family legacy."

"And in front of all of your sexist asses, I would like to say she is one of the youngest ever CEOs. Girl power!" Roxy cheers.

"Roxy, that's not why we're here," Xander groans.

"It warranted the mention though." She shrugs.

"Can you all leave finally? I don't want to talk about Lily."

"Listen, fucker, she's your wife." Corm pushes me back to my seat and swirls it, leaning on the armrests. "Two weeks ago, you were buying her a ring. You wouldn't buy her a ring if she wasn't special."

"I can't make her choose me." I push him away.

"I'm far from a relationship expert here," Xander says, and everyone else murmurs their agreement. "But didn't she choose you already? She married you."

"And then moved to London." My gaze finally lands on the bottle. The only problem: Roxy is holding it. She doesn't look like she'd want to give it back.

"Not to point out the obvious, but we're about to open offices in London," Xander deadpans.

"Don't fucking try to take advantage of my situation." I push to stand up, but my legs are not following my brain, so I stumble back into my chair. "You know I can't—"

I don't finish the sentence. What's the point?

"Just start with a shower. We will wait downstairs." Corm pats my shoulder.

"I don't need you to babysit me," I growl, completely lying. I'm way past taking care of myself.

Or caring in general. Maybe sending the twins to the Hamptons wasn't the best idea. They would have kept me focused on moving forward.

"I beg to differ." Roxy smirks.

They loiter around until I exit the office and enter my master bedroom. What's next? They will get into the shower with me?

I hate having people around. Other than her.

I should have never let her go.

"Daddy," Zoya shouts and runs to me.

Zach and Mom exit the elevator behind her.

"We had such a great time," Mom chirps, ruffling Zach's hair. When her gaze collides with mine, she flinches. "Zach, Zoya, why don't you go wash your hands so I can talk to your dad?"

"I missed you, Daddy." Zoya gives me a sloppy kiss on my cheek.

"I missed you, too, sweetheart." I hold her for a moment longer, hoping to feel stronger for them.

I'm not, but I will pretend the shit out of it. These two don't need yet another absent parent.

"Why do you have a beawd?" She pulls at it.

"I didn't have time to shave."

She scrunches her nose. "I don't like it."

"Neither do I." My mother scrutinizes me, not even hiding her judgment.

"How is your wrist, Zach?" I turn to him before they leave.

"Itchy, but good. We had a good time with Grandma." He nods and follows his sister upstairs.

"What happened to you?" Mom asks the minute they are out of sight.

"Nothing, just a rough day." I don't think I've ever blatantly lied to my mother.

"Okay, if that's the story you want to feed me." She purses her lips, looking hurt.

"Look, Mom, I just—"

"Is it about Lily?"

Fucking mothers and their sixth sense.

"Why would you say that?"

"You punched a man at my event, and then dragged her from there like a caveman. The romantic in me couldn't be prouder of you, but I had some damage control to do, so I'm not going to praise you."

"Sorry about that." I sigh and shuffle to the kitchen. "Do you want a coffee?"

"Cortado, please." She leans against the kitchen counter. "You know who the man you punched is?" Her tone suggests she knows who he is.

"Yes."

"Why is Lily in London and you're here?"

"Mom, just drop it." I push the cup to her.

"The way you look, I'm not sure I want to leave the twins with you at the moment. This is the first time I've seen you not being fit to parent them, and you went through a lot before."

I pinch the bridge of my nose, sighing. "I have things under control." Wow, the lies keep piling up.

She steps closer, pulls my hand away from my face, and cups my cheek. "My love, you don't have to try to control everything. Sometimes, we just need to lean into the crazy, spontaneous and chaotic to feel alive. You can't control all the outcomes. You have already proved that you can face any and all challenges. But darling, you can't always plan ahead for them."

*Life is not always predictable.* The memory of Lily's words hurts like hell.

"It's too late, anyway." Acid gnaws at my stomach, sharp and relentless.

To my utter shock, and in such contrast to my current emotional turmoil, Mom laughs. "It's never too late. Didn't I teach you that?" She pats my cheek and turns to finish her coffee. "I talked to my friend Bernadette."

"The countess from England?"

"Duchess."

"Mom, I really don't feel like chitchatting about your friends." Especially the ones that are geographically closer to Lily. "I should go and be with the kids."

"That Spinelli man you punched? He's back there, weaseling his way in. And he's not a good man."

A sour burn rises up my throat as I clench my fists. I turn to the windows, the anger blinding my vision.

"Anyway," Mom says, "he might be one of those situations you actually want to have under control." She squeezes my shoulder. "I'm going to say goodbye to the kids."

"Good night, Zach." I kiss his forehead.

"Can I still play for a bit?"

"It's late, buddy."

"But I can't play piano with this cast. And I couldn't swim at Granny's, so my airplane is all I have left—"

"Okay, okay, Zach, you can play with your airplane." Jesus, is he becoming as dramatic as his sister? I walk to the door.

"Dad?" He stops me. "Is Lily coming back?"

Fuck. "Her dad is sick, and she needs to run their company while he recovers."

He nods, luckily not pressing the topic. "I miss her."

*Me too.* "Good night, Zach."

I rush away from there, scared of another question.

Zoya is half-asleep when I enter, so I kiss her forehead, and she mumbles something before turning to her side.

"Good night, sweetheart."

Let's hope that, at least, they can have a good night.

I take a shower and shave, but it doesn't make me feel whole or normal. The hollow feeling keeps spreading, eating into my organs.

Instead of my bed, I go to my office. The housekeeper cleaned and aired it after Corm and the Merged entourage left yesterday.

I turn on the show, the comedy laughter becoming the torturous background of my time in my personal oasis. The armchair in the corner immediately sparks flashes of Lily crossing her legs.

The memory immediately moves my attention to the shelves, and how sweet and hot she was that night.

So much for my personal sanctuary. I exhale slowly, dragging a hand down my face. My muscles are tight, my head pounding. I should sit down. I should drink something. But if I learned anything this past week, alcohol doesn't make the gloom go away; it deepens it.

Behind my desk, I first torture myself with some past footage of Lily in my house, and then try to work on the family tree I've been ignoring.

*He might be one of those situations you actually want to have under control.*

Mom's words redirect my attention, and I start searching and making phone calls. She may no longer be here, but she's still my wife. Mine to protect.

Two hours later, I have a few leads, and for the first time in days, the fog in my mind lifts slightly. Maybe I should try to sleep. I'm sure Zoya will wake me up at dawn.

I reach to turn off the lamp, and notice a folder peeking out from under the other paperwork. I don't use pink folders. That's Roxy's specialty, to diffuse the amount of testosterone in the office, as she puts it.

I pull it out and immediately recognize it. The idiots left the signed offer here, and the housekeeper must have tidied it under the other paperwork. God, my desk has never been this messy.

I take the folder to bring it downstairs, so I can have it delivered to our office tomorrow.

The city flickers beyond the terrace, and I stop dead halfway on the staircase.

The fairy lights flicker on the terrace. Lily hung them there. I drop to sit on a step. She's everywhere. But the patio holds many special memories. I can practically see them all, as if the glass wall was a movie screen.

Lily in her purple dress. Me discovering her scars. Her blushing. Her arching her back. Laughing. Sharing a glass of whiskey with me. Looking so serene when she watched the city.

I don't know how long I sit there, but for the first time, my reminiscence brings more than just pain, regret, and grief. It sparks determination.

I may not be able to control the situation, but am I going to let that prevent me from acting?

The folder in my hands is wrinkled from holding it in a white-knuckled grip. I pull out my phone and take a first step on the uncertain journey.

# Chapter 32

## *Lily*

**CELESTE**

I miss you.

**SAAR**

Stop being whiny, she doesn't need that on her plate.

**CELESTE**

I'm a breastfeeding sleep-deprived mother, I get to be as whiny as I want.

I can tell her I miss her.

> You know I'm a part of this conversation.
>
> And I miss you too.
>
> Have you seen him?

**SAAR**

Not answering that.

> **CORA**
> How is your asshole cousin?

> Scheming and trying to get through my security team.

> **CELESTE**
> How is your dad?

> Better.

> **SAAR**
> Is the job still overwhelming?

> They will find out I'm faking it soon.

> **SAAR**
> BS. You're smart.

> **CELESTE**
> You've got this, Lils.

> **CORA**
> Can we ask how you are?

> The same.

> **SAAR**
> Fuck

"You work too hard." My father coughs in his bed. He takes off his glasses and puts down the paperwork he's been reviewing.

I look at him from the makeshift desk I set up in his room. "Really? Says the man who should be resting."

"Oh, the doctors are just being extra-cautious," he

complains, as he's been doing for the past four days since he returned from the hospital.

"I think that's a good approach." I return to the spreadsheet on my screen.

"You're deflecting, Cookie."

"Don't call me that. I'm not five anymore." But I can't help but grin at his use of my childhood name.

"Doesn't change the fact that you're deflecting." He pins me with that fatherly gaze of his that always makes me sit up straighter. Even at almost twenty-six.

"Okay, I'm working extra hard because I have no choice. Because, for whatever reason, you decided none of your colleagues can run the company."

"Oh, they can run it just fine, but none of them is you."

"I don't even know what that means. I'm not qualified."

A part of me suspects my father insisted on my highly unusual appointment as CEO to force me to stay here. Another part hopes it was more a seal of approval rather than manipulation.

At the end of the day, it doesn't matter. I accepted because I want to make some changes. My family's business is extremely successful, but not necessarily progressive in its internal policies, marketing practices, or business dealings.

I observed that as an intern, and now I've grabbed

the chance to, at least, start implementing changes.

The position terrifies me. But it's demanding enough to help me go through this life without breaking into pieces.

So yeah, my father might have manipulated me, but I beat him at his own game and took advantage of the situation.

I've been working fourteen hours every day, either here or in my father's office. Burying myself in this work is the only way to banish certain thoughts from my mind.

It's the only way to live with the agonizing pain that my bleeding heart injects into me at regular intervals. It's been two weeks, and I feel only worse.

So I dive into another analysis, financial projection, expansion plan, marketing campaign, litigation case. Anything to keep the brain working hard enough not to leave any space for memories.

As much as I try, my heart is pumping beats of regret, grief, sadness, and often anger. At him. At me. At us. At Tim. At the media. At my father. At the world.

Even fourteen-hour workdays don't tire me enough to fall into a dreamless slumber. I'm running on coffee and energy drinks. I try to kill myself in my private gym before bedtime, or right after I get up, but nothing works.

"You are a Spinelli."

"That's hardly a qualification. Let me remind you that Timothy is a Spinelli, too."

"No, he's not."

"Dad, we had this argument so many times. I stepped in because you asked me to. I appreciate your trust in my abilities. But don't ask me why I work this hard. Your trust and my name aren't enough to get the job done."

"I think you work hard to take your mind off something."

I close my eyes and take a deep breath. I didn't exactly assume I was hiding my grief well, but I hoped my father would avoid the topic.

"Dad, I have to finish this before I leave for the office."

"Come here, Lily." He pats his bed.

Sighing, I climb beside him, resting my head on his chest as he wraps his arm around me.

"I failed you." He kisses my crown.

"Dad—"

"No, let me finish. I have always been hard on you, especially after..." He peters out, never able to say my brother's name. "After your mother left, I was always more focused on business than you."

"Dad, you don't have to—"

"I do. I guess facing one's mortality brings some

things into sharper focus. I'm sorry I didn't consider Tim an actual threat. I should have protected you better from him, but I was so focused on work, on protecting the company from the in-family fighting, that I didn't see... or maybe I chose not to see what was really going on."

"I never blamed you for anything."

"You should. I almost lost you because I had the wrong priorities. I'm not going to let that happen again."

I sit, turning to face him. "Did you give me the job to atone?"

"No, I still love the company." He smirks. "I just took everything else for granted. I'm glad to have you back."

"A part of me is glad to be back, Dad." I wish it was more; things would be so much easier.

"You left the other part in New York?"

I look away, and he takes my hand, patting it.

"You don't have to tell me the details, but I hate seeing you this unhappy."

"I'm not unhappy, Dad. I'm happy to be back home, and I love the job. I didn't even realize how much I cared about the company. I'm not going to lie, I am heartbroken, but I guess that is a rite of passage at my age."

"If he is half as smart as you, he'll realize soon what he lost and come crawling back."

I roll my eyes.

"But if that happens…"

"Dad, don't—"

"Are you sure you want an instant family, an older divorced man with kids?"

"As opposed to my conniving, no-morals, corrupt cousin?" I slide from the bed to return to my work, done with this conversation.

"Touché."

Okay, fuck it, I'm not done with the conversation. I turn back. "For the record, Declan Quinn is a wonderful, caring, and loving man and father. He listens, and makes me feel safe. He's smart, loyal, passionate, confident, and honest—" My voice breaks. I can't claim the last one.

I hurry to collect my things and flee from here before I bawl in front of my father.

"If he's so perfect, then where is he?"

"One more signature here." Someone shoves another contract in front of me. I scan the pages and scribble my name on the last one.

"Okay, let's start." I look around the room, at people who are the trusted advisers of my father.

Most of them have been with the company for a very long time. They all look at me like I'm a nuisance.

Their vision, when they suggested me as their interim boss to the board, was that I'd bring over Daddy's to-do list and they would happily go about their own business.

Dad clearly has enough sway with the board to outvote his half-sister. The problem with that is that Timothy is now trying to get to me, because with me in power, however temporarily, his undying love for me has bloomed. He's been whining to the reporters about how grateful he is for my return, and can't wait to plan the wedding. What an idiot.

At least Dad is on my side this time, understanding better the level of evil his kin can stir.

Regardless of the turmoil of my personal life, to the people in this room, I'm a glorified messenger. A poster child for nepotism. Mostly I'm just trying to grasp what's going on here. But there are certain things where I can't help, but want to contribute, to breathe fresh air into the traditional operation.

I'm excited about this company, but it's hard to harness passion when one's heart is bleeding.

The gaping wound festers and spreads like a disease, infecting my every waking hour. A part of me wants to call Declan, and another part waits for his call.

What is worse, there is no part of me that hopes to forget and move on.

I've navigated mistrust and manipulation all my life. I want to be surrounded by people I can trust.

And therein lies my problem. Because deep down, I trust Declan. I trust the man who made me feel cherished, protected, beautiful, and smart. Who let me care for the most precious people in his life.

God, I miss Zoya and Zach.

I miss him.

I miss him so much.

Someone clears their throat and snaps me back to the reality of the boardroom.

Shit. Daydreaming—or rather day-nightmaring—isn't really a CEO groove.

I take my time looking around, resting my gaze on every single person in the room. In some ways, this is familiar. I sat in at these meetings when I was an intern. But as an intern, I sat in the corner, soaking it all in.

Now, I'm sitting at the head of the table. Equipped by my father's advice, a lot of theoretical knowledge, and little practical experience, I try to lean into my drive to continue growing this company, because I have nothing else to back me up.

That drive surprised me, to be honest. I didn't expect to care so much. I didn't expect I'd take the job with such a sense of responsibility and purpose. If I wasn't hurting so much, I would love it all.

Before, Liliana Spinelli took on her duty. Now, it's different. My stay in the US, my quest for some resemblance of independence, allowed me to assess my options better. And I fucking love this opportunity.

I look down at my notes and start the meeting, ticking off the topics my father wants an update on. I ask questions and challenge the reports, but my game is fully orchestrated by my father.

Finally, we get to the end of the list, and I look at the last two items. Items I added there. I consider adjourning the meeting. Who am I to pretend I know better?

*Can you be any more perfect?*

"Before we wrap up, I have two more things. I would like to see at least three new directions for our Christmas advertising, because frankly, updating our print ad from the fifties with a modern housewife is embarrassing."

The marketing director's face reddens. "We have been successful with that image for years. It's part of our brand. People expect it."

"People who are our customers may take comfort in it, but it doesn't speak to anyone else. It certainly doesn't speak to the younger generation. Let's challenge the team to bring the campaign into the twenty-first century."

Shocked faces stare at me. My heart beats so fast, they must hear it.

"Is this what your father wants?" the Head of Marketing scoffs.

"I'm the CEO at the moment, and that's what matters. I want to see your proposals next week."

He opens his mouth, but I turn to the head of HR. "I would like a proposal on how to create a more inclusive environment to attract female talent to the top positions at the company."

I don't know her, but she's been silent at all the meetings, trying to blend into the background. A smile grows on her face at my words, and she nods.

"Okay then. Good job, everyone." I stand up, my hands only slightly shaking.

The HR director approaches me. "I will send you my proposal today."

I frown. "You knew I would ask?"

She shakes her head. "No, but I have tried to present it since I started a year ago."

"I look forward to reviewing it."

"It's good to have you on board." She leaves, and I smile for the first time in two weeks.

"Ms. Spinelli, I'm sorry, but Mr. Quinn is here,

claiming he's your husband." My father's assistant shrugs. "I told him that he has no appointment, but he just sits in the reception, refusing to leave. Should I call security?"

Her words penetrate my brain, and spread like a livewire dropped in water—sparking, hissing, sending shockwaves through every nerve.

My pulse trips, a wild rhythm of thrill and anxiety, while my stomach tightens as if bracing for impact. The rush is electric, overwhelming.

Heat spreads over my face as I try to find a regular rhythm for my breathing, and look like a reasonable person at the same time.

People who had booked a meeting here start wandering in, hesitating at the entrance when they see me.

"Right," I croak. "Give me five minutes before you show Mr. Quinn to my office."

I dash from the boardroom, forgetting my tablet and all my documents. Entering my father's suite, I run for the bathroom.

Fuck, why didn't I wear makeup? I'm dressed for the job, but my face looks like... well, like I haven't slept, or taken care of myself.

I open the mirror cabinet, but of course my father doesn't have blush or lipstick hidden here.

I splash my face with water, more to cool myself

than to improve anything. What am I doing?

I hear the door of the office open. Fuck, it's been five minutes already? For weeks, time has glided like molasses, and now, when I need a minute, it flies.

"Ms. Spinelli?" the assistant calls.

Okay, I just stood up to a room full of men in suits; I can face one more. I step out, my heels sinking into the plush carpet that covers the lavish office. Immediately, I realize how wrong I was.

I can't face him.

The sight of him knocks the air out of me. He looks the same and different. Familiar broad shoulders, immaculate suit, mussed-up hair, and that dark gaze of his. His confidence spreads through the room, but there is something hesitant in his entry.

For a beat, time stops, and we stare at each other. I'm rooted to the floor, trying to tame my racing heart. It's like all my bodily functions have narrowed into the loud pumping in my temple, so there is no energy left to breathe, think, speak, or anything else.

Declan turns to look at the assistant, and she shrivels under his scowl before she rushes out, leaving me alone with him.

Another lifetime passes as we just stand and look at each other. I will my legs to stay put, and it takes an inhuman effort not to run toward him.

"Seagull," he rasps, and there are so many emotions

behind that name, my knees buckle. The reverence and pain in his tone are almost my undoing.

And his voice. That voice has owned me for over a year. And at this moment, it arrests me with the same need as always.

But he isn't just a voice to me anymore. And I'm not the girl I was then—as much as I wish for things to go back to one of those beats of time when we were whole.

"You came," I breathe, as if it isn't obvious.

"We need to finish our last conversation properly." He puts his hands in his pockets. I wish that posture didn't affect me as much.

It's just a man with his hands in his pockets. I can repeat that to myself endlessly, but that doesn't make it true. He's way more.

"Declan, nothing we can say will change the fact that I'm here and you're there."

"We will get to that part. Do you want to sit?"

I definitely need to sit, but I resist. "I'm good." That's a gross exaggeration. "What are you doing here?"

"First, I came to apologize." He pulls his hands out and clenches his fists, but then puts them back into his pockets.

Once I would have considered it an arrogant gesture. I know he does it to control his reactions. I wish he wouldn't because I want to see his reactions. I want to feel them. I want to experience them.

I want him to be vulnerable with me.

I want to see he's hurting as much as I am.

"For what?" I lick my lips, and his gaze drops there briefly before he locks it with mine, and I regret I didn't take that seat.

The intense longing in his eyes hits me like a wrecking ball.

"For letting you leave."

I blink. What the hell? And suddenly, the latent fury that I've been stifling blasts into a fire. "*Letting* me leave? This is exactly why I left, Declan, because I'm not your property, or your employee."

"Technically, you never quit."

"Are you for real?" Thank God I'm not closer, because I want to slap him. I can still throw a stapler.

"Fuck, Lily, please just let me say what I came to say before I fuck it all up."

I fold my arms over my chest, glaring at him.

"Maybe I wanted to own you. But only because you owned me first. Completely, painfully, unconditionally. Without you even knowing it, you owned me. I'm not going to apologize for that. But I'm sorry for keeping things from you. I'm sorry for not believing we might have a chance. For thinking my only chance with you was so brief, I needed to trick you into it."

My chest constricts, burn searing my throat and itching my eyes. He didn't think he had a chance with me? As far as apologies go, this one is the worst, but in some twisted way, the best I could have imagined.

"I kept things from you too." I don't say it to absolve him, but to put our relationship into perspective. We didn't communicate well.

"To protect me and my kids. Don't try to share the blame. The blame is on me. Only on me."

He lifts his chin, challenging me. Even his admission of guilt carries an air of confidence. Why do I find it so attractive?

"Declan." I sigh, not even sure whether I want to unwrap all my reservations.

He eats the distance between us and takes my hand. I need to snatch it away to protect myself, because his touch has never resulted in sensible behavior or logical choices for me.

He tugs me gently, so I'm forced to step closer. As soon as I'm in front of him, he squeezes my hand, but doesn't invade my personal space. On some level, it's almost worse.

I withdraw my hand from his and hug my arms.

He hangs his head, the pain we share palpable in the air. We share it without talking about it. We feel it without naming it. What we don't know is how to get out of this limbo. Well, I don't.

"I want to put an oversized photo of you on my wall," he says.

I frown. "What?"

He shakes his head. "I'm not expressing myself properly, but I'm on Rachel's side."

Okay, maybe his cologne wiped my brain, because I really don't follow. "Who is Rachel?"

He shifts from one foot to the other, frustration clenching his fists. "That episode of *Friends* where they argue whether Ross cheated. There is no such thing as a break when you love someone the way I love you. I can't possibly imagine being with any other woman.

"You might be on the other side of the world, not talking to me, but that changes nothing. There is no break from you, Seagull. You're it for me. Whatever you decide, I will only ever love you."

God, how I wish these were the words he would have said before I left. "I wish you wouldn't have said that." My voice trembles.

He flinches, his face falling and rearranging itself into a stony expression. "Oh, I see." His voice is still the voice I adore, but the tone is like a cold shower.

"Do you? Because I don't see how this could work. I never knew being in love hurts so much. I've been miserable without you. Without Zoya and Zach. But my father needs me here, and I don't see how this could work. So I appreciate that you came to finish our last conversation, but let's not torture each other any longer, Declan."

"You want to stay here?" he asks curtly.

I sigh. "I'm hurt by your actions, but I believe you. I believe you did it because you wanted to be with me. It's the most fucked-up way to start a relationship, but I believe you did it because you saw something in me that pulled you in.

"You say I owned you before we married. Well, until I moved into your house, I didn't even know you knew I existed—"

"You must know by now that's not true." He takes a step closer, but thinks better of it.

His touch would be devastating.

"We can't continue where we left off, Declan. But I'm not sure if I know how to redefine the dynamics between us. I come from a family where I only witnessed that when you want something you take it, no matter what, and not in an ambitious, healthy way, but in a domineering, rotten way."

I glimpse the photo of me, my dad, and my brother on the shelf behind Declan. "I know firsthand that love can make you overlook a lot of that. Forgive, accept, make excuses. I don't want to live like that. I don't want my children to live in such a toxic environment and grow up believing that's the only way."

"What are you saying, Lily?"

"For the past two weeks, I pictured you showing up and hugging me. And then everything would be better. Only I realized that I don't want to be that girl who is silently waiting for your touch and attention. I want to be the woman who deserves it. But I also want to be the woman who makes her own choices."

He stares at me, and I wish I could see what's happening behind his stormy expression. I wish things were different. I wish I could know I'm making the right choice.

I wish I could know if one can function with their heart shattered.

Finally, he nods. "You want to stay." This time it's not a question; it's a statement.

I nod regardless, and the last whole piece of my heart cracks.

"Okay," he says and whips around.

"Where are you going?"

But my question reaches the open door as I watch Declan storming down the hallway. And, just like that, he is gone.

I close the door behind him and slide down, wondering whether I'll ever stand up again.

## Chapter 33

## *Declan*

"I understand she's not accepting the flowers, but I'm paying you to have them delivered three times a day, so you do that," I bark into the phone, pacing around my hotel room.

"With the same note, sir?"

"Yes." The card says "Just because" and has no signature. I hope it's enough for now. I hope she gets it.

The person on the other side sighs.

Why is she not accepting the flowers? *Come on, Lily, hang in there for a moment longer.*

I disconnect the call and answer the video on my laptop.

"It's nice to see you're still shaved." Xander snickers.

"It's not so nice to see you're still an asshole." I sit on the sofa, holding the notebook in my hands. It's not the most comfortable, but I'm not taking a call in my bed. There is only so much disorder I can handle.

"Oh, you miss me, Dec."

"Like herpes."

"Enough." Corm turns his camera on. "Update quickly. I have things to do."

"Nice to see you, too," I say.

"Fuck off," my brother murmurs.

"Someone is in a mood." Xander snickers.

"Fucking dog destroyed my new shoes this morning."

Xander almost falls off his chair laughing.

"Are we waiting for Caleb?" I ask, hoping this meeting will end already.

Roxy's face appears on the screen. "Caleb won't make it. He's on a call with Japan, and it's running late."

"At least this time his excuse isn't his domestic situation." Xander pops something into his mouth.

"One day you will have a family, and you'll shut up." I glare at him. "What's on the agenda, Roxy?"

"Just the London update." She shoves a pencil behind her ear. The woman uses writing utensils as her accessory.

"Okay." I lean back. "The offices look good, fully furnished, and designed with Merged branding. I'm meeting with Vivienne Drake in half an hour."

"Let's hope it all goes smoothly, because we need to hit the ground running." Corm checks his watch.

"I agree. I will send you an update, hopefully by the end of the day London time." I stand to grab my jacket.

"What about some Lily update?" Roxy asks, grinning.

"None of your business," I growl.

"But things are going okay?" Corm leans forward like he can see what's going on here through the screen. "How is she?"

I blow the air from my cheeks. "I only saw her once."

"What? At this rate your kids will graduate from college by the time you win her over." Corm frowns.

Just because he's in a committed relationship for the first time in his life, he feels he has the moral ground to mock me.

"As I said, none of your business. Lily told me what she needs, and I'm making it happen."

"So you're going to roll over for her? That's manly." Xander chuckles.

"I'm going to compromise, you idiot."

"That sounds like sacrifice," Roxy says. "It almost rhymes." She wiggles her shoulders.

*It's like a kindergarten,* I swear under my breath.

"The two of you are chronically single, so you have

no right to comment." I put on the jacket, ready to disconnect the call.

"It still begs the question: when are you coming back?" Corm stops me.

I wish there was a straightforward answer. "Soon."

I snap the laptop shut and head to the first important meeting of my day.

* * *

I adjust my tie as the server cleans our plates. "Look, Ms. Drake—"

"Call me Vivienne." She smiles.

The woman in front of me has confidence, qualifications, and, judging by our twenty-minute conversation, sharp intuition. She would fit the shoes well.

"Vivienne, this is probably not what you expected when you came today—"

"You're going to offer the job to someone else, aren't you? A man, probably. You could have saved me the trip."

She grabs her briefcase and pushes her chair back.

"I would appreciate it if you let me finish. Or for that matter, stop interrupting me. Sit down," I growl. "Please," I add, and almost can feel Lily's smile.

Vivienne frowns at me, glaring for a beat too long, but then sinks back into the chair.

"The job is going to a man, but that man would love if you joined his team as his second-in-command."

She folds her arms across her chest. "I don't think I'm interested in playing second fiddle to someone who stole the job from me. I've been there, done that. There is always someone more qualified because they have a penis."

"Thank you for your opinion. I would prefer we would not mention cocks in our future dealings. The man is more experienced than you, though."

She scoffs. "Who?"

"Me."

Finally, she loses her gumption and just gapes at me. "I don't understand. Wouldn't I report to you anyway?"

"Let me explain."

\* \* \*

"Where is my wife?" I ask the receptionist on the Spinellis' executive floor.

"Mr. Quinn," she stammers.

"Good, you remember me. Now, could you kindly tell me if my wife is in her office?"

"Ms. Spinelli is in a meeting."

"I think it's time you start calling her Mrs. Quinn. Which way?"

"You can't—"

"Watch me." I march down the corridor, not sure where I'm going.

When I was here last week, I noticed the boardrooms here have glass walls, so I'll take my chances.

"Mr. Quinn, please." The receptionist strides behind me.

I stop, and she collides with me. I grip her elbow, so she can find her footing. "What's your name?"

"Lavinia."

"Look, Lavinia, I've done many idiotic things in the last few weeks. I'm not going to add to them and barge into my wife's meeting. I just want to wait for her and get her attention when she is done."

She heaves like she's just run a marathon. "I don't want to get fired."

"You won't, I promise. When is her meeting over?"

"I don't know."

"Take me to her assistant then."

She relaxes and leads me to the corner of the floor. Two things immediately surprise me.

One of them is pleasant. Lily's meeting is taking place in that part of the building, and she looks positively arresting presiding over the table. Fuck, I'm proud of her.

I want to savor the view through the glass wall, but the second surprise requires my immediate attention.

"I told you to never even so much as breathe her way." I keep my voice down, but my tone leaves no room for interpretations.

Timothy fucking Spinelli turns on his heels and flinches when he sees me. He schools his expression quickly. "What the fuck are you doing here?"

"None of your business, and I strongly suggest you get the fuck out of here before you regret it."

I was never someone who causes a scene, but this dickhead just asks for it.

"This is my company, you twat." He puffs out his chest.

"No, it's not. Your mother owns some shares, and you believe that gives you some privileges. Let me correct that belief." I step closer.

He flinches again, stepping back. "You're going to regret this, Quinn. If you think you can steal what's mine, you are mistaken."

"The only person making mistakes here is you, Timmy. First, nothing here is yours. Second, the only person regretting their actions will be you. And that's a promise. Now get out of my sight."

As he stumbles away, spitting empty threats, I find several people left their offices to watch the exchange. Shit, I hope nobody recorded it.

"What's going on?"

Lily's voice is like a drug hitting my system, permanently addictive, immediately coloring the world in high definition.

I whip around. "Sorry about that."

All eyes are on her, the people from her meeting rooted to the floor. She shakes her head. Okay, she's pissed.

"Go back to work, everyone." She eats the distance between us and gestures toward her office.

She waits for me to enter, and before she joins me, she turns to her assistant. "Call my security and fire them. He was not allowed to come to this level. Organize me a new security team."

She walks in and shuts the door behind her.

Fuck, she is hot when she is in charge. When I saw her last week, after the painful days full of doubt and regret, it was like coming home.

Her small frame that she carries with such confidence, her slanted nose, those beautiful intelligent eyes, and her smoking-hot body—it all takes my breath away.

Seeing her now, seething like a goddess of war, is even hotter.

The air is unusually heavy with fragrance, and when I look around, I realize she's been accepting the flowers. I smile, which only spurs her indignation.

"What are you doing here, Declan? You think you

can just waltz out of here and keep sending flowers without a word—"

"There was a card."

She rolls her eyes. "What do you want? I have work to do."

"I brought you something." I reach into my pocket.

"I don't want any gifts."

"It's not a gift, Lily. And I guarantee you'll want this." I hand her an encrypted data stick.

She takes it, frowning. "What is this?"

"Everything I could collect on your cousin. Enough to put him away. Not for what he did to you, but enough for a decade behind bars."

Her eyebrows rise. She looks at the stick before her gaze returns to me. "Thank you. Is this the reason you came?"

"Will you use it?"

"I don't know. I need to see what it contains and discuss it with my father. Tim is still a Spinelli; it's not just my decision."

"When you see what's he been up to, you will want to disassociate yourself from him."

"Okay, I will review it. Thank you. Though I don't understand why you went to all this effort—"

"I need you to be safe. Even if you never accept me back, I need to know you are safe."

"Declan, if I accept you back? You came here last

week, declared your love, and then stormed out." This fired-up version of her is fucking attractive.

"You told me you want to stay; I didn't have anything to say to that, so I needed to fix that."

"What are you talking about? You don't just leave in the middle of a conversation." She flails her arms in the air.

Fuck. "I see how that looked. A tactical mistake. I'm sorry, when I'm on a mission I tend to... act less... polite." I wince.

She shakes her head. "Yeah, I've noticed that." She walks over to the sofa and opens her laptop. "Thank you for this." She waves the stick before she throws it on a stack of folders beside her.

"Why don't you work behind the desk?"

She sighs, like she's faced with an annoying child who keeps asking questions. "It's my father's desk."

"Technically, it's your father's job, and you're slaying it. Don't hide in the corner, Seagull. It doesn't suit you."

She opens her mouth, ready to argue, but then she gives up. A hint of vulnerability flashes through her face. "You don't know if I'm slaying it."

"I do. I make a lot of money sniffing problems in a company, and your appointment didn't cause any concerns. The share price confirms that."

She closes her eyes and leans back. She looks exhausted. Fuck, I wish I could take some of her load.

"It's exhausting. I'm so worried I'll make a wrong step, I want to throw up half of the time." She looks at me, and the overwhelming need to fix everything for her rams through me like a freight train.

But she doesn't need me to fix things for her. She might have been forced into shoes that don't yet fit, but she will fill them just fine.

"It means you care, Seagull."

She chuckles humorlessly. "Care about not making a fool of myself."

"Can I take you out for lunch?"

My own words surprise me. That's not what I came for. I planned to explain how I see our future, but suddenly it feels essential to spend time with her, sharing a meal.

"I don't think it's a good idea."

"Let me change your mind."

She closes her eyes. "Okay, let's go. Where are you taking me?"

If only I knew. "It's your city; you choose."

She stands up, studying me. "Have you just invited me for lunch without having reservations?"

I shrug.

"You didn't plan this?"

I shrug again, and the corner of her lip twitches.

"Are you about to do something spontaneous?"

"A very smart person told me once that it's good to try sometimes." I turn to the door. "Now let's go, because we'll be late."

"You said you have no reservations." She grabs her purse.

"We still need to eat at noon."

She laughs, and a bit of my uprooted life rearranges itself back into place.

* * *

"Where are we going?" Lily asks for the fifth time, this time not hiding her annoyance.

"We're here."

She looks around the street, and then up at the white stucco house. "What's here?"

The door opens. "Mr. Quinn."

I lightly touch Lily's back to usher her up the few stairs. "Jonathan, this is my wife. Lily, Jonathan is showing us this house."

She narrows her eyes, looking from me to the realtor and back. "Why?"

I follow her into the air-conditioned foyer. "Jonathan, could you give us a moment?"

"Of course. I'll be in the kitchen." He leaves us, and I take Lily's hand to pull her into the sitting room.

It's empty, like the rest of the house, but the light streaming from the street makes it inviting.

"I get it, Seagull."

She cocks her head. "You get what?"

Fuck, again, I'm not saying the right words. "Last week, I didn't understand why you would choose the life you ran from. Regardless, I decided to accept it. I found a school for the twins, and this morning, I officially told the new London CEO that she has no job. Well, not the one she wanted."

Lily gasps, her hand flying to her mouth.

"I was going to buy this house and just bring you here, but—and I'm sorry it took me a moment—as I was making all these decisions that I refused just a month ago, I kept reminding myself that I'm doing it for us.

"But really for myself. That the need to be close to you is much stronger than my need to maintain the carefully planned status quo in New York. And it dawned on me, you wanting to stay here wasn't about choosing your family and past full of trauma. You chose you. And that is so fucking sexy."

She blinks a few times, and a tear rolls down her cheek. "You're moving to London?" She utters the words slowly like they are too fragile.

"Yes."

"Because of me?"

"Were you not listening, woman? I'm moving

because of me. I want this. I want to be close to you, and I hope to God you decide to take me—take us—back, so really, I'm doing it for us. For my family."

"Why?"

I step closer to cup her face. "Just because."

"Just because," she whispers.

We stare at each other, suspended in the tenderness of our uncertainty. Of the future that is unknown, unplanned. A future we are unprepared for, but so fucking ready for.

"Let's look at the house." She takes my hand.

Ten minutes later, we join Jonathan in the kitchen.

"We'll take it," I say.

"Wonderful. Congratulations." He shakes Lily's and then my hand. "I will contact the owner and get all the paperwork ready."

"Can I have the keys now?" I suggest rather than ask.

"But we haven't even drawn up the purchase agreement."

"I'll transfer the purchase price to your company's escrow account. Give me the account number."

"What?"

I sigh. "You heard me."

Lily folds her arms across her chest, glowering at me. "Sorry, Jonathan." She smiles at him.

But the man smells money, and dutifully types the

banking information into my phone. I fire it off to my waiting lawyer.

"Can I have the keys now?" I'm being an asshole, but there is an urgency to my spiel.

Jonathan's phone pings, and he checks it before he looks at me wide-eyed. "That's ten percent above the agreed price."

"A bit of an incentive to give me the keys and leave finally."

"Declan," Lily warns.

"Jonathan, technically I own this place, and you're trespassing."

His phone rings.

"That's probably my lawyer to discuss the paperwork." I gesture for him to answer.

"Hello?" He listens, and without disconnecting the call, he drops the keys into my hand and leaves.

"That was reckless. Not to say rude." Lily turns to me.

"I couldn't wait any longer."

"To own a house?"

"To be alone with you."

# Chapter 34

## *Lily*

I roll my eyes, but a smile stretches across my face. I've tried all day long to resist, but it is a lost battle.

A devil on my shoulder is reminding me he's being crazy to uproot his life for me. That he will regret it and hate me for that.

But leaning into that fear will rob me of potentially a lifetime of happiness with this grumpy, controlling man whom I love.

When he left last week without explanation, I stopped crying, my sadness replaced by anger and frustration.

When the first bouquet arrived with his "Just because" card, I was torn. A part of me got even more upset about his complicated way of communicating, or lack of it.

But a much bigger, significant part of me accepted that he needed to do things his way.

I place my hand over his where he is leaning against the kitchen island. "I'm sorry I ever compared you to Tim. I know that whatever you did, you never meant to hurt me."

He takes my hand and kisses my knuckles. "Lily, I know I still have years to prove to you that you can trust me. I understand that you must have reservations, and all of this seems too fast, too spontaneous. Believe me, I feel the latter too."

I smile. "I like spontaneous."

He yanks me to him. "Then I really hope you like to be fucked right now. Because I can't wait another minute without being deep inside you."

Oh my. His arms around me dissolve every last hesitation I might have harbored. I missed his touch so much. "There is no furniture here."

He pivots us and lifts me to the counter. "No problem." Bringing his forehead to mine, he traces my lower lip with his thumb.

The anticipation crackles in the air. My heart thumps in my temples. It's almost like we're doing it for the first time.

I slide his jacket off his shoulders, and he lets it drop to the ground. He unzips my dress and traces my shoulders, my clavicle, and then my arms as he pulls the top down to my waist.

His gaze drops to my bra, and a guttural sound makes its way from deep in his throat. "My wife has the most perfect tits." He cups them, flicking his thumb over my hard nipples. "So beautiful."

"Declan," I moan, arching my back, his touch not enough.

He dips his head to my neck, kissing me gently. "What does my Seagull need?"

Without hesitation, I grip his hair and force him to look at me. "Have me, wreck me, own me, but first, kiss me finally."

His pupils dilate, and then his lips are on me, and the sound that comes out of me is feral.

Declan devours my mouth like it's the first meal he's had after a long time of starvation—savoring it, pacing his attack, but making sure he enjoys every single moment.

The kiss ignites every nerve in my body. I jerk his belt, trying to unbuckle it while I bite his lip.

"Someone is needy." He chuckles.

"I need you inside me, Declan, I need it. Now." I practically yell at him.

"Lift."

I push off the counter and he grips my dress, sliding it down without grace. It ends up on the floor beside his jacket. I kick off my shoes while I concentrate on his tie and buttons.

It feels inadequately long before his shirt is off, and I attack his collarbone. "I missed you," I breathe.

"Don't ever walk out on us."

"Don't ever give me a reason."

He lowers his lips to my nipple and bites hard. I yelp, but the pain provokes lust to spread through my body, coiling in my core.

"Show me how ready you are for me." He straightens, his eyes burning with need. "Slide your fingers into your panties, Seagull, and show me how much you need me."

I lick my lips and do as he says, groaning at the contact of my own fingers with my sensitive center.

Declan grips the counter like he needs purchase to control himself. God, I love making this man lose it.

"Now show me," he growls.

I lift my hand to my lips, smearing some of my arousal on my bottom lip.

"Fuck, Lily. If you only knew what you do to me." He takes my hand and licks my fingers. "Mine."

"Always."

He pulls out his cock, already glistening with pre-cum. It seems larger than I remember, but I have no time to hesitate, because Declan rips off my panties and yanks me to the edge. Guiding his tip inside me, he thrusts in an inch.

We both groan.

"Don't go slowly. Take me like you hate me, Declan."

I don't know where the words come from. Perhaps the agony of the past weeks and his absence inspired my need.

"I love it when you ask for what you want. And you should have everything you desire, Seagull." He thrusts in, burying himself deep inside me, and we both groan.

I look down at where we're connected, and Declan starts moving, both of us entranced by the connection of our bodies.

"Look how well you take me, baby." He lifts my chin and kisses me.

Things escalate quickly, and the room fills with our slapping bodies, moans and sighs, while Declan fucks me in our new kitchen.

He dominates the pace, the timing, and really, the entire experience, and I love every moment. Because that's who we are. I make him lose control, and he helps me find mine.

Declan lifts me and moves us to the island in the middle of the room. "Are you going to be a good girl and come for me?"

My back hits the cold marble, and Declan's hand snakes under me, his finger prodding my other hole. My eyes snap at him. He's already searching for consent.

"Let me make it explosive for you, baby."

I nod.

He smiles. "Relax for me."

He swipes his finger through my folds, coating it in my own arousal. He circles around the opening before sliding in. The sensation is foreign, but not completely unwelcome.

My body yields to his finger faster than my mind, and the lightning bolt of pleasure that shoots through me has me lifting from the counter.

"Easy, love, relax and enjoy it. I will get you there."

Oh, fuck, he starts moving, and my mind fogs. "Declan!"

"That's right, let the world know who you belong to. Come for me, Seagull."

The orgasm is earth-shuddering, and I almost lose my voice screaming. Declan fucks me through it with his cock and finger, prolonging the pleasure.

"Look at me, Seagull."

What? My foggy mind barely captures the command, and I find his eyes, blinking. He pulls out his hand and grips my hips. "I want you to see what you do to me."

So I watch. I watch as my beautiful, powerful, flawed man comes undone, giving me his vulnerability as a gift.

Just because.

* * *

"I found a hand towel." Declan comes back to the kitchen with a damp cloth and helps me clean up.

The light reflects on his chest, and the sight just spreads another wide grin on my face.

"What are you smirking about?" He drops the towel to the sink and starts opening the cabinets.

His broad shoulders shift, muscles flexing beneath the glow of the under-cabinet lights. Delicious.

"I think you in your suit pants, bare-chested, is my favorite version of you."

He bangs the cabinet closed and turns, leaning against the counter. "I thought it was me being balls deep inside you."

I cross to him and snuggle against his chest. "Okay, fair enough. But it's a close second." I kiss his collarbone.

He nudges my chin with his finger. "My favorite version of you is spread on this kitchen island."

I giggle. "You didn't own the island a minute ago."

"Well, I bought it just in time." He kisses me. "And it's *our* kitchen island."

My smile may split my face by now. "What were you looking for?"

"A glass. You need to hydrate."

"My, my, Mr. Quinn, your aftercare game is impeccable today."

"What aftercare?"

I roll my eyes. "What you do for your partner after you've fucked their brains out. Like helping me clean up and get me water. Or cuddle."

He looks at me like I'm speaking an unfamiliar language. "So, common decency."

I shake my head. "Let's hydrate."

"There are no glasses."

I run the water in the sink and bend over to drink from the faucet.

"Now that's just plain barbaric."

I giggle and splash him.

His eyes widen. "You didn't."

"Maybe we need to christen our new home." I flick more water at him.

"Lily," he warns. "We will christen it when the kids are here."

I stop the water. "Okay, party pooper. Wait? With confetti?"

He belts out a laugh. "Sure."

"I love you, Declan Quinn."

"I love you, Lily Quinn."

And just like that, I'm no longer Lily Thorne or Lilianna Spinelli. I'm Lily Quinn.

"We never said the vows, though." I wrap my arms around his waist.

"I vow to protect, respect, love, and fuck you for the rest of my life."

"Fuck me?"

"That's an important vow."

"Of course. I vow to love you in all its forms, as my soulmate, as my lover, as my partner, as my husband. I promise to communicate better with you, and never keep secrets."

He kisses my forehead. "I won't keep secrets from you either. Never. I came close to losing you once, Lily, and I will never make the same mistake again. And I will share my thoughts with you instead of assuming you know where my head is."

"It's interesting how you're the chatty one when we're having sex, but lose that ability in other situations."

He looks at me, horrified. "I'm not chatty under any circumstances."

I laugh. "If you say so."

"Enough talking." He captures my lips, whips me around, and walks us to the window. "Hands on the glass."

* * *

"I meant to ask you, have you watched *Friends?*" I pick up my dress, stepping into it.

He groans. "Some of it."

I try not to grin. "Why?"

"Because I missed you. I never found the Seagull episode though."

My heart swells, emotions clogging my throat. "I think you found the right ones, anyway."

I turn, and Declan zips up my dress and then wraps his arms around me, pulling me back to his chest. "This kitchen will hold the best memories. I can't wait to fill it with our family."

"Do you expect me to learn how to cook?" I crook my neck to look at him.

"God, no. You're only allowed here naked."

"That would scandalize the staff."

"We'll have to hire resilient, blind people."

I laugh, but it dies quickly when I realize we're about to walk out of here. "Are you sure you're ready to deal with the media, and my family?"

"Lily, I think once your cousin and his mother are dealt with, your family can slowly transition away from the public eye. They have been the ones instigating the scandals. But our boring little family will hopefully soon lead a more-or-less normal life."

I sigh, letting out a long breath. That might be very naïve. "It may not be that easy."

"I didn't say I expected it to be easy. I don't expect it to happen overnight. I hired a very discreet security company for the kids and for us. I didn't handle things well in New York, but I learned from that experience."

"Promise not to shut down and push me away if things get out of control." The knot in my stomach tightens again.

"I promise. But if I fail, know that it's only my reaction to the situation. Promise me that you will help me through that, even if I'm an ass."

"Will you always apologize with mind-blowing sex?"

He nods, slapping my ass. "Do you understand I was never truly upset with you? Never."

"I know."

"I'm sorry you were the collateral of my helplessness. You didn't deserve that."

I rise to my tiptoes and kiss him. "We will both try to communicate better next time."

He takes my hand, and we leave our new home.

"You do know you will have to attend our family functions?" I tease as we walk down the street.

"By your side, anything is doable."

"On second thought, I may use that dreadful scowl of yours to scare people off. I guess everything is doable by your side."

He kisses my knuckles. "Talking about families—"

"Let's go get the kids."

He lifts me, twirling us around. "Can you be any more perfect?"

# Epilogue

# Lily

SAAR

So you're officially Mrs. Quinn, @Lily.

CELESTE

So are you, by the way.

> We're related now, aren't we? All three of us.

CELESTE

Best family ever.

CORA

Should I leave the chat?

SAAR

We love you.

CELESTE

Don't you dare.

## Epilogue

> I miss you so much.

"Daddy, I don't want to go to school tommowow." Zoya bounces on our bed.

Declan groans. "Tomorrow is Sunday. What time is it, Zoya?"

"Don't know, but Zach says it's five hours later than in New Yowk." She climbs between us.

"That means it's still early," Declan says, making no sense.

I open my eyes, smiling at her sleepily. "Good morning, sweet girl." I kiss her shoulder.

Fuck, I'm tired. Between work, moving, and sharing a bedroom with Declan, I don't think I've slept for more than four hours a night in weeks. I've loved every moment of it.

"Why can Lily sleep with you and I can't?"

Oh shit.

Declan scrambles to sit, running a hand down his face. "Because this is mine and Lily's bedroom, and it's an adult-only bed."

"But I'm hewe now." She snuggles up to him.

"Yes, you are." Declan sighs. "Why don't you go downstairs and have some juice? I'll be right there to make your breakfast." He kisses her forehead. "Is Zach up?"

"Yes, he's building something."

*Epilogue*

"Okay, if you don't come in here for the next ten minutes, I will make you waffles."

"Yummy." She sprints from the room.

"Good morning, Mrs. Quinn." Declan throws the covers off and pounces on top of me.

"Good morning, husband." I stretch languidly, his body a delicious weight on mine.

"We have ten minutes." He thrusts his hips.

"Are you crazy? I'm not having sex with you when they're up and can come in any minute. I'm already on the edge at night."

"Welcome to parenthood." He kisses me, his hands finding my breast.

I moan into his mouth. "Stop it. You know how hard it is to be quiet?"

"I do know." He smirks. "Don't worry, they start school on Monday, and we will have a day-sex marathon."

"A day-sex marathon? How does that fit your work ethic?" I wrap my arms around his neck.

"I'm the boss, and so are you, so let's make the rules." He rolls us around so I'm on top of him. Swiping my hair from my face, he smiles at me. "I never thought I would find happiness again."

"I love you."

"Correction, actually: I never knew happiness like this exists."

*Epilogue*

"Daddy," Zoya yells from downstairs.

"They are kissing again," Zach responds, and I giggle into Declan's chest.

"Fuck, I guess it's waffles time," he groans.

The sun filters through the trees, casting golden light over the park. The air is crisp but not cold, the kind of perfect London day that makes everything feel soft and unhurried.

Zoya and Zach run ahead, their laughter bright and carefree as they chase each other toward the Round Pond, their giggles mixing with the distant sounds of ducks splashing.

Declan's hand is warm, his fingers lacing through mine. Weeks later, and these quiet moments still feel surreal to me.

"Have you decided what to do about Tim?" Declan asks. He's been impatiently patient about the topic.

"I spoke to my father and the lawyers."

"And?"

"And he will be dealt with."

"Publicly, legally?"

"He won't be a threat to us anymore. Or to the company."

*Epilogue*

Declan makes a clicking sound of displeasure. "I should have dealt with him myself," he mumbles.

"Thank you." I turn to kiss him.

"For what?"

"For allowing me to take my time and fix it myself. For providing me with the evidence, and for protecting me while giving me the space to stand up for myself."

He grunts like he isn't happy with the situation, but hugs me tighter, which makes me smile. We're a work in progress. But we're together.

"Can we find whewe the pwincess lives?" Zoya shouts.

I wave at her. "Okay, this way."

"I can't believe I was worried about them adapting to a new place." Declan abandons the former topic.

"I think their home is where you are." I look at him sideways. "How are you adapting?"

I know I have nothing to fear, but I still wonder if him moving so fast won't put a strain on our relationship.

"My home is where you and the kids are. And I didn't realize how much I love starting something new."

I scoot closer, leaning my head against his shoulder.

"It doesn't look like a castle." Zoya wrinkles her nose, assessing the Kensington royal residence skeptically.

## Epilogue

"This is her city residence; they have castles, don't worry." I chuckle. "But if you're ready to have hot chocolate and scones, we can go to the Orangery where queens used to hold their parties."

"Yes." She claps.

"For real?" Zach frowns.

I nod, and we head over to the Orangery when one of our bodyguards approaches. "Sir, Ma'am, reporters are ahead of us. Probably not for you, but I wanted you to be aware."

"Thank you," Declan says as we turn the corner.

We put our heads down, huddling the kids against us as our two security guards escort us to the entrance.

Relieved we're getting in undetected, I look up, and immediately there is a mic in my face. "Can you comment on the arrest of your cousin Timothy, Ms. Spinelli?"

Declan freezes, pushing the kids toward the entrance and snatching my hand. But I don't move.

"Actually, it's Mrs. Quinn, and that's the only comment you get." I smile and turn away. Amid blinding flashes and shouted questions, I lead my family inside.

"He got arrested?" Declan whispers as we wait for the hostess.

"Apparently." I grin.

*Epilogue*

"I thought we said no secrets." Declan narrows his eyes.

"This wasn't a secret; it was a surprise. But we can talk about that later. Let's enjoy the family time."

We are ushered to a secluded table, and Declan orders way too many cakes for the kids.

"Is Lily ouw mommy now?" Zoya takes a huge bite of her scone.

My heart stumbles, and I glance at Declan, but his gaze is locked on his daughter, his expression soft.

"Lily is my wife, and that makes her your stepmom. Is that okay with you?"

Before she can answer, Zach's sharp voice cuts through. "What if our real mom comes back?"

"I don't want Lily to leave." Zoya's eyes dart between the two of us.

"My point exactly." Zach deadpans.

"Oh," Declan utters, looking stunned.

The baggage this family carries; the fear that has been buried beneath their excitement over new adventures, new homes, new routines; the fear that all of this —the safety, the love, the family—can be taken away.

I swallow against the burn in my throat. "Oh, baby. Come here."

Zoya launches herself into my arms, and I hold her tight. Zach hesitates, but after a second he presses into my side, silent but seeking reassurance.

*Epilogue*

Declan wipes the corners of his mouth and drops his napkin. "Lily is my wife. That means she's part of our family forever. She's not going anywhere."

I nod, pressing a kiss to Zoya's temple. "No matter what happens, I will always be here. I love you both so much."

Zoya sniffs against my shoulder, her small fingers gripping my coat. "But ouw weal mom—"

Declan's voice turns firm, but still very kind. "Don't worry about it, sweetheart. Neither of you. Lily chose us. And we choose her."

Zach's shoulders relax slightly, his expression contemplative. He looks up at me, assessing, as if testing the weight of Declan's words. "Promise?"

I cup his cheek, my heart cracking a little at the seriousness in his eyes. "Promise."

Zoya wipes her nose, then asks with all the confidence of a six-year-old, "So we can call you Mommy now?"

I blink. Declan chokes on a breath beside me.

Zach groans like his sister just ruined the moment. "You don't have to call her that, Zoya."

She shrugs, turning back to her scone like we didn't just have a life-changing conversation. "I'm gonna twy it out."

Declan huffs a quiet laugh, wrapping an arm

*Epilogue*

around me, pressing his lips to the side of my head. "You okay?"

I exhale, warmth spreading through my chest. "I think I just got promoted."

"I think I like the carrot cake the most," Zoya says, fluidly moving to another topic.

"Me, too." Declan scoops up a bite from the plate in the middle of the table.

"Wait a minute." Zach turns to his sister. "Say it again."

She frowns. "I like carrot cake." Her eyes widen. "Carrot. Carrot."

"Zoya, say perfect." I practically bounce in my chair.

"Perrrfect." She smiles proudly, her *R* sharp.

"Well done, sweetheart. Let's order more carrot cake." Declan leans into me, his breath tickling my ear. "With you, Seagull, everything is perrrrfect."

"How is it that you're married and we never went to a wedding?" Zoya asks, and I tense while Declan clears his throat.

"We only had a small ceremony at the courthouse," I say quickly, heat spreading through my cheeks.

"Courthouse?" Zach frowns. "Like criminals?" He looks at us, unimpressed.

"Zach," Declan warns, but then he smiles at his son. "Actually, you're right, Lily deserves better."

## Epilogue

My heart stutters. "I got the three of you, and that's the best."

Declan takes my hand and kisses my knuckles. "But you also deserve a large wedding."

"Can I be a flower girl?" Zoya claps her hands.

A smile tugs at the corner of my mouth as I find Declan's gaze. It's like finding your true home. The love. The admiration. The pride. I love this man so much.

"What do you say, Mrs. Quinn?" He squeezes my hand.

"I think Zoya will be the most adorable flower girl." I grin.

"Is that so?" he grumbles, his eyebrows furrowing.

"Well, yes, and that is fortunate, because I always wanted a big wedding."

Zoya claps, and even Zach makes a sound that may be a cheer—masked with a grunt.

Declan leans in, his breath fanning my ear. "And you shall have everything you ever wanted, Seagull."

**Thank you for reading Declan & Lily's story.**

Someone *will* turn Xander Stone into a one-woman man... eventually.

While you're waiting for his story, why not binge another grumpy billionaire?

*Epilogue*

**Reckless Deal** is a workplace, billionaire, enemies-to-lovers romance readers call *"incredibly captivating,"* *"satisfying to the last page,"* and *"an absolute page-turner"*.

### *Want more Declan and Lily?*

*If you though Declan couldn't get any more protective... think again. Get a glimpse of their life in this exclusive bonus scene here: www.maxinehenri.com/declan or scan:*

## Author's Note

I spent years fulfilling others' expectations. Deep down, without realizing, I believed that's the only way to be seen, heard, loved.

It took me a while to recognize I didn't need to do anything. I just needed to be myself. I hope Declan and Lily showed you that as well. They were hiding some of their actions. They were hiding part of themselves. But it's a love story, so ultimately their love helped them grown together.

In real life, we can find that strength within ourselves. We can grow and shine as long as we believe in ourselves. When we stop chasing and start accepting. And that's what I wish for all of us.

While writing is a solitary job, this book got to your hands, gorgeous reader, as a team effort. I'm always terrified I will forget to name someone, but here is my

## Author's Note

best effort to express my gratitude to everyone who helped to bring this story to life:

1. My wonderful editor Kathy
2. My proofreader Dan
3. Fabulous cover designer Jaycee
4. My brainstorming buddies and incredibly talented author friends: Mila Kane, Kat Bammer and Sienna Judd
5. A wonderful group of content creators **Maxine's Billionaire Babes**—you, ladies, are there for me during the highs and lows and I appreciate you so much

And last, but not least, **you dear reader**—whether you reviewed an early copy, gave this book a shout-out on any platform or in real life or just picked it up to escape into the wonderful world of fiction full of devastating emotions—you mean a word to me!

Love,
    Maxine

# Also by Maxine Henri

## Reckless Billionaires Series

**Reckless Fate** (Massi and Gina's Second Chance Romance)

**Reckless Deal** (Gio and Mila's Grumpy/Sunshine Bosshole Romance)

**Reckless Hunger** (Andrea and Ivy's Age Gap Romance)

**Reckless Bond** (Paris and Finn's Accidental Pregnancy Romance)

**Reckless Vow** (Brook and Baldo's Marriage of Convenience Romance)

**Reckless Desire** (Sydney and Hunter's Single Dad Romance)

**Reckless Dare** (Lo and Dom's Fake Relationship Romance)

## Untamed Billionaires Series

Fall in love with the morally grey heroes obsessed with their women

**Chosen by The Billionaire** (Art and Violet's Enemies

to Lovers Romance)

**Chased by the Billionaire** (Ness and Rocco's Age gap/Innocent Heroine Romance)

**Stolen by the Billionaire** (Phillip and Lena's Forbidden Love Romance)

**Tempted by Charlie** (A Fake Relationship Novella)

# Merged Series (Billionaire Marriage of Convenience Novels)

**A Temporary Forever** (Cal and Celeste's story)

**A Forgotten Promise** (Saar and Corm's story)

**A Convenient Secret** (Declan and Lily's story)

Book 4 coming in 2026

*If you loved this book, please spread the word and leave a review. One sentence is enough to help other readers and make me very happy.*

# About the Author

Maxine Henri is a contemporary romance author who infuses her stories with steamy passion and complex characters. When she's not crafting stories that will have you swooning, she can usually be found sipping on a cup of black tea while reading a good book. Or traveling to new destinations.

Maxine believes that stories matter. They facilitate emotional journeys, inspire and entertain. And when it comes to books and fiction, stories are a great escape and probably the most beneficial addiction on this planet.

Her billionaire romances are the perfect escape, offering a taste of luxury and adventure. Maxine introduces heroes who may have a dark past, but are always balanced by a lighter side. And her leading ladies? They're strong, independent women who may be a little broken, but always find their way in life.

You can connect with her on any of these platforms:

- facebook.com/maxinehenriromance
- instagram.com/maxinehenriromance
- bookbub.com/profile/maxine-henri
- amazon.com/author/maxinehenri

Made in United States
North Haven, CT
31 December 2025